"HELP ME, DAVID," VALERIE WHISPERED "PLEASE..."

With a groan of long suppressed yearning, David captured her mouth in his lips, and Valerie opened herself to him, her body yielding to the warmth he was igniting in her. Feelings, everything was feelings, she thought wildly... her blood throbbing, her bones turning to liquid, her need awakening more fully with each feather stroke of his fingers.

"Oh Valerie, Valerie, I've waited so long for this," he murmured against her hair. "Are you sure? Tell me, darling, are you sure?" he asked hungrily, stilling the flight of her fingers as they tried to push apart his now unbuttoned shirt.

Valerie said nothing. She stepped away from David, and slowly began to unbutton each pearl button on her silk blouse. David did not move to touch her, and she did not take her eyes from his, burning into him the extent of her desire. The blouse made a soft rustle as it slipped from her shoulders onto the floor, and still he did not move nor did she look anywhere but into his eyes, drawing encouragement from their heat.

"I'm giving you my answer, David..."

PROMISES & LIES

PROMISES & LIES

Susanne Jaffe

BANTAM BOOKS
TORONTO • NEW YORK • LONDON • SYDNEY • AUCKLAND

PROMISES & LIES

A Bantam Book / March 1985

For information address: Bantam Books, Inc.

ISBN 0-553-24866-9

Published simultaneously in the United States and Canada

Bantam Books are published by Bantam Books, Inc. Its trademark, consisting of the words "Bantam Books" and the portrayal of a rooster, is Registered in U.S. Patent and Trademark Office and in other countries. Marca Registrada. Bantam Books, Inc., 666 Fifth Avenue, New York, New York 10103.

PRINTED IN THE UNITED STATES OF AMERICA

H 0 9 8 7 6 5 4 3 2 1

BOOK I

Chapter 1

The strains of "Heartbreak Hotel" by that new singer Elvis something were indistinct to Valerie Cardell from where she sat on the far side of the sports-equipment shed, a small, rippled-aluminum hut that held two volleyballs, a few baseballs, bats and mitts, and a deflated football. The good athletic equipment was kept in a locked room next to the phys-ed teacher's office. The gear in this prefab building, which was not quite as large as an outhouse, was intended for the students of the Galesville Public School to use during their recess, but no one ever went near it, preferring to fill their spare time telling secrets if they were girls or listening to rock and roll and sneaking cigarettes if they were boys.

The lack of interest in the shed was the reason Valerie had chosen it as her shelter from the rest of the eighth-grade class. She would have preferred to be closer to Tommy Walkerton and his transistor radio, but that would have meant hanging around with the other kids, and that she could not do. It was safer this way, some distance from them. The children from the lower grades were always monitored by a teacher, and those from the upper grades, like her sister, Alice, and her brother, Billy, would never bother with her. So, except during the cold winter months when she would sequester herself in the school library, Valerie spent her thirty-minute lunch recess outside the shed, sure of being undisturbed. Usually she would read a book—a different one every three days—but some days she would simply stare past the scratched white fence and scraggly green hedges that surrounded the school to the dusty dirt road; to the rusty tractor that had been on the edge of the Lamberts' property ever since she had started going to school; to the marshmallow-plump clouds protecting the eighty-six hundred inhabitants of Galesville, Indiana, from the real world beyond.

In this April of 1956, the people of Galesville did not care much about the rest of the world. They had a crop surplus; they planned to vote for Eisenhower again; and Grace Kelly had just become an American princess. Galesville was small-town even by 1956 standards: the six-thousand-volume library doubled as the town hall; there were two doctors, six veterinarians, no dentists. There was a main street—really two streets on either side of a small square. Here one could find a grocery store; a drugstore/luncheonette; three general stores that sold everything from fertilizer to buttons, blue jeans, and boots; a small post office; and eight bars, seven of which were really roadhouses since they were beyond the main streets. There was one gas station about four miles out of town, and three churches. The people who lived here bought by mail order, read the *Galesville Courier*—a twelve-page weekly gazette—for its death notices, and used the church as the fulcrum of their social lives. They were an insulated population, and they liked it that way.

If the parents of the twenty-three boys and girls in Valerie's class had any concerns, they were about that new singer Elvis Presley, who incited reactions, in their daughters particularly, that were utterly frightening. That music, the increasing popularity of television, the flirtatious clothes, and the availability of cars made mothers and fathers whisper urgently to each other in the night about morality and sex and children who were rapidly getting out of control. They would have been much happier if the outside world had intruded even less. Fortunately, they would say to each other, the next largest town was eighty miles away, and the sins of Eddington—with its bowling alley and movie theaters and bookstore selling who knew what trash—were far enough away to be inaccessible except to the most enterprising youths. Still, with only church and school socials to occupy their time and energy, the teenagers of Galesville could be enterprising.

This afternoon, Valerie dreamed, as she often did, of going to Eddington. Not to find mischief or to tease temptation, but to satisfy a craving constant and deep. Eddington, then Indianapolis, perhaps even Chicago someday: it was all out there, unavailable, haunting in its imagined vitality, enticing in its fantasized mystery. The world beyond Galesville throbbed with LIFE for Valerie. She never saw it smaller than billboard-high letters; never dreamed but that it danced with exuberance and energy; never imagined but that it shimmered with romance. Out there was everything she wanted, and nothing she could have. So she indulged her fantasies in these thirty-minute escapes, reading any book she could borrow from the school or public library, especially romances, and then projecting herself into a similar situation in a city inexhaustible in its delights.

A sudden rush of girlish giggling made Valerie jump to her feet. She quickly brushed off the back of her pleated skirt, which had long ago faded into dullness from its original cherry red. She wished she had one of those pretty, starched full skirts with the ruffled crinoline underneath like Merry Spitzer and Caroline Wheeler wore; like Alice wore, too, but Mama refused, said she couldn't afford enough material for two, and since Alice was older, she got it. And the white ribbed socks with enough elastic to stay up; the wide red cinch belt that made a waist look as big as a kiss; the black patent-leather pocketbook with a special see-through plastic purse for lipstick and mirror. Maybe, Valerie thought, these would be handed down to her before they went completely out of style.

"Valerie Cardell, we just knew we'd find you here. Your nose buried in a book, I bet."

The remark had come from Merry, surrounded as usual by her coterie of thirteen-year-old sycophants. Valerie wanted more than anything—well, almost more than anything—to be one of them, part of their unending silliness that made the teachers furious and the boys wild. But Valerie, even at thirteen, knew she was an outsider.

"Hi, Merry, hello, Caroline," Valerie said in a voice scratchy from disuse. "I thought you'd be over with Tommy listening to the music."

"Oh, we were, but then he and a couple of the boys decided to go 'round near the back and sneak some cigarettes. We didn't want to be there if they got caught." Caroline, a startlingly pretty blonde, had not stopped running her hands over the starched folds in her electric-blue full skirt, playing with its perfection as if it were a new, velvety plush stuffed toy. Valerie's eyes were riveted on the mesmerizing motion, and a small shiver ran down her arms when Caroline's soft voice stopped.

Valerie looked at the two girls, the leaders of the eighth grade, and did not know what to say. It was so rare that they bothered to acknowledge her existence, outside of asking her a history or English question, that she did not know how to respond to their friendliness. So she said nothing, and felt even more awkward. It was better when they left her alone. At least she was used to that.

"What're you reading?" Merry asked, pointing to the book Valerie was holding by her side.

"*Wuthering Heights*. It's a wonderful love story that takes place on the moors about this man who—"

"I *hate* moor stores," Merry said with finality. "Come on, let's go. See ya, Valerie."

The group was giggling again and did not hear the strained whisper of Valerie's goodbye.

Valerie's mother reached over to her side of the bed for a cigarette, not bothering to cover her breasts with the now-rumpled sheet. At forty-one and after four children, Edith Cardell knew her breasts were still more than good; a lot better than her roughened hands and lined eyes and mouth. She would rather have Mack concentrate on what was appealing about her, not on what was aging.

She glanced over at the man who had initiated her into the mysteries of sex back in high school, the same school her children now attended. After Mack's first visit home from college, Edith had known she had made a mistake in marrying Eli Cardell. Mack Landry came from money, and had gone on to make more of it with his machinery-parts company in Chicago. She was sure that if she had waited, she could have been Mrs. Mack Landry, wife of this gentleman farmer who owned the big bed in which they had just made love, the beautiful white brick and shingle colonial house, and the 250 acres surrounding it. Instead, she lived in his caretaker's cottage rent-free, a gift Mack had persuaded his parents to make when he realized that Edith had married a man who would never be able to afford a home of his own. When Mack's wife had died six years ago and he had returned to Galesville from Chicago with his two sons, Edith had been more than willing to take up where they had left off in high school. She would continue to go to bed with him indefinitely if it would bring her closer to becoming his wife. Mack had told her from the beginning that he would never remarry, but Edith was not willing to accept that. She had his body; the rest was just a matter of patience.

"You look thoughtful," he commented.

Edith stubbed out her cigarette. "I've got to do something about Valerie." She turned on her side, propping herself up on her elbow. "She's impossible, Mack. Just impossible. That child has the most devilish way of doing everything Eli and I give her to do, and then sneaking off somewhere to read." She leaned back against the brass headboard and reached for another cigarette. "Why can't she be more like Alice? I never have any trouble with my little princess. That girl is my salvation. But Valerie... I swear, I don't know where she gets her strangeness."

"You call reading strange?" Mack replied lightly. He was used to Edith's complaints about her family. Her eighteen-year-old son, Ned, was always getting into trouble with his fists; Billy, at sixteen, was so quiet that she sometimes forgot she had him. Valerie could do nothing right: if she asked questions, she was too smart for her own good; if she obeyed, she was being sly. Only Alice, her oldest daughter, pleased Edith consistently. From what Mack knew of Edith and her children, he attributed her opinions—both negative and positive—to a total lack of understanding.

"You and Eli are too hard on that girl," Mack went on. "Leave her be, why don't you?"

"You don't understand, you never do. I've got her so busy around the house, and Eli has—"

"What do you mean? What exactly does she do?"

Edith's hand fluttered dismissively. "Oh, you know. Cooking and cleaning, and whatever else there is."

"Why can't you and Alice help out?"

"Because Alice is a young lady of fifteen now and she can't be spending her time at home," Edith said matter-of-factly. "And I'm not as strong as I once was."

"Come on, Edith. That's ridiculous and you know it. You're certainly strong enough to tire me out," he said with a grin.

"Besides," she continued, ignoring his remark, "idleness isn't healthy. Too much time to herself can lead her into trouble."

"If I remember correctly, when Alice was thirteen you let her go to town after school with friends and to parties. Why not let Valerie start doing that?" When Edith did not answer, Mack went on, "Valerie has energy to spare, Edith. She's at that age. Let her use some of it by becoming a teenager instead of your personal housemaid."

"It's her duty!" Edith flared, defensively tugging the sheet to her chest.

"Then why isn't it Alice's duty too?"

"Alice is different. She's special, beautiful, a princess. She's going to get everything I never had."

Mack stared at her, slowly shaking his head at her pathetic dream. "It won't work, Edith," he said softly. "You can't stop Valerie from becoming who she must be."

"I knew you wouldn't understand!"

"I understand plenty, Edith, believe me. I understand that Valerie hasn't done things according to pattern and so you get angry at her even when she obeys you. *You're* the one who doesn't understand, Edith. You don't understand your own daughter."

"Well, I never know what she's thinking," Edith admitted. "And I don't like her taking walks and sneaking off to read. *Read*, Mack, when she could be doing something useful with that time, like earning money."

Mack sat up, too startled to speak. He ran a hand through his disheveled light brown hair, which was beginning to be flecked with gray, as was the hair on his chest. As he often had over the past six years, he wished he liked the person who was Edith Cardell instead of only her services.

"You can't mean that," he said. "Edith, the child is only thirteen."

"So what? Nothing wrong with her working at the Lamberts' place a couple of times a week or at Enderby's grocery in town. I was working at her age, and my folks were grateful for the money."

Edith's expression of smug belligerence made Mack regret ever having started with her. "I thought parents were supposed to try to make life easier for their children," he remarked dryly.

"That's easy for you to say, with all your money."

"Money isn't the only answer." He looked at her intently. "Giving them more as a parent than you got when you were a child is the best way, Edith."

"I don't see where that's done you much good with Wayne."

Mack shut his eyes briefly against the truth of her words. His youngest son, Wayne, seemed unwilling or unable to benefit from all that Mack could give him. At fifteen, he was completely enthralled by Ned Cardell, following him blindly, often into trouble. Wayne was used to looking up to his older brother, Ty, and Mack supposed Ned was the substitute now that Ty was away at college. But Ned was a poor substitute and a worse influence.

"It's wrong, Edith," Mack said.

"Right or wrong has nothing to do with it. Besides, you've no cause to be so self-righteous. You've got Mae's little girl over here twice a week and she's only eleven."

"For your information," Mack said, losing patience, "my housekeeper's daughter does not work for me. She comes over when her brother has to work late at the gas station so she isn't at home alone. She isn't out earning a living at eleven years of age, and I'm sure she won't be at thirteen, either."

Edith slid closer to him and began to plant little kisses on his bare chest. "I don't see what you're getting so upset about," she murmured against his skin. "All I want is for Valerie to use the talents she was given. If she's so smart that she's got all this free time, why not put it to some good? I don't mean any harm to the child, you know."

Gently, Mack lifted Edith away from him and got out of

bed. He put on a bathrobe and went to stand by the window that overlooked the front yard and the blossoming dogwood tree. He could not let Edith do this to her daughter. Too idle, too smart, reads too much—distorting virtues into sins, gifts into failings. Give the Cardells another shallow blonde like Alice, another Milquetoast like Billy, another bully like Ned; they were familiar with those types, knew how to handle them. But Valerie was different—different with her ink-black hair and olive complexion and eyes the color of the deepest sapphires, instead of blonde and pale. She did not look like them, so she was different. She wanted to learn, so she was different. And different was unfamiliar, so it was bad and had to be crushed in order that it would not be frightening. Well, not if he could help it.

"I have an idea, Edith," Mack said, going to sit at her side of the bed. "You seem pretty set on Valerie getting a job, right?"

Edith nodded. "That's right, and you can't make me change my mind."

"I don't want to change it. In fact, I'm going to help you out." At her questioning look, Mack smiled. "Why not have Valerie come over here a couple of times a week? She can . . . oh, I don't know . . . she can dust or help Mae with the polishing—whatever. What do you think?"

Edith stared into the deep brown eyes that were now waiting for her agreement. Valerie work for Mack, in the house Edith visited as often as possible? Never.

"No. Out of the question."

"Why the hell not?" Mack asked, his voice rising with frustration.

"What about us, then?" Edith whined, stroking his thigh where his robe had parted. "Mack, honey, I can't come over here if *she's* around."

"It won't be every day," Mack pointed out. "Besides, I'll pay her."

Edith's hand stopped its stroking. "How much?"

"Three dollars a week, how's that?"

"I don't know," Edith replied slowly.

"It's the perfect solution," Mack pressed, knowing he had her hooked. "You'll be getting what you want, and as for us, we'll just have to be more discreet."

"Three dollars a week, huh?"

"Why send her to somebody's house miles from here when she can be right next door? Edith, you can't have any argument against it."

Ultimately, she did not.

"No, I won't permit it."

Valerie was about to open the front door to her house when she heard her father's booming voice. She had dawdled walking home from school and was prepared for her mother to yell at her. She was not prepared to face her father as well, who needed little excuse to demonstrate the stinging power of his belt.

She did not want to go into that house. Did not want to listen as her parents accused her of being lazy; as they thought up some new work for her so she would have less time to herself; as they forced her deeper into a Cinderella existence from which there might never be an escape.

"You're being mule-headed and foolish, Eli. It's a wonderful idea!"

"No!"

Valerie wondered what her mother wanted badly enough to fight her husband so strongly. Usually Edith Cardell was obedient; the only times Valerie could remember her arguing even slightly with her husband had been about Alice's needing a new dress or a new pair of shoes. Invariably, her father conceded.

She entered and stood to the side of the archway that separated the kitchen from the living room. Her father was sitting at the table where the Cardells ate all their meals; her mother was leaning against the chipped white porcelain sink.

"Think of the extra money, Eli. We can use it, can't we?"

"That's not the point. I won't take charity from that man. It's bad enough we gotta live here on his land. I ain't about to take more than I have to."

"But this isn't charity, Eli. She'll be *workin'* for Mack, I tell you. She's too smart, too quick. We gotta get her away from those books and doin' somethin' useful with her time. Why not workin', just tell me why not?"

Valerie was sure her gasp was audible. She had no doubt that they were talking about her; Alice never read anything more lofty than *Photoplay*. So now they were about to take her books, her time alone, away from her too. But what did Mr. Mack have to do with it? And why would they be getting money for it?

"I don't care if she works," Eli said. "But what would she be doin' over at his place? And how much time would it take? Lord knows I got enough here to keep her busy."

"But it's *not* enough," Edith insisted, coming to sit next to her husband. "I'm telling you, she's too quick. Look at the house, always clean. The meals always ready, the darnin' always done. Whatever you got for her is always finished fast, too. She does it purposely, Eli. Gets everything over with one-two-three and then disappears with her books. That kind of idleness is no good and you know it, and if Mack Landry is generous enough to pay for her time, well, I say you'd be some kind of idiot not to accept."

Valerie felt tears well behind her eyes and swallowed hard to keep them from spilling over. She had thought Mack Landry was her friend. Whenever he saw her, he always took time to ask her how she was and what she was enjoying in school, and seemed genuinely interested in her answers. Now he, too, was turning against her. Why couldn't they all just leave her alone? Why did they think it was so dangerous for her to be curious about what existed beyond Galesville, beyond farming and this family? Well, they could take her time and her books. She *knew* there was more out there and she was determined to find a way to get it. They couldn't take that knowledge or that determination away from her.

She walked into the kitchen, muttering hello to her parents as she placed her schoolbooks on the table.

"You're late," her mother accused. "It's almost four o'clock and you haven't even begun to prepare dinner. How many times do I have to tell you to get home right after school."

"I'm sorry, Mama, but—"

"Sorry! Sorry!" Edith mimicked in a high voice. "You'll be sorry all right when you have no time tonight for your homework. I got two baskets of socks that need darnin', and your father here is missing buttons from three shirts. So tell me, Miss Always Sorry, when are you going to do your schoolwork?"

"I don't know," Valerie mumbled. "I guess I'll get less sleep. But, Mama, I really couldn't help it," she added in a rush, ready to spill out the fib she had created on the slow walk home. She had needed to take her time coming home today. For her, there was no going into town for a soda after school; no visiting at a friend's house; no membership in the 4-H Club. For her, the hours at school were really just a respite from work; she often had the feeling that it was only the law that forced her parents to send her to school. But on this particular afternoon—maybe because of Elvis Presley's song or because Merry and Caroline had spoken to her, or maybe because Grace Kelly had become a princess, which meant dreams could come true—Valerie had wanted to savor the pleasure of the spring air and a false sense of freedom for a few minutes longer.

"Why couldn't you help it?" Edith demanded.

"Mrs. Ingstrom kept me and Wally Divers after class to go over some questions we had on Mark Twain," Valerie said, eyes round with innocence. She did not like to lie; she liked less being yelled at or beaten.

"Likely story," Eli put in. "Since when do you have any questions about your schoolwork. So darn smart, aren't you? Too smart, that's what I say."

"Eli, I'll handle this," Edith said. "Fix me some tea, Valerie. For your papa, too. Then come and sit down, we want to talk to you."

She prepared their tea, then poured herself a glass of milk, not sitting down with it but standing, as her mother had been, against the sink.

"Your mother said to sit down," Eli ordered.

Valerie obeyed. She placed both elbows on the table, holding her milk glass in hands rigid with fear and rage.

"Valerie, honey, a great opportunity has come your way and your papa and I want to tell you about it."

Valerie knew this was going to be even worse than she had imagined. Her mother never called her "honey" unless she was about to ask her to do still one more chore; and if this was really a fine opportunity, Alice would have gotten it, not she.

"Stop beatin' around the bush and tell her. I still got work to do today," Eli barked.

"Valerie, Mr. Mack has this big house with only Mae to help out, and mainly in the kitchen, and her daughter coming in twice a week for some of the heavy work." Edith smiled encouragingly as she lit a cigarette to hide her lie and avoid her daughter's eyes. "I was talking to him the other day about how smart you are and how you always seem to get all the work done over here and how maybe it would be a good idea if you used your spare time to earn some extra money for your family."

Valerie hesitated. "Aren't I a little young to be out working, Mama? I mean, isn't sixteen the state law?" she asked softly.

"Whadda laws have to do with this? Just shut up and listen to your mother. You're too idle, Valerie Agnes Cardell, and that means too much time to get into trouble. Now don't you say another word until your mama and I are through talkin' to you."

Valerie caught her bottom lip between her teeth and gnawed gently at it like a puppy with a sock; she did not speak.

"You're a big girl, Valerie," Edith went on. "Mack has offered to have you work for him a couple hours a week, and he'll pay you three dollars for it. Think of that, Valerie, three whole dollars just for going next door to that house you love so and helping out with a little dusting."

Valerie looked from her mother to her father, back to her mother. She wanted to scream out that Alice should do it; Alice had more free time to be with her friends than Valerie had hours to sleep. She wanted to shout out against the unfairness. But in a low, even voice she said, "Mama, I really don't have all that much time, what with the chores and schoolwork. There aren't enough hours to sleep at night as it is."

"That's a lie!" Edith cried, standing up. "I know you're always out by the wood shed reading, and I've seen you take long walks across the fields, *slow* walks. That's wasting time, girl, and your daddy and I won't stand for it. If we can't find enough to keep you busy, then somone else will!"

"What about Alice?" Valerie dared. "Since she's older, she'd do a better job for Mr. Mack than I could. I'll probably break something, and then what?"

"Then you'll pay for it."

"Sure," Valerie said, her eyes alive with knowing. "Out of the three dollars I'll never see." She glared at her mother. "I want to know why Alice can't do it."

"Your sister is too busy. She's a young lady now and can't be frittering her time away."

"Now, Edith, that doesn't sound quite fair," Eli put in, to Valerie's surprise. Usually when her mother was this obviously discriminating, Eli went along with it. "What your mother means, Valerie, is that Alice is at that age when a social life is important so she can meet some nice boy and settle down."

"But she's only fifteen."

"Fifteen is old enough," Eli said. "You're still too young to have to worry about such things."

"But I'm old enough to go out and earn a living, is that it?" Valerie burst out, unable to control her anger any longer. "Why me? Why is it always me?"

"Because it's your duty to do what we want," Eli stormed, pounding his palm against the table so hard that Valerie's books jumped. "Because your mother is too weak and too tired since the struggle she had giving birth to you, and it's your duty, your obligation, to help her and me out whenever we want. And right now your mother wants you working at Mack's place, so that's exactly what you'll do. If you weren't too damn smart for your own good, you'd have done the chores at a normal pace like Ned and Billy do theirs, and then your mother never would have known how much time you're off by yourself." He gave a short bark of mirthless laughter. "So much for being smart. Seems to me you're a whole lot stupider than you think you are. It's called outsmartin' yourself, isn't it?" He laughed again as he pushed back his chair and stood. "I'll be back for dinner in two hours. Make sure it's ready." Then he left.

Valerie slowly got up, washed her milk glass and her father's cup, and began the preparations for dinner. She did not look at or speak to her mother.

"You start tomorrow, right after school," Edith instructed. Then she sat down, took out *True Story* from where she had it rolled in the pocket of her housecoat, and began to read.

That night, Valerie did all the chores and her homework, and even stole twenty minutes for herself by letting the water run in the shower after she had quickly washed herself. Often, she would wait until everyone was asleep, then take a flashlight she kept at the bottom of her bed, underneath the blanket, and her current book, into the bathroom, willing to deprive herself of sleep in order to be alone and read. Sometimes she would take a book with her when she fed the animals, and grab a few minutes by the shed, rejoicing in the snatched moments as a woman on a diet delights in finding a cache of chocolate bars. She rarely dared so audacious a move as letting the shower run longer than her allotted ten minutes, but tonight's injustice was a tight band of frustration around her heart, and she needed to make one small gesture of defiance.

Wuthering Heights, however, was too far removed from her reality this night. Not even Heathcliffe and Catherine could relieve the weight of this latest inequity. Why should the burden of running the house and now earning a living be placed on her small shoulders? Why did Alice never have to share the responsibilities? She used to ask her parents these questions; they had called her a spoiled brat, a selfish, ungrateful child. And when she had asked for the same simple liberties as Alice had, of going to a friend's house or being with a group of boys and girls for a weekend picnic, refusal and a slap had been the swift response.

So, at age ten, Valerie had begun to explore the pleasures in her imagination and in books, aware that these solitary enjoyments did not take the place of friendship. She knew what the other children whispered about her: that she was strange, always off somewhere with a book, *alone*. But didn't they know? she often wanted to cry out. Didn't they understand how much she longed to be with them, talk with them, share with them? Didn't they realize that she had no place to turn but to herself and her books? She was not permitted anything more.

They did not understand, of course. As her parents did not understand why she had become more obedient. They could never know that by doing everything they asked of her quickly she bought herself precious time. They could never know that by doing what they asked of her without question, she guarded herself against hurt. Rebellion brought not only physical pain but the kind that lasted longer, went deeper:

the anguish of feeling their injustice. Yet, acquiescence had its own price: it insidiously crept into every aspect of her life so that she quietly accepted no friends, Alice's liberties, the companionship of daydreams, because it hurt too much to fight for more and repeatedly be denied it. But now it seemed that obedience was not enough; they had managed to twist even that to their own advantage.

When she went into the bedroom, careful to hide her book underneath her bathrobe, Alice was brushing her hair at the vanity Eli had made for the girls. It consisted of two orange-crate chairs and a large, pine-framed mirror above a pine shelf. On the shelf were a variety of creamy coral lipsticks, brushes sticky with caked mascara, and small round metal-topped compacts of powdered rouge—all Alice's.

"That's a long shower you took," Alice remarked, not taking her eyes from her reflection.

Valerie slipped her book under the blanket, then got into bed watching Alice methodically brush her long blonde hair.

"Alice, what do you do when you're not in school or with your friends?" Valerie asked suddenly.

Alice turned around. "What do you mean what do I do? Who has time for anything else after school and boys?" Her laugh rasped against Valerie's nerves, a musical instrument out of tune. "I'm not smart like you. I don't have time to read and wouldn't want to even if I did. 'Sides, look where it got you—more work."

That was the second time today someone had told her that being smart had caused her more work, Valerie thought. But she did not believe she was smart. Smart would be figuring out a way to leave all this. Stupid was realizing you wanted to leave but not knowing how to do it.

"Did you tell Mama I sometimes read outside by the wood shed?"

Alice went back to her reflection. At fifteen, she was acutely conscious of her looks. She was Alice in Wonderland—that was what everyone called her, and that was how she saw herself—a storybook princess with blonde hair, an upturned nose, and a smile that she had learned, at an early age, to work as if it were a windup toy.

Valerie watched Alice watching herself, and begrudged

her none of her vanity. The only thing her sister had that Valerie wanted was liberty. If she could have just one fraction of Alice's freedom, she would be so happy that she might never want to read by flashlight again.

"Well, did you?" Valerie persisted.

"Why should I tell Mama?" Alice answered without turning.

"I don't know why you should. I'm only asking if you did."

"Of course not." Alice paused, and Valerie saw the mirror image of her sister's lips slowly edging into a smile. "And I won't tell her about you reading by flashlight in the bathroom, either. Now why don't you go to sleep and let me brush my hair."

Valerie was fast asleep when Alice tiptoed over to her, so she was not aware that Alice stood watching her for several long beats, studying the way the black lashes rested on the softness of her skin, the way two thick wavy strands of hair fell casually upon her cheeks, the way her swan's neck made her look regal even in rest. Valerie had no idea that, just as she would trade her stolen moments alone for some of her sister's freedom, her sister would trade everything she had for the promise of Valerie's beauty and the potential of her mind. Those weapons, Alice knew, were the means to the escape they both craved.

Chapter 2

"You gotta go over to the big house now?"

Valerie, getting her books from her locker, straightened and turned sharply.

"Billy, what are you doing here?" she asked her brother. "Don't you have shop club today?"

The sixteen-year-old boy, thin as a whisper and already as tall as his eighteen-year-old brother, leaned against the adjoining locker. "I do, but Ned's gonna pick me up and take me into town." He grinned shyly and looked down at the cuffs of his chino pants. "I've outgrown my pants again so Mama said he can take me to buy another pair."

Valerie smiled. "I don't know which is worse, spending time in shop club or being with Ned."

"Oh, he's not so bad, Val."

"I suppose not," she admitted.

"So is today your first day at Mack's?"

Valerie nodded, then went back to putting her books and looseleaf binders in order.

"I'm real sorry about that, Val," Billy said softly. "It's not fair, not at all."

"Fairness doesn't seem to make much difference when it comes to my life," Valerie said sharply, slamming her locker door.

"It'll be different, you'll see."

"When, Billy? When I'm too old to care anymore?"

He reached out and gently squeezed Valerie's shoulder. "Someday, Val, really. And soon, too." He removed his hand and gazed into his sister's eyes. "You know I hate it too, but the twenty-five dollars I've managed to save wouldn't last me very far, and even an artist has to eat." He shook his head at the sad reality of their situation. "I wish I could run away and paint and I wish I could take you with me. But I can't do it yet."

Valerie smiled at him; he was the only member of her family who ever showed her kindness. "You think you'll do it someday, Billy? Really go off and paint?"

Billy's eyes shone with excitement over his fantasy. "I want to, Val. That's what keeps me going—the thought that I have my whole life ahead of me and there'll come a time when I'll be free to do whatever I want. Meanwhile, whenever I can do it without risk of getting caught, I paint and draw, and that helps me get through the rest of it."

Valerie started to walk toward the door. "You're such a dreamer, Billy."

"I'm not," Billy replied fiercely, stopping in his steps, forcing Valerie to do the same. "The difference between you and me is that I know what I want and it's a goal that protects me. You don't know what you want so you have nothing to look forward to, nothing to hope for. Well, you gotta change that, Val. You gotta tell yourself that you're gonna get what you want someday and keep believin' that no matter what. But you gotta know what you want and keep that dream ahead of you to reach for like the ribbon at the end of a race." He stared at his sister's expressionless face. "Do you understand what I'm sayin'?"

"I understand. And you're wrong. I do have a dream. I do know what I want."

He tilted his head, waiting for her to explain.

Her smile was close-lipped and deeply knowledgeable, her eyes bright with belief. "I want to get out of Galesville, Billy. That's what I want. Just to get out."

"But that's not enough, Val," Billy said as they began to walk. "You've got to want to *do* something, *be* somebody."

"Oh, but I do, Billy. I want to be me, whatever that may be."

Valerie never could have imagined how devastating an effect her words had on her brother. He looked down at the linoleum floor of the school corridor; he was sure that if he met his sister's eyes he would see someone much older than thirteen.

"There's Ned," Valerie said when they got outside. "Aren't you scared to drive in that broken-down heap of his?"

"Oh, the Rambler's okay," Billy said, glad for the change of subject. "'Sides, it beats walking."

"What're you still doin' here?" Ned asked Valerie as she and Billy approached. "I thought you were supposed to be over at Landry's place."

"I'm going now."

"Too bad I can't give you a ride, but I'm goin' in the opposite way." His voice and eyes held no regret. "Come on, Billy, let's go. I been workin' out in that damn field all day and I need a coupla beers. And don't ask if you can drive, 'cause you can't."

"See ya later, Val," Billy said, then got into the car. Ned gunned the motor, and Valerie saw him laughing as the brown dirt dusted back into her face. She stared after the car, slowly turned, and began to walk. *To work*, she thought with growing resentment. *To work*. Alice didn't work. Her mother didn't work. Billy didn't work except on weekends and during the summer, helping out on the farm. Even Ned's working full-time with their father wasn't the same as what she had to do. He was eighteen; that was his job. Dusting and polishing was to be her punishment.

You're wrong, Billy, she thought as she quickened her pace. I love you because you're sweet to me and you mean well, but you're all wrong. I have that dream, and I'm going to make sure it comes true.

Valerie hesitated before pressing the door chime. She had been inside the big house only a few times—at Christmas, when Mack invited her family over for eggnog and to give them each a little gift. She loved the house, with its rich, gleaming woods, its carpets that looked like fields of flowers, its soft, fat sofa cushions that pillowed your body in an embrace. She had never dreaded the house before; had never felt anything less than eager to be with Mr. Mack. But this afternoon her heart ached.

What would he want her to do? And for how long? She had to be home to prepare dinner, and she had to wash the dishes afterward, feed the animals, and probably do some darning too before she could get to her homework. Don't think about it, she told herself as she pressed the bell and waited for the door to open. Remember what you said to Billy about your dream and don't think about not having time or sleep, don't think about—

"Hello there, Valerie. Come in, I've been expecting you."

"Oh, Mr. Mack, I thought Mae would be here."

"She is, in the kitchen getting Wayne's and my dinner ready so all I have to do is heat it up. I'm a terrible cook." He smiled at her, but Valerie could not respond; she stayed planted on the brick entry.

"Well, come in, come in," Mack said, reaching for her. Valerie managed to move before he touched her, slipping past his outstretched arm and onto the shiny peg-and-groove wooden floor of the foyer.

"Mae," Mack called out, "Valerie Cardell's here. We have some fresh cookies, haven't we?" He looked down at Valerie and smiled again. "You do want some cookies and milk, don't you? Wayne always bolts first for the kitchen when he comes home. And that's after Mae has packed him a lunch that would feed two men my size."

Valerie opened her mouth to speak, but her throat was so dry that nothing came out. She swallowed and tried again. "No thank you, Mr. Mack. My mother said you have work for me to do, so I better get to it or I won't have time to make dinner and do the chores and get my homework ready and—"

"Whoa," Mack said, putting a hand that felt to Valerie like a large, warm comforter on her shoulder and leading her into the kitchen. "We'll talk about your work after you've had time to recuperate from your hard day at school."

"But—"

"As your new employer, I insist you have milk and cookies. Now, you can't refuse me or I'll fire you, how's that?"

From that moment on, Valerie Cardell could refuse Mack Landry nothing. It was the beginning for her: of having a large desk and the right lamp for her homework—which Mack insisted she finish before doing anything else. It was the beginning of laughter, when she would sit in the kitchen with Mae and her daughter, having cookies and brownies or sometimes a peanut butter and applebutter sandwich and a tumbler of milk so cold she was convinced it had been kept in a bucket of ice. It was the beginning of a friendship that buoyed her life to a level where her perspective was richer, broader; where the world itself was laid out before her, beckoning.

And Mack did lay out the world for her. That first afternoon, he spent most of the time convincing Valerie that there really was no work for her to do; they could talk, he would help her with her homework, or she could just sit and read. She began to cry, something she had not done since she was nine years old when her father had taken her to the wood shed and beat her for a solid fifteen minutes with his belt. She had burned his stew, which she would not have done if she had come home from school immediately with Alice instead of staying behind to play in the schoolyard. Neither he nor her mother had believed her when she told them that Alice had never shown up for her and she had waited and waited, which was why she had been late. Alice never admitted that she had not shown up, saying instead that when she had tried to find Valerie she wasn't at the spot where they were supposed to meet. The injustice of that incident had become welded into the core of Valerie's emotions, so that after the tears shed for the lashes of her father's belt in her soft child's skin, there had been no more. Until that afternoon with Mack Landry.

The tears were initially due to fear: Was this a game—was he doing this to punish her for something? Mack was taken aback by her distrust, but he understood it, too; she had come to expect anything but kindness from adults. Gently, with a tenderness that Valerie had instinctively sensed in the older man but had never imagined could really exist, Mack gained her trust that afternoon. For two hours they sat in his study, he in his worn brown-leather desk chair, she on an equally worn brown-leather couch, and they talked—about Valerie's loneliness at school because she was not permitted to have any social life; about how she would read and wonder what the world was like; about how she loved her sister Alice, but it did not seem fair that a mere two years could make such a difference in what their parents allowed each of them; about how her father and mother could not like her very much or they would not keep punishing her for having made her mother so weak during her birth. If Valerie saw the surprise this last caused in Mack, she did not speak of it; it was more important to tell him everything she thought and felt and sensed and wanted. When she had finished, he rose from his chair and sat next to her.

"From now on, Valerie," he said softly, taking both her hands in his, "you will do your homework right here, at that desk, and when you're finished, I'm going to tell you about the world. I'm going to give you books with beautiful pictures and some with beautiful words, and I'm going to prepare you for all that lies beyond Galesville that you're so hungry to discover."

On the third day, Mack spent two hours discussing New York, Chicago, and Los Angeles with Valerie, and when she got back to the cottage she was eager to share her new knowledge.

"Did you know people travel underground in New York, in things, trains actually, high-speed trains called subways," she said to her mother as she peeled and sliced potatoes. "And they put a token in a machine and get on the train and it can take you anywhere, from New York to Yankee Stadium in the Bronx to almost as far as the Statue of Liberty, except that's on an island so you have to take a ferryboat."

"Where'd you hear all that garbage?" Ned demanded, coming into the kitchen. Their mother had not spoken, rapt as she was in *True Confessions*.

"It's not garbage!" Valerie retorted hotly. "Mr. Mack told me. He said—"

"Oh bullshit, what does—"

"Ned Cardell! Don't you dare use that language in this house!" Edith said, finally rousing.

"Well, what *does* he know about New York and subways? I bet he made it all up."

"Mack Landry doesn't lie, young man. Believe me, he knows a lot of things."

"Oh yeah, like what else? What else makes the great Mack Landry so great? Wayne says his daddy can't even shoot a rifle, so how smart can he be?"

"Oh, Ned, that's silly," Valerie said. "What does knowing how to shoot a gun have to do with being smart?"

"Listen, you little brat—"

"All right, you two, that's enough," Edith said. "Ned, go on out to the east field, your papa needs you there, and leave Valerie to make dinner."

Ned threw Valerie a gray look of menace and stormed out. She was not to be deterred in her enthusiasm to share what Mack had taught her. "You know what else Mr. Mack told me, Mama? He said lots of the houses in Los Angeles have their own private tennis courts *and* swimming pools, can you imagine that? And the people in Chicago are always trying to be as sophisticated as New Yorkers and never are!" She laughed with delight at such an idea, and waited expectantly for her mother to join her.

"I hope you're doing the work Mack wants and not just wastin' time askin' dumb questions," Edith said sternly.

Valerie was about to blurt out what her afternoons had been like, but she stopped herself. This had to be her secret, one that they must never take away.

"Yes, Mama, I'm doing all the work I'm supposed to. It's just once in a while I ask a question or two because Mr. Mack has been to so many places."

The answer seemed to satisfy Edith, but when she told her husband at dinner that night, Eli took a different view.

"I don't want that man fillin' your head with no fancy ideas about Chicago and California. From all that readin' you always do, you think you're too smart as it is."

"But, Papa—"

"You're gettin' paid to work, not ask questions. And don't let that Mack get you to thinkin' you're better'n the rest of us just 'cause you're polite enough to listen to him. Who else would listen to his tales but a little girl."

"Eli, that's unfair!" Edith said.

"Papa," Alice said, making the word sound like a nougat roll on her tongue, "there's no need to jump to any conclusions that Val is getting too big for her britches. That's what you meant, isn't it?"

"Yeah," he answered gruffly. "That's what I meant all right."

"Well, I'm sure Valerie knows her place."

"She better."

Alice smiled at her, but Valerie looked away. She was grateful to her sister for getting her father to stop picking on her, but she felt she had somehow been insulted.

"I'd love to go to California someday." That came from Billy, normally silent during meals.

Ned laughed rudely. "*You!* What would you do in California, draw pictures of the Pacific Ocean!"

Billy blushed, the freckles on his face fusing into an orange glow. Only Valerie knew about his sketch pad. He shot her a quick look and she shook her head slightly to indicate that she had not revealed his secret.

"I don't draw," Billy said softly.

"Don't lie," Ned bellowed. "I know you do 'cause I seen that book with your little drawings in it."

"You went into my drawer!" Billy cried.

"Is this true, Billy?" Eli asked. "You wastin' time drawin' pictures when you're supposed to be workin'?"

Don't tell him, Valerie ordered, but it was a silent command, and not even the imploring look she gave her brother could stop him from blurting the truth.

"Only once or twice, and never when I got a chore to do," Billy admitted, avoiding Valerie's eyes.

She played with the stew on her plate. She wanted to scream at Billy to stand up to their father, but she knew it would do no good. Weakness was as much a part of her brother's nature as was gentleness. How many times, after she had been victim of her father's belt, had Billy crept into her room to console her, and how many times had she begged him to speak out *before*, to help her *before* she had to feel the pain? Billy would shake his head and say, "I can't be like you, Val. He'd go after me then, and I can't take it like you can."

"I promise, Papa," Billy said now. "No more painting."

She would forgive Billy his weakness, this time and at any time. To keep their dreams alive was an awesome task, probably impossible. Billy was not smart enough to lie well or brave enough to fight back. Neither, really, was she. Perhaps it was more a question of desperation than desire, she thought. Hers gnawed at her so constantly that it sometimes frightened her. But most of the time she was scared that even desperation would not be enought to sustain her and, like her brother, she would crumble.

For the next two months, Valerie spent all her free time at the big house. When school let out for the summer, she managed more than the usual two or three days a week, so that Mack one day jokingly complained that he would have to give her a raise or her parents would think he was working her too hard.

"Am I taking up too much of your time?" Valerie asked.

"I've never enjoyed myself this much," Mack answered. "You make me feel younger and smarter than I have for years."

"Why?"

Mack hesitated, staring into that smooth-skinned face, with those unwavering, deep blue eyes so filled with trust for him that he shuddered inwardly at the staggering responsibility he had taken on. He wondered if she realized what a beauty she would be someday. Only thirteen, and all the bloom still to go, while her sister had blossomed quickly and would fade just as fast. He shook his head, not wanting to think of the woman Valerie would become and how much she still had to learn about that side of life. It was one thing to teach her about Europe and the Russian revolution and theater and ballet, red wine and champagne. People and their mystery he believed he had no right to discuss with her; but who then?

"Why?" Valerie repeated. "Why do you feel younger and smarter?"

Mack laughed. "Because you help me see everything as if for the first time again, and that's a nice feeling."

Valerie was silent a moment, then: "Why doesn't my father like you?"

"Well, I certainly wasn't expecting that," Mack said, trying to put a lightness in his voice.

"I'm sorry, I shouldn't have said that."

"Val, honey, don't apologize for anything you say to me. We're friends, and that means we share when we feel good and when something's troubling us. Okay?"

She nodded and waited for him to go on.

"I think your father doesn't like me," Mack began slowly, "because he's a very proud man, someone who wants to feel independent, never needing anyone else. And that's wrong, Val, because everyone, at some point in his life, needs someone else, even if it's for something as small as holding a door when your arms are full of packages." He smiled, knowing she understood that his insignificant example represented much more. "Your father doesn't like the idea that it's my land he works, my cottage he's living in, maybe even the fact that your mother knew me before she knew him. It's not that he doesn't like me, I don't think. It's more that he doesn't like that I've given him what he hasn't been able to get for himself."

"But he says you're making me too big for my britches," Valerie said, eager to communicate how troubled she had been lately. "He says you're filling my head with ideas about things and that I'm going to turn into a snob. He says that I have no friends anyway and that with all these notions about books and theater and Paris and all, I'll never have any friends and no boy will want to marry me. He says that it's bad for me to learn these things because they'll never do me any good here in Galesville."

Suddenly, unexpectedly, hot tears filled her eyes. "I try to keep what you talk to me about to myself," she said, "but sometimes I can't help it. It's all so interesting that I just want to share what I learn with everybody at home."

"Valerie, please—"

"I don't care what he says," she said with a fierceness that surprised her. "I *will* get out of Galesville! I will! I don't care how long it takes, but I'm going to get out!"

Mack reached out to her, but she turned away, embarrassed by her tears and her outburst. When she faced him again, her eyes were dry.

"I'm sorry," she mumbled.

Mack shook his head, dismissing her words and her embarrassment with that single gesture. "Valerie, your father means well. He just doesn't understand that you're not like him and your mother, not like your brothers and sister, either. And he doesn't know how you can get out of a future that seems pretty well laid out for you—but you can, Valerie. Believe me, you can."

For a moment the sapphire eyes widened and glowed with the hope of Mack's words. The Valerie looked down. "I'll never get out," she whispered. "I'll be just like my mother, living in some little house, taking care of children, never seeing anything more of the world than maybe a movie in Eddington."

Mack put his hands on her shoulders. "Hey, where's that determination I just heard? What happened to that?"

She gazed up at him, desperately wanting to hold onto his encouragement as if it were a lost wallet filled with money. "Sometimes it's just so hard. . . ."

Mack nodded. "I know, but you've got to be patient, Valerie. You're still very young, you're not ready for all you want. When you're old enough—"

Valerie pulled away from Mack's grasp. "That's what Billy says—when we're old enough. But I don't want to wait that long. By then it'll be too late. By then I won't have any hope left in me!"

Mack moved away, bruised by the poignancy of her insight. How he wished he could keep her with him, away from Edith and her harping, away from Eli and his eternal demands. "Valerie, it won't be that much longer. You trust me, don't you?"

"Yes, but—"

"Listen a minute. I'm telling you that you *will* get out of Galesville. You will see Paris and Rome and New York. You'll watch the great dancers and actors, dine in the best restaurants, satisfy all your curiosity about the world. When you want something as badly as you want to leave here, you'll get it."

"Promise?"

Mack smiled at the childishness of the question, then shook his head. "I won't make any promises to you, Valerie. That way I'll never tell you any lies. Just trust me and be patient. And don't give up. Don't give up your hope or your determination. Both of those will be more valuable to you than anything I can teach you."

She stared into the face of this man who had come to be father and best friend to her in a short time. She would believe him because not to would be too painful.

"I want to hear again about the Metropolitan Opera House in New York, okay?" she said brightly. "About the curtains that are as thick as a mattress and . . ."

Mack laughed lightly, and knew it was as forced as her change of mood.

One evening the next week, Valerie was late getting home. Ty Landry was back for a short vacation. He was planning to play professional baseball after he graduated from the University of Indiana, and this summer he was going to be with a farm team in Illinois. That afternoon, Valerie had sat rapt as Ty told her about college life. When he had left the house, she and Mack had pored over Ty's college bulletin, and Mack had told her a few of his own college-day anecdotes. The time had slipped away as Valerie's mind whirled with scenes of dorms and science labs, fraternity parties and beer blasts.

Walking home now, she smiled to herself, thinking how nice Ty had been to her today, talking to her as if she were an adult instead of a little girl. He was so different from Wayne, who always made her uncomfortable. Whenever Wayne saw her, he would laugh or try to scare her or do something that would make her want to get away from him as quickly as possible. It was as if he were looking through her, imagining things about her that instinctively she knew were not good.

A squealing noise stopped Valerie as she neared the wood shed behind the cottage. At first she thought it might be a stray animal, then the sound came again, and she realized it was human. She approached cautiously, knowing that each second she took would make her later and would undoubtedly mean criticism or worse from her parents. But maybe someone was hurt; she had to find out.

Valerie stood by the half-open door to the shed and peeked in. What she saw would be seared into her memory forever. Her sister stood with her blouse off, her bra dangling from one hand. Her other hand was unbuttoning Ty Landry's shirt.

"Oh, c'mon, Ty, don't be so shy. Don't you want me?"

"That's not it, Alice, and you know it," Ty said, pushing away her hand. "You're underage. There's a law about that, you know."

To Valerie's ears, Alice's laugh sounded like poured syrup. "I won't tell if you won't. Besides, I'll be sixteen in a couple of weeks. Come on, Ty, please."

Valerie stood transfixed as Alice began to kiss Ty's chest, as she took his hand and placed it over her bare breast. Valerie's initial reaction was disgust that someone like Ty Landry, older, sophisticated, practically family, would do this to her sister. Slowly, Valerie realized that Alice was the instigator: *she* was seducing Ty. Disappointment burned in Valerie's chest like hot liquid gulped too quickly. How many nights had she and her sister lain awake in their room, Alice telling her that the reason she was so popular was because she never gave in to boys; sex was something sacred, to be shared only with your husband; any girl who did it before marriage was not a good girl. Now Valerie was eyewitness to her sister's duplicity, and that was what hurt. Alice did not have to lie and pretend to her; they were sisters, and to Valerie that meant she would love her and be loyal to her no matter what. She trusted Alice, so why did Alice have to tarnish that trust by preaching what she herself did not believe?

Valerie turned and walked back to the house, dismay, confusion, and a strange resentment weighing down her steps.

"Where the hell have you been!"

She should not have been so startled by her father's thunder, but her mind was still on the scene in the shed, and she jumped at the loudness.

"I'm sorry, I was . . . I was—"

"I know what you were doing," Eli yelled. "You were letting that damn know-it-all fill your head with more high-falutin' ideas while I'm sittin' here after a hard day's work waitin' for my supper. Well, that's it, young lady, that is it. You and Mr. Mack High and Mighty Landry have seen the last of each other!"

"Papa, please—"

"Eli, now wait a minute."

"Stay out of this, Edith. I've had all I'm gonna take from this smart aleck. She belongs here, in this house, doin' what we need her to do." He punctuated every few words with a hard pounding on the kitchen table. "You hear me, Valerie Cardell, no more workin' for Landry. You got any time to spare, you fill it here, where you belong."

"What's goin' on?"

Ned had just come into the kitchen, Billy behind him. Ned was grinning, and Valerie recognized it as the delight he always took when someone else was on the receiving end of Eli's fury. Billy's face was pale; she knew she could count on no help from him.

"Your little sister here thinks it's more important to be over with the great Mack Landry than in this house makin' dinner for her family."

"Now, Valerie, that wasn't too bright, was it?" Ned said, his grin widening maliciously. "You know how hard we work and how we need to have a hot meal on time. Guess you outsmarted yourself again, didn't ya?"

"Mama, please . . ." Valerie implored, going over to her mother at the table.

"Your papa's right," Edith said. "Ever since you been goin' next door you been comin' home late, rushin' through the chores. *I've* even had to catch up on some of the darnin' you haven't had time for, and me with my eyes not as good as yours. If your papa says no more workin' for Mack, then that's that."

"And just to make sure you know I mean it, I think a good whippin' and a night without dinner will do just fine," Eli said, getting up and grabbing Valerie by the upper arm.

"Papa, please, don't. I promise it won't happen again."

"It's what you deserve," Ned said with authority.

Valerie flashed him a look filled with poison. "You're going to get what you deserve too someday, Ned. And it's going to be much worse than a whipping!"

"Hey, you shut your mouth or I'll finish what Papa starts!" Ned threatened, moving toward her. Billy reached out to stop him, but Ned shoved him out of his way.

"Ned, Billy, both of you stop this now," Edith commanded. She glanced at Valerie; there was no regret in her expression for what her daughter was about to endure. "Take her out to the shed, Eli. The boys'll have dinner ready when you get back."

At the mention of the shed, the scene Valerie had witnessed came rushing back to her. "No. Not the shed. Please!"

"Why the hell not?" Eli demanded. "You think a whippin's gonna feel any better right here?"

"Please, Papa, not the shed."

"I'll take you where I please. Now shut up or you'll get worse than the strap from me!" He yanked her hard toward the door.

"Papa, don't . . ." Valerie heard Billy's faint protest, but as usual it was too late. She knew Billy was not mean like Ned, but his weakness proved just as dangerous and provoked even more anger in her.

Valerie did not drag back as her father pushed her toward the shed. She would withstand the whipping without tears. The real pain would come later, in the days without Mack Landry.

When they reached the shed, Valerie's heart was racing. What would happen to Alice if their father caught her? But Alice wasn't there; there was no sign that she had ever been there. And then, as Eli was unbuckling his belt, Alice appeared in the doorway.

"Mama said to hurry or dinner'll get cold," she announced, her voice honeyed, her smile guileless.

"Where you been?" Eli asked.

"Feeding the cats and dogs and chickens. When Valerie didn't show up, I didn't want you to have to do it, so I got the food for them."

"Thank you, Alice, that was thoughtful. Go back inside now and tell your mother I'll be along shortly."

Valerie had been staring at her sister while she spoke, willing her body to stop quivering, but her rage could not be bridled. "That's a lie!" she shouted. "You were right here in this shed. I saw you!"

Alice turned to her, wide-eyed with surprise. "Well, of course I was here. Ned told me Wayne Landry had lost his new pocketknife when they were in here the other day getting wood to make ducks for their target practice, and I told Ned I'd look for it before I fed the animals." A brief cloud scuttled over the innocent expression, then quickly disappeared. "I didn't know you were out here, Valerie. You must have been real quiet."

"Or maybe looking for that pocketknife took all your concentration," Valerie replied evenly.

"Oh, it did, it did. And I couldn't find it after all."

"The more you two jabber, the longer I'm goin' without my supper," Eli barked. "Go back inside, Alice."

Valerie expected a curtsy to accompany her sister's smile before she left. She then watched as her father rolled the metal buckle of the leather belt around his fist. She closed her eyes. When it was over, even her anger at her sister's deception had been whipped out of her; it was, after all, just another injustice.

"You got exactly what you deserved," Alice said later that night when they were alone in their room.

Valerie did not answer. Her pain had been eased by some balm her mother had put on her, but she did not have the energy or the will to speak to her sister. All she could think about was the pattern of her days without those visits to Mack; the dreariness, the sameness, the claustrophobia.

"You should know by now how Papa hates Mack Landry and that your going over there every day is like a prickly thorn in his skin. And when you're late like you were tonight . . . well, he was just looking for a reason to stop you. I don't understand why you can't learn to do what he wants, Valerie. I don't know why you can't just be satisfied with things instead of always trying to make them different. You've got to learn to compromise, to give in sometimes."

She had been giving in all her life, she wanted to say;

she never had any choice but to give in. "Like you wanted Ty Landry to give in this evening?" she blurted.

If Valerie had expected her words to startle Alice, she did not get that reaction. Alice laughed shortly, a sound so harsh and patronizing that Valerie winced as if from another lash of her father's belt.

"So you did see us," Alice said with no trace of guilt. "He *is* a hunk, isn't he? But what a prude. I couldn't get him to... Uh, it's just as well, I guess, since Papa might have caught me and then who knows what would have happened." She laughed again. "Have I shocked you, Val? Is that why you're not talking to me?"

"You told me you never did that, Alice. You said nice girls don't do that before they're married. I don't care whether you do or you don't, but why'd you lie to me? Why'd you tell me one thing and then go and do something else?"

Alice turned off the light on the table between their beds, and the sisters lay in the silent, darkened room. Alice wanted to tell Valerie that Ty Landry had not been the first; that at thirteen, she and Brandon McLintock had given each other their virginity in the back of his father's pickup truck, and that since him, there had been at least four others. She wanted to tell Valerie that Ty Landry was older, rich, handsome, going to be somebody, and if she could snare him, as she had those other, younger boys, then she could be somebody with him and leave Galesville behind her. She knew she had no way to escape other than through a man, and no way to capture a man except with her body. She knew, too, that she had to do it while that body was still fresh and young. Valerie would not need to use sex, while she had nothing but that.

On the third day that Valerie did not show up, Mack Landry went to the cottage. It surprised him that Edith had not been by, and he wondered if Valerie was sick—sick enough that Edith had to be with her.

When there was no answer to his knock on the front door, he went around back, to the kitchen door, and looked in through the top-half window panes. What he saw disgusted him. Valerie was on her hands and knees, scrubbing the kitchen floor. There was no sign of Edith or anyone else. Rock and roll was blasting from a radio, so he did not bother to knock again, just walked in. Valerie did not look up until he snapped off the radio.

"What happened?" he asked dully.

"Please, Mr. Mack, I can't—"

"Tell me what happened, Valerie."

She shook her head and continued scrubbing a section of linoleum that already sparkled. Mack bent down, gently took her by the elbows, and drew her up. "Sit down, Val."

"I can't," she whispered.

"Where's your mother?"

"She went into town with Alice to buy some material for a new dress."

"Won't you please sit down?"

"I told you, I can't."

"Valerie, no one's going to yell at you for sitting down."

Shame blotched her face, and she couldn't look him in the eye as she said, "I can't because it hurts."

"It hurts? What do you mean? . . . Oh no, oh Jesus, did your father—?"

"Please, Mr. Mack, you better go. If they know you're here and I'm seen talking to you, I don't know what'll happen."

"Nothing will happen, that I promise you," he said firmly.

Suddenly Valerie flared. "Don't make promises you can't keep. You told me that, remember—no promises, no lies. Well, don't do it now!"

Mack shook his head sadly and sat down, grasping one of Valerie's hands in both of his. "This is a promise I *can* keep, Valerie. No one is going to hurt you. Now tell me what happened."

"My father won't let me go see you anymore," she said, loving the warmth of his grip. "He thinks you're filling me with ideas that are turning me away from him, making me think I'm better than everyone."

"Is that why he beat you?"

"Not exactly. The other day when Ty was with us and when you and I were going over his college stuff, I was late getting home and didn't fix his dinner on time." She pulled her hand away then, and Mack suspected she was not telling him everything.

"Valerie, where's your father now, out in the cornfield?" She nodded. "Okay, I'm going to have a little talk with him—and, Valerie?" She looked at him expectantly. "You come over tomorrow, okay? Anytime in the afternoon. I'll be in town in the morning, and when I come back I want to see you at the house. I think it's time you learned about the wonders of Japan."

"Mr. Mack, I don't know—" Valerie hesitated.

"Be there." Then he turned on the radio again and left.

Mack found Eli and Ned at the far end of the Landry property, where they were supervising the cutting of the corn stalks. "Eli, come on over a minute," Mack called from his station wagon. "I want to talk to you."

Eli lumbered over. "Yeah, Mack, what is it?" he said with ill-disguised distaste.

"Eli, I've just been to your house. Saw Valerie there scrubbing floors, too sore to move. You got an easy choice to make, Eli. That girl starts coming back to see me or you're fired."

"Now wait just one damn minute—"

"No, you wait." Mack's voice crackled with anger. "That girl's been beaten so bad she can't even sit down. And for what? For being late with your damn dinner! Well, I don't believe that, not for a minute. You whipped her to get back at me—and, Eli, it just won't wash, understand? You got something special in that little girl, and you're not going to beat it out of her—not while I'm around. So you decide, Eli. Your job or your damn stupid pride."

He put the car in gear and left Eli Cardell gritting his teeth, words of rebuttal lost in the brown dust thrown back at him from the car.

Mack felt enormous satisfaction as he drove away. In some small measure, he had staved off another attempt to mold Valerie into a model of mediocrity. What might have spoiled his pleasure, had he thought about it, was that while Valerie might adore him for what he had done, her father would see that she paid even more dearly for it.

Chapter 3

On March 24, 1958, Valerie turned fifteen. She was sure that now that she had reached that magic age, she would finally be permitted the elusive, longed-for freedom.

While satellites were being launched into space, and *American Bandstand* fixed teenagers to their televisions, Valerie was developing into an exceptionally appealing young lady. The contrast between her almost exotic coloring and the whitewashed blondness of the other girls around her was fascinating to the boys in her class. She had no idea how promising her full mouth could seem, how charming when it broke into a smile; she did not fully appreciate her flawless skin, nor quite understand the temptation of her long legs and full breasts. While Alice never forgot her own good looks, Valerie was oblivious to hers, and in that was an appeal of itself.

The boys were increasingly aware of Valerie but made no move to approach her until one day when she came to school wearing a scooped-neck white blouse tucked into a red and white plaid skirt. The lower neckline showed off enough of Valerie's satiny skin to give Carl Enderby goosebumps when he looked at her. So, three weeks after her fifteenth birthday, the town grocer's son and leader of the tenth-grade class invited Valerie to a party. She immediately and delightedly said yes. When she got to Mack's that afternoon, she eagerly told him what had happened.

"That's great, Valerie. I knew it was only a matter of time before those young fellas saw what I've been seeing for a couple of years now. Be careful, though. Remember, you don't owe them anything except a thank-you, and that only if you want to."

Valerie averted her eyes, knowing that he was referring to the subject she and Alice had never again spoken of since that night with Ty Landry. She was curious about sex, but mindful of how her sister misused it, and she did not want to make the same mistake. For all her popularity, Alice never went out with the same boy twice, nor did she ever have a steady boyfriend. She was always with someone new, always had a criticism to make when he did not call for a second date. Valerie understood too well why they never called: why come back for seconds when they had had appetizer through dessert the first time around?

That evening she shared her news with everyone at dinner. It was as if, in her happiness at finally being included, all the refusals and denials of her parents had been erased, leaving her with a clean slate to begin enjoying her life. Reality intruded as abruptly as a knock on the front door from Death.

"Out of the question," Eli stated.

"But why not, Papa? Carl's a nice boy. You know his father and—"

"You have no time to go gallivantin' around, that's why not. You have enough time to yourself visitin' that pal of yours next door. Your mother has to do more than is good for her health as it is. The answer is no."

"But you let Alice go out when she was fifteen," Valerie persisted. "I don't see what the difference is."

"The difference is, young lady, that Alice understands about responsibility, always has, and you don't. When there's a job to be done, your sister does it without complainin'. Every time we ask you to do somethin', it's like having to apologize to a queen for intrudin' on her precious time. You're too full of yourself, that's the problem. I woulda thought hard work might teach you a lesson or two, but it hasn't."

Valerie said nothing, but her eyes darkened and she was sure her father could sense the hatred she was feeling for him. She had tried rebelling when she was much younger, and that had not worked. She had tried obeying, and that had not worked. Nothing would ever satisfy her parents when it came to her, she understood that now; nothing would ever get them to treat her fairly.

"The reason I complain is because I'm the only one around here who does anything, and I'm tired of it!" she said, her voice hard, steel-edged, much older and almost unnatural-sounding. "All I'm asking now is to go to a party with a boy, something you've let Alice do for years." Her resentment, long dormant, welled up uncontrollably. "It's unfair, that's what it is. It's because you don't like me, never have, and you're not going to stop punishing me for being born!"

"Valerie!" Edith gasped.

"I'm sorry, Mama, but it's true and we all know it. For years I've kept quiet, but no more. I'm tired of the criticism and I'm tired of all the refusals, and I'm tired of the unfair way you treat me. Let me tell you something. You still have the right to force me to obey you, to listen when you say I can't go someplace or can't see someone. That's because I'm only fifteen now and I have no choice except to listen. But pretty soon I'll be old enough to do exactly as I please. Who're you going to get to do your darning and cooking and cleaning then, Mama? Who're you going to whip then, Papa? Just wait, all of you. A few more years and then I'll be gone—away from your complaints and your orders, away from your unfairness. You're wrong, Papa—hard work *has* taught me a lesson. It's taught me that only the people who can't fight back are forced to do it. Well, all right, then. I may be forced to listen now, but not forever. Not forever!"

She waited for the slap across her face from her father, the outrage from her mother, the jeering from Ned, the knowing smirk from Alice. There was only shocked silence. Trembling with anger, with relief for not being beaten, and with surprise at herself for the defiant outburst, Valerie pushed back her chair and got to her feet. "Excuse me," she murmured, and went to her room.

Billy came in to see her later that night.

"You okay?" he asked.

She was sitting Indian-fashion on her bed, leaning against the headboard, staring into nothing. At his question, she nodded, but did not look at him. He sat down on Alice's bed, facing Valerie.

"I'm proud of you, Val. I was scared there for a while, thought you were gonna get it for sure." His smile was filled with admiration. "You really told 'em. They didn't say another word after you left. Only sound was them swallowing their food."

"And you ate, too, didn't you, Billy?" she asked quietly.

"Well, sure, what else—"

"I figured maybe you'd get up and leave too. Kind of a silent protest, you know?" She was looking at Billy now with an expression of sad resignation.

"Hey, Val, I couldn't do that."

"Of course not, Billy, I'm sorry. It's just that I thought... oh, never mind."

"No, tell me. Tell me what made you think I'd suddenly have the guts to stand up to them." Billy got up from the bed, went to fiddle with the makeup on the vanity a moment before facing his sister again. His voice was brittle with anger when he spoke.

"I'm almost nineteen, Val, and I still don't have the courage to break away."

"You will, Billy. One of these days—"

"One of these days, hell! Working on the farm for a couple of bucks and tending bar on weekends isn't filling my pockets with anything more than loose change." He ran a hand through his fine, wheat-colored hair. "I hate it, Val. I hate the farm and our father and every day I have to live here, but I don't know what to do about it. I just don't know."

Valerie said nothing. She and her brother were victims, and words of false encouragement could not protect either of them.

"I'm sorry," he said, calmer now. "You didn't need to hear that. It's just that I don't want you to hate me when I disappoint you." He smiled ruefully as he moved toward the door. "Truth is, I guess, that I don't want you to hate me when I disappoint myself."

"I love you, Billy," Valerie whispered.

He left without answering, and Valerie returned to the silence of her thoughts. Before her brother had come to see her, she had been thinking of what had occurred tonight and the lesson she had learned. She savored her new insight as if it were the juice of a ripe fruit.

Tonight she had gained knowledge that, while it might

not gain her the immediate freedom to go to a party with Carl Enderby or anyone else, it had made her aware that she, of all the children, frightened her parents. Alice's obedience had turned her into a sexual baton, passed from one twirler to another until she would lie discarded from overuse. Billy's acquiescence had made him a shadow personality, wise enough to admire strength, too scared to draw from it. Ned was his father's son; Eli and Edith could easily accept his spasms of straining against the parental ropes: too much drinking and brawling. Immorality, cowardice, trouble-making—all could be understood and discounted as youthful energy or ignorance. Nothing to fear.

But in the hush that had greeted her explosion, Valerie had suddenly understood the power she possessed, the threat she posed to the wall of self-delusion they had striven so hard to erect. She alone dared to voice her claim for more than what was planned for her, and her intention to get it. When the time was right, they would not be able to stop her, and that was the threat: they knew they were impotent once that day arrived. All they could do in the meantime was try to postpone its arrival.

The pride and self-satisfaction Valerie felt that night struggled to stay alive when she told Carl Enderby the next day that she could not go to his party. Her determined vow to one day get out faltered each time a boy invited her somewhere and she said no; each time a girl tried to be friendly and she deliberately shunned the overture. What was the point of pretending she could be one of them? Soon enough the invitations and friendliness stopped, as they had when she was younger. Now, though, the explanation was not that Valerie was a bookworm, a daydreamer. Now Valerie was too big for her britches, thought she was better than they were.

She wrapped loneliness around herself with an ease born of familiarity. She forced herself not to think of what she was missing, only of what she could have someday. She told herself she did not mind forfeiting her adolescence if it would mean an adulthood she alone controlled. But the loneliness hurt, the aloof posture she forced herself to adopt hurt; even the dreams began to ache, weighing down her fierce determination so that it became a millstone instead of an amulet she could call upon for strength. By the time she was sixteen, Valerie's hope had become scar tissue, itching occasionally, fading rapidly.

Then two incidents occurred that rekindled Valerie's desperate determination. It might have been better, she often thought afterward, if they had never happened: they only served to make her aware again that wanting out was one thing; having the means to get out was quite another.

Valerie awoke the morning of the junior-class outing with her heart pounding. She could not remember being this excited since the first time she had been allowed to go to Mack's house for Christmas. She dressed with deliberate care, wearing a turquoise and white polka-dotted full skirt Alice had given her, a wide black patent-leather belt, and a fuzzy, white angora sweater. Around her wrist she wore a pink and white baby bracelet with her name spelled out on individual beads—Mack's Christmas present to her last year and a special joy to her. It was the only article she had that was fashionable at the right time; all the girls in school were wearing them.

Now she sat at the makeshift vanity, brushing and rebrushing her hair until it gleamed like lacquered ebony.

"You'd think you were going on a date instead of the stupid class outing," Alice remarked from bed. "And would you please be a little quieter. It's only seven-thirty and you know I don't have to be down at the paper until nine."

Since Alice had graduated from high school in June, she had been working as a girl friday at the *Galesville Courier*, taking a course in Eddington on Saturdays to learn how to type and take shorthand so she could become a secretary. Usually Valerie was considerate in the morning, but today she was too full of the promise of the day to think of anyone but herself.

"I'm sorry, it's just that I'm so excited," Valerie bubbled. "Do you realize this will be my first trip to Eddington?" She put down her hairbrush and turned on the orange-crate chair. "Alice, you can't imagine what this means to me because you've been there so many times, but Eddington is like another world to me. Eighty miles from here. I bet the bus trip takes hours."

"It takes two, to be exact," Alice said. "Which is hardly worth the effort once you get there," she added with a tone of worldly sophistication.

"Well, I don't care how long it takes, I can't wait." She stood up and held out the sides of her skirt. "How do I look?"

Alice let her eyes run from the top of her sister's glossy hair to the full lips that had been lightly colored with peach lipstick, then down to the narrow waist made narrower by the wide belt. Valerie looked lovely, doing more for the skirt than she ever had, more for the sweater than she ever would. "Fine," she said shortly, "you look fine. Now let me get back to sleep." She put the pillow over her head to avoid any further conversation.

But there was no more sleep for Alice that morning even after Valerie had left. She kept seeing the image of her sister, the freshness, the promise; and fear for what was happening to her own life washed over her again, as it had with growing frequency. She was eighteen years old, with no husband in sight; no one to rescue her from the tedium of her days at the newspaper, the idiocy of the secretarial course. She had no idea what her future held except more of the same. She had to find a man and get out of Galesville, but she had gone through all the available ones, and had even started to see what was possible in Eddington. It was always the same: a few beers, some groping, and either she would go to bed with them because she was bored and had nothing better to do, or she would refuse, the man's prospects not desirable enough to be seductive. Seeing her sister as she was this morning—eager, hopeful, tarnished by nothing more serious than a family who was wary of her—made Alice acutely aware of how desperate her situation was and how powerless she felt to change it. She hated her sister this morning, hated her viciously for not having committed the same mistakes she had made, not having had the opportunity to make them. She hated her for the beauty she would grow into, for her intelligence, and most of all for her innocence. Until this morning, she had resented Valerie, been jealous of her, but seeing her today had somehow intensified those feelings until they had become loathing. She told herself, as she flung the pillow and cover from her, that the feeling would go away; it was temporary and would vanish once her own life gave her satisfaction.

The expectancy and joy with which Valerie greeted the day was as ephemeral as Alice's brief hatred of her sister. As soon as Valerie boarded the school bus, an overwhelming sense of loneliness threatened to dissolve her into tears. Merry and Caroline, inseparable, were chattering with the other girls, all pairing off and claiming seats together. Carl Enderby and his friends sat near the back of the bus, an invisible rope marking off their male domain. With the exception of Ashton Rampole, the anemic, greasy-haired class "genius," and herself, everyone had a friend to sit with, laugh with, make plans with. Ashton sat with Mrs. Fingers, the teacher, which Valerie had known he would do because he was that kind of boy. Even he would have been preferable to taking the seat behind the driver, the emptiness next to her a mocking companion.

With the same willful determination that had seen her through other disappointments, Valerie vowed that she would let nothing spoil this day for her. As the bus trundled along, she kept her face against the smudgy window, exhilarated by being on the move, unmindful of the dullness of the flat farm landscape. And when the giggling and chattering became the lusty singing of "A Hundred Bottles of Beer on the Wall," and "Red Red Robin," Valerie joined in.

After about an hour and a half, she began to see signs of life. There was a drive-in movie, a small church, then a shingled house with a sign in the window saying VETERINARIAN. The highway soon became a paved road with shops on either side: a uniform store, a luncheonette, a small grocery, Eddington Stationers, and the Eddington Jewel Theater, where *Bridge on the River Kwai* was playing. The bus lurched around a corner and up a hill, past the biggest supermarket Valerie had ever seen, with a parking lot she was sure could hold thousands of cars. Next to the supermarket were a pizza parlor, a bakery, and a card shop. The bus lumbered farther up the hill, then down another and into the Eddington Center. There was a J. C. Penney and a Sears, just doors from each other, and at one end of the sprawling concrete city was a Montgomery Ward. Valerie could not believe what she was seeing. There were even more parking spots here than at the supermarket, and stores . . . she had never dreamed there could be so many shops in one place. A bookstore, four shoe stores, a bowling alley, two movie theaters, a Chinese restaurant, an ice-skating rink! She wanted to bolt from the bus, go into every single place and sample their wares as if they were different flavors of ice cream.

"All right, class, here we are. Our first stop will be J. C. Penney, so those who need to may use their facilities. Now remember, there is to be no going off on your own," Mrs. Fingers instructed. "We are to stay together as a group throughout this outing, and for anyone who dares to do otherwise, I promise you the punishment will be severe. We will take in the shopping center this morning, have lunch—which I assume you all brought with you—at some lovely outdoor tables, and then there will be a friendly game of bowling before we return here promptly at four o'clock. Are there any questions?"

Ashton raised his hand.

"Yes, Ashton?"

"I don't bowl, Mrs. Fingers. Could I spend that time at the bookstore?"

"Hey, Ash, give it a rest," Carl called out.

"No, Ashton, you cannot. You can sit and cheer," Mrs. Fingers said. "And, Carl, no more of that."

With a stern look around at her charges, she nodded at the bus driver, and the group alighted.

Valerie could not stop touching the pretty dresses, ogling the perfumes and costume jewelry. The chirping of the girls and the snide remarks of the boys were lost to her as she exulted in her first acquaintance with freedom. As the day progressed, she grew giddy with the sensation. She was alone, on her own. No one paid any attention to her; they were all too busy flirting with one another, or looking for dirty books in the bookstore, or chortling over the contemporary cards in the card shop. At lunch she sat with two girls who were on the fringe of Merry's group. When she tried to express to them the awe she had felt in the bookstore, they started talking about the adorable boy behind the cash register, not about the books. Valerie pretended she had noticed him too, but she hadn't; she hadn't seen anything all day except life without limits. She felt like laughing, like wrapping her arms around herself and dancing down the street. It was all just as she had dreamed it, and she knew Eddington was just a small part of that magical LIFE.

It was during the bowling game that she made her decision. She was part of the cheering squad, and this seemed a waste of precious time to her, time she could have to herself, exploring. While everyone was concentrating on the players, she told Mrs. Fingers she was going to the ladies' room. Since Mrs. Fingers was keeping score, she simply nodded, not even looking up to see who was speaking to her. After that it was easy.

Without hesitation, she headed back toward the bookstore, stopping to splurge fifteen cents of her dollar on a chocolate marshmallow ice-cream cone with chocolate sprinkles from a tiny shop that sold only ice cream. It was while she was walking to the bookstore, licking her ice cream, observing the people bustling about with packages, that she made another decision. It was not enough just to be away from the group and then return to them at four o'clock. She would not be on that bus when it left. She would not return to Galesville and her parents and her frustrating life. Even if it meant giving up Mack, she would do it. Somehow, she would get a job and earn money and move on. It wasn't as if she was running away from anyone who really cared about her, she reasoned. After the initial shock, her parents would probably be glad to have her gone.

At four o'clock, Mrs. Fingers took a head count and found one missing. She counted two more times and the number did not change.

"Who's not here?" she called out. "We can't leave until we're all accounted for."

Because Valerie was not a prominent member of the class, no one missed her immediately.

"Come on, Mrs. Fingers, I got a two-hour trip ahead of me," the bus driver said from his perch.

"I have a responsibility to bring home the same number of children I started out with!" Her voice rose with nervousness. "Each of you call out your name, and then we'll see who's missing."

They were midway through the class when Carl said, "It's Valerie Cardell, Mrs. Fingers. She's the one."

"Valerie?" Mrs. Fingers repeated, disbelieving. Valerie was so quiet, so obedient.

"Oh, dear me," she fretted. "Well, all of you get on the bus. I'm going to take a quick look around and see if I can find her. Carl, you come with me; Caroline, you take charge until we're back."

"Hurry up, Mrs. Fingers, I'm losing valuable time," the driver warned.

For twenty minutes Carl and Mrs. Fingers scrambled around the shopping center, backtracking to the outdoor tables and to the bowling alley, where Mrs. Fingers went into the ladies' room looking for Valerie. Finally, Mrs. Fingers said, "Come along, Carl. I don't know what might have happened to her, but we have to get home. I'll notify her parents and the police if she hasn't called home by then. I can't imagine what has happened. It wouldn't be like her to run away."

"I don't know, Mrs. Fingers," Carl said slowly. "Valerie can be . . . kinda different."

Mrs. Fingers' eyes flashed. "If you mean she's very bright and likes to read and doesn't carry on like the rest of you, yes, Carl, then you're right, she's different. That is a young lady I'd like to see go on to college. There's a lot of promise there."

"Maybe we should check out the bookstore again," Carl offered.

"There's no time now. We really have to leave."

Had Mrs. Fingers checked the bookstore, she would not have found Valerie there. She had left almost thirty minutes before to wander through the cosmetics department of Sears, then to sit and watch the people ice skating in the huge indoor rink. By six o'clock, she began to get hungry.

She wandered around some more, staving off her hunger until the coming darkness, chill, and cries of her stomach propelled her into a small coffee shop. She had only eighty-five cents—not enough to buy a real meal. She ordered an English muffin and a glass of milk, and then two large jelly doughnuts; the dime she had left over she would leave as a tip, she decided. She ate slowly and sparingly, savoring the events of the day. It was when the proprietor of the restaurant began to wipe the tables, then stopped to answer the pay telephone, looking at her occasionally as he spoke, that Valerie realized she was the only customer. The clock behind the counter said it was seven-thirty. She had had no idea it was so late, and for the first time since embarking on this adventure, concern began to creep into her thoughts. Where would she sleep? How would she get money to eat? If her parents found her, she knew she would get the beating of her life. But it had been worth it; was worth it if they never found her and she had to scrounge and scramble for every meal.

"Am I keeping you?" she asked the man when he got off the telephone.

"Nope. You can stay as long as you like."

The smile on his face masked his lie. He had been on the phone with the Eddington police; they had called, as they had called all the shopping-center establishments, to ask if a girl matching Valerie's description had been seen. The proprietor of the coffee shop promised the police he would keep her there until they arrived.

"I better be going. I'm sure you want to go home," Valerie said, making no effort to rise.

"Just stay where you are. Here, have another jelly doughnut," he offered.

"Oh no, I couldn't. I don't have enough money."

"It's on the house, okay?"

Valerie smiled shyly. "Okay."

"Waiting for your parents?" he asked.

She shook her head.

"Boyfriend?"

Again, a silent negative.

"Where's home?"

Fear darkened Valerie's eyes, and she slid back into the corner of the booth.

"Hey, I'm sorry. I didn't mean to upset you."

"I'm not upset," she muttered. Then, proudly: "I've run away from home and I'm not waiting for anybody." She spoke the words as a challenge. "I'm going to get a job and I'm just trying to decide the best place to begin."

"Well, you can't do anything until morning, you know. Where you planning on sleeping tonight?"

Valerie looked guardedly at the paunchy, bald man and

decided his words were without ulterior motive. "I don't know, but I'll find a place."

"Don't you think your parents are worried? Maybe you should call them?"

"I was going to," she admitted, "but I used up my money on food. I'll call them in the morning, after I get a job."

"Meanwhile, there's tonight."

Valerie gazed down at the scratched formica table and a lone powdered crumb from one of her doughnuts. "I'll think of something," she whispered.

Ten minutes later, the door to the coffee shop was swung open with such force that it shook on its hinges.

"You damn no-good brat! I'm gonna kill you for this!"

Valerie's eyes widened as her father stomped over to her, his normally gaunt, hollow-cheeked face swollen with fury. "Papa!" she gasped, getting to her feet.

Eli Cardell had her by the upper arm and was yanking her away from the protection of the table. "You won't know what a beating is when I'm through with you! Runnin' away like a common tramp! Whaddaya think you were doin'? Driving your poor mother half-dead with worry. You're gonna—" He raised his hand, palm open, way behind him, aiming to meet her face with the full force of his body. Suddenly his arm was stopped in mid-air by the policeman who had come in after him.

"That's not going to solve anything," the policeman said. "Maybe it's that kind of thing that made her run away in the first place."

"You mind your business," Eli barked, but he lowered his arm, although he did not relinquish the tight grip his other hand had on Valerie's arm. "Come on, you... you bitch! I'm gonna take you home and teach you a lesson without any interference!"

Abruptly, unexpectedly, Valerie pulled away, her eyes smoldering as she faced her father. "You can do whatever you want to me. You can beat me till I can't move. But I escaped once and I'm going to do it again. Remember that, Papa, again and again and again until I reach that place where you won't ever be able to find me!"

With that, Eli did slap his daughter, and there was

nothing the policeman or the coffee-shop owner could do to stop him. Valerie never shed a tear, not then, nor on the way home when he went on relentlessly about what he was going to do to her. And not when he did beat her, first with his belt, then with a wooden board. Not when she was forced to go to school, forced to do chores when her entire body shrieked in agony. Not when her mother stopped speaking to her or when Ned opened the door to her room the second evening and laughed callously in her face; not when Billy sat by her bed and held her hand, telling her how sorry he was; not when Alice said nothing, not one word, acting as if the entire incident had never taken place. There were no tears throughout this ordeal; Valerie gathered strength instead from the memory of that almost-perfect day and the hope it held for her.

Then, on the fourth day, she overheard a conversation.

"Where is she, Edith? She sick or something? I heard about her running away. What happened?"

"It's none of your business, Mack. And I suggest you don't come by to see her anymore."

"Edith, let's not forget I own this farm and I'll see anybody I damn please. You know why she ran away. And she's going to do it again. You and Eli don't let her breathe. Christ, I'd be worried if she *didn't* try to get out."

"What're you sayin'?"

"I'm saying that you got at least one child who isn't willing to roll over and play dead for the rest of her life just to make it easier on you and your fool husband."

"Well, Mack, it doesn't matter a damn what you think, because Eli and I are Valerie's parents and we're the ones who'll teach her how to behave."

"Don't try to stop her from seeing me, Edith," Mack warned. "I won't stand for it."

"You don't have no choice."

From where she was crouched at the top of the stairs, Valerie realized her father had come in. Her body trembled with anxiety for what would happen now. There had been no mention of her visits to Mack; she had assumed that once she felt better she would start to see him again. She had meant to go over a day ago, but she had been so sore that just walking home from school had been an effort. Now she wished she had.

"What do you mean I have no choice, Eli?" Mack was saying. "I told you once before, your job was on the line if you ever raised a hand to her again. I'm guessing that the reason I haven't seen her is because she's in too much pain to move."

"That's right, so now fire me if you want. Because I'm gonna keep on beatin' that girl till I get some sense into her. And until I knock out all the damage you've done."

"*I've* done!"

"Yeah, you and your high-falutin' ideas about big cities and fancy restaurants and theater—nothin' she'll ever know about. Fillin' her with these dreams so it's impossible to even talk to her anymore. That's why she ran away. *You* caused it. She was perfectly happy doin' what she was told till you came along and put those fool ideas in her head. She ran away so she could look for all you told her about."

Eli took a deep breath, his sneer contemptuous as his eyes darted from his wife to the man who was his boss, his wife's lover, his enemy. "I'm warnin' you, Mr. Landry, *sir*. I learn that Valerie is at your place one more time, I'll break her arm. And I'll break every bone in her body till you and she understand that *I'm* her father and that you can't have nothin' more to do with her!"

Mack knew that he could threaten Eli about his job, he could even come to blows with him, but the man would never back down. And firing him would not help Valerie in any way. Mack had no right to her except as someone who loved her; in this family, that was no right at all. Loving her, it seemed, had put her in jeopardy, and he would not risk that again.

"All right, Eli," Mack said softly. "Valerie is no longer welcome in my home."

"And don't try to do anything sneaky behind my back," Eli went on belligerently, feeling cocky in his triumph. "She's forbidden to see you anywhere, anytime, understand? Forbidden!"

Mack's answer was to slam the kitchen door as he left. As that door shut, friendship and hope and courage went out of Valerie's life. For this pain, finally, she cried.

It was not until the following autumn that Mack and

Valerie spoke again, under circumstances that both wished had never taken place.

Valerie had spent the worst summer of her life; not even books eased her depression. The only relief from the sameness of the days and nights was the increasingly frequent quarrels between Ned and Eli. At twenty-one, Ned was no longer satisfied with the temporary amusement derived from petty thievery, or Saturday-night brawls after too much beer, or drag racing halfway to Eddington in his third-hand Rambler. It was not that he wanted to leave the farm, at least not yet; he liked the free meals and having his shirts ironed and his socks laundered. What he did not like was watching the boys he hung around with leave Galesville, one by one, until only Wayne Landry and Ralph Danziger were left, and Ralph was semi-retarded. In his restlessness, Ned started to drink more, which led to more fights and to more property damages for which Eli had to pay. And that was what caused the quarrels.

After a particularly bad one toward the end of the summer, Eli grounded Ned for a week, but he sneaked out to seek solace with Wayne. At the back of Mack's house was a detached garage; usually Mack kept his wood-sided Ford station wagon there, while Wayne left his red Thunderbird convertible—also Mack's, but Wayne had permission to use it anytime—in front of the house. Ned went to the garage knowing that sometime during the evening Wayne would show up for a few beers. He was there when Ned walked in.

After Ned finished complaining about his father, Wayne broached a subject he had tried before that Ned had always refused to discuss: Alice and Valerie. That night Ned was so angry at his father that the emotion extended to every member of his family. So, when Wayne again began to graphically describe the anatomies of Ned's sisters and what they did to him, Ned did not shut him up.

"Well, why don't you do somethin' about it then instead of always talkin' about it?" Ned encouraged.

"You kiddin'?" Wayne replied with a dry laugh. "Your father'd kill me. Jesus, *my* father'd kill me!" He laughed again before taking a deep slug from his beer can.

"How would they know?" Ned asked, warming to the subject.

"Whaddaya mean?" Wayne said, looking at his older friend curiously. "Course they'd know. Alice would tell them."

A slow grin spread across Ned's face. He should have thought of this before: watching ugly Wayne Landry make it with one of his sisters would be terrific fun. But he knew Alice hadn't been a virgin for years. The real amusement would be with Valerie. His "better than the rest of 'em" little sister. Now *that* would be worth the price of admission.

"But Valerie wouldn't tell," Ned said now, keeping a keen eye on the younger boy.

"Valerie? You're outta your mind!" Wayne exclaimed, beer spilling from his mouth as he choked on the preposterous idea.

Ned grabbed Wayne's arm. "Why not? Why the hell not? You're so hot for her, why not do it? She'll never say a word. She'll love it, I bet."

"You're crazy." But the words were spoken with less conviction as Wayne's mind busied itself with images of Valerie . . . naked, writhing under him . . . scratching him. He began to laugh, a high, nervous giggle. "You really think so? Jeez, what a pair of jugs on her. Hey, you ever seen 'em?"

"Sure," Ned lied. "They're even bigger without clothes on. You'll probably come just lookin' at 'em."

"Well, I don't know," Wayne said, shaking his head. "What if she does tell?"

"No way. She and my old man hate each other. She'd sooner die than go to him."

"Yeah, but what about my old man?"

"What about him? I'm tellin' ya, there's nothin' to worry about."

"Ned's right."

Both Wayne and Ned jumped to their feet, their eyes, accustomed to the dark, not immediately able to make out who had spoken.

"It's me, Alice," she said, moving closer to them, a wide smile on her face.

"What the hell you doin' here?" Ned snapped.

"Oh, I was just taking a walk and then I decided to see if Mack was home, and when I heard laughing in here I thought I'd see what was happening. I was wondering if maybe Wayne was with a girl." She laughed lightly.

"Why'd you want to see my father?" Wayne asked suspiciously.

"Oh, no special reason, just to pass some time." She would never tell anyone that the idea had come to her to seduce Mack Landry. She would then have her claws into someone with money, and she would certainly have bested her sister. But on the way over she had had second thoughts. She preferred not to consider what would occur if her father ever found out; besides, Mack might turn her down, and that she would not like at all. What she had just heard might be more fun anyway.

"So, Wayne, you going to listen to Ned and see what you can do about Valerie?" she asked.

"Hey, Alice, this is no business of yours," Ned said.

"Oh, stop being so dumb. I'm telling you Valerie will love it. It's about time she knew what a real man was like, isn't that right, Wayne?" And she smiled again, taunting him with all her female promise. Then, suddenly, the smile was gone, and her sky-blue eyes hardened as she envisioned Valerie's loss of innocence.

"Do it, Wayne," she urged breathlessly. "Do it."

And so the seed was planted, not to reach fruition until the second week of October, when Wayne insisted on giving Valerie a lift home from school.

Ned and Wayne and Alice were wrong: Valerie fought viciously. She had not abided injustice for so long to fall victim to it again, not when she had a choice. Wayne became frightened enough to open the car door and shove her out. Then Valerie proved Ned and Wayne and Alice wrong again. She did go to her father, who went to Mack, dragging Valerie with him. Her shame and embarrassment were heightened as her father embellished the story of the attempted rape. Eyes glistening with unshed tears she beseeched Mack not to blame her, not to believe for one minute that she had encouraged his son.

There could be no question of blame when Mack was faced with her torn sweater, the two missing buttons of her blouse, the faintly discernible imprint of fingers around her slender neck. When Mack summoned Wayne to the living room, the evidence of guilt was equally apparent. A long scratch on his cheek was freshly caked with a bloody scab, and his right hand had unmistakable teeth marks on it. Wayne did not even try to deny what he had done; instead, he attempted to share the blame.

"Ned and Alice said she'd never go to you! They said she'd like it!" he whimpered, straining against the pressure of his father's fingers digging into the soft flesh of his arm. "I told them it wouldn't work. I told them, but they both said it would be okay!" Then he began to cry.

"Go up to your room, Wayne. I'll deal with you later," Mack said stiffly. When he was out of sight, Mack said, "I don't know how to begin to apologize to both of you. I promise you that the boy will be severely punished. I'm very sorry this happened. Very sorry."

"That makes two Landrys forbidden near my daughter, hear?" Eli said in a voice gravelly with hatred. "You and your perverted son."

"What he did was wrong, Eli, but let me tell you something. Wayne doesn't have the wit to think up such a scheme himself. If he says Ned and Alice put him up to it, then by damn I believe him! That makes *your* kids perverts, Eli, not mine!"

"You can just go to hell!" Eli shouted. With Valerie in tow, he moved toward the front door. "You and your whole rotten family can just roast in hell!"

There was no further mention of the incident in the Cardell home. In fact, Ned and Alice were never more caring and considerate toward Valerie than in the days that followed. The possibility that they had had anything to do with the incident seemed ludicrous to Valerie. She might not always get along with Ned, and maybe she and Alice sometimes got on each other's nerves, but there was no way they would have tried deliberately to hurt her; of that she was sure.

Less than a week later, Mack was standing midway between his house and the Cardells' cottage, waiting for Valerie to come home from school.

"Valerie, come on over here a minute. I want to tell you something," he called out, waving to her before she went up the path to her house.

She looked around like a trapped squirrel, checking to see if the predator that was her father was around. Tentatively, she approached Mack.

"I shouldn't be here talking with you. If my father sees me—"

"Don't worry about it, Valerie." Mack looked at her closely. "Feeling any better?"

"I'll be okay," she answered, avoiding his eyes.

"I've been waiting here for you because I wanted you to hear this from me and not from anyone else. I'm leaving Galesville," he said gently. "Wayne and I are going back to Chicago."

"But why?" Valerie cried. Although she had not been able to visit him, she had known he was there, and that had been a comfort. What he was saying now chipped away at the last piece of her dreams.

"You can't go, you just can't!"

"I have to. I don't want to, but what happened with Wayne . . . Well, I don't see any alternative. I want him working for me in the office—maybe that'll give him some sense of responsibility. I don't think he's a bad boy at heart, just too easily influenced, and I don't want to risk his doing to someone else what he tried to do to you."

"I thought you didn't like Chicago," Valerie said, the words an accusation. She was hurt and needed to strike back. "You said you love the farm, love living here. Why did you lie to me?"

Mack slowly shook his head and put his hand on her shoulder. Out of hurt, she wanted to pull away, but it had been so long since she had felt the warmth of his touch that she did not move a muscle for fear that he would let go.

"You know I didn't lie, Valerie, and if you weren't so hurt you wouldn't say such a thing. I do love it here, but I've got to give Wayne some room to grow. He needs the playground of a big city now." He hesitated, and his expression grew more serious. He removed his hand and glanced briefly at the flat landscape.

"I'll be back, Valerie, I promise. Just as soon as I can. And in the meantime, you have to give me your word on something."

She waited, silent.

"Don't give up, Valerie, not for one minute. I know I told you this once before, but it's even more important now. Don't let any of them get you down—not your parents, the kids at school, your brothers and sister, none of them. I know it's been difficult for you lately, worse than it used to be because I haven't been able to help. I'm sure you've felt sometimes like forgetting all those dreams of yours. But don't forget them. Keep wanting, keep believing, and try to be patient a little longer. Sometimes it's going to be really tough, Valerie, but if you keep that determined spirit of yours, you'll get what you want."

There was no sound but the rustle of the falling leaves for several long seconds. Tears began to fall down Valerie's cheeks.

"Well? Do I have your word?"

"I won't give up," Valerie whispered fiercely. "I promise."

When the orders for the class rings were taken, Valerie's name was absent.

When the yearbook was distributed, under Valerie's picture it said: "Quietly defiant, but who knows what she's *really* thinking?"

When the college acceptances were proudly announced in the auditorium, Valerie stayed in the ladies' room. Eli and Edith had told her, her teacher, and her principal that Valerie had no need of a college education for life on a farm.

When the graduation dance was held, Valerie was not invited. Alice said it was because she was too smart and scared the boys. Edith said it was because she was such a snob, always off by herself.

When her classmates began to brag about the graduation presents they had been promised—a second- instead of third-hand used car, a wristwatch, a record player—Valerie thought of the two books her family had bought her: *Wuthering Heights* and *Jane Eyre*. She had read them both years ago.

She had no one to tell of her disappointments or her loneliness, or that it was getting more and more difficult to keep her promise.

Chapter 4

Valerie hoisted the metal tray with its dishes covered with dried sauce and sticky crumbs, and trudged back into the restaurant kitchen. Like the two other waitresses and the kitchen help, she was entitled to a free lunch, but on this steamy August afternoon, food held no appeal. She wanted only to leave the stifling restaurant for an hour to go to the man-made lake that Galesville used as a public swimming pool.

Listlessly, she walked outside where the heat shimmered off the ground and the humidity kept it in place like a plane in a holding pattern. Her dark hair stuck damply to her forehead, and her skin was pasty with the kind of sheen that comes from fever or chill. Her yellow sleeveless blouse was ringed with perspiration under the arms; she pulled it out of the waistband of her white Arnel sharkskin pleated skirt, waving the shirttails in a futile bid for a breeze.

Twice a day every day since graduation, except Sunday nights, Valerie waited tables at the restaurant of the Hotel Golden, which was really a motel rather than a hotel. Between her lunch and dinner shifts, she usually went home to prepare the family meals and do her chores, which had not lessened in the intervening months. She had finally begged permission from her parents to have Sunday nights as her own, to do as she wished. Usually this meant a solitary walk by the lake or an equally lonely hour in the playground by the school, swaying slowly on one of the children's swings, wondering if, at seventeen, her future had already been canceled. Until July, the only respite from the monotony had been an occasional date with one of the local boys, but these had quickly proved as unsatisfactory to them as to her. Their clumsy, predictable gropings, her equally predictable refusals, and her lack of guile, which made it impossible to pretend interest when she had none, soon returned her to the isolation she had come to know so well. Then, in mid-July, Mack came home, and Valerie's heart lightened.

Wayne too was back in Galesville, driving his new red Volkswagen to his job as a shoe salesman in the Eddington mall. The few times Valerie had accidentally run into him, she had not acknowledged his presence; not even Mack's insistence that his son deeply regretted what had happened and had changed, was more mature, persuaded Valerie to recognize Wayne's existence. As she had done in the past when Eli beat her, Valerie tuned out reality and concentrated on something fine and pure beyond the pain. That was how she treated Wayne Landry—as someone who had no meaning, no effect; not even Mack could soften her determination regarding his son. Other than that, Valerie and Mack were quick to reestablish their special friendship. But it was a careful relationship, one that had to be conducted with all the skill of secret lovers since Eli was ever watchful of the influence his boss had on his daughter. Often Mack had dinner at the restaurant and lingered until she was off duty so that they could walk home together. Occasionally they went swimming together, and as they lolled under the summer sun, Mack told her about Chicago, and she haltingly shared the hurts of the past year.

She was wondering now if Mack would be at the lake this blistering afternoon when suddenly she heard her name being called. She turned and saw Alice coming down the steps of the building that housed the *Galesville Courier*.

"Hi. What are you doing out at this hour? Did the office close on account of the heat?" Valerie asked with a smile, admiring the way the sun seemed to create a halo around her sister's blonde hair.

"I wish. No, I have to go to the post office and get some stamps for Teddy. You on your way home?"

"Thought I'd head over to the lake for a while," Valerie told her. "Who's Teddy?"

"You're impossible," Alice said with exasperation, falling in step beside her sister. "He's the new reporter I've been telling you about. Don't you remember anything?"

"Oh, that's right. He's the one from out west somewhere, isn't he?"

"Boise," Alice supplied with a pout of her coral-painted lips. "Don't you pay any attention? Honestly, Val, he's all I've been talking about since he started last week, and you can't remember a thing. You've got to be the most self-centered person I've ever met."

Valerie smiled. "Come to think of it, you haven't been complaining as much about your job lately," she said, feeling no rancor at her sister's accusation of selfishness. Valerie had learned to treat most of her sister's remarks with an indifference that she had finally come to feel.

"I hardly think being aware of the inferiority of one's position is complaining," Alice said archly, and Valerie laughed.

"What's so funny?" Alice asked, stopping outside the post office.

"Nothing. Tell me more about this new reporter. Is he good?"

Alice's grin was sly and knowing. "Ask me that tomorrow. Tonight we're going into Eddington to see *To Kill a Mockingbird.*"

"I meant as a reporter," Valerie said stiffly, disliking it when her sister brought her sexuality out in the open.

"Oh, well, sure, I guess he's good. He's planning to work for a big paper in Indianapolis or Chicago soon, but he wants to get some more experience under his belt. That's why he took this job with the *Courier*. He's only twenty-two and he says he doesn't want to be just some cub reporter on one of the important papers and that it's worth being stuck in Galesville for a while to prove himself." She started toward the post office. "Tell Mama I'll be home late," she instructed, then disappeared into the building.

A small smile tugged at Valerie's mouth as she continued walking. Sometimes she wished she could be more like her sister. Alice wanted only to get married and live away from Galesville; to have her own pale blue Chevrolet Impala, her own house with a backyard barbecue, lots of pretty clothes, and a mirror-topped vanity table reflecting colorful bottles of polish and paint. It was all there waiting for her . . . she had only to find the man to supply it. And that, Valerie knew, was the challenge for her sister. There had been many men interested in Alice, but none had been good enough for Edith's little princess, or the little princess had not cherished herself dearly enough to prove valuable in a lasting way. But Valerie knew that if it was not this young man Teddy, there would soon be someone else to rescue Alice from Galesville.

If only there could be such a simple way out for herself, she thought, her smile fading with the brief breeze that floated down to her from a lone apple tree. But it was not the kind of escape she sought, and even had it been, Alice's beauty was too dazzling to compete against. Besides, Valerie thought with the sharp perception she frequently ignored, even if there was a Prince Charming for her, he would have to show up after Alice found hers. Mother and sister never would permit it to be any other way.

Valerie climbed the two flights of marble steps that led to the *Courier*'s offices. For a few weeks now Alice had been asking her to visit her there, but Valerie had always found an excuse to avoid what she felt would be an uncomfortable situation for her. There were still too many piercing memories from school, when Alice would flutter like a butterfly around her friends, either ignoring her sister to the point of embarrassment or whispering about her aloofness with the same cruel humor as did strangers. Since Valerie's graduation, the two had become closer, the fear for their individual futures a mutual bond, but it was a fragile tie, and Valerie expected it to be broken as soon as Alice attained what she desired.

Early this morning, before Alice had left for work, she had again asked Valerie to drop in to see her; her insistence made Valerie feel too guilty to refuse. Now, as she stood in front of the frosted-glass door of the newspaper's office and listened to the cricket chatter of the typesetting machine, Valerie wondered if the repeated invitation was to give Alice an opportunity to show off Teddy rather than to be friendly. Valerie admitted to herself that she was interested in meeting him, primarily because Alice was so enthusiastic about him.

Valerie pushed open the door and stepped into the spacious room. It was divided by plastic walls into several separate cubicles, not all of them for *Courier* business. Since the paper only came out weekly, Fred Brickley, the publisher and owner of the entire building, rented out space to a few businessmen, including the town's one insurance agent, the TV-and-radio repairman, and Galesville's sole undertaker. Valerie heard the honeyed giggle of her sister's laugh, a sound as recognizable as the chiming of the United Methodist Church's bell on Sundays, and followed it to a cubicle in the rear. She poked her head around the opening and saw Alice seated in a chipped wooden chair, leaning forward, elbows on the desk in front of her, face posed prettily in the palm of one hand. She was smiling at a young man who was smiling back at her from the other side of a wooden desk. Valerie determined that this was Teddy.

"Alice?" Valerie said tentatively.

Alice turned around. "Valerie! What in the world are you doing here?"

Valerie stared at her sister, not understanding. Then she realized that this was the way it had to be with Alice. She had to make sure Teddy knew that here, uninvited, was one of the bit players in the never-ending drama that starred Alice. For a moment as fleeting as a sigh, Valerie contemplated not playing her designated role, but thought better of it. Alice's need for center stage was greater than her own curiosity about what would happen if she didn't do it.

"I was on my way home and thought I'd stop by and say hello," Valerie said as if on cue. "I've always wanted to see where they put the *Courier* together."

Alice was beaming like a lighthouse beacon. "Val, I'd like you to meet Teddy Chambers. Teddy, this is my sister, Valerie."

The young man got up from behind his desk, and Valerie really saw him for the first time. He was tall, seeming to tower over her own five feet seven inches, and rangy, as if his height had come in a few quick spurts and his breadth had not yet had time to catch up. He had a shock of dirty-blond hair, close-cropped but not crew-cut. He had the kind of clean good looks that reminded Valerie of Archie, from the comics, but the watercolor blue of his eyes was anything but funny. She was drawn to them as if magnetized; only when he offered his hand to shake hers was she jolted back to earth.

"Hi. Nice to meet you," he said, his eyes holding hers. "Alice told me she had a younger sister, and I had this vision of a little kid." He gently removed his hand, leaving his stare. "But you're no little kid, are you?" he added softly.

Valerie managed a tremulous smile. "I'm not interrupting anything important, am I?" she asked, looking at Alice.

"Well, we were—"

"Of course not," Teddy cut in. "We were just going over some article ideas. Nothing that can't wait." As he spoke, Valerie could feel him studying her, and it took an effort not to squirm as his eyes lingered on the soft rise of her breasts under her skimpy pink T-shirt, then wandered down to where her khaki bermuda shorts fanned over her hips, and on to her firm, slender, tan legs. When he finally came back to her face, she forced herself to shift her gaze, to concentrate on Alice, to smile with a fluorescent-false brightness.

"I really should be going," she said. "I've got to buy some groceries and there's dinner to—"

"Alice told me you work over at the Golden, waiting tables," Teddy said, sitting, gesturing that Alice should do the same. Since there were no other chairs in the cubicle, Valerie had to remain standing, suddenly feeling gawky and ungainly looking down at these two beautiful people.

"You work both shifts?"

Valerie nodded, wrapped in a desperate misery as acute as she'd felt the day Mack had told her he was leaving Galesville. Her sister's eyes were frosty with wariness, the smile on her mouth a patent lie.

"You like it?"

"It's okay."

"Valerie wanted to go to college, but her grades weren't good enough. I told you I got an academic scholarship to State, didn't I, Teddy?" Alice bubbled, her glance a dagger challenging her sister to refute the outrageous lie. "I couldn't go, of course. Even with an academic scholarship, my parents wouldn't have had enough money. So here I am at the *Courier*, trying to earn enough money to go back to school. Everyone said it was such a shame that someone with my grades couldn't go right on to college, but I don't mind waiting. Having to work will make me appreciate college even more."

As Alice constructed lie upon lie, like Chinese baskets, Teddy never took his eyes from Valerie, and she was helpless to look away. It was when she heard Alice laugh—a sound stained with venom too sweet to be detected by Teddy but too familiar to her own ears—that Valerie knew she had to leave immediately and never return.

"Val'll probably end up marrying Carl Enderby, the grocer's boy, won't you?" Alice was saying, still laughing. "And stay here in Galesville the rest of your life." She strained back in the hard chair, hands clasped behind her head so that her small breasts thrust forward in her blue-checked shirtwaist, demanding—and finally getting—Teddy's attention.

"Not like us, Teddy," she went on, her voice a caress. "People like us who have ambition know there's more out there."

"Oh, I don't know, Alice," Teddy said slowly, grinning as he gazed back at Valerie. "Seems to me like Galesville has a lot more to offer than I originally thought."

Valerie did not have to observe her sister's face to see the tightening of her lips and the rush of hot color to the pale skin. Her own throat was dry. "It was nice meeting you, Teddy," she said, edging out.

"Do you have to go?" he asked, getting to his feet again.

She nodded. "See you later, Alice," she said, but Alice found the cuticle on her right forefinger of too much interest to answer.

After descending the first flight of stairs, Valerie stopped and leaned against the cold stone wall. She shut her eyes and breathed deeply, and marveled at what had just occurred. For the first time in her life, she had been in the same room with her sister and someone, a *man*, had liked her. *Her*. The wonder of it made her heart race, and she wanted to rush out and look at herself in a full-length mirror. Instead, she glanced down at the swell of her breasts, took her hands and circled her waist and let them slide to the curves of her hips. Then the moment of vanity vanished, and she was left with the terrible reality of what had happened. The man her sister wanted had been attracted to her: there would be hell to pay. She would be blamed for showing up in the first place; for wearing shorts and a snug T-shirt, for letting her dark hair hang wildly about her face instead of tied back in a ponytail. But there was nothing to be concerned about, she told herself. She was a seventeen-year-old girl, Teddy was a twenty-two-year-old man. She interested him the way a pretty necklace in a shop window would catch the eye of a passer-by. Alice would understand that: it would be ridiculous not to.

Satisfied with her logic, Valerie skipped down the remaining flight of stairs, again permitting herself to feel wonder that a man—not a boy like Carl Enderby, but a handsome newspaperman in his twenties—had liked her. With the innocence of both her youth and her nature guiding her, she decided to talk to her sister about it.

It began the next evening after dinner, and then every evening for the following several: Teddy was waiting when Valerie finished the dinner shift. The first few times, her concern was obvious. "Where's Alice?" she would ask. "Let's get Alice and go down to the lake." Or: "Alice is so beautiful, isn't she? I wish I had hair like hers."Or: "Alice is a terrific sister. I can't imagine any sister being better."

No matter how often Valerie invoked her sister's name or how honorable her words, there was no lessening of Teddy Chambers's interest. And, despite the fear she felt, she knew she welcomed his attention and would be heartsick if it stopped.

"Will you go out with me Sunday, Valerie?" Teddy asked on the seventh evening he walked her home.

"Teddy, I can't—" Valerie began automatically. There was a light on in her house; was Alice there, watching them?

He placed his hands firmly on her shoulders and twisted her around to face him. She looked up into his blue eyes, wanting to lose herself in their heat.

"Listen, Val," he said, his voice a husky throb that seemed to echo in her heart. "I know what's worrying you, but it can't be helped. Alice is a great girl, and she's gorgeous. But you're the one I want. From the minute I saw you I wanted you. Do you understand? It's you."

She watched the way his lips moved over every precious word. Her resistance, born of loyalty, finally vanished. Alice had many boyfriends, and would have many more after Teddy. There could be nothing wrong with her having just this one. And it wasn't as if she had pursued him; it wasn't as if she hadn't done everything possible to dissuade him.

With his hands still on her shoulders, Teddy lowered his head, and his lips brushed Valerie's mouth with the lightness of a wheat stalk fluttering in the wind. Then his grip became a little firmer, and when he kissed her again, there was a controlled intensity about it that thrilled Valerie even as it scared her. Fleetingly, as if recalling a dream, she was reminded of Alice and Ty Landry in the barn and the cold harshness of her sister's demands. What Teddy was doing was subtle and sweet, a promise of infinite possibilities.

"I'll pick you up at the restaurant tomorrow after lunch," Teddy said, bringing his hands back down to his side. "Take your bathing suit and we'll go down to the lake."

Valerie nodded; then, before he could kiss her again or say another word, she turned and dashed into the house. She hoped she would not have to face anyone in her family until the morning; hoped she could cherish the glow of Teddy's kiss for at least as long as that. But when she went into the kitchen, there was her mother, reading one of her confessions magazines and drinking Scotch. Valerie had known her mother to drink at Christmas; seeing her drinking at nine o'clock on a Saturday night shattered Valerie's joy as devastatingly as a slash of Eli's belt.

"Mama?" she asked tentatively.

Edith's head bobbed up from the magazine, and Valerie noticed that her blue eyes were glassy. "Are you okay, Mama?"

"Course I'm okay. Why?" Edith's voice was thick, her movements jerky as she lifted the glass to her lips.

"Where's everyone?"

"Your papa's in Eddington with the boys, and Alice is out with that reporter fella of hers, Teddy-what's-his-name."

"But—" Valerie stopped. "Well, I guess I'll go on up to bed. You going to stay down here awhile longer?"

"Yeah, I want to finish this story," Edith said, taking

another sip of the Scotch and lowering her eyes to the magazine.

Valerie got into bed, but she was too confused to sleep. Alice had lied, saying that she was out with Teddy. Why? And whom was she really seeing? Her mother was drinking alone at night. Why? For how long? And her brothers were with her father, following in his footsteps as sure as the corn came up every season. When would Ned break loose? Why didn't Billy leave? How much longer could they all pretend to themselves and to one another that they were living the life they wanted? Then there was Teddy—a handsome, ambitious young man who had decided that he wanted her, not her sister; Teddy, whose kiss still warmed her lips. It was the memory of that, and of the touch of his hands on her, that formed the pillow of her dreams that night.

Downstairs, Edith Cardell kept drinking, knowing there would be no sleep for her unless the liquor led her into it. There was no confession story she had to finish; tormented by rage and frustration, she had been staring at the same black-and-white page for more than an hour. Damn Mack Landry! Damn him! She had waited while he was in Chicago, fully expecting the separation to make him realize how necessary she was to his life. But he'd been back long enough now, and there was no change in their relationship. She still went to his bed at least three times a week, as she had tonight. As soon as Eli and the boys had left, she had fixed her hair and her face and gone, unexpected, to Mack's; given the freedom of the night, she had not been able to resist. He had not been glad to see her, had told her he was working on some important papers. Edith had taken care of that quickly, toying with him until he surrendered. So what? Going to bed with him didn't take her closer to becoming his wife. Within the hour she had come home and begun to drink to dull the anger.

It was her children's fault, she decided. If they had amounted to something, she wouldn't be relying so desperately on Mack. But not one of them, not a single one of them, thought of anybody but himself. Ned was a slob, a bully who was so afraid of his father that he would follow him into hell if it would pacify him. He released his own pent-up emotions by drinking and brawling. And Billy was a weakling—a skinny little weakling who kept talking about moving away from Galesville. As if that were any answer. He should have been working in Eddington instead of on the farm; making good money like Wayne Landry was earning at the shoe store, and sharing it with her. Valerie was hopeless; Edith knew she could expect nothing from her unless she forced her to marry Carl Enderby. Maybe that wasn't such a bad idea. At least she'd get free groceries that way. It was Alice, though, her little princess, who was proving the most disappointing, and Edith didn't understand why. Alice should have been married by now, married well, and taking care of her mother like they had talked about so often. Maybe this Teddy fellow would be the answer. But Edith still needed someone of her own, and Mack Landry was the one she wanted. Why was he taking so long to marry her?

The answer to that was too painful for Edith to consider. So she took another swallow of Scotch . . . and another.

While her mother was silently fuming at the injustice of her existence, Alice the princess slipped her arms through her cotton Maidenform bra and fastened it. Then she put on her panties and fumbled for the rest of her clothing, which was scattered around the floor of Dennis Rich's trailer.

"What's your hurry, babe?"

"Let's go dancing, Dennis. I'm in the mood."

The brawny, blond mechanic from the gas station between Eddington and Galesville shrugged his muscular shoulders but made no move to get dressed. Instead, he reached out with one hand whose nails still were black with grease and unbuttoned the blouse Alice had just put on. With his thumb and forefinger, he began to pinch her nipple, at first gently, then harder.

"Dennis, stop it, you're hurting me," Alice complained, pushing away his hand. "C'mon, I said I want to go dancing."

"From what I can tell, babe, what you like to do is what we just did."

Alice shut her eyes. *No, you fool. I don't like it. I just don't know how to do anything else.*

"Denny, honey, please. Let's go dancing, have a few beers, and then we'll come back here and I'll show you how much I like it."

"Show me now," the mechanic said, pushing away her blouse, yanking up her bra so that her breasts bobbed free, then wrapping his hand around her neck and bringing her face down to him. "Do it the way I showed you, Alice. Nice and slow. That's it, babe. Mm, yeah..."

Alice hesitated only briefly against the pressure of the boy's hand on her neck. But in that moment other images came to her... the back seat of a blue Pontiac; a parking lot outside the movie theater in the Eddington mall; a deserted dirt road; the lakeside... and with a smile she lowered herself to Dennis Rich, knowing that whatever Teddy might see in her sister right now, he couldn't forget those nights. He'd be back. She'd make sure of it.

Chapter 5

"Val, please. Please, honey. You know how much I love you. I just can't stand this. You're driving me crazy."

"Teddy, don't.

"You want it as much as I do. I know you do."

"Don't talk like that, Teddy. Please."

"Val, I can't take much more of this. Don't you know what you're doing to me. Come here, feel this." He reached for her hand across the front seat of his blue Pontiac, but she pulled away.

"Stop it, Teddy!"

With a snort of disgust, he shifted his position and stared out at the inky lake before him.

"Teddy, don't be angry," she said in a small voice, wrapping her arms around herself; the chill came less from the October night than from the ache of fighting with Teddy. "I just—"

"I don't know what the hell you're saving it for. Your sister sure gives it away quick enough."

At Valerie's gasp, Teddy turned his head, then inched closer to her. "I'm sorry, Val, I didn't mean that. It's just that

I want you so bad I can't think of anything else. Sometimes after we're together, I can't even get to sleep for wanting you so."

Valerie was not listening, her mind on what he had said about Alice. Had he been to bed with her sister? She gazed at him and saw the anguish in his blue eyes. No, he couldn't want her so badly if sex was such a casual thing to him. He had said that about Alice because that was the reputation she had acquired, and he had needed to shock her, had wanted her to think that if she didn't give him what he desired, he could get it elsewhere. But Valerie knew that Teddy was not that kind of person. She was sure he had been with plenty of girls, but never just for the sake of sex. He wasn't like that. A girl had to mean something to him—maybe not love, but something. That's why he could never have gone to bed casually with Alice and then started dating her. He was too much of a gentleman for that.

If a small part of Valerie's mind did not fully accept this rationalization for Teddy's remark, it was not yet sufficiently strong to take command. What was much stronger in her was her longing to give in to him. Every time he touched her, she wanted him to touch her more. Her body strained with need. But she couldn't do it. And so they argued; lately it seemed to Valerie that they argued more than they had regular conversations. Their evenings together invariably ended with Teddy pressuring her to go all the way, and with Valerie having to stop him. It wasn't that she didn't love Teddy. She had known she loved him after only six dates; but now, two months after that first glorious day swimming in the lake and then having dinner at a small Italian restaurant in Eddington, proving her love had become more important to Teddy than avowing it.

"Maybe we should just not see each other for a while."

Valerie's eyes grew wide. At seventeen, she was all innocence and trust. Teddy Chambers had opened up the world of romance for her; with him, there were quiet dinners and silly evenings at a local carnival; with him, there were dreams, the joy of walking home after work hand in hand, and the sweet yearning after a good-night kiss. Valerie began to hear the words of the popular songs and feel they were meant for her; she began to doodle "Mrs. Valerie Chambers" and wonder how many children they would have. To hear him speak now of not seeing her was to darken her blue sky and make the flowers wilt in her garden. With those few words, Valerie realized how close she still was to the despair of only a few months ago.

"Teddy," she said softly, "is it really that important to you?"

"Oh, Val, it's only because I love you so much," he said, taking her in his arms. His lips began to move against her hair, his breath hot along the side of her neck. She closed her eyes and let herself enjoy the warmth of his hand on her breast; she willed herself not to flinch as that hand went beneath her skirt and his mouth teased hers, his tongue prying open her lips, his hand moving farther up until it reached the edge of her panties. She heard his heart beating hard against her own, the raggedness of his breath as his head lowered to her neck, then to the soft curve of her breast. She so wanted to please him; she so wanted him to believe she loved him . . . but not like this. Not like this.

With her palm against his chest, she pushed him away. "No, Teddy. I can't. I just can't!"

"Jesus H. Christ!" he exploded, running his hand over his face. "I'll take you home now," he muttered soon after.

They drove in silence, continuing a pattern that had been going on for some time: a lovely evening, an argument, silence. Each night at this point Valerie felt breathless with fear. Teddy would no longer tolerate her reluctance; he would tell her it was over. But when they arrived at her house, he would take her in his arms, hold her, and kiss her gently, and everything would be all right again. Still, she had come to dread the evening's end, knowing that they would argue, that she would be battling her conscience and her desire to please him. She couldn't deal with the pressure much longer; the worry and the dread were too confusing; loving Teddy was becoming too difficult. And tonight it was as if he had reached within her and pulled on the string that would get her to do whatever he wanted. He had voiced the threat that she had come to expect, and in doing so had made her apprehension real.

Valerie sat with eyes straight ahead as Teddy turned off the motor of the car. She would not let him see her pain. No one had the right to see so deeply within her. And there would be no tears. She loved Teddy, and she wanted him to go on loving her, but if not doing what she did not believe in meant losing him, then she would have to risk that.

"Come here," she heard him whisper, and out of the corner of her eye saw his arm reach out for her. She turned her head fully, and the resigned smile on his lips sent a drumroll of joy through her. They moved toward each other, and he planted tender little kisses on the top of her head. He put his hand under her chin and tilted her face to his.

"I do love you, Val, and that's what makes it so hard sometimes."

"Then you didn't mean what you said before—about not seeing me for a while?"

He shook his head. "No, I was just angry and frustrated and I wanted to hurt you. I'm sorry."

He kissed her softly, the kind of kiss she had come to associate with another evening saved. "Dream of me," he said as he reached across her to open the door.

She nodded, her smile filled with relief and trust.

"That's not true, Mack. It's not!"

"Why are you being so damn headstrong, Valerie? I haven't steered you wrong before, have I?"

"You haven't been so right, either," Valerie retorted.

They were in his kitchen, sitting at the old pine table, dipping apples in melted caramel; Valerie was making them as a surprise dessert for her family's Thanksgiving dinner. Her difficulties with Teddy had neither abated nor increased. They were a constant, and she needed to share her anguished confusion. Mack seemed the most likely person, but instead of confirming the rightness of her emotions and her actions, he had been trying to convince her that what she felt for Teddy was not love; that she had been confusing the new world of romance with a feeling of much deeper intensity. He wasn't only telling her that she shouldn't go to bed with Teddy; he was telling her that Teddy wasn't right for her.

"What do you mean by that, Val?" Mack asked, wiping his hands on a red-and-white-checked dishtowel as he looked at her. She kept her eyes glued to the apple stick in her hand, her black hair a cascading camouflage around her face. "Val?" he prodded.

She shrugged, but said nothing as she continued dipping the apple. Suddenly Mack clamped her wrist, stilling her hand. "Look at me, Val. And answer me when I speak to you."

Her eyes met his with a defiant gleam. "When you left for Chicago, you told me I'd get out of Galesville one day," she began. "Well, you were wrong. You'd been telling me that for so many years that I believed you. I really did!" She shook off Mack's grip and dropped the apple into the bowl of caramel, putting her hand in her lap to hide its shaking.

Mack frowned. "But it is true, Valerie. You *will* get out. You just have to be patient."

She jumped to her feet. "It's *not* true! And now you're doing it again. You're trying to get me to believe something because *you* believe it, not because it's right for me."

"You're being unreasonable, Val. Getting out of Galesville is one thing. Sleeping with Teddy Chambers or marrying him is something—"

"See, I told you you were wrong," she interrupted with a bitter smile of triumph. "If I listened to you, I'd just be going to work as a waitress, trying to save enough money to take a bus into Eddington once in a while. Sure, that's really getting out!" Valerie tossed her hair back over her shoulders, an arrogant gesture that, to Mack's eyes, seemed incongruous with the childish confusion he knew she was feeling.

"If I listened to you," she continued, "I could wait around a long, long time. Where would all that fine patience you're always preaching get me when I'm thirty years old? I don't want to get out when I'm too old to enjoy it, Mack. I want to get out *now*."

"And you think Teddy Chambers is the way to do that, don't you?" he asked softly as he began to understand.

"That's beside the point. Teddy is someone I love, and

that's what you refuse to believe. Sure I want to leave Galesville, and with Teddy I'll be able to do that. But the fact is I love him."

"Would you still feel that way if he weren't a reporter with plans to move to one of the big cities?"

"What?"

"You heard me."

"Yes, I heard you," she answered, not flinching from Mack's hard stare. "And I can't believe what you said. I'm not like Alice, Mack. I don't use people, and I don't pretend to feelings I don't have."

Mack nodded with approval. "Interesting. I hadn't realized you had become so aware of your sister's methods."

She sat down again and leaned toward him. "Alice wants to get out too, Mack, and she does what she has to toward that end. Maybe it's not what you or I would do, but she manages with what she has. Don't fault her for it."

Mack said nothing, seeing only the loyalty in the beautiful young face before him—a loyalty that was powerful enough to smother intelligence. He shook his head at the potential danger of such a sentiment, but Valerie misinterpreted.

"You think I'm using Teddy, don't you?" she asked, incredulous. "You think all I want Teddy for is a ticket out of here. I—"

"No, Valerie. I know you're not like that."

"Then why can't you believe I love him?"

Mack sighed heavily. He knew how much his approval meant to her, but he could not give it to her this time.

"Valerie, I believe you *think* you love Teddy. All I've been trying to say is that he's the first boy you've ever been with. Your growing up so far has been secondhand, watching Alice have dates, seeing your schoolmates go to parties and dances while you've been forced to stay home. Now along comes this young man and he's smitten with you. I can't say I blame him, either," he added with a grin.

"So?" Valerie pressed, her glare unwavering, challenging.

"So what you're feeling may not be love, but infatuation with romance—a fantasy notion of how love is supposed to be. I'm not saying it would be wrong to have sex with Teddy, whether you love him or only think you do. I'm saying you should question your feelings, not your actions." He paused, then continued in a voice firm with conviction.

"I'm also telling you that you don't need Teddy Chambers to get yourself out of Galesville. Seventeen may seem old to you, Val. You may be thinking that each day that goes by, each day you serve another meal at that restaurant, is another day you're missing out on life. Give yourself a chance, and give me some of that trust you've always had. You *will* leave here, and you don't need Teddy Chambers to do it."

The air seemed to crackle with hostility. Neither moved for several moments; then, with great care and deliberation, Valerie rose, removed the apron she had been wearing, and folded it neatly over the back of the chair. She stood with both hands on the top of the chair, her fingers gripping hard around the pine slat.

"You ask for my trust," she said hoarsely, "but I don't think I can give it to you anymore, Mack. It's not that I mind your disapproving of Teddy or of how we feel about each other." She swallowed, and her eyes glistened with tears. "I can't give you my trust because you don't deserve it any longer."

"Valerie, what in the world—" Mack said, starting to rise.

"You've had your say, now let me have mine."

Mack slowly sat down. "You're jealous, Mack. I realize that now, and that's why I can't listen to anything you've said. For the first time, there's another man in my life, and you can't stand the competition."

"Valerie!"

"You always knew Papa and Ned and Billy didn't count. And until Teddy, there hadn't been anyone but you and them. The only reason I'm even allowed to go out with him now is because Alice convinced Mama that it was time for me to date and that she had dumped him, so Mama thinks I've got discarded merchandise. Well, I don't care what Mama thinks as long as she lets me see Teddy. But I did care what you thought, and now I see I was wrong to put so much faith in you. You're just jealous, Mack, that's the truth of it. You want me all to yourself, here in Galesville where you can play the big man of the world to the adoring little girl. I'm sorry, Mack, I really am. But I'm not a little girl anymore, and trying to keep me one with your false promises and your twisted reasoning just won't work."

She moved toward the door, then turned to face him as she took her jacket from the coat hook. "I guess Papa will be real happy about this," she mumbled, gazing around the warmly familiar kitchen. "He finally won't have to worry about your influence on me."

"Valerie, don't go. You're wrong," Mack urged, but he made no move to get up; Valerie had left before the words were out of his mouth.

She let her tears flow freely as she ran across the property to her house and stumbled into the kitchen. Her heart pounded with a pain fiercer than any she had ever known before. She had said horrible things to the one person who had never been anything but kind and good to her. How right could her love for Teddy be if it caused her to lose her best friend?

"Val? Hey, whoa there!"

She felt a strong hand reach out and grab her arm, stopping her escape upstairs. "Valerie? You okay?"

All she could do was stand there silently as Billy regarded her. "What happened, Val? You have a fight with Teddy?"

She shook her head and tried to pull away, but Billy held on. For his sister to cry meant something was troubling her deeply, and he couldn't bear that. "Sit down, Val. Come on. Papa and Ned are in town, and Mama's at the church pie sale."

"How come you're home?" she asked, her voice thick with tears.

"I'm being a sneak," he admitted with a wry grin. "I told Papa I needed to go into Eddington for some supplies. Course, what I'm really doing..." His eyes, followed by Valerie's, went to the sketch pad on the kitchen table. He had been making pencil drawings of a bowl of gourds on the table.

In spite of her misery, Valerie smiled. "They're good, Billy. But what're you going to tell Papa when he comes home and asks for the supplies?"

"Oh, I've got them. Last time I was in town I bought

extra, figuring I'd need them for a day like this." He paused and released his hold on her arms. "You gonna tell me what's hurting?"

"I can't, Billy," Valerie whispered.

"Is it Teddy?"

"Not really. No."

"Whaddaya mean not really? Either it is or it isn't."

Valerie opened her mouth, but no words came out. Then, without warning, she bolted from the kitchen. Upstairs, she hid in the bathroom. The tears had stopped, but the sense of loss throbbed through her like a living thing. She wished she could tell Billy, but, sweet as he was, he could do nothing to help her, not with Mack, and not with Teddy. She still needed someone to help her through the morass of her feelings.

Billy could never do that for her; he was too frightened to face his own feelings. Her mother would never understand, nor would she particularly care. That left Alice, who had been surprisingly supportive of Valerie's relationship with Teddy. Alice was very different from her in her approach and attitude toward men, but Valerie was sure that her sister wouldn't laugh at her sexual reluctance, and would understand that being in love required a special set of values.

Valerie splashed cold water on her face and tied her hair up in a ponytail, then went into her room, sat on her bed, and flipped through last month's issue of *Seventeen*, waiting for Alice to come home. She would not think about Mack, she told herself firmly. He had failed her when she needed him most.

She told herself this each time her eyes threatened to spill over with tears.

Valerie had to wait a long time to speak to Alice. She did not come home for dinner, having called to say she had a date with Dennis Rich. Valerie worked the evening shift at the Golden, knowing she would not see Teddy later because he was in Indianapolis, covering a big murder trial. He had convinced Fred Brickley that it would make a better story if he was there in person instead of getting the news from the wire services. She loved Teddy's ambition.

There were so many things she loved about him: the way

he made her laugh by walking like Charlie Chaplin; the way he described his dreams and plans; the way he held her against him when they danced so that she felt safe from all harm; the way he sometimes lifted a strand of hair that had fallen over her eyes, then kissed the tip of her nose; the way he talked about his family and how he wanted them to be proud of him. So many things . . .

"I thought you'd be sleeping by now. It's past midnight."

Valerie looked up. "I was waiting up for you."

"How come?"

Valerie hesitated. It was so unusual for her to take Alice into her confidence that she did not know how to begin. Should she start with the argument with Mack and go back, or just plunge right in and ask her if she thought she should go to bed with Teddy? And then, unbidden, came the memory of Teddy's remark about Alice. If they *had* been to bed together, how could Alice possibly give her sincere advice? But they hadn't been together; hadn't, hadn't, hadn't!

"Alice, I need to talk," Valerie said, playing with a loose thread on her worn comforter, but keeping her eyes on her sister as she undressed and removed her makeup. "It's important. Real important."

Alice put down her hairbrush and turned to face her sister. "You pregnant?"

A sharp, brittle sound that was meant to be laughter pierced the room. "Not exactly. Same subject, different approach."

"Oh. Then Teddy must be putting pressure on you to have sex with him. Is that it?"

Valerie nodded, feeling heat creep up her neck and into her face.

"So what's the problem? Don't you want to?"

"But, Alice, it's not right," Valerie said, hating the childish whine in her voice. "We're not married yet and—"

"Yet? What do you mean 'yet'? Has Teddy asked you to marry him?"

"Well, yes, in a way. And I think we ought to wait until—"

"Has Teddy asked you to marry him or hasn't he?"

"He hasn't formally proposed, but we talk about it all the time."

"Then he hasn't asked you to marry him," Alice stated firmly.

"I already said that," Valerie snapped irritably. "The thing is, we *are* going to get married when he has some more money put aside. But I don't know if we can wait until then. I love him so much, Alice, he's so good and kind and generous and smart. You have no idea how smart he is."

"I work with him every day, remember?" Alice said dryly.

"And he loves me so much, that's the thing, he loves me so much and I don't know how much longer I can refuse to give him what he wants."

"What makes you think he loves you so much?" Alice's voice sounded tinny, but her eyes were clear and wide and innocent. "You know, Val, men say those things when they want to take advantage of a girl. You can't be too careful. Teddy strikes me as being no different than all the rest. Horny, that's all. Just plain horny. And telling a girl he loves her is the oldest game in the book."

Valerie shook her head. "Teddy's different. You know him, Alice. You know how honest he is. He's just not like other guys."

"I know he's a twenty-two-year-old man with an itch," Alice said derisively. "So far you haven't told me a thing to make me think he's anything else."

"He's willing to wait."

"You just said—"

"I said we love each other and I don't know if we *can* wait. I want him, Alice! I love him and I want him and just kissing in his car isn't enough. But he says he knows how much it means to me, and he's willing to wait until we're married. That's how I know he's different."

In Alice Cardell's gut, a blade as sharp as a stiletto was twisting and slicing. She turned away from Valerie and lowered her head, her hair spilling forward over her face as she began to brush. Her voice was calm and even as she spoke, and the raging jealousy blazing from her eyes was hidden from view.

"Well, I think you just may have convinced me, Val," she said. "Any guy who says that has got to really be in love. But you realize, don't you, that you're risking a whole lot. A man's got needs, Val, and if he doesn't satisfy them with the girl he loves, he may have to go elsewhere. How would you feel about that? There're plenty of girls who wouldn't think twice about getting into bed with Teddy, love or no love."

There it was again . . . this time, an image of Alice's blonde hair spread out on a pillow, Teddy poised above her, both naked. *Stop it!* Valerie screamed at herself.

"That's a risk I've been taking, I guess," she admitted, "but Teddy says that though he may be frustrated, he'd rather suffer than be with anyone else. He says he'd only be thinking of me and that he wouldn't enjoy it with anyone else."

"He said that to you?" Alice's head jerked up, her hair whipping back from her face as she swiveled on the stool.

Valerie nodded. "You see what I mean? We really do love each other, and that's what's killing me. He's so good to me, Alice, and I don't want to hurt him. I just don't know what to do anymore."

Alice stared at her sister for several moments; then, putting on a smile of understanding like a fresh coat of lipstick, she went to sit on Valerie's bed. Gently, she brushed down her sister's hair, the smile so perfectly in place that its absence from her eyes went unnoticed. "I think you're a very lucky girl, Val. Here you are with your very first boyfriend, and the two of you are truly in love. I'd call that very lucky." Her voice was like honey, spilling sisterly devotion with every word. "You know, I had quite a crush on Teddy myself. And I was kinda jealous of you in the beginning."

"You were? But you encouraged it—you always seemed so supportive of my dating him."

"Well, sure." Alice laughed lightly. "If I couldn't have him, then my sister should, instead of some strange girl!"

What she did not say was that she had encouraged it because she had believed that Valerie was safe, offering no real competition for Teddy's affections. Everything about her sister was still so unformed; she had assumed that only *she* could see what would someday be there. She had underestimated both Teddy and her sister.

"Now I know I did the right thing," she went on. "You two are meant for each other. If I had stood in your way it would have been a mistake. Teddy and I could never feel about each other the way you two do. I'm really too sophisticated for him. Wonderful as Teddy is, he's still a little boy."

Valerie pulled tighter on the loose thread in her quilt, the familiar, angry resentment welling in her. Why was it always necessary for Alice to diminish what Valerie had? Why did she always have to seem to win at Valerie's expense? Well, it was unimportant in the long run, she told herself. When they both got what they wanted, Alice would stop this petty oneupmanship.

"So you think I should sleep with him?" she asked, tilting her head so that it was beyond her sister's reach.

Alice got up from the bed and into her own. "I think you should do what you want to do, depending on which influence is stronger—your conscience or your body."

"Alice, that's no answer!"

"Oh, but it is. Look at it this way: you know you're going to marry Teddy, so on one hand there's no point in saving it. Of course, your virginity means something to you, and Teddy is willing to respect that. Either way, he's still going to love you, so it's up to your body or your conscience."

"What would you do?"

"Me? I'm the wrong one to ask, Val. I gave up fighting that battle a long time ago."

"I mean if things were different. If you were still a virgin."

"Well, I guess I'd go to bed with him. After all, if he loved me as much as you say he loves you, it would be a gift, and he'd probably love me all the more for giving it to him."

Valerie turned off the light on the bedside table. "Thanks, Alice. Goodnight."

"Night, Val."

Valerie lay awake, sure in her heart that she would not heed her sister's advice. Within the words of comfort and encouragement was something she did not quite trust.

Alice lay awake as well, the demon of jealousy stirring her senses.

A few hundred yards away, Mack Landry listened to the sounds of his son getting ready for bed, hearing him bump into the hall table, then throw his sneakers into his closet, where they thudded against the back wall. He was drunk again. But worrying about Wayne getting home safely had not caused Mack's wakefulness. He had mishandled an important situation; more to the point, he had forgotten what it was like to be seventeen years old and in love for the first time. He refused to believe he had lost Valerie forever; yet, he could n't stop brooding over what he would do if, indeed, he had.

Chapter 6

It was five-thirty, and the *Courier* office had emptied for the day. Only Alice and Teddy remained; Teddy was polishing an editorial, the first he had been permitted to write, on the wholesome values of the holiday season. Alice was at her desk, waiting until she was sure everyone was gone.

Almost three weeks had passed since that midnight conversation with her sister; weeks of rage; of becoming so intimate with jealousy that it seemed it was always there, laughing over her shoulder like a cruel fiend relishing her misery. It had become impossible to sit at the same table with Valerie and keep up a facade of pleasantness; to share the same room had become torture. In the past, when she would acknowledge her sister's beauty, her intelligence, and her surprising strength of character, the jealousy would flare, then abate, a mere spark of animosity that extinguished itself. But since that conversation, since the full understanding of what her sister meant to Teddy and how seriously she had fooled herself—since realizing that it could be her sister who would marry first—the jealousy had turned into a hatred of such unrelieved intensity that she thought she would go mad.

Sometimes when she sat at her desk in the office, about to type a letter, a mere word would trigger a thought of Valerie, and she could no longer work. Her blue eyes would glaze and she would stare past the typewriter into a space that had suddenly become crowded with images of her sister destroyed, mutilated, ugly. Often, when she was out on a date, maybe even about to have sex, a chance remark from her partner would make her stiffen as if with fear, or shiver as if with cold. Her mind again would travel elsewhere, away from the immediate pleasure to the pain within her and the desperate need to alleviate it, to rid herself of the obsession by eliminating its source. As the days passed, she was driven by only one thought: to hurt Valerie, to make her feel the torment of acute disappointment as she herself was feeling it. Valerie's seventeen years of deprivation and punishment meant nothing. For Alice, any second that provided her sister with more than what she had was a second to be avenged.

Valerie would have to pay for getting what Alice wanted, for having what she needed. Most of all, Valerie would have to pay for her innocence. Only through tarnishing that purity could Alice find relief.

She had had no plan in mind until two nights ago, when she and her mother had been alone in the kitchen, the rest of the family already asleep. Alice had come home from a date with Dennis, her lips swollen, her bra in the pocket of her jacket. She had not expected to find her mother still up and was in no mood for one of her drunken chats about the perfidy of men, which occurred whenever Edith could get Alice alone. That, and Edith's whining complaints about Alice's lack of a marriage prospect. The last thing Alice wanted was for her mother to remind her of how she was failing.

"Givin' it away for free again, huh?" Edith had said, her Scotch-shiny eyes taking in Alice's appearance and the telltale signs of sex. "I didn't raise you to give it away. We're not goin' to get what we want doin' that."

Alice's heart thumped with the effort of self-control. She would have loved to take out on this weak, selfish woman all the pent-up fury she felt toward Valerie. But she needed her mother, the way a bully needs a coward to encourage and reinforce his cruel acts.

"I like Dennis," she said stiffly.

Edith laughed harshly. "Since when does likin' somebody mean anythin'? Is he goin' to marry you?"

"I don't want to marry him," Alice said. "Why don't you go to bed, Mama. It's late."

"Sit down a minute, Alice. I want to talk to you."

"I'm tired, Mama. I don't feel like talking now." She started out of the kitchen.

"Well, I do," Edith said firmly. "Sit."

Alice obeyed, keeping her jacket buttoned so that her mother would not see that she was braless. Not that it mattered, she thought, watching her mother take another gulp of Scotch. For all that Edith might drink, her sharp cunning never diminished. It was difficult to fool this woman: she had been too instrumental in forming Alice not to see through her clearly. "You're drinking too much," she said.

Edith shrugged. "And you're givin' it away for free. So now that we both got problems, what're we goin' to do about 'em?"

"Mama, please, let's go to bed."

"I've given that man the best years of my life, and where's it gotten me? Sittin' here drinkin' alone and gettin' older."

Alice stared at her mother, confused. "What're you talking about? You and Papa have a fight?"

"Your papa and I don't fight anymore, Alice. You can't fight with someone you don't talk to."

"I don't understand."

"Course you don't. I been real careful."

Alice leaned across the table and gently removed the glass as her mother was about to bring it to her lips. "Real careful about what?"

"Never mind, it don't matter. What matters is you. You're almost twenty-one, Alice, and the way you're goin', the bloom is gonna be off the rose mighty quick. You've had your pick, so how come you're still comin' home, still sleepin' in the same room with your sister? What about our dreams, Alice? You were supposed to be married by now, married to someone who could take care of you *and* me. Well, I don't hear you tellin' me to send out any invitations."

"Mama, we've been through this a million times," Alice said wearily. "We both agreed that I can't marry just *anyone*. And in this town there isn't much to choose from."

"You could have had that nice reporter fella, Teddy what's-his-name. Why'd you let him go? And don't tell me he wasn't good enough for you. If he's good enough for your sister, he's good enough for you.

"I don't want to talk about Teddy. I want to talk about you," Alice said, hoping to divert her mother's attention. "Who'd you give the best years of your life to? Who's making you hit the bottle every night? I want to know, Mama."

"I said it doesn't matter," Edith snapped.

"Well, it does to me." Alice sat back, scrutinizing her mother, trying to see her as a woman, as someone who might be appealing to a man. She saw a woman ravaged by disappointment, and it dawned on her that that was how she might look if she did not get out of Galesville. Her blonde hair would fall lusterless on a face lined with unsatisfied desires; her lips would draw in on themselves in a slash of regret, and her blue eyes would be dull and hopeless. She found herself trembling.

Suddenly Edith cackled, and Alice was jarred back from her terrifying vision of her future. "You're thinkin' you don't want to end up like me, aren't ya?" Edith said. "I don't blame you, and you won't have to if you stop behavin' like a damned fool. Don't pin your hopes on one man, and then you won't end up like me."

"Is that what you did?" Alice asked softly.

Edith nodded, and this time when she lifted the glass of Scotch to her lips, Alice did not stop her. "Since high school, there's been only one man I ever wanted. And I was a fool. A fool for letting him go, a fool for taking him back, a fool for still wanting him."

"Who, Mama? Who're you talking about?" Alice's voice was barely a whisper, and her eyes glowed with curiosity.

"You really don't know, do you? It's Mack Landry."

"Mack!" The name cracked through Alice's lips like a bullet.

"You don't believe me?"

"No, no, it's not that. I'm just surprised. I had no idea." She swallowed. "Do you and he—" She could not finish the question. She knew the answer, but she did not want to hear it; did not want confirmation of her mother's weakness, a portent of her own.

"It don't matter what we do or don't do," Edith said. "I'm tellin' you this now so you don't make the same mistake. I know you don't think any of the fellas you been with are good enough for you, and I'm sayin' that don't matter. You should've kept that guy Teddy around. At least he's gonna make somethin' of himself. Don't wait around for what you want, Alice, take what you can get, that's what I'm talkin' about. I've been waitin' all these years, and what good has it done me?"

"Didn't you love papa when you married him?"

"That's the funny thing. I did love him. And I didn't even care about Mack till he came back. That's when I realized what a mistake I had made. And I been waitin' all these years for him to ask me to leave Eli. But he won't, I know that now, he won't. And I'm stuck."

"Did Mack ask you to marry him when you were younger?"

"How could he? His folks were dead set on his goin' away to college," Edith said defensively. "But he would've. I know he would've."

With those words, Alice realized the far-reaching dangers of self-delusion. Whatever her mother and Mack had been to each other, and maybe even still were, potential husband and wife had never been part of the picture. What her mother did not realize and probably would never accept was that Alice was not waiting for the right man; she was waiting for any man who would have her. But she could never tell her mother that. Edith saw her as the crystallization of her own dreams. She would never believe Alice could not get anyone she wanted, would never accept the fact that Alice could not hold a man once the sex had lost its excitement. Edith thought Alice had dismissed Teddy because he was dull, not sophisticated enough for her—that had been Alice's explanation when he had begun to call on Valerie. And Alice had truly deluded herself into believing that if she wanted him back, she could have him anytime.

She would prove that now. She would use Teddy to destroy her sister. Through him, she would prove that she was different from her mother; she would prove that she *could* have any man, whether she wanted him or not, even if he thought he wanted someone else. She would prove that her future would not be sitting around a kitchen table in Galesville, drinking cheap Scotch from a jelly-jar glass, regretting the waste she had made of her life, sleeping with a man and calling it romance. She supposed she could get Dennis or any other man to marry her if she truly put her mind to it, but it was Teddy she wanted. No—she didn't want him, but she would take him. He belonged to her sister, and he would be leaving Galesville. Those were two of the best reasons she could think of for having him.

"You look like you used to when you were a little girl, Alice, when you were about to do something rotten," Edith remarked. "What're you thinkin'?"

Alice smiled sweetly and patted her mother's hand. "Oh, about what you've been saying. You're right, Mama, I made a mistake letting Teddy go."

"It's too late now. Your sister's got him."

"So?"

A smile spread in the wrinkles around Edith's mouth, and her blue eyes shone briefly with a gleam of understanding. "Is he the one you want?"

Alice shrugged. "Like you said, Mama, I'm not going to wait around for the one I want. But he's the one I'm gonna take."

"How?"

"Does it matter?"

"What about your sister? Don't her feelings matter none?"

"You tell me, Mama. Do they matter?"

Edith Cardell paused, looked into her Scotch, then back at the daughter she had fashioned into her instrument for future satisfaction. "She's young, she'll find someone else," she muttered. Then she put down her glass, and her eyes were hard as they locked with her daughter's. "Do what you have to do, Alice. Get someone to marry you now, before it's too late. The hell with your sister."

After that, it had been a matter of coming up with a plan. It had to be something that Teddy would not doubt; something that could not be traced back to her; something that would devastate and humiliate Valerie. And it had to be something that would make her shine so brilliantly by comparison that Teddy would be blinded by what he almost lost, and then grateful for a second chance. . . .

She no longer heard his typewriter now, so she stood up, tucking her white angora-and-rabbit-hair sweater more tightly into the waistband of her glen plaid pleated skirt. She ran her tongue over her lips, then walked to the doorway of his cubicle. "Teddy? Got a minute?"

"Sure, but I'd like to get out of here before the snow starts. The sky looks full of the stuff."

"Mind if I walk a ways with you? Or were you planning to meet Val this evening?" she asked, knowing her sister would be working late, helping to put up the holiday decorations.

"No, Val's busy tonight. Sure, walk with me. I'd like the company. Besides, I wanted to talk to you about a Christmas present for Val."

Had Alice had any second thoughts about the treachery she was about to commit, Teddy's innocent remark erased them. When they got to the street, she wrapped her arm in his. "It's cold," she said shyly. "You don't mind, do you?"

"Uh, no, of course not."

"We never get to talk anymore, you know."

"Sure we do, Alice. We work together every day."

"Not like that, silly," she said, pressing her breast against his arm. "I mean like we used to, when you first came to Galesville."

"Well, that was different. And if I remember correctly," Teddy said with a warm chuckle, "we didn't do much talking then, either." He shook his head. "I wish your sister were a little more like you in that regard," he mumbled.

Alice smiled to herself; he was making it so easy. "You and Val having trouble?"

"No, not really, it's just that—well, you know, she's kinda old-fashioned. Not like you."

"We did have some good times, didn't we, Teddy?"

Teddy Chambers looked down at the petite girl holding on tightly to his arm and thought how lovely she was, with her blue eyes like stars in a night sky and the first snowflakes dancing off her golden hair. How sweet and tempting her mouth was, parted slightly as if waiting to be kissed. And her smooth cheeks were stained pink from the cold. She was beautiful, he thought, and very different from Valerie, a colder, more unreachable kind of beauty. But he had reached her, several times, and briefly the memory of those couplings came racing back to mind. Damn Valerie, he found himself thinking. Damn me, too, for loving her so much that I'm letting her convince me to wait.

"You haven't been listening, Teddy," Alice chided gently. "Daydreaming about my sister?"

"Sorry. Guess I was," he admitted. "What were you saying?"

For the rest of his life Teddy would regret asking Alice Cardell what she had been saying. For the rest of his life he would loathe himself for being a gullible, naive fool, a stupid, callow man who did not have the sense to trust his own judgment of human nature. What he prided himself on as his ticket to fame as a newspaperman was his ability to distinguish the truth from a pack of lies. His mistrust of that self-proclaimed ability would haunt him for a long, long time.

"I don't believe you."

"Oh, Teddy, it's true. Do you think I could make up such a thing?"

"But she told me she was a virgin."

"What else could she tell you? Abortions are illegal, silly. Mama and I had to go all the way to Indianapolis to find a doctor who would do it. And she was only fourteen. We don't even know yet if she can *ever* have children."

"She said she'd never been to Indianapolis."

"Of course she said that. Did you expect her to tell you the truth? Valerie is a very proud girl. She just can't help herself, that's all."

"Why are you telling me this now?"

"Because I care about you, Teddy, and I know how much you love Valerie. I just want you to know that there's more there than you might think, and you deserve to know what you're getting yourself into. It's been quite a problem, you know. Mama has really had her hands full."

"There's more?"

"Oh, Teddy, it's been just awful. After the abortion, we were sure Valerie had learned her lesson, but it's like she can't help herself. Sex is as necessary to Valerie as eating three meals a day is to normal people like us."

"I don't want to hear any more."

"I know I've hurt you, Teddy, but I'm telling you this for your own good. Valerie's a wonderful girl, she really is, but she's got these *needs*. Why, when she was fifteen, she tried to seduce Wayne Landry, and Mack had to move away, back to Chicago, just so there wouldn't be trouble. I tell you, my parents were beside themselves. It's like Val has this sickness, you know. She can't seem to help herself when it comes to men."

"But... but she's not like that with me."

"Of course not, Teddy. That's because she loves you so much. She's trying. She wants things to be right between you two, and I'm sure they will be. But still, you've got to wonder how long it will be before that itch gets hold of her. It's like a fever, Teddy, I swear. I just don't know how she's controlling herself around you unless... No, she would never do that, she loves you too much."

"Do what, Alice?"

"No, it's ridiculous. She would never hurt you like that."

"Like how? Alice, you've got to tell me. What would she do?"

"Well, go to bed with other guys. But she wouldn't. She—"

"Jesus Christ. Oh shit."

"Teddy, please, don't get upset. Oh, I should never have said a word. I know she loves you, really. She just can't help herself."

"And all this time I thought you were the hot number. Alice, what in hell am I going to do? You've got to help me, you've just got to."

"Of course, Teddy, but what can I do?"

"I don't know! Dammit, what an idiot I've been!"

"Then you're not angry with me for telling you?"

"Angry? Of course not. I don't know what I would have done if you hadn't. Alice, you're gonna have to help me get out of this mess."

"Well, if you really want my help, of course I'll do whatever I can."

A week later, Valerie put on the new aqua taffeta dress she had scrimped and saved to buy. The dress had puff sleeves and a low cutaway neckline that more than hinted at the promise of her full breasts. She had used some of Alice's makeup, and her eyes were luminous, fringed lightly with mascara. She had swept up her hair, leaving a few dark ringlets to dangle beside her face and down the nape of her neck. There was a regalness about her tonight, and a glimpse of the kind of proud beauty she could someday be.

In just a few minutes Teddy would pick her up and take her to Eddington to a big, lavish Christmas party that a friend of his, a reporter on the Eddington paper, was giving. It was still a week till Christmas, but Teddy was flying home to Idaho to spend the holidays with his family so they had decided that this would be the night to exchange gifts and celebrate their own Christmas.

Valerie had not known what to get Teddy as a gift. She did not want to knit him a scarf or sweater the way so many girls did for their boyfriends. She wanted something special, something that would always remind Teddy of her. It was Billy who came up with the idea of a charcoal portrait of her, done by him. Valerie had initially thought it was too vain a gift, but Billy convinced her that it would be a loving gesture. She had spent much time wondering what Teddy would give her. She did not want to dwell on the idea, but she could not help hoping that it would be an engagement ring. Of course, they hadn't spoken much of marriage lately. In fact, they had seen each other only twice in the last ten days; one night he had told her he was sick and they had made it a short evening. The other time they had gone into Eddington for a movie and then straight home. They hadn't even stopped to neck by the lake. She hadn't had the nerve to question him about it or about his unusual quietness during the evening. She had assumed he had work on his mind and let it go at that. The rest of the week he had been so busy with the newspaper and with buying presents that they hadn't had time to get together. Valerie was certain that things would return to normal after the holidays.

Teddy was due to arrive at seven o'clock; a few minutes before, she went downstairs to wait in the kitchen. She wished Alice were there, approving the way she had put herself together, but her sister had called earlier to say she had a date and would go right from work. Ned was out somewhere with Wayne Landry. Billy and her father were watching television in the living room. There was no one to see her except her mother. Edith was in the kitchen, reading one of her magazines.

She glanced up when Valerie entered. "You don't look too bad," she remarked disinterestedly.

Valerie would not let her mother spoil her good mood. "Thanks. What're you doing?"

"What does it look like?"

"Come on, Mama, be happy for me," Valerie said gaily. "Teddy's going to be here soon and this is my first new dress in years, and I'm happy! So be happy with me."

"Your sister would look good in that color dress."

Valerie stopped trying.

At seven-thirty, she began to get restless. At eight o'clock, worry set in. By eight-thirty, she had chewed off her lipstick and shredded some of the wrapping paper on the portrait and there was moisture staining the underarms of her taffeta dress.

At nine o'clock, Billy and her father joined the vigil in the kitchen. "I'm sure there's a good explanation for this, Val," Billy offered.

"Yeah, like he probably had a few too many and passed out," Eli remarked.

"Oh stop it," Edith put in. "Valerie, why don't you call him? It's better than sittin' here worryin'."

Valerie nodded, not seeing the sly, cold glint in her mother's eyes. Something terrible had happened. Teddy would never be this late without calling. She went over to the wall phone and dialed the number of the *Courier*. As she had suspected, there was no answer. With trembling fingers, she began to dial his apartment, then stopped. Why hadn't he called her? If he was home sick in bed, he still could have called. She turned abruptly and looked at her mother, who was staring hard at her with an expression in her eyes that raised goosebumps on Valerie's bare arms. She knows something, Valerie thought. She knows, and wants me to find out for myself. She dialed his number. The phone rang four times before Teddy picked up.

"Teddy? It's Valerie. What's wrong?"

"Wrong? What do you mean?"

"Don't you remember? This is the night of the party."

"Oh yeah, I guess I must've forgotten."

"Teddy, are you okay?"

"Sure, why shouldn't I be?"

"Well, this isn't like you."

"Val, honey, no one's like they seem, are they? You ought to know that better than anyone."

"Teddy, I—" Valerie stopped as the sound of a honeyed giggle assaulted her ear with the force of a cannon blast.

"Who's there, Teddy? What's going on? Why are you doing this to me?" It suddenly seemed stifling in the small kitchen, the three pairs of eyes riveted on her back, the three pairs of ears listening to every nuance.

"Hey, Val baby, I'm not doing anything to you you haven't been doing to me. It's the old goose-and-gander routine, know what I mean?"

"No, I don't. Teddy, are you drunk?"

"No, baby, I've never been more sober." Again, that liquid laughter. She knew it . . . there was something familiar about it, but she couldn't place the source.

She gripped the phone hard and said breathlessly, "Teddy? Have I done something? Are you angry with me? I don't understand."

"Yeah, you've done something. Seems like with everybody but me. What a fool I've been. So long, Val. Next time maybe you'll get lucky and trap the sucker."

"Teddy, wait. Teddy? she said urgently, her throat tightening. Only the dial tone answered her. Mechanically she replaced the receiver. Teddy was no longer there. And would never be there again. She stood facing the phone for several long seconds. . . . *Everybody but me . . . trap the sucker . . . so long . . . so long . . .* She understood none of it, only that Teddy did not want her anymore.

With robotlike precision, she turned around, picked up her portrait, and left the kitchen, tearing the picture into pieces as she walked.

"Val? What is it? What happened?" she heard Billy ask.

"I knew it couldn't last. Too big for her britches. Would scare any fella away," Eli remarked with satisfaction. "Got just what she deserved."

"Yes, she did, didn't she?" Edith muttered, knowing that her firstborn daughter had succeeded.

Valerie spent the holidays working. When she wasn't waiting tables, she did nothing. Food held no interest for her, nor did sleep. She spent Christmas Eve in her room, staring at the ceiling. She accepted the late shift at the restaurant on New Year's Eve. She spoke when addressed, never first, except to request an order from a diner. The family steered clear of her as though her failure were a contagious disease and they did not want to be contaminated by it. Billy tried to communicate with her, but he was met with glassy-eyed silence. Alice tried, too, voicing her pity and concern, and her confidence that there would be someone else. Valerie did not respond.

It was not that her mind kept reeling with questions about what had happened and why. It was that she had retreated into herself because to deal with anyone required more strength than she had. And when Alice came home one evening to announce, jubilantly, her engagement to Teddy, Valerie's pain had so impoverished her that she never for one second suspected how she had been victimized and by whom.

When Teddy returned from Idaho, he and Alice were married in a quiet ceremony, with all the Cardells, including Valerie, in attendance. It was an effort to wish Teddy well, but she managed to do so, not able, however, to go so far as to kiss him. There was a little part of her heart that felt relieved to have lost him to her sister and not some stranger, but it was a very tiny part.

She communicated with Alice as infrequently as possible before the wedding, not wanting to spoil her happiness; after the marriage and their honeymoon to Chicago, Valerie turned down Alice's repeated invitations to join them for dinner at Teddy's apartment, which was now her home. She knew Alice wasn't deliberately being insensitive, but to have dinner with the man she still loved sitting right there, married to someone else, would be too painful to endure.

So the days and nights continued to blend one into the other. Life had become a relentless carousel, and Valerie just went around and around in an endless circle of despair.

Early in March, Valerie slowly began to heal. What prompted it was the realization that in a few weeks she would be eighteen years old, with no indication of a change from the life she was currently leading. All that she had held dear had disappeared with the loss of Teddy. She had not once, in this time, thought about leaving Galesville. She had not once recalled the vivid images Mack had painted for her when she was a child, images that had kept her going through other disappointments. She had put in Teddy all that she was and wanted to be, had invested him with the caretaking of her future, and when he had misused that trust, she had forsaken herself.

The quiet defiance that had permitted Valerie to withstand rejection by her schoolmates, the solid determination to make something of her life, the resolute belief in herself that had enabled her to be whipped and shed no tears slowly began to reassert themselves. Like a spring flower pushing forth through the hard winter crust of earth, Valerie began to come alive again. She did not feel the sun's growing strength on her back, or notice the gradual greening of the grass or hear the songs of the birds as they returned from their winter's vacation; she did not become part of life around her, but she was becoming alive again in herself. And as she did, she knew that the days of patience were over, as was the passivity that she had let claim her. There was only one person who could help her help herself. She had hurt Mack terribly, had not spoken to him since that horrible night before Thanksgiving, but she would go to him now, apologize, ask for his help. If he didn't give it to her, if he again told her to be patient, she would find another way. . . .

"Valerie, of course I forgive you. How could you ever have doubted it?"

"Then why didn't you come see me all this time? Why didn't you try to talk to me?"

"Would you have let me?"

Mack and Valerie were in his study, the room where she had first discovered the warmth of his friendship. She smiled, embarrassed, and shook her head. "I guess not," she admitted. "Oh, Mack, I've been such a fool."

"Not really. Just very young and terribly romantic."

"I'll never be that way again," she vowed.

Mack laughed. "Well, maybe not as young and maybe not quite as romantic, but some things don't change much."

"I have," she insisted. "I'll never let another man be that important to me. You'll see. The only man I'll ever trust is you."

Mack reached for her hand as they sat on the worn leather couch. "Don't say that, Valerie. Teddy was a first love, and nothing is quite as intense or hurts quite as much when it's over, but there will be other men and you're going to love again, next time even better."

"Promise?" Valerie asked, echoing the routine she and Mack had shared since she was a child.

"Now, Valerie, you know what I've taught you. Don't ask me to make promises and I won't have to tell you any lies."

"No promises, no lies. Is that how it always has to be?"

"Not always. I can make you one promise right now and I know it won't be a lie."

"Mack, please don't tell me to patient again. I don't think I could bear that," she said, pulling away her hand and getting to her feet. "I need help, Mack. I need you to help me. I can't stay here any longer. You understand that, don't you?" She turned to him, her eyes eloquent in their appeal.

"I've had an idea, Val. You may not like it, but I think it night be the answer. And you won't have to be patient much longer, believe me."

"Tell me, Mack. Whatever it is, I'll do it. Just get me away from here. Please."

It was 1961, a momentous year. The Soviets would be the first to send a man into space. Roger Maris would hit sixty home runs. The United States would establish the Peace Corps and sever relations with Cuba. John F. Kennedy's presidency remained America's fairy tale, and names like Fellini, Resnais, Bergman, and Truffaut changed movies into "cinema." But no event affected Valerie as strongly as her birthday party on March 24, 1961.

She had baked the cake herself and festooned crepe paper aound the living room. She felt no sense of deprivation that only Billy had given her a gift—a watercolor of the lake at sunset. She had insisted that everyone come to help celebrate, including Teddy.

She smiled cheerfully as she cut the cake and served it. She kept the smile fixed in place as her mother and sister spoke about new furniture, as Eli belched loudly, as Ned popped his fourth beer, as Billy ate a second piece of cake. When they all seemed to have forgotten her presence, she rose to her feet.

"I have something to tell you," she started, the smile never wavering, her midnight-blue eyes impenetrable as they went from one member of her family to another, challenging each of them to ignore her.

"Since it's my birthday, I decided to give myself a present."

"Shit, Valerie, what now?" Ned griped. "Another book? Who the hell cares."

"No, Ned," Valerie replied calmly, "not another book. If you'll just wait a sec, I'll show you what it is."

She walked out of the kitchen, raced upstairs, and came back with a sky-blue Samsonite suitcase. She held it up proudly. "Here's my birthday present."

"What the—" Eli said.

"Big deal," Ned muttered. "A suitcase don't mean a thing unless you're goin' somewheres. Can't see where you'll need it for waitin' tables at the Golden." His laugh was a crude innuendo as he added, "Maybe you're plannin' to work overnight, huh?" Eli joined his son in the laughter, as did Teddy until he was silenced by a glare from Alice.

"You're right, Ned. A suitcase is meaningless unless I'm going somewhere," Valerie continued. "That's the other part of my birthday present." She paused, and the smile became a line of determination as hard as her eyes.

"Tomorrow morning at eleven o'clock, Mack is driving me to Indianapolis, where I will take a plane to Dallas, Texas."

"Now just one minute—"

"Please let me finish, Papa, then you can have your turn," Valerie said. "In Dallas I will have my interview with Universal Airlines. They could, of course, turn me down, but I don't think they will. Mack is very good friends with the president of the airline, and there should be no problem getting accepted in their stewardess school."

She sat down, her palms itchy with nervous tension, her stomach gurgling with the acid of anxiety. She willed herself to keep her gaze steady, to meet each face before her with absolute self-confidence. She hadn't known it would be so difficult. She hadn't planned on the fear of leaving home. Finally having a way out was all she had thought about since Mack had first suggested she become a stewardess, but now, confronted with the reality of it all, a terrible fright came over her, gripping her so painfully that all she wanted to do was shout that she wouldn't go, that she was joking, that it was all a mistake—anything to free her heart from its galloping terror of the unknown. But she forced the empty smile to reappear as she said, "Now, Papa, you were saying?"

"You little bitch! Who the hell do you think you are! And how the hell do you plan on paying for this?" Eli shouted.

"Mack is loaning me the money."

"In exchange for what—sleeping with him?"

"I would think you'd be glad to be rid of me, Papa. No matter what it took."

"What about me?" Edith whined. "Who's gonna help me now? You can't go. I won't let you."

"Won't *let* me, Mama?" Valerie shook her head. "You can't stop me. Not anymore."

"You're nothing but a slut," Eli accused. "Nobody but a whore becomes a stewardess."

"Papa, don't," Alice said. "That's not fair." She exchanged a look with Teddy that Valerie did not understand but that she did not like.

"Alice, why do I always feel that when you try to rescue me you're condemning me even more. I never have quite understood that."

"Valerie, why that's—"

"Ned? Surely you have something invaluable to say, don't you? I can't remember when my big brother hasn't added fuel to the fire if it meant burning his little sister."

"Papa's right. You gotta be some kind of slut to do what you're doin'," he said, but without enthusiasm.

"And what are you, Ned? Some kind of man, right? Drinking and carrying on and getting your papa to bail you out of trouble as if you were still a teenager." Her smile was bitter. "Poor little Ned. A boy in man's clothing."

Ned bolted to his feet, but Billy restrained him from going after Valerie. "Sit down and shut up," he said with more force than he had ever before used. He looked at his sister, and his grin was wide, warm. "Bravo, Val. I wish you all the luck in the world."

"Thank you, Billy," she said softly. She glanced at Alice. "You're awfully quiet. Don't tell me *you* think I'm a slut, too."

Alice's eyes flashed a warning, then she shrugged. "I

think you're a big girl now and if you want to make a fool of yourself, I'm not going to try and stop you."

"First a slut, now a fool. My, my, you people really do think a lot of me," Valerie said, her belief in the rightness of her decision returning fully.

"Well, I'm sorry I don't have anyone's blessings except Billy's but then again, if I waited for that from any of you, I'd never do anything with my life."

She stood and picked up her suitcase. "I'll send a postcard from Dallas," she said, then walked out of the room. Drained by the effort of keeping her voice strong, her attitude sure, she had to hold on to the banister as she climbed the stairs.

She had waited for this day, dreamed about it, but never could she have imagined it having such an effect on her. Would it have been that ugly if Teddy had not been sitting there as her sister's husband? she wondered. If her father had not tried to demean her, her mother to control her? Would she have had the courage to speak to them as she had if they had not performed quite so true to form?

But they had, and so she would take the only course open to her. Galesville. Family. Even Mack. The good, the safe, the frustrating, the hurtful. All of it would be behind her by tomorrow.

A shiver ran through her. She wondered if it was a tremble of fear about leaving. Then she smiled as she recognized it for what it really was: the thrill of a new beginning.

BOOK II

Chapter 7

Week 1

Four days later, Valerie was in a large dressing room, seated in front of a huge mirror framed with theatrical light bulbs. The glow they cast was glaring and unkind, judging by the moans of the fifteen other girls in the room. Valerie peered closer into the mirror but saw nothing unusual there.

"What are you looking for? You wouldn't know an enlarged pore if you fell into one!"

Valerie grinned at the girl sitting next to her, who was grimacing at her own pert, skin-perfect reflection. Linda Donahue was Valerie's roommate for the next five weeks of stew school. A redheaded moppet with enormous china-blue eyes and freckles across a short ski slope of a nose, Linda would have been cloyingly cute were it not for a peppery wit and often foul mouth that left no one thinking she was a little girl for long.

Since Mack had been able to waive her first interview with Universal's head of personnel, Valerie's call-back interview four days ago had been pro forma, more a lookover to make sure that Mack had not misappraised her. Valerie had found the thirty-minute screening with Martin Corning, a tall reed of a man with a black shoebrush mustache and a remarkable ability not to blink, terrifying. Why did she want to be a stew? How many in your family? Good, we like stews from large families, they're used to serving others. How big is Galesville? Good, we like stews from small towns, they're eager to learn. Stand up. Hmm, posture could stand a little improvement. Walk. Sit down. Cross your legs. Good legs. Okay. Here's your Stew Manual; tomorrow you'll have a quiz on the Civil Aeronautics code designations for every major airport in the United States. Your instructor will be Patricia Harnell, one of our best. Good luck. And since each class has a thirty-percent failure rate, you'll need it.

Legs trembling, Valerie had followed the instructions, given to her by Corning's secretary, to the motel across the street. The Universal Motel was the "dormitory" used by the airline to house the stews during training. The school itself—a one-story building—the motel, and the adjoining cafeteria that served the training personnel and the girls were about a mile from the Dallas airport and, Valerie soon found out, about an eternity away from civilization. With classes from eight o'clock in the morning until five in the evening, and then rigorous studying for exams in which a grade of ninety percent was passing and automatic termination resulted from two failures, there was little time or energy for the class of sixteen to wonder about the attractions of Dallas, or to test the eleven-o'clock weekday curfew by hanging out at the various bars frequented by the airline's male personnel.

Struggling with her suitcase in one hand and the hefty manual in the other, Valerie had entered her room to find it already occupied. A redheaded girl swung herself off one of the beds and quickly helped relieve Valerie of her suitcase. "Hi, I'm Linda Donahue, your roomie for the next five weeks. You're—?"

"Valerie. Valerie Cardell." She was tongue-tied at the sight before her. Besides the wayward cap of red curls and the kewpie-doll face, which had a racoon ring of black make-up around each large eye and a dollop of pink rouge on each cheek that matched the pink on her lips so that her face seemed to be all eyes, the tall vision before her in tight shorts and tighter T-shirt made Valerie blush. Linda Donahue had the kind of figure that no exercise and no diet could create, and no bra and girdle could contain. Some women are born with that kind of perfection; Linda Donahue was that kind of woman. If she had been beautiful instead of cute, Hollywood would have been stampeding to her door.

Linda laughed at Valerie's expression of stunned admiration. "Thanks. I think what you're not saying is supposed to be a compliment."

Valerie nodded, dropping the huge looseleaf Stewardess

Training Manual on the other bed and sitting down beside it. "Do all of them look like you?" she couldn't help asking. Then: "I mean, uh, I know stews have to be good-looking and all, but you could be a model."

Linda laughed again. "Not with these tits, sweetie," she said, taking a deep breath so that the perfection of her chest became even more pronounced. "Besides, I did that gig for a while and I don't like it. No *real* men, if you get me."

Valerie did not get her at all; in fact, her reactions were on a rollercoaster, from embarrassment at the girl's crude reference to her breasts, to ignorance of words like *gig*, to uncertainty about what "real men" meant. She sat staring, mute.

"Oh, honey, you don't understand, do you?" Linda said, plopping onto her bed and sitting cross-legged against the headboard. "I used to do some runway modeling in New York for some of the Seventh Avenue rag houses—clothing manufacturers—but I didn't like it because most of the men I met were either more interested in other men or too devoted to their wives. Now do we understand each other?"

Valerie nodded sheepishly, then began to unpack. Her heart was pounding, and she felt a trickle of perspiration between her breasts, despite the fact that the air-conditioner was blasting. She knew that what she was experiencing was utter fear.

"Where you from?"

"Galesville, Indiana."

"Galesville! Do they really still name towns with 'ville' at the end?"

"It's a small town about a hundred twenty miles west of Indianapolis," Valerie answered stiffly. A slow thread of anger began to weave through her. She might not understand all this hip jargon, and she might be from a small town, and she might not be sophisticated, but she was qualified enough to make the Universal stew school, and that counted for something; for quite a lot, in fact.

"I'm from Long Island. Know where that is?"

Mack had, on more than one occasion, told her all about the suburbs of New York: Queens, Long Island, Westchester, and the beautiful homes on the south shore of Long Island, abutting the Atlantic ocean. "Sure. Where in Long Island?" she asked.

"A place called Syosset. It's about thirty minutes from Manhattan."

Valerie had never heard of it, but its proximity to New York City gave it a magic that erased any feeling of anger or resentment. "Did you ever live in New York?" she asked.

"For about a year. While I was modeling."

"Why did you leave?"

Linda shrugged. "I told you. I was in a dead-end job, and besides, I've always wanted to travel. Becoming a stew seemed perfect, even though it's about as glamorous as waiting tables."

"Nope, you're wrong about that. I *know*," Valerie said with more liveliness than she had so far shown.

Linda laughed with understanding, and Valerie smiled. "You're excited about all this, aren't you?"

Valerie nodded. "Aren't you?"

"I guess. The truth is I'm eager to get into the air and meet some fabulously rich man and get married. Or meet lots of not so fabulously rich men and have a good time." She propped her hands behind her head and smiled knowingly. "Shocked?"

When Valerie did not answer, Linda went on, "Don't tell me you're doing this for the glory of serving?"

"I'm doing this because it was a way of getting out," Valerie said softly, meeting Linda's amused look with an almost challenging intensity.

"After the next few weeks you may want to go back to wherever you're trying to get away from," Linda said with a short laugh to dispel the tension. "I hear they're grueling, and the poop on Harnell is that she's a bitch on wheels. 'Tough' is a compliment."

Valerie sat back on the bed and lifted the manual onto her lap, running her hand reverently over the top of it. "I don't care how tough she is or how tough she is on me. I don't care what they make us do or how late I have to stay up studying. I'm going to make it. I'm going to become a stewardess no matter what it takes. You don't know how much—" Valerie stopped herself from revealing more. This girl was a stranger; she could not possibly understand the gift Valerie had been given by being here.

But Linda Donahue did understand. And in the next several days, as the girls met Patricia Harnell and were frightened by her rigid manner and her dire warnings about failure to adhere to the rules; as they got to know one another and groan together over the rigorous regulations, the endless things to be learned, the lack of time to have fun, Valerie realized that Linda, April Mayhew, who came from a farm in Oklahoma, Dorothy Bennett from Spokane, and Didi Winters from Chicago, and all the others wanted to be Universal stewardesses as much as she did. For each of them, it was a way out of a life they no longer wanted, and a way into a future that could be filled with nothing but promise.

The first afternoon, after a scary morning of listening to Patricia Harnell, there had been the quiz on the code designations, and Frannie, a petite strawberry blonde from Bennington, Vermont, had not made the passing ninety. The next morning she had her one chance for a makeup, and flunked again. One more failing grade, and no matter her sparkling, bubbly personality, her sincere eagerness, her charming looks—she would be out. That was why when Linda and Didi invited Valerie to go bar hopping the second night, she refused. She understood that she was risking the same thing that had happened to her back in Galesville: that to distance herself from the other girls could get her a reputation as being aloof, a snob; but nothing meant more to her than getting her wings—*nothing*. If that meant studying all night, she would do that. If it meant not having any friends, so be it. Besides, she had never been to a bar in her life, let alone to meet men. And after her experience with Teddy, men held little interest for her.

The first few days had been a constant whirl of classes, studying, and exams on everything from the functions of the Civil Aeronautics Board to the history of Universal Airlines. In a way, Valerie had been looking forward to this afternoon since it would be devoted exclusively to grooming, one of the most important aspects of a stewardess's professional life. They were weighed in every morning; a few extra pounds, not lost after the proper warning, could be grounds for dismissal. As could going without a girdle or wearing too much makeup or too much jewelry. Almost anything, it seemed to Valerie as she sat there peering into the mirror, could be grounds for dismissal.

Patricia Harnell entered the room, and the buzz of voices quickly stopped. With her was a tall, thin woman of about thirty-eight, with black hair done up in a perfect chignon. Valerie decided that she now understood what the word *stately* meant.

"Class, this is Adele Verona, head of grooming for Universal. She'll take over for the afternoon. Don't be surprised when she tells you that everything you've been doing to make yourselves beautiful is wrong." With a rare smile, she left.

Valerie and Linda exchanged raised eyebrows and grins. Despite Linda's breezy attitude toward her studies—which did not stop her from passing every exam—and a propensity for getting back to her room a safe second before the eleven-o'clock bed check, Valerie liked her. She was two years older but often seemed more, with her sophisticated, occasionally hard-edged wit. Underneath, Valerie quickly realized, was a warm and generous person. Linda tried to include Valerie in whatever she did, but Valerie usually refused her invitations, whether it was to go to one of the other girl's rooms for a gab fest or to go to a bar. Her excuse was that she had to study, but that was not the real reason and she suspected Linda knew it. Valerie did not want to explain that loneliness had made her shy and heartache had made her solitary, and Linda never pushed. Only once had she seemed put out by Valerie's constant refusals to join her, and that had been last night, when she had tried to persuade Valerie to go to the Clipped Wing, the hangout bar, for a drink.

To Valerie's mumbled excuse about studying, Linda had said, "First of all, there's no exam tomorrow. And second of all, you can't keep hiding. Look, I'm not about to take up causes, but you ought to get wise to something. Just knowing what's in the books doesn't make a good stew. You've got to know how to deal with people, all kinds of people. And like it or not, Valerie, men are people."

That had hurt, but this morning Linda had acted as if nothing unusual had occurred. In fact, she had made a comment about Valerie having been smart not to go with them last night since the hangover she was now suffering wasn't worth it, and Lily, one of the girls who had been with them, had gotten sick in the ladies' room and missed bed check. She had been automatically terminated from the program.

"What?" Valerie had said, aghast.

"Harnell came around as Lily stumbled into the room."

"Couldn't Bobbi have stalled somehow?"

"Lily's dear roommate was already asleep, as were you, by the way."

"I can't believe it," Valerie had whispered.

"Those are the breaks, kiddo. If you can't land on your feet, don't try to fly."

"But, Linda, she wanted to be a stew so badly. Couldn't they have given her one more chance?"

"Remember what Harnell said that first day? This is a job of responsibility, and if we can't be responsible for ourselves, we sure as hell aren't fit for an airplane full of people." She shrugged. "I guess she's right. Come on, don't look so glum. A goody two shoes like you has nothing to worry about."

"I'm not a goody two shoes, and I—"

"Just joking, just joking. Actually, you're smarter than the rest of us. Either that or just born with a weaker sex drive." Linda's mischievous grin had made Valerie look away without answering.

But now, waiting for Adele Verona to begin, Valerie found herself replaying that conversation as well as what Linda had said last night. She knew the older girl had had several sexual experiences; Linda was more than open about them. Was it possible then that Valerie did have a weaker sex drive, or had something vital died when she had lost Teddy?

There was no more time to dwell on that or on Lily's dismissal as the grooming instructor began to lecture the group on hairstyles, girdles, brassieres, color of hose, length of skirts, quality of slips, jewelry. Then she took each girl individually and tore her apart. When it was her turn, Valerie thought she would pass out from embarrassment. All eyes were on her as Adele began to inspect her like a scientist scrutinizing a new specimen of bug.

"Your hair has to go," she said emphatically, lifting a handful of Valerie's thick, heavy black hair. "Long hair is not allowed unless you want to wear it up the way I do." She began to brush Valerie's hair away from her face, making a severe French twist in the back. "What do you think?"

Valerie stared at the reflection of this suddenly urbane-looking woman that was herself. She seemed to have aged by about ten years and that many experiences. She caught Linda's eye and saw that her roommate was having a difficult time keeping a straight face. She was wrinkling her nose and shaking her head slightly, and Valerie had to agree with the negative assessment of this new look.

"Maybe I should get it cut?" she ventured.

Adele Verona nodded. "Yes. I think that would be better. Now, what about makeup. Why don't you use any?"

"Well, I use lipstick, of course, and—"

"Class, look at those eyes. Big, deep-blue eyes. Just beautiful. They should be the focus of attention. Now, let's see if you've learned anything from what I've been teaching the past two hours. What should Valerie do about eye makeup?"

A rash of suggestions followed that would have had Valerie circling her eyes with liquid black eyeliner, curling upper and lower eyelashes, and wearing violet eyeshadow even to sleep. When April, the Oklahoma farm girl, a pallid blonde with no lashes at all, suggested false eyelashes, Valerie groaned aloud.

"That's not such a bad idea," Adele said, "but you don't need them, Valerie. You happen to have lashes like spider legs. Others are not as fortunate."

"I'm sorry, it's just that—"

"I think what I'm going to recommend is that you get your hair cut, and do your own makeup, using the principles you've learned here today. Does that sound reasonable?"

Valerie nodded, chastised and relieved. "All right," the grooming instructor continued, "stand up and walk from one end of the room to the other. Let's see how your posture rates."

As Valerie walked, Adele's voice rang out: "Shoulders back. Stomach in. Chin up. Up. That's it. Good. Tummy in. Better, a little more. That's it. Now stand there a minute." She walked over to Valerie, who stood with her stomach sucked in, buttocks muscles tightened, shoulders back, chin up in a paralysis of good posture.

"Now this, class, is the perfect example of how each of you should walk up and down the aisles of an airplane. Anything less does a disservice to your Universal uniform."

That night, April and Didi joined Linda and Valerie in

their room, and laughed themselves to curfew reviewing Adele Verona's admonishments to each of them.

"Why the hell do I have to wear a girdle when I don't have an ass to begin with?" April complained.

"You think that's bad," Didi retorted. "It's taken me three years to grow my hair." She swung her long, straight blonde hair so that it rested between her shoulder blades. "No way am I getting it cut."

"You'll never make it in a bun, Didi," Linda pointed out, smiling.

The barely five-foot-five regulation-height blonde shrugged. "I'll buy a wig and tuck this under it. I don't care, I won't cut it!"

"Shorter hair might make you seem taller," Valerie suggested.

"A low center of gravity can be very useful in the air," Didi said straight-faced.

"Where did you hear that?" April asked.

"I just made it up, but it sounds good, doesn't it?"

When they all stopped laughing, Linda said, "Listen, you guys, I've got a bigger problem than all of you."

Since her beauty and her glorious figure seemed to be problem-free to the eyes of the others, they looked at her as if she were crazy. "Makeup. I'm talking about makeup. That old witch says I wear too much. Did you ever hear anything so ridiculous!"

"She's not so old," Valerie pointed out.

"She's got to be over thirty-five," April said.

"Automatic dismissal time. I guess old stews go to the big grooming school in the sky when they have to be retired," Didi said, laughing.

"That, or the big bitch school of stew instructors," Linda remarked. "Harnell must have been valedictorian of her class." She shook her head and looked around at her friends. "Now seriously, what am I going to do with all my makeup? I've got fifty bucks' worth of crap that I can't use anymore."

"Give it to me," April volunteered. "I'm so washed out I can use all the color I can get."

"And don't forget the false eyelashes," Valerie reminded her, grinning.

"Puh-*leeze*. Can you just picture it. Serving some old geezer his martini and instead of an olive he gets an eyelash in his glass."

The bantering continued for more than two hours before the girls heard Harnell doing her check down the hall. April and Didi scampered out with a quick good-night. Later, when Valerie and Linda were in bed, with the lights out, Valerie said, almost as if she were thinking aloud, "That was fun."

"What?"

"Tonight. With the girls. I enjoyed that."

"Val, honey, all you've got to do is give yourself a chance. Believe me, you can have a lot more fun. You've got looks, brains, personality. You can't imagine how much fun is out there waiting for you."

Valerie said nothing. She wanted to share her secrets with Linda, but she did not know how to begin. Tonight she had been part of a group, laughing, having fun, being young and alive and carefree. She had liked that feeling, loved it, and she felt closer to Linda Donahue, whom she had known for only four days, than she had ever felt to anyone else, even her sister. Still, she could not take the step from friendliness to intimacy; what if it was more than Linda wanted? Rejection from this newfound source of warmth would devastate Valerie.

"Val?"

"Huh?"

"Mind if I ask you something personal? I mean, really personal?"

"I'll let you know after you ask it," Valerie replied lightly.

"Are you a virgin?"

"That's not so personal," Valerie said, grinning in the dark.

"It isn't?"

"I figured you already knew the answer."

Linda snapped on the light on the table between them and saw Valerie's smile. "Well, I did, but I wanted to make sure, I guess. Are you really?"

"Yup."

"Incredible. In this day and age."

"You sound like my sister."

"I didn't know you had a sister."

"And two brothers. What about you?"

"Are you kidding? My folks didn't want to risk having another like me."

"So. That was your big question?" Valerie reminded her.

"Well, yes. I mean, it's none of my business, of course,

but how come? Are you afraid, or hasn't there ever been anyone?"

Valerie hesitated, but only briefly. "There was someone. We broke up." Her voice was a husky whisper and every nerve in her body tightened with the desire to be silent, to volunteer nothing more, but she knew how important it was to share this with Linda. She had to offer this token of trust if the friendship was to blossom. She understood that, and fought the well-honed instinct to shut herself off protectively.

"It hurt, huh?" Linda asked gently.

"Yes. It hurt."

"Did you break up because you wouldn't go to bed with him?"

Was that it? Was that why Teddy had treated her so shabbily and then married her sister? No, she did not think so, but she had been wrong about so many things when it came to him. "I don't know."

"Did you want to? Go to bed with him, I mean."

"Yes, yes I did," Valerie said. "But I really believe in saving myself for marriage. At least I did," she amended.

"You'll never find anyone to marry if you stay in this room every night," Linda pointed out.

"Is that what this is all about?" Valerie asked, not knowing whether to be annoyed or amused. "Are you still trying to get me to go to the Clipped Wing with you?"

Linda grinned. "Well, it can't hurt. Besides, I'll make sure you stick to flight engineers and avoid all captains."

"How come?"

"You don't know? Boy, you *are* innocent. Val, never *ever* get involved with a pilot. Either they're married or they're so in love with themselves they can't spare any of that precious affection for anyone else. Their attitude toward stews is something like mine toward makeup. I like to try them all out, but I never stick with one kind for very long. Understand?"

"And how do you come by all this knowledge?" Valerie asked.

"There are some things, dear child, that one doesn't have to experience firsthand to know they're true. And having anything to do with a pilot is one of them. It's just a rule of the game, like wearing those damn girdles."

"You're impossible," Valerie said, laughing.

"Does that mean you'll go to the Clipped Wing with me?" Linda asked hopefully. "Come on, Val, we'll go Saturday night when curfew's extended to one o'clock and there's no exam on Sunday. Just try it once. Think of it this way—you'll have a new haircut by then, and you'll be wearing all that fancy new makeup that I'll probably end up giving you. You've got to show yourself off. What do you say?"

She couldn't study all Saturday night, Valerie reasoned. And it was fun being with the girls. This was part of why Mack had worked so hard to get her here; part of why she had defied her family. Fun. She had to learn how to have fun.

"Okay, I'll go."

"Great! And remember, no pilots."

"Right. No pilots."

At eight o'clock Saturday evening, Bobbi, Didi, April, and Frannie were in Linda and Valerie's room, chattering with the nervous energy females get when they know they are going to be around men. Linda had arranged for everyone to meet in their room so they could see the "new" Valerie. They all looked different from the way they had when they first arrived at Universal: April had started to wear very discreet false lashes and looked much better for it; on a whim, Didi had tied her hair up in a Victorian knot, seen how much better she looked, and promptly had it all cut off in a layered style; Bobbi, who had been told that tweezed and shaped eyebrows would do much to enhance her round hazel eyes, had done so, and what had been a rather blandly pretty face now was a striking one. Frannie, the strawberry blonde who was having academic difficulties, knew without being told that weight would be her biggest problem, but tonight, in a tight-fitting pair of white pants slung low on her hips and a midriff-baring striped T-shirt, every pound seemed inviting.

"Okay, guys, get ready!" Linda announced, arms outstretched as she emerged from the bathroom.

"Where's your new image?" Didi asked. "You could put the makeup you've got on in a tube and sell it as a full package."

"Very funny. Look, I'll do what Halitosis Harnell wants when I'm on the aisles, but the rest of the time belongs to me."

"Poor attitude, Donahue," Bobbi said. "What was it Harnell told us—oh yeah, we're stews every minute Universal pays us, and a bad image at any time is a bad reflection on Universal."

"That's right," Frannie chimed in. "Universal would just die if they saw you now."

"Frannie, Universal is a name, not a 'they,'" Linda snapped, "and I would appreciate it if you would all kindly shut up. Valerie's going to fall asleep in the tub if you don't let her come out." She glanced around at the group, making sure she had their attention. "Okay, Val!"

"Linda, this is ridiculous," she muttered as she came out of the bathroom.

"Now turn around slowly. Give 'em a full view," the redhead instructed.

"Come on, this is—"

"Turn."

With an exaggerated sigh, Valerie pivoted slowly so that her new friends could see what the hairdresser had done for her, along with Linda's expertise with makeup and her suggestions about clothes. Despite being unused to the limelight, Valerie had to admit to herself that her racing pulse had less to do with anticipation of the girls' reactions than to her own deep pleasure at the transformation.

Gone was the mane of thick, wavy black hair. Now there was a sleek but saucy cap of different layers, soft tendrils cupping her face so that her cheekbones were more pronounced, her magnificent eyes magnetic. Linda had been subtle but effective with the makeup: a thin line of midnight blue above and below the eyes, and lots of mascara; a blush of brush-on powder in a berry color to bring out the olive in Valerie's skin tone; and a brownish-pink lipstick. What had looked strangely exotic in Galesville now was desirable, exciting, and unabashedly sexual, the full lips inviting, the skin creamy with warmth. Wearing a slim white skirt that Linda had loaned her the money to buy and a pink camisole sweater with matching short-sleeved oversweater that she had let her borrow, Valerie had looked at herself enough times to know that the butterfly had begun to emerge from its cocoon. Although she had made halfhearted objections as Linda had worked on her, Valerie could no more have gone back to her old image than she could have gone back to waiting tables. Her embarrassment now was from the thrill of self-pleasure, the healthy awakening of vanity in an eighteen-year-old young lady.

"Faan-tastic!" Didi said.

"Not to be believed. Just not to be believed," Bobbi commented.

"See! I told you, didn't I?" Linda said to Valerie with delight.

"I'm terribly sorry, girls," Didi said solemnly, rising from the bed and walking to the door. "I'm afraid I won't be able to join you tonight."

"What!"

"Look, Frannie, and the rest of you idiots, if you think I'm going into the Clipped Wing with competition like those two," she lifted a shoulder in the direction of Linda and Valerie, "you're all crazier than I thought."

"Oh come on," Linda said, striding toward her and taking her arm. "We won't be selfish. You can have any guy we don't want!"

Laughing, the group left.

Cold fingers of trepidation gripped Valerie as the girls walked the quarter mile to the pub. At lunch on any given weekday, the restaurant did a brisk business of beers and burgers. Starting at five o'clock with a happy hour, during which all drinks were sixty cents, business was even better, going strong until the eleven-o'clock curfew for the stews in training. But it was on Friday and Saturday nights that the place jumped, the rickety floorboards of its small dance area throbbing with the rock-and-roll beat from the jukebox, the noise level shattering as people tried to connect in conversation, or perhaps something more. On this first Saturday night for class 62-9—each class was designated by the year and the number of their class so far that year—the Clipped Wing was packed with technicians, flight engineers, and even some pilots, all eager to see the new batch of stews and prey on their beauty and eagerness to please. Although Linda, Didi, and a few of the others had already made their debut appearance earlier in the week, this Saturday night was their real "coming out" party.

Gnawing on her inner lip and clutching her handbag as if it were a lifeline, Valerie found an inch of space by the bar, determined to have just one drink and make her escape. Much as she wanted to be one of the girls, talking to strangers in a dark, loud bar was simply beyond her abilities. It was not because of her sensitivity after Teddy or even her shyness; it was because of her ignorance: What do you say to a stranger? What kind of drink should she order? If someone asked her to dance, what would she do? All she knew of dancing was what she had seen on *American Bandstand*. She and Teddy had, on occasion, gone dancing, but they had danced only to the slow songs; the twist, the stroll, the monkey were awkward embarrassments for both of them. She did not know how to behave in this new social situation, and she was scared.

By the time she finished her second brandy stinger—recommended by Linda as sweet, smooth, and guaranteed to relax her—Valerie's oversweater was off, one spaghetti strap of the camisole had slipped down her shoulder, and she was flushed with the power of pleasing. Everything was amusing; it was easier to laugh than to make conversation. She discovered that after a few drinks her body warmed to the heavily sexual rhythm of the music, and when one blond fellow in a checked shirt and chinos dragged her from the barstool onto the dance floor, her feet and body had no inhibitions about moving to the music. After him there were others, and two more stingers, until she was forced to weave her way into the cubbyhole that served as a restroom, with Linda at her heels.

"You okay?" her roommate asked with concern as she watched Valerie grinning at herself in the dirt-caked mirror.

"*Grrreat*, as Tony the Tiger would say!" Valerie answered with a sloppy giggle. "I'm so glad you made me come with you tonight."

"Yeah, well, I think you've had enough to drink, kiddo."

"Oh no, definitely not. Definitely not!"

Linda shook her head. "You're blitzed. Soused. Also known as drunk as a skunk. Come on, we're going home." She tried to take Valerie by her upper arm, but Valerie shrugged off her grip.

"Nope. I'm not going back until it's one second before curfew. Just like you do. I'm having fun. Fun! Fun! Fun!"

Her giggling became so uncontrollable that Linda helplessly joined in. When the two girls managed to wipe away the tears, Valerie said, "I *am* high, Linda, but I'm not drunk, at least not from the liquor. I'm just having a really good time. For the first time in my life, I am really and truly having fun."

She gazed at Linda, a lucid part of her brain wondering if the import of her words meant anything to this girl who seemed so comfortable in a bar, who had no difficulty talking to strangers, making jokes, being witty and charming and sexy. She couldn't possibly understand that for Valerie to discover she had the same abilities was tantamount to discovering an entirely new human being residing within herself. For so long, all pleasure had been secondhand through her sister; then there had been Teddy, and whatever firsthand knowledge she had had of joy disappeared with him. But tonight there was the boy in the checked shirt, and the tall, curly-haired flight engineer with the bushy mustache who whispered in her ear about what he would do to her if she left with him. And there had been the stocky redhead whose hand kept slipping to her side to feel her breast as they danced slowly in a tiny dot of space. Outrageous, obscene, delicious. The young of America had been calling themselves the population of Camelot since Kennedy had taken office; she had envied that feeling of privilege and endless possibility. Now she understood it.

"Okay, kiddo," Linda said gently, her eyes warm with understanding. "The night's yours, but watch the booze, huh?" Valerie nodded happily. "And watch that guy with the mustache. I think he could even get Harnell into bed!"

"Oh, Linda!"

"I'm serious. He's gorgeous."

"I know, I know!"

Week 2

Despite a wicked hangover the next day and a fervent vow never to set foot in another bar as long as she lived, Valerie accepted Linda's invitation on Wednesday, which was Ladies' Night. Although she switched her drink to rum and Coke with lots of ice, she still managed to dance wildly, laugh a lot, and increase her familiarity with flirtation and fun. On Friday night, Didi, Linda, and Valerie decided to have dinner at the Wing—forbidden greasy burgers and fries, which would have to be dieted off the next day—and then settle down for the regular Friday night action.

"Class of Nine?"

"Sorry?"

"I was asking if you're part of the training class now in session."

Valerie only nodded in reply, unable to get her voice to work properly as she stared, wide-eyed, at the man who had addressed her. It struck her that if John F. Kennedy had been cloned, his double was standing right here at the bar of the Clipped Wing. Sandy hair, brush cut; pale blue oxford-cloth shirt, little tendrils of sandy hair peeking out where the top two buttons were undone, and more golden hair on the muscular wrists and tanned forearms where the shirt sleeves had been rolled back. Blue eyes the color of the French flag, looking at her as if he understood what she was feeling, her delight in him. In those eyes and in the smug set of his firm, full lips was an arrogance that Valerie, in the infancy of her social awakening, did not discern. As the blue eyes crinkled at the corners and the mouth moved in a closed-lip half-smile, she saw only incredible handsomeness, a physical appeal that made her gulp her drink, savoring the cooling sensation of the ice. She did not know that the crinkling and the half-smile were practiced props of Roger Monash's narcissism.

"Looks like that drink's all ice. May I get you another?" he offered, taking her glass as she was about to put it back on the bar top, the soft hairs of his hand teasing her skin. As he turned to get the bartender's attention, she noticed that he was tall, about six foot two, and tautly muscular, his neck thick, his shoulders straining against his shirt. After ordering, he leaned on one elbow against the side of the bar, and she forced herself to look at him fully as he smiled at her.

"Roger Monash."

"Valerie Cardell."

"How do you like training?"

She shrugged, willing herself to find her voice and use it. The spring of wit and humor she had thought was limitless a few nights ago had dried up on her, leaving her with the disappointing emptiness that had marked her former social personality. Just because he was the most unbelievably good-looking man she had ever seen; just because he must be at least thirty-three or thirty-four, so much older than anyone she had ever known; just because he seemed so sure of himself—these were hardly good enough reasons for her to retreat back into her mousehole. She knew that if the new face she wore was not matched with an equally bright charm, she might as well forget being a successful stewardess. After all, wouldn't she be meeting many kinds of men when she started working the aisles? And wouldn't some of them be older, worldly, good-looking, charming, and wonderful? And would that mean that she would spill their drinks, be tongue-tied and clumsy? So, when her new drink arrived, she took a very healthy swallow, got more comfortable on her barstool, and smiled at him with a naturalness that revealed none of her nervousness.

"I haven't seen you here before," she said.

"My loss," he replied smoothly, and Valerie felt the hairs on her arms stand up as if they had been caressed. "I just got in from Paris," he went on, "and thought I'd stop by before heading home."

"Paris! Do you go there often?"

He leaned closer to her. "Would you like to go there sometime?"

Valerie managed a light laugh. "Of course. Who wouldn't?"

"I might be able to help."

"How?"

"Oh, I know a few people."

"First-year stews rarely get anything but domestic flights."

"Like I said, I know a few people."

Valerie's eyes locked with his, and suddenly, unbidden, unwished for, a warning went off in her mind. She kept her smile in place as she asked, "You're not a pilot, by any chance, are you?"

Monash straightened. "Of course. What did you think I was, a technician?"

"I'm sorry, I didn't know. I just wanted to make sure, that's all."

"Make sure of what?" Monash asked, a hard edge in his voice. "Don't tell me you're one of those pilot groupies?"

"Pilot what?"

"Those broads who only make it with the captains. I hate those women."

Valerie's outrage was immediate and undisguised in the rigid set of her back, the cold glitter in her eyes. "No, Mr. Monash, I am not a pilot groupie," she said coldly, not surprised but disappointed at this man's egotism. "In fact," she went on, "I was warned against having anything to do with pilots, so I was asking out of self-protection. And since you've had your trouble with adoring stews, maybe it would be best if we ended this conversation right now." She took her glass and swiveled on the stool, about to leave. Linda's arrival stopped her.

"Well, Roger Monash, as I live and breathe. Come to pluck another blossom off the bush, Jolly Roger?"

Monash glared at Linda but said nothing. "I didn't know you and the Jolly Roger knew each other, Val," she went on, a strange, tight smile on her face that Valerie did not understand. "Has that Kennedy charm of his gotten to you yet? Has he told you how much he hates pilot groupies, never once, of course, admitting that he's got a rep as a stew pirate? That's how he got the name the Jolly Roger—because he hits each new class and takes the one he wants, the purer and stupider she is the better. Obviously you qualify on both counts, kiddo."

"Linda!"

"Donahue, why don't you make a visit to the trough where the rest of the pigs go," Roger hissed.

Linda's odd little smile did not waver. "Ah, Roger, you haven't changed a bit. Still the face of a choir boy and the mind of a pimp." She turned her brittle blue glare on Valerie. "Roger and I go back a long, long time, Val. We're what is known as old friends. Isn't that right, Rog? Or should I say 'intimate strangers'? Yes, I think that would be better. I can't imagine you being anyone's friend. Well, forewarned is forearmed, as they say, so be careful, Val." And then she was gone, a stunned Valerie staring after her.

"Don't mind her," Roger said with a small laugh. "She's got a lot of the bitch in her."

"I've never seen her like that before," Valerie remarked quietly. "Would you mind telling me what it was all about?"

"As a matter of fact, I would mind," he said evenly,

reaching out and pushing a loose wisp of hair back from her face. "Now that I've found you, I don't intend to spend the rest of the time until your curfew talking about people I don't like." The back of his fingers began to lightly caress her cheek, and she was lost, her eyes unable to look anywhere but into his, her body unable to move away from the heat of his touch. The confusion left by Linda was quickly forgotten. Valerie was drowning in a quicksand of sensation and she did not want to be saved.

When she arrived at her room that night at fifteen minutes before bed check, Linda was there, reading a magazine in bed. She did not look up when Valerie entered.

"Oh, Linda, I'm so glad you're still up," Valerie said gaily, walking over to sit on her bed, a smile as bright as a moonbeam lighting up her face. "We've just got to talk."

"I'm tired."

"But, Linda, the most wonderful thing has happened to me—"

"I said I was tired!"

The sharpness of her roommate's tone and the unexpected coldness were as effective as a slap in the face. Valerie felt herself disappearing into the shadows again, the beauty of her friendship with Linda just a warm memory, like that of the summer sun on her back in the middle of winter. Slowly, she got up from the bed and began to undress.

When she came out of the bathroom, Linda was still pretending to read; when Valerie got into bed, Linda snapped off the light. Minutes ticked by, with no sound of the even breathing of sleep.

"I'm sorry," Linda muttered finally.

Valerie shut her eyes quickly, feeling relief cover her as if it were another blanket. Pride prevented her from responding, though. She could not turn her emotions on and off; she had neither the practice nor the inclination. There had been too many false promises in her life for her to give of herself with ease or to withdraw without truly meaning it. Linda had scalded her tonight, had made her go back in time and memory to where she did not want to be, and she could not shed the pain casually, nor did she want to. Linda had abused her trust, and Valerie could not easily forgive that.

"I said I was sorry," Linda repeated more loudly.

"I heard you."

"Well, say something, damn you!"

Valerie turned on the light. "What do you want me to say?" she snapped, angry at having her night with Roger Monash ruined, at having her friendship with Linda jeopardized. "You come over to me at the bar acting like some . . . some shrew. I couldn't believe you. Then you yell at me and treat me like dirt when I come in. Well, I'm sorry, Linda, but a few words of apology from you doesn't make everything right again."

Linda pushed her pillow against the headboard and propped herself up. "Oh, Val, I'm sorry, I really am. I know I acted horribly, but seeing you with Roger Monash, you can't imagine what that did to me. He's so bad, Val. Seeing you with that bastard . . . well, I guess it made me kinda nuts."

Valerie did not want to ask, did not really want to know, but the words came out. "What's wrong with him, Linda?"

"Everything! He's the worst kind of scum, the lowest form of creep, the vilest kind of—"

"Either tell me something substantial or let's just go to sleep!" Valerie said, her voice shrill, her pulse racing.

Linda got out of bed, walked over to the dresser to rummage for a cigarette from her purse, lit it, then got back into bed.

"I thought you gave up smoking," Valerie remarked.

"Not when I'm aggravated."

"I see. And I'm aggravating you?"

"Yes, because you're falling for that bastard! Do you have any idea how he can destroy you?"

"I thought that's what you were going to tell me."

"You're not going to like it," Linda warned.

"Let me be the judge of that." But even as Valerie spoke, she felt a strange dread run through her, and her palms turned clammy.

Linda then explained that she and her roommate in New York, Wanda Eberle, had met Roger Monash at a party. Roger had put the make on Wanda, who was almost as innocent as Valerie, and she had fallen like the proverbial ton of bricks. One weekend when Wanda was home visiting her folks in Syracuse, Roger had a layover in New York, and came over without calling first. By this time, he and Wanda had been seeing each other for about three months, and he knew she was crazy about him, but that didn't stop him from making all the moves on Linda, or from telling her that Wanda was a sweet, dumb kid good for one thing only, and that thing had already gotten boring. He wanted to try something new—like Linda. Linda kicked him out, and Wanda continued to pine for him, even when he stopped calling and she heard he was seeing someone else. Eventually she moved back to Syracuse, but not before having a nervous breakdown and trying to kill herself.

"That's horrible!" Valerie said, eyes wide with incredulity.

"I told you, he's a first-class bastard. He uses women the way other men use their handkerchiefs, and he'll use you, too, Val."

"Maybe—"

"No maybes," Linda said firmly. "Listen, I know the guy's good-looking, no question about it. And charming—*whew!*—let me tell you if it hadn't been for Wanda, I might have been tempted when he was pouring on the charm. But then he got ugly, Val, real ugly, and that's what he's really like. He just doesn't care about anyone, and you're not going to be any different for him. You're the kind he likes best—fresh off the farm and oh so innocent—until he does his number on you."

"Well, I'm not going to bed with him, if that's what's worrying you," Valerie said self-righteously, wondering even as she spoke if she was lying. The thought certainly had crossed her mind during the evening. She was embarrassed now as she recalled her graphic imaginings . . . wondering what it would be like to have those full lips on hers . . . that mat of sandy hair against her bare chest . . . those strong arms wrapped around her. Not even with Teddy, at their most ardent moments together, had her thoughts been so vividly erotic.

Linda stubbed out her cigarette, and when she spoke her voice was filled with sincere caring. "Val, honey, you're a virgin and you've told me you want to stay that way until you're married. Don't let a louse like Roger Monash get you to change your mind."

"You're a fine one to talk," Valerie said with a nervous laugh.

"That's exactly what I mean. Okay, so I've given it away

when I shouldn't have, and I'll do it again. But it never meant that much to me anyway. You're different, Val. You can never recapture that innocence once it's gone, and Roger just isn't worth it. You're better than he, deserve better. He's going to hurt you, Valerie, and I don't want to see that happen. Not over him."

The only sound in the room was the ticking of the bedside clock until Valerie, with a forced lightness, said, "At least he's not married."

"Divorced."

"What!"

"What did you expect—the guy's thirty-two years old. And that's another thing," she added knowingly, "he's too old for you."

"I see, and from your ripe old age of twenty, that wouldn't have been a consideration?"

"I was nineteen at the time, and I told you, with me it's different."

"You remind me of my sister when you talk like that," Valerie said thoughtfully. "Before she got married, she was a little too, oh, I guess you'd say easy, and I think she regretted it."

"I don't regret it, believe me," Linda said. "I like sex, but for me it doesn't have to be part of a steady relationship. It's just fun, pure and simple fun. But for you, well, if you've been saving it because it means something, then save it for someone who deserves you."

"Maybe I think Roger is that someone."

"Then I feel sorry for you, kiddo, but I'll be here to pick up the pieces."

Since there was nothing further either girl could say that would not take them back into the same argument, Valerie reached over and turned out the light.

Week 3

By day, Valerie gave all her attention to her studies; on the evenings when Roger was flying, she gave all her attention to writing letters to Mack and her mother and Alice, studying, or being with the girls. But on the evenings when Roger was in town, she concentrated solely on him.

Saturday of the third week was particularly devastating

for Valerie. Frannie, bright as neon in her personality, simply could not absorb all the rules and regulations on which the daily exams were based. When she flunked her second makeup test, she was suspended from the school. That afternoon, Didi, Linda, Bobbi, and Valerie had gathered in Frannie's room, tearfully watching her pack. Her roommate, Andrea, had been so shaken that she had gone to the Clipped Wing, vowing to be sickeningly drunk for the rest of the weekend so that she would not have to face the room without Frannie.

The group was now down to twelve, since two girls had left voluntarily at the beginning of the second week; with two and a half weeks left to go, there could be others who would not complete the course. During this time, the girls had lived, cried, laughed, studied, and gotten drunk together; it was a sorority whose initiation would not be over until each was given her wings. The tension that had been so acute the first week had not lessened; rather, it had become more a part of their daily existence, so that they were not as aware of it until something happened to one of them. Then, their vulnerability and their desire to succeed became too real, frightening them. That was how Valerie felt this Saturday evening as she waited for Roger at the Clipped Wing. She needed his masculine assurance that she would make it; wanted to hear him say, with his advantages of age and experience, that she would not fail.

By eight o'clock, Roger still had not shown up. As the minutes after their appointed time of six o'clock ticked by, Valerie experienced the most nauseating case of déjà vu, remembering that awful night in her kitchen, waiting for a Teddy who never showed up. But then Roger was there with a "Hi ya, gorgeous. Sorry I'm late, but we had a heart-attack victim and had to stop down in Philadelphia to get him to a hospital."

"Is he all right?" Valerie asked, not really caring about anything except that Roger was with her.

The pilot shrugged disinterestedly. "I've missed you, babe," he whispered huskily, bending down and nuzzling her neck. "I feel like I haven't seen you in months. You must really be getting to me."

Valerie smiled, warming to his words. They had been

together last Saturday night, and Tuesday and Thursday evenings for a few hours. Each time it had proven more and more difficult for her to refuse his importunings to go to bed with him. She wanted to; of that she was sure. She felt none of the hesitation that she had felt with Teddy, ascribing it to the fact that she was somewhat older, much wiser, and more in touch with her own needs. Also, she realized that what she felt for Roger was far different from what she had felt for Teddy. Mack had been right: Teddy had been an infatuation. What she felt for Roger was love. When he smiled at her, her blood raced. When he kissed her gently, she felt like Cinderella being claimed by her prince. When he kissed her intensely, letting her know how much he needed her, she felt as if her toes would never again touch earth. Linda's warnings were as distant as the moon.

"I missed you, too, Roger," she said. "I had an awful day."

"Let's grab a table and order some food, I'm starving," he said as if she had not spoken.

"Frannie flunked out," Valerie said when they were seated.

"Who?"

"Frannie Collins. You know, the cute strawberry blonde. You met her."

"Oh yeah. So what? You stews aren't exactly known for your brain power," he remarked, grinning at her.

Valerie looked down into her glass, hurt. "That's not fair. I'm not stupid. Linda's not stupid."

"Linda's a whore," he said with a hiss.

"Don't say such a thing! She's my best friend and—"

"Listen, babe, I've had a rough day and what I don't need is to hear you whining in my ear."

Valerie did not speak. Her heart was pulsing so painfully that she thought she might black out. She began to make excuses to herself: he had had a difficult flight; he was tired; he was under terrible pressure. Why was she being so selfish?

"I'm sorry," she said in a small voice, her eyes downcast.

When Roger did not answer, she glanced up and saw that his attention was on a statuesque blonde who was smiling at him from the bar. He was smiling back at her.

"I said I was sorry," Valerie repeated more emphatically.

"Huh? Sure, sure. Forget it." Valerie never totally recaptured his attention until the blonde left and the Clipped Wing began to fill with the regulars. Linda and Didi came in and said a terse hello, then stayed by the bar. At nine-thirty, Roger suggested they leave.

"But my curfew's not until one," Valerie reminded him.

"I have a surprise for you. Come on."

"Where are we going?" she asked as they got into his red Corvette.

"A place where we can be alone." He pushed up her skirt and rubbed the soft flesh of her inner thigh. "If I had to sit in that damned bar one more minute, wanting you the way I do, I would have gone crazy. Christ, how I want you. Come here." And he wrapped his hand around her neck, pulling her to him, not able to get close because of the bucket seats and the gear shift. But his kiss left both of them wanting more.

They drove in silence, Valerie pretending to herself that she did not know what was about to happen. He was taking her to his apartment and he was going to make love to her. That's what she wanted too, wasn't it? He would kiss her, whisper encouraging love words to her, and touch her and touch her and touch her until her skin was on fire. He would find out she was a virgin. She had to tell him. Would that turn him off? No, he would be proud that she was giving him such a special gift. And he would be gentle with her. But he might also be disappointed, and she could not bear the thought of that.

Valerie had gone out with Teddy for more than three months, and had considered getting married, but had not been able to have sex with him. She had known Roger Monash for less than two weeks, and she was worrying about not being able to please him in bed. She never questioned her feelings for him or what the outcome of this intimacy would be. Irrational, illogical, uncharacteristically impetuous as it might be, Valerie knew she loved him. She could not conceive of his feeling differently. The very intensity of her emotion bespoke its rightness. She did not think she was being naïve, only truer to herself than she had ever been before. And she was too innocent and inexperienced to understand the vast difference between longing and loving. She had no qualms, therefore, about doing the right thing, only about doing it right.

"Is this where you live?" she asked tremulously as they climbed the stairs of a small apartment building near downtown Dallas.

"Uh, no, this belongs to a friend of mine."

"Why can't we go to your place?"

"I loaned it out to a buddy. I wasn't sure you and I would be using it, and besides, he's married, so if I can help the poor sucker out, why not?"

Valerie nodded her understanding, but her stomach gave a funny little lurch.

"Roger, maybe we should wait," she said when they entered the apartment. It was a dismal place, with a hodgepodge of dusty furniture and a view of a parking lot. "I'm sure your place is much nicer and—"

"Who gives a shit about nice. All I care about is that I want you." He crushed her against him and kissed her deeply. "Now tell me," he whispered against her ear, "do you really want to wait?"

She shook her head and smiled up at him, eyes glistening with love. "Roger," she said softly, stepping slightly out of the circle of his arms. "I'm a virgin."

His laugh was a crude, harsh snort that Valerie pretended not to hear. "Sure. And I'm Santa Claus. Come on, get serious. If there was ever a stew who was a virgin she'd be kicked out for poor job performance."

"It's true," she said, ignoring the quick stab of hurt.

He looked hard at her. "You're telling the truth, aren't you?" She nodded. "Why me?"

She tilted her head, surprise evident on her face. "Because I love you."

Roger Monash did not answer immediately, but a frown flashed across his Kennedy-like face, as if he was considering just how much of a bastard he really was. What he saw as he looked at Valerie was a lovely young face filled with trust, and a body that had been tormenting his dreams for a week. She had to lose it sometime, he thought selfishly; it might as well be to him.

"I love you too, baby," he said as he took her back in his arms. "And I won't hurt you. I promise."

"Could I have a drink?"

"Sure."

She followed him into a sliver of kitchen and watched him fumble around looking for the liquor and glasses. Without asking what she wanted, he poured her a glass of Scotch, neat, and she gulped it down, grateful for its warmth. She was beginning to feel chilled, as if only now the cold reality of the situation was dawning on her.

Then she was being led into a bedroom, and Roger was kissing her, his tongue prying her lips apart, his hands roaming over her back, to her shoulders, down to her hips. "Val, oh, Val, you feel so good, baby," he murmured against her ear. His hands were on the cool skin of her back as he pushed up her sweater; then he was unhooking her bra, lifting it away. He lowered his head, and his tongue caressed first one nipple, then the other, his breath scorching her as much as his touch.

"Take off your clothes. I can't stand this another minute."

"Roger, maybe—"

"I said get undressed." He turned away and took off his clothes, unaware that Valerie had not moved. She tried to unbutton her skirt, but her fingers were trembling so badly that she could not grip the button. Her sweater and bra were still bunched up above her breasts, her hands dangling by her sides. She felt miserable, foolish, incapable of doing anything to help herself.

When Roger was naked, he faced her. Whatever embarrassment and awkwardness she might have experienced during her first encounter with a naked man was mitigated by her awe at his physical beauty. His muscles rippled like those of a thoroughbred stallion. Shoulders, chest, tapering waist; lean, firm thighs: this was a body of power, a body almost audacious in its perfection. Her eyes followed the mat of sandy hair on his chest to its thinning trail, then darted up again to meet the grin on his face.

"Come on, honey, don't be shy," he said softly. "I'll help you."

Seconds later she was naked, on her back, willing herself to feel the warmth that Roger's kisses and touch usually inspired in her. But she felt oddly dispassionate as he murmured in her ear, kissed her neck and breasts and nipples and stomach, touched her in secret places and sacred places. Was it fear that had taken control, or was it something deeper, more vital? Thoughts suddenly fled as she felt him throbbing against her thigh, and then he hoisted himself above her.

"It'll hurt for a second and then it'll be fine," he assured her, and she kept her eyes wide open, nodded, wishing it was over, wishing more that she would feel something, even the pain.

Week 4

On Tuesday, Linda and Valerie walked to the dressing room where they would be fitted for their uniforms. It should have been an exhilarating time for them, the culmination of what they had been striving toward. Instead, there was a strained silence between them, a tension that had been there since Saturday, when Valerie's disheveled appearance in the room at three minutes before curfew had left no doubt in Linda's mind about what had occurred.

Since then, Valerie had managed to avoid her. On Sunday she had been with Roger until curfew. Yesterday had been filled with classes and a surprise exam on emergency exit procedures. Afterward, she had gone to their room to take a short nap, only to sleep straight through dinner; she had finally awakened, fully rested, at three in the morning.

It was from three this morning until five that Valerie had permitted herself to dwell on what she had done. Until then, she had found things to occupy her thoughts, to keep her from remembering how pleasureless Saturday night had been, and how a repetition of the sex Sunday afternoon and evening had left her similarly unmoved. She told herself that it was her fault; she was inexperienced and therefore scared, inhibited, inept, inadequate. She still loved Roger, she told herself; he had been kind and thoughtful each time. If it bothered her that Sunday they had gone straight to his friend's apartment and had stayed there all day, she let herself be convinced that Roger's needs were more urgent than her own, and that once the newness became part of a practiced routine, they would do things together, things that had nothing to do with sex. She told herself that he would never grow bored with her as he had with Wanda Eberle. She told herself that she had not been used.

In those two hours when night was at its unfriendliest and morning seemed a light at the end of an infinite tunnel, when time turned threatening and thoughts turned to unavoidable truths, Valerie was thankful that Linda was sleeping. Whatever she was telling herself, she knew she would not be able to say it to Linda with any conviction. But now, as they walked together silently to get their uniforms, she had a feeling that the confrontation was imminent.

"Should I start or will you?" Linda asked quietly, keeping her eyes straight ahead.

"I suppose it will have to be you because I have nothing to say." Valerie despised herself for acting this way. She did not resent her friend's prying because she knew it came from caring. She was scared of Linda—scared to hear her speak with knowledge that Valerie would refute without sincerity.

Linda stopped and reached out to hold Valerie back from walking ahead. The two girls faced each other, Valerie's expression challenging and proud. Linda's eyes shone with anger.

"You went to bed with him, didn't you?"

"Who?"

"Who! How many could there be?"

"If you mean Roger, the answer is yes."

Linda shook her head in amazement. "Didn't I warn you? Didn't I tell you what he did to Wanda? How could you be so stupid, Val? How?"

"If you think it's stupid for two people in love to do what's only natural, that's your problem, and I'm sincerely sorry for you," she said haughtily.

"In love! You're an even bigger fool than I thought," Linda yelled.

"I don't have to listen to this!" Valerie started to walk away, but Linda's hand was on her arm, keeping her there.

"Do you really think he's in love with you? Be honest, do you?"

"He said so and I believe him."

"'He said so and I believe him.' You're incredible, you really are."

"I would appreciate your not repeating everything I say.

And I suggest that we save this little chat for another time. We're going to be late."

"We have plenty of time, and besides, this won't wait. You've been deliberately avoiding me since Saturday and I—"

"I haven't noticed you trying to be with me, either," Valerie cut in.

"Of course not, you idiot. What did you want me to do, rush up and ask for a blow-by-blow description! I figured that you would *want* to talk with me—that what happened to you was important and you would want to share it with a friend. Obviously, you're so ashamed you can't even face me. That's why I knew I had to bring it up first."

"I am *not* ashamed!" Valerie retorted hotly. "What Roger and I did is beautiful and special. We're in love with each other. Why won't you believe me?"

Linda took a deep breath, briefly shut her eyes, and said, "I do believe you, Val. I believe you love him and that you think he loves you. But let me just ask a few questions, okay?"

Valerie nodded, dreading what was coming.

"Did he take you to a friend's apartment, saying his was too far or that he had loaned it to a married friend? Did he tell you that he couldn't fly for wanting you so badly? Did he just take you to bed Sunday and stay there with you all day? Did he say he can't make plans for when he'll see you next, it depends on his schedule? Did he—"

"Stop it, stop it!" Valerie shrieked, covering her ears with her hands. Gently, Linda lowered them and took Valerie in her arms. Soundlessly, Valerie sobbed, for being a fool and a coward.

"I'm sorry," Linda said softly. "I didn't want to have to hurt you this way, but I didn't know what else to do. You had to see what was going on, what kind of bastard you were getting involved with."

"How did you know he said those things to me? How did you know about his friend's apartment?"

"The answer to the first question is easy. He used the same lines on both me and Wanda. As for the second, while you've been out of it these past few days, I asked around a little. It seems that Mr. Swinging Singles Monash shares an apartment with three other guys, two to a bedroom. When he's in Dallas, he hits on anyone he knows who has a place to himself."

For a moment Valerie said nothing, staring at her roommate but seeing beyond her to the dingy, dreary, unkempt apartment with its parking-lot view. "What am I going to do?" she whispered.

"What do you want to do?"

"I *don't* want to go to bed with him again."

"Not good, huh?"

"Well, I'm sure it's my fault, but no, not too good."

"Why do you think it was your fault?"

"I'm not very experienced, after all, so I probably don't know what I'm doing."

"Your pleasure comes from *his* knowing what to do, kiddo, not you."

"Well, still, I think I'll save sex for another time."

"Another man, Val, not another time. Roger Monash simply was not the right man. Not for someone like you."

"Why *not* someone like me?" Valerie demanded, tired of being different, of being unable to do what other young women did. What made her so special? What made her so unable to pretend?

"Because your innocence won't disappear no matter how many men you have, even if they're all like Roger Monash," Linda said with a small smile. "You deserve someone who can appreciate that innocence. I'm not saying he has to love you, Val, but there are men who will recognize your purity and admire it. If you want to experiment with sex, do it with them, not with selfish bastards like Monash."

Valerie thought about what Linda said. "You're not like that, are you?" she asked gently. Linda shook her head. "Why not? What makes me this way, and why am I so embarrassed by it?"

"Oh, Val, don't ask me questions like that. I'm not smart enough to answer them."

"You're smarter than I'll ever be," Valerie said miserably.

"No, just not as nice."

The girls looked at each other and broke into laughter, but for Valerie the sound was bittersweet. She would be seeing Roger the next night and she did not know how to tell him there would be no sex. She had a feeling that telling him she did not love him would not matter as much to him.

"What the fuck do you mean you won't go to bed with me! Listen, you little bitch, I'm in no mood to play games. I had a brutal flight from Puerto Rico, turbulence that made me feel like my balls were coming out of my mouth, and I don't want to hear you tell me you don't want to go to bed with me. Why the fuck do you think I'm here anyway!"

Valerie felt as if she were shriveling within her skin, each squeeze of his fingers around her wrist, each brittle snap of his words making her wince with anguish and anger. They were seated at a booth at the Clipped Wing, early enough that none of the other stews were there yet and only a few of Roger's colleagues were at the bar, occupied with their own conversation. Valerie could not believe she had been so devastatingly mistaken about Roger. Was her lot in life always to be mistaken about men?

"I thought you cared about me," she whispered.

Suddenly Roger began to stroke where he had gripped, his fingertips making little feather-light brushes on the inside of her wrist and then on her palm. Where a moment before his mouth had been a mean, thin line, now it wore a smile and his eyes seemed to caress as warmly and invitingly as did his fingertips.

"I do care for you, baby. How could you doubt that?"

"You make it sound that if it weren't for the sex you wouldn't have anything to do with me. Just because I don't feel like it for one night you get crude and abusive. Can't you understand that I just don't want to tonight?"

The feather touches stopped and the eyes went cold, but only briefly.

"Of course I can understand that, baby, I just want to know why. You haven't stopped loving me, have you? I couldn't bear that, Val, honest, I couldn't." His voice was a smooth coax, and Valerie wanted desperately to be coaxed. "Do you love me, baby?"

"Roger, please, let's not—"

"I asked you a question," he said more harshly.

She managed to pull her hand away from the warm blanket of his touch. "Do you love *me*?"

His laugh was short, and he sat back in the booth. "Of course I love you. How can you doubt it? Don't I want to be with you whenever I can? Don't I show you how much I love you—when you let me?"

"I'm not talking about sex, Roger, I'm talking about love. Linda thinks—"

"Don't tell me what that bitch thinks!" Roger raged, slamming his hands down on the table, eyes blazing. "She started this, didn't she? She told you about her dumb roommate, Wanda whatever the hell her name was. Listen, baby, you want to fuck, great. If telling you I love you will get you to do it, fine, I'll tell you I love you. But don't think old Roger here is going to get tied down. I played that number once and never again. You stews give away pussy as if it were drinks in first class, and, baby, if you don't want to play, there're plenty of others who will." All pretense at wooing was gone. The Roger Monash whom Linda had warned her about, the Roger Monash whom she had deliberately blinded herself to, was totally visible, and he made an ugly, distorted image of what she had believed was romance.

Propping both hands on the table top, he rose to his feet and leaned over, his face close to Valerie's. "You were a lousy lay anyway," he spat out, then walked over to the bar, within seconds laughing coarsely with his friends.

Started, blossomed, dead—and not even a month had passed. Her virginity was the least she had lost. She had gut instincts and she had measured responses. Gone forever was ignoring one in favor of the other. That was a loss she did not regret.

Week 5

For the rest of the time until graduation, Valerie went through the motions of preparing for the end of school. Linda made sure the other girls kept their distance, knowing their pity would be a poor balm to Valerie's pride. She performed superbly on the familiarization flight, passed her final exam with only two wrong, and had no argument when Linda suggested they ask for Los Angeles as their first—and unlikely to get—choice for a base assignment. Valerie and Mack had spoken of New York or Washington, D.C., as exciting home bases for her, but Los Angeles could be equally interesting. Anywhere but Dallas would be fine.

She ran into Roger only once after that infamous Thursday night. She had permitted Linda and Didi to drag her back to the Clipped Wing, just to prove that the fiasco with Roger had not left her a social invalid. She had sat at the bar, chattering charmingly when a man approached but refusing all invitations for drinks, dances, or future dates. About an hour into the evening, Roger entered, his arm around Leslie Vernon, one of the girls in Valerie's training class. Their heads were close together, and she heard his laughter, saw him smooth his hand down her hip, watched her lean closer into him. She heard Linda's whispered, "She's what he deserves. She's been sleeping with two of his friends since school started." She felt nothing. No rancor toward her classmate, no regret at falling for Roger's shallowness, not even anger at her own naïvete. Nothing. And that dull emptiness seemed more invidious to her than the worst kind of emotional anguish.

It struck her, as she sat there that night, that lack of genuine feeling had marked her brief time with Roger. She had thought she loved him, but hadn't that simply been an acceptable explanation for wanting him physically? And when that desire had taken her to its natural conclusion, the hollow reality of their relationship had returned, only to be shunted aside as if it were an inconvenience. She smiled pastily at the young man next to her, and then, while he was talking, slipped from her stool and, without a word to Linda or Didi, left the Clipped Wing. It would be some time, she thought, before she would be able to trust herself again, and until that time she did not see how she could possibly allow another man, no matter how casually, into her life.

Finally, this morning, she would receive her wings. By tomorrow she would have her base assignment, and then she could leave Dallas and Roger Monash behind her. It would not be as fresh a start as leaving Galesville had been, but perhaps, she thought now as she readjusted her cap, any beginning, no matter how lacking in freshness, was all right.

"I'll be ready in five minutes," Linda said from the bathroom, where she was applying the last of her makeup.

"Do you mind your parents not coming?" Valerie called out.

"Are you kidding? I'd mind if they did show up. Listen, my parents and I are not exactly what you'd call close. I think they paid for stew school just because they were hoping I'd die early in a crash."

"Linda, that's a terrible thing to say!" Valerie said, rising from the bed to lean against the doorjamb of the bathroom. "You can't mean that."

"Well, maybe I am exaggerating a little, but there isn't any love lost between us, I've told you that. What about you and your crazy clan? From what I've been able to gather, you should be thrilled they're not here."

"They're not so bad," Valerie replied defensively.

"Not so bad, ha! They're worse! You've got a sister who married your boyfriend, a mother who forgets she has two daughters, and a father who makes Simon Legree sound charming." Linda smiled. "At least you have Billy; he sounds okay. Weak but okay."

"He's terrific," Valerie said. "They're all okay, Linda, really. It's just that sometimes they didn't quite understand me, that's all."

"Keep fantasizing, kiddo, if it makes you feel better. As far as I'm concerned, they sound like creeps and you should be grateful you got away."

Valerie turned slowly and went back to sit on the bed. She supposed, if she was being completely honest with herself, that Billy was the only Cardell who lived up to her idea of family. Aside from Mack, he was the only one who wrote to her, filling her in on family news like Ned's moving to a small suburb of Indianapolis where he was managing a bowling alley, and Alice and Teddy's weekly dinners at the cottage. But she and Billy had always enjoyed a special closeness, and she could not fault the rest of her family simply for not understanding her the same way. That didn't mean they didn't love her or want the best for her.

She moved to the small window and looked out, still hoping that Mack would show up. His last letter, received three days ago, had indicated that he planned to be here, but there had been no further word from him. It was now ten o'clock in the morning, only two hours until the ceremony, and she still did not know if he was coming.

"I'll get it," Valerie said, hearing a knock at the door.

A young delivery boy was standing there, his arms balancing a massive flower arrangement in its own glass vase. Tiger lilies of blazing orange, red roses, snow-white chrysanthemums, all set against a sea of lacy green ferns, lit up the drab motel room as the boy entered.

"Wow!" Linda exclaimed, peeking out from the bathroom. "Hurry up and open the card."

"No card, ma'am," the boy said. "These flowers came with a telegram. Which one of you is Valerie Cardell?"

"I am," Valerie said, color draining from her face as she took the cable. Linda gave the boy some change, and when he left, she and Valerie sat down on Valerie's bed.

"Relax," Linda assured her. "It can't be bad, it came with flowers."

Valerie nodded, then took out the telegram and read aloud:

"'Cannot make grad. Chicago emergency. My heart is with you. Let me know your base. You have fulfilled a promise and I love you. Stop. Fly proud. Mack.'"

"I'm sorry," Linda said. "I know you were counting on his coming."

Valerie said nothing as she got up to smell the flowers. It was as if Mack had magically appeared in the room. She could feel the strength of his support for her, giving back to her that sense of herself that she had relinquished to Roger Monash. She was so fragile, so young, he would say, and his only disappointment would be if she did not learn and move on. And she had learned, hadn't she, about desire, about friendship and sharing and trusting? That was all part of the promise, all part of why Mack had given her this chance. She would be cheating him if she did not accept her lessons and move on.

Slowly she turned to face her roommate, the telegram clutched against her heart.

"You okay?" Linda asked.

"For the first time in too long, I'm fine. Really fine," Valerie answered, her midnight-blue eyes glistening. "For a while there I almost forgot about . . . oh, I don't know. I guess

I had let myself forget about all the tomorrows." She gave a small laugh. "Leave it to Mack to remind me of what's really important."

Later, as she stood for her class picture and then for her own portrait, Valerie decided to have both pictures framed for Mack. She hoped that he would keep them on his mantel, next to the photograph of Ty in his college football uniform. As her name was called out, as she walked with her black hair shining in the sun, her Universal cap tilted saucily, her eyes bright with the moment, she hoped that she would always deserve Mack's pride in her. When the small silver wings were pinned to her uniform lapel, and when Patricia Harnell shook her hand and congratulated her, Valerie felt, for the first time in her life, a deep sense of pride in herself. And she knew too that these weeks had not been a beginning but a mere preparation. Fly proud, he had said. *Oh yes, Mack, I will. I will.*

Chapter 8

"Hey, Linda, you going to the party tonight?"

"What party?"

"I thought I told you when we checked in. This guy I met on a flight last week is the Mamas and Papas' roadie. He called last night to invite me and any friends I wanted to bring to a party at Mama Cass's house in Laurel Canyon. Should be wild. You know what those musician types are like."

"No, but it sounds like it might be fun finding out. I'll see if Val wants to go, too," Linda said to Beverly, the senior stew who was handling first class with her on this New York to Los Angeles flight. It was Linda's third time in first class, and she loved every minute of it, especially all the miniature bottles of liquor she was able to take for the apartment.

"I'm inviting you, not your roommate," Beverly said pointedly.

In the year that Linda and Valerie had been living together in their small West Hollywood apartment, Linda had often heard that kind of remark about her roommate. Her face now took on a determined expression. "Look, Bev, Val is my roommate and I like her. If you invite me somewhere, I invite her. That's the way it goes."

"I don't know what you see in her," Beverly said, buckling herself into her seat as the pilot announced the impending landing. "I mean, she's a good enough stew and all that, but 'friendly' is not exactly a word I'd use to describe her."

"You don't understand her."

Beverly shrugged. "What's there to understand? She's a snob, pure and simple. She shows up at a party, nurses one drink all night, won't touch dope if her life depended on it, lets the guys fall all over themselves for her, and then drives home alone in that little Mustang of hers. I swear, she's probably still a virgin. Or a lesbian." Beverly's eyes narrowed. "Is that it, Linda? Are you two—"

"Oh shut up and stop sounding like the ass you are," Linda snapped. "Valerie's gun-shy, that's all. She's not as tough as we are, and not as, uh, shall we call it experienced?" she added meaningfully.

"Don't make enjoying a good time sound like a sin. That's the feeling I get from *her*—as if she's judging me and I always come up short. A lot of the other girls feel the same way."

Linda shook her head. "She's not like that at all. Believe me, if you make the effort to get past the wall, there's a terrific person there. Don't be put off, Bev, really."

"Yeah, yeah, I've heard all this before. Well, I don't care, bring her to the party if you want to, but you'd better warn Miss Purity that there're going to be drugs and who knows what else. This isn't a Sunday-school outing we're going to."

Linda said nothing to Valerie about the party until they were on the San Diego Freeway, heading toward Hollywood. The two girls did not often get to work the same flight, but this had been an exception, although Valerie had been in coach. Now, in Valerie's red Mustang convertible, the top down, the Los Angeles smog blanketing them, Linda told her about the party, knowing what her response would be.

"I don't think so, Linda, I'm kinda bushed. I had a group

of slightly drunk conventioneers in econo class and they ran me ragged. Maybe another time."

"There's never another time with you," Linda said more heatedly than she had intended. "I swear, outside of this car of yours and planes, you don't do a damn thing. I regret ever suggesting you get your driver's license!"

Valerie chuckled as she moved into the fast lane of the huge freeway. A gold Porsche with the license plate MACHO-1 almost cut her off, but she outmaneuvered him, as Linda covered her eyes with her hands. "Jeez, you're getting to be a menace behind the wheel."

"I love it," Valerie admitted. "I probably should have been a pilot. Now, *that's* freedom!"

"You're nuts."

"Entirely possible," Valerie joked.

"Listen, about the party," Linda began again. "Beverly said—"

"Beverly Steener?"

"Yes."

"I don't like her," Valerie said. "Very unfriendly."

"That's funny, that what she says about you." Valerie shot Linda a quick, sharp glance, then turned her attention back to the road. "Anyway, she said this party was going to be wild, and Lord knows we could do with a little excitement. Lately I'm beginning to feel like a virgin again. Hey, do you think maybe it closes up again if it's not used regularly?"

Valerie shook her head and laughed. "You're gross."

"That's beside the point." Linda reached into her purse and, bending down to shield herself from the wind, lit a cigarette. "So what do you say? Will you go with me?"

"I say let me take a long bath and I'll think about it, but I doubt it."

"Val, what is it with you?" Linda said, losing her patience. "You're almost as remote these days as that first week of stew school. I mean it—even the other stews complain. You go through the motions but there's no one home. It's like you locked yourself away or something."

As much as Linda loved Valerie and, even more, respected her, there were times when her self-possession and her distance got to her. Usually Linda accepted it as the odd mixture of shyness and maturity that it was. Occasionally, though, like now, she knew Valerie was deliberately holding herself back—in punishment? expectation? She did not know.

Valerie did not answer as she moved from the fast lane to the Santa Monica Boulevard exit, which would take them to Laurel Drive near the Beverly Hills border. Their small apartment, with its regulation courtyard and pool, was in West Hollywood—also known as the swish alps for its preponderance of homosexuals—but the apartment was cheap, the neighborhood safe, and it was close enough to the major freeways to be convenient.

"Look, Linda," she said finally, "I like my life exactly the way it is. I love living in L.A., swimming when I get a chance, driving the old bug here, and flying. There's nothing more I want, at least for the present. And I do go to some of those parties with you."

"Sure, and you always go home alone. Do you have any idea how many guys ask me about you? Why won't you let one of them get close?"

"Why is it so important to you whether I date or not?"

"Because I want to see you happy, having fun."

"Have all the men you've been with made you happy?"

"That's not fair."

"Well, have they?"

"Okay, okay, have it your way."

"I'll think about the party," Valerie said. "I promise."

She did not go to the party at Mama Cass's Laurel Canyon house that night, nor to the many others to which she was invited. She preferred to spend her evenings writing letters to Mack and to Billy. Her brother was now living in San Francisco, working as an apprentice in a commercial art studio. He had sneaked out of Galesville in the middle of the night four months ago after a vicious fight with Eli, had hitched his way to Indianapolis, and then had taken a bus west. Periodically she also dropped notes to her mother and to Alice, but not often. In the year since she had left home, she had heard from them only twice. Once had been a Christmas card from her sister and Teddy; the other time had been a brief letter from her mother telling her that Alice had suffered a miscarriage.

Other nights, whether Linda stayed in or went out on a date, Valerie would fill the hours by reading—everything from biographies of artists to the latest trashy fiction—and experimenting in the kitchen. Whatever she cooked, she brought most of it to various neighbors so that she and Linda would not be tempted to overeat. Occasionally one of the girls from stew school, like April or Didi, would have a layover in Los Angeles and would stay at the apartment. On those nights they would all laugh and reminisce, eat, and compare horror stories of passengers and flights.

Valerie had no complaints about her life. If she was protecting herself a little more than was necessary—and she granted to herself that she might be—she believed that she would emerge from her self-imposed cocoon when she was ready. For now, there was no man who particularly interested her, and she did not find the endless sameness of the parties more fun than staying home. She knew that Linda often was forced into a position of defending her, of explaining that her roommate was not a dud, just a little different. By now, Valerie herself was no longer dismayed by her difference. She liked to have fun, liked to dance and drink and carry on, liked to be one of the girls, but privacy was important to her, too. Sometimes she would listen to the stews talking about men, or she would meet a man who wanted to date her, and she *would* feel remote, as Linda had said. It was as if she would don a costume and mask, prance at the ball in disguise, and then return to the cool comfort of herself when the others were still pretending. Was it that innocence Linda had once spoken of that made her like this, or just an awareness of her own inability to take things—and people—casually enough to be safe from harm? Perhaps both, or maybe neither. Maybe it all came down to the fear of not being accepted, or, worse, of being rejected. Whatever the reason, she felt neither strong enough nor curious enough to test the deeper waters of social play.

There were also times, in these past months, when her mind would drift back to Galesville. No matter how close she and Linda were, Valerie occasionally felt homesick for her sister, her mother, her small-town life. She would forget the sadness that had come from them and remember only the warmth and security of familiarity. It was foolish, she knew, to recall them with fondness, because her family knew her far less well than did Linda, but as she flew from coast to coast, or down to Mexico or to the Caribbean, visiting places she had only heard of through Mack and had never dreamed of seeing for herself; as she drove into Beverly Hills, strolled down Rodeo Drive, peeked into the windows of Giorgio's but shopped at the Broadway, she could not help but think how much her mother and Alice would enjoy all this and how she would love to share it with them. And then return with them to the safety of the farm where each day was the same, conversations were predictable, futures preordained; where uncertainty did not exist. And sometimes, when Southern California's magnificent flowers bloomed too wildly, when the air seemed particularly oppressive, like a mantle of despair, when avocados and horoscopes and special license plates and rock-and-roll billboards the size of a mountainside screeched desperation, she wondered about going home because she also wondered where she was heading. She sometimes felt as if she was waiting, marking time, on the brink of her future, and yet on the other side of the highway was so much unknown that she preferred the waiting to the discovery. It was at these moments, when life seemed alien and she saw herself as a stranger, that she most wanted to run home again.

Valerie was airborne on her twenty-first birthday, but she was planning to celebrate that evening in New York City. Both Linda and Valerie worked in first class exclusively now, their status as senior stews secure. Linda had not really expected still to be flying. As she often bemoaned to Valerie, she had thought she'd be married by now to a rich business-man who would be keeping her in furs and charge accounts. And Valerie, over the past three years, had not known what else she would do except continue to fly. Both girls had vacationed everywhere from Aruba to Hawaii, and while Linda's social life had kept up its frenetic, hit-or-miss pace, Valerie's had, if not rebounded fully, at least developed to the point that Linda did not complain as much. But as frequently as Valerie dated, she did not maintain a relationship with any one man long enough to go to bed with him. Parties and dinner dates were one thing; involvement was something else entirely. And a party like the one tonight at Angela DiChico's luxurious townhouse was something else again.

Angela was a phenomenally wealthy and well-connected

fashion designer/dilettante, Linda had informed her. They had met during Linda's New York modeling stint. Although in her mid-forties, Angela was the kind of madcap, Auntie Mame personality that made friendship with someone much younger easy and comfortable. They had corresponded over the years, and whenever Linda was in New York, she always made a point of calling Angela, more often than not getting a message from the housekeeper that Miss DiChico was off in Guatemala or Biarritz, Juan-les-Pins or Ibiza. Valerie and Linda had rearranged their schedules so that they could both be on this flight to New York and attend the party that Angela was throwing for herself to let everyone know that she was back from wintering in Barbados. Valerie and Linda were staying in an apartment shared by four Universal stews based in New York. They had splurged a month's salary on new outfits, and it took all their concentration to attend to their flight duties instead of chattering about the party.

"Thank goodness it's a light flight," Linda said as she took down the champagne and brandy bottles for first class. "I'm so excited about tonight I can't think straight."

"Miss Party Girl herself excited! I can't believe it," Valerie teased, putting ice cubes in a bucket.

"I told you, this one's different. There's no telling who might be there. She knows everybody, Val, and I mean everybody. I bet Rudi Gernreich'll be there and Bill Blass and Kurt Vonnegut. Maybe even Leonard Bernstein and Truman Capote. Wouldn't that be something!"

"That would be something all right," Valerie said dryly.

Linda glanced at her, then grinned sheepishly. "Okay, so I'm acting like a little kid. I'm allowed."

"You are," Valerie conceded with a smile. "Now, do you have the first-class manifest?"

"Yup, right here. Why don't you get the orders and I'll mix?"

Valerie made her way down the almost-empty first-class compartment. "Miss Carsons?" she said to the passenger in seat 1A, after checking her name on the passenger manifest. "May I get you a cocktail or some champagne?"

"Double Scotch on the rocks," the woman replied. "And then another one fifteen minutes later."

Valerie had learned by now not to be surprised by any

passenger's request, so her face reflected only the automatic smile she had been trained to wear.

"May I get you something to drink, sir?"

"Champagne," was the next passenger's request, a Lyle Endicott; and from his seat companion, a frosted blonde in her late twenties, a nod indicating that she wanted the same. Valerie guessed, by the lack of a ring on her finger and the obvious one on his, and the intensity of the looks they shared, that this was an illicit outing for Mr. Married and Miss Single. She resolved not to disturb them during the long flight.

"Cocktail, sir? Champagne, wine?" she asked the remaining first-class passenger, a Mr. David Kinnelon. When she caught the man's eyes, her smile deepened and became more sincere. Judging by his appearance, he was her favorite kind of passenger, well dressed, in his mid-to-late forties, with an attaché case opened on the empty seat beside him. He had dark hair, graying at the temples, a hawklike nose that went well with his firm, square jaw and solid mouth, and deep-set gray eyes crowned by almost bushy eyebrows. The man seemed to radiate power and success, the kind of passenger who wanted nothing more than to be left alone. Or, as she had found out on occasion, the kind who thought he could make every stew in sight. She had a feeling that this man would concentrate on the papers in front of him, interested in nothing else. Good, she thought; an easy flight.

"I'd like a brandy with a splash of soda," the man said, his voice deep and mellifluous.

Valerie returned to the galley with her orders. She might have been surprised had she known how the passenger in seat 4A, who she had decided was interested only in his work, had studied her retreating form, approving what he saw and deciding to pay more attention to the rest of her when she reappeared.

"What do you have?" Linda asked as Valerie turned in the orders.

"Easy, should be quiet. One businesswoman who's scared of flying, one couple who want to be left alone, and one businessman, successful, I'd say, by the cut of his suit."

"Since when did you become such an expert on the cut of men's suits?"

"Just fill the orders," Valerie said with a grin.

"Which one's the businessman?" Linda asked when the drinks were ready.

"The one in 4A," Valerie said as they stood in the archway of the galley. "I think his name is David Kinnelon."

"Not *the* David Kinnelon!"

Valerie sighed with exasperation. "Don't tell me you know him?"

"Well, not personally, but I've heard of him, of course. Who hasn't?

"Me."

"That figures. You still think the Beatles are musical insects and that Vietnam is an oriental dessert."

"Very funny. If I remember correctly, you didn't know Kennedy had been shot until the morning after."

"That's an unfair comparison. It just so happens that I was otherwise engaged while history was being made."

"Right. For more than twenty-four hours!" Valerie joked, remembering back just a few sad months ago to that tragic day when she had been off duty, eager to talk to Linda and share the horrible grief that had gripped not just a country but each individual citizen. Linda had managed to miss the assassination, Ruby's murder of Oswald, Johnson's swearing-in—everything of that historic nightmare—because she was in Antigua with one of the soap-opera stars of *As the World Turns*. It amazed Valerie now that she could even think of that time with anything less than total despair, yet here she was teasing about Linda's absence. She shook her head.

"What's wrong?"

"Nothing," Valerie said. "I was just thinking how short our memories are."

"No, not short, just protective," Linda replied gently. "Come on, let's get to work."

When Valerie served the brandy and soda to the passenger in 4A, he was so absorbed in his paperwork that he forgot his intention to reappraise her. As the founder and chairman of the board of the vast network of businesses that comprised Kinnelon Enterprises, David Kinnelon's interest in the passing form of a pretty female was akin to his interest in hors d'oeuvres at a cocktail party. He never sampled for the sake of tasting, only to appease his appetite, and when that was accomplished, he moved on to more satisfying pleasures, usually sports, politics, and, always, making money.

David Kinnelon had started as a salesman for a Seventh Avenue low-end dress manufacturer when he was seventeen and going to New York University at night. Through friends, he met a young Parsons School of Design student named Angela DiChico, and persuaded his boss to try two of her designs in the upcoming collection. They were far more upscale than anything Gruen Togs had ever done, but they worked far more successfully. After another season, this time a full collection of Angela's designs, both she and David were offered backing for their own company. Lovers briefly, they remained loyal friends as Angela went on to become internationally renowned and David went on to buy out their backers and begin acquiring businesses that, over the years, included vineyards in the Napa Valley, a soccer team in Brazil, a buying office in Detroit that serviced three major department-store chains, and an oil-drill parts manufacturer in Louisiana. When Angela gave up designing to become a full-time international playgirl, a lifestyle paid for by her own success and the generosity of men she would never marry but always say thank-you to, David continued to acquire, including two women whom he married.

The first was Carla, an eighteen-year-old from Tulsa. When David was twenty, he arranged a junket to Las Vegas to woo a few investors for an offshore drilling operation he wanted to buy out. Despite his youth, he was rapidly gaining a reputation for having a Midas touch, so finding backers was never a problem. Carla was "performing" at the Desert Inn—if being lowered, topless, from a cage could be called performing. David had never seen a chest or legs like hers, and he abandoned his gambling just to have the sensation of those long legs wrapped around him. He was sexually smitten. She was as crude as the oil in her home state, an unpolished, raw specimen whom David believed he could mold into a scintillating object of envy. One week after they met, they married, and David brought her back to Manhattan, to his penthouse apartment on East Seventy-second Street and Park Avenue.

David had come from a working-class family on Long Island, people whose idea of a special occasion was eating at a

Chinese restaurant. Even while he was going to school at night, David made a point of studying the people around him to learn the right way to conduct himself. When his business with Angela started to take off, he dropped out of school and spent his nights socializing and learning more about the rarefied set to which he aspired to belong. A fascination with and an aptitude for makeover was in his soul, and when he met Carla he had a willing subject. He performed magic on her, but it was all on the surface. The beehive hairdo went, replaced by an Italian cut; the rabbit-hair sweaters were discarded in favor of Ungaro and Courrèges suits; Charles Jourdan replaced the stilettos, and Elizabeth Arden was the substitute for Maybelline. But Carla's transformation did not extend to her mind. There was nothing David could do to get her to be an interesting dinner companion or a gracious hostess, and her dullness became so irritating to him that her sexual appeal diminished. Within the first year of their marriage, she became pregnant, and David hoped that somehow the birth of little Ray would make things all right. It did not. Fortunately, Carla was an indifferent mother, and when David suggested a divorce and his taking custody of the child he adored more than anything in the world, she agreed. Instead of alimony, David paid her a healthy settlement, and his first marriage was over by the time he was twenty-two.

For the next few years, David was one of the country's most sought-after bachelors; his fatherhood pleased the mothers of available debs, as well as the models, actresses, stewardesses, showgirls, and socialites who thought he might be looking for a new mommy for his little boy. None of these women lasted longer than a few weeks, time enough for the sex to become predictable and the conversation tedious. He did not believe Ray was missing anything by not having a mother; between his British nanny and Angela DiChico's zany influence, the child learned both the proper and the improper. And David realized that he did not have the makings of a good husband. He loved to work; loved to pore over profit-and-loss statements, to gamble on risky businesses, to buy up losers and turn them around; loved to make money. His success opened new social doors for him, and his intelligence, wit, striking good looks, and acquired sense of style made it possible for him to charm and be comfortable with senators and judges. athletes and actors, financiers and best-selling authors.

Then, when he was thirty-three, he went to Cap d'Antibes for a brief vacation, and met Giselle, a twenty-four-year-old chanteuse from the provinces, whose husky voice aroused him almost as much as did the ingenuity of her mouth. Having participated in most varieties of sexual activity and priding himself on his astute judgment of people, particularly women, he ignored his gut instinct and married her, believing he could transform her into a polished French diamond, a social jewel that would make his friends and associates wince with envy.

He brought Giselle home to his duplex off Fifth Avenue and taught her perfect English, where to have lunch and what to order, how to create the proper dinner party, how to dress with French flair and American discretion. He led a very social life with Giselle and enjoyed the product of his Pygmalian efforts. Renovating, he discovered, gave him almost as much pleasure as acquiring. Then, only eight months after they had married, David came home early one afternoon to pack for a sudden trip to Hong Kong. When he arrived home, called out his wife's name, and got no answer, he went to their bedroom to pack. He found her in bed, moaning ecstatically as the wife of the junior senator from New York State energetically made love to her.

The divorce was amicable and not costly since Giselle was in a poor bargaining position, and David returned to being a sought-after bachelor.

Now David was forty-five years old, and there was gray in his thick, wiry dark brown hair and more muscular flesh on his powerful six-foot body. Aging had done nothing to diminish his attractiveness. Instead, his awesome self-confidence, his blatant virility, and, of course, his reputed wealth had increased with the years, making him even more sexually appealing. And for those women not interested in an older man, there was his son, Ray, now twenty-four, a graduate of Harvard, and president of Kinnelon, Inc., a branch of Kinnelon Enterprises devoted exclusively to real estate development. As far as David was concerned, this was a throwaway part of the business, but Ray had done his apprenticeship in various other operations, always returning to his father with requests to buy more property, especially in rundown areas. The concept appealed to David's delight in renovation, so he permitted Ray to purchase tenements, vacant lots in bad neighborhoods, and row houses in black neighborhoods. At first the land lay fallow, not providing even a tax advantage. But in the last year or two, Ray had been getting more ambitious, especially with the arrival of Grant Hollander, a young, smart, forward-thinking building contractor David had hired.

In fact, the papers he was poring over now were from Grant, concerning the feasibility of constructing a shopping mall near Columbus, Ohio. Ray had found the acreage, Grant had developed the plans, and the cost analysis that David was now studying seemed reasonable, if not ultimately profitable. He had heard and read about the wave of the future being shopping malls. Esthetically, he objected to them—rows of little shops surrounded by an island of parking lot set in an ocean of highway. Still, both Ray and Grant thought it could work; thought, in fact, that Kinnelon was overdue in getting into that market. And David supposed that an auto-dependent area like Columbus had a good chance of making a mall work. He respected Grant and he loved his son; maybe investing in developing one of these places wasn't a bad idea. Besides, he could easily afford to lose money if the plan did not work.

"May I get you another drink, Mr. Kinnelon?"

David looked up at Valerie's face with its professional smile, and quickly determined that front and rear views of this stew were more than acceptable. His eyes traveled down her body, and when he again met her eyes, he noticed that her expression had not changed, despite his bold scrutiny. Her poise pleased him. He briefly toyed with the idea of engaging her in conversation, then decided against it. He still had to study the acquisition of an expensive new soccer player, as well as put his signature to the contract finalizing his takeover of Eldee Leasing, the third-largest car-rental agency in America. He would have no time to work tonight, he knew. If he didn't show up at Angela's party, he'd never hear the end of it.

"Linda, darling, I'm so glad you could make it." Angela DiChico wrapped her former model in a hug of genuine warmth, and her kiss was planted firmly on Linda's cheek instead of the air. "You look stunning. I love that dress, but then you've got the legs for it."

Linda was wearing a black sequined shift that stopped four inches above her knees, or three inches below her crotch, depending on the measuring starting point. Her long legs were sheathed in glittery silver hose, ending in black *peau de soie* sandals with four-inch heels. The years had brought a slight edge to the cuddly cuteness of her face, enhancing her looks rather than hardening them. She had had her hair straightened professionally, and it was now a long, sleek Jean Shrimpton-like mane that fell loosely to her shoulders.

"You haven't changed a bit," she said, holding Angela at arm's distance and shaking her head. "Did you have a face lift?" she asked bluntly.

"Shame on you!" Angela scolded. "It's living well that brings the blush to my cheeks."

"Sure. And what's his name this time?"

"You are totally impertinent," Angela said with mock severity, then grinned. "And it's wonderful to see you. Now, introduce me to this lovely young woman whom I'm sure we have embarrassed completely." Angela, raven hair done up in a series of swirls and curls atop her head, turned the full force of her radiant smile on Valerie.

"Angela, this is Valerie. Val, Angela," Linda said.

"Well, at last," Angela said. "I've been hearing about you for years, and for once I can say that Linda has not exaggerated."

"Thank you," Valerie said, smiling warmly as she took the woman's offered hand. "Your home is remarkable," she added, her eyes sweeping the exquisite twenty-foot living room. Valerie had never seen such a place before. The black-and-white marble floor, the marble fireplace, the lighting recessed into the ceiling, the glimpse of garden with its gas lamps illuminating what seemed to be a perfect little Japanese rock garden—all of it was dramatic yet magnificently tasteful. The entry hall was white marble with a vast bevel-edged round mirror on a wall painted in lacquer red. A bonsai tree was the only other touch of color as one entered the townhouse. The colors and furnishings of the living room were no less stark and were equally attractive, with pewter-colored velvet chairs surrounding an immense lucite cube table. There were no paintings on the white walls, only black-and-white photographs of Angela posing in exotic places like the casbah of Morocco or the ruins of the Parthenon. On the floor near the fireplace was a breathtakingly beautiful oriental rug heaped sybaritically high with large velvet pillows. Valerie was speechless as she surveyed the room, and her hostess left her no less in awe.

Valerie found herself hoping that she would look half as good at forty-plus as Angela did. With her hair piled high, the skin on her face was taut, emphasizing her huge, almond-shaped black eyes with their heavy layer of silver eyeshadow. Her nose was longer than would be considered beautiful, but everything about her was larger than life and seemed right that way. Her mouth was a broad slash of sensuality, painted in blood red, the same color as her long nails. Her makeup, while theatrical, was artfully applied, and Valerie marveled at how the woman got away with what would be considered outrageous and cheap on someone with less presence and self-assurance. Tall, almost skeletally thin, Angela wore diaphanous black harem pants cut wide in the leg and low on the hip. Her midriff was bare, and there was not a ripple of extra flesh. The top was a halter made of several layers of the same sheer black material, tied behind her neck by a thin black string. Her only jewelry was a gold chain that ended in a large ivory elephant floating in the valley between her breasts. Exotic, and just a little bit frightening, Valerie decided. This was a woman who knew her own mind, whose sense of self was irrefutable. She wondered, fleetingly, why someone with Angela's looks and talent and taste did not use these assets, as she once had with her designing. If Valerie had been so gifted, she would not have squandered her money or her life away just traveling and indulging in mad affairs.

Valerie did not know that as she was studying the room and her hostess, Angela was doing the same to her. Her oddly wholesome yet voluptuous beauty impressed her. Youth sparkled from her face with almost blinding purity; innocence and expectation seemed to shine from incredible blue eyes that would have been just as wonderful without the touch of makeup. Valerie's face, Angela realized, was still not fully formed, but she could see the woman the girl would become.

The nose was perfectly straight, the cheekbones high but still covered with some girlish flesh, the mouth wide, seductive. And that incredible thick black hair should be long, Angela thought; a dark velvet whisper of wildness, not that dreary Italian cut-up look that made every brunette look like a cheap imitation of Gina Lollobrigida.

"What's so funny?" Linda asked, noticing the small smile on Angela's face.

"Your friend is beautiful," she said, nodding toward Valerie, "but I was thinking she should let her hair grow long. It would be more becoming."

Valerie touched her hair self-consciously. "Don't mind her," Linda said. "Angela has a designer's eye. If she says you'd look better a certain way, trust her. She's never wrong."

"Thank you, my dear," Angela said. "Now, why don't you two circulate and help decorate the room. It should be a lovely party and I want you to enjoy yourselves. We'll talk more later." With a peck on Linda's cheek and a smile for Valerie, she glided to the entry of the living room to welcome another guest.

"What do you think?" Linda asked as she took a glass of champagne from a butler circulating with a tray.

"She's something else," Valerie said, also taking a glass. "I was expecting a critique of my dress next."

"No, she rarely does that. Clothes don't make the woman, she always told me, it's the other way around. You could be wearing a burlap sack and she'd see what you really look like."

"I'm afraid what I'm wearing leaves less to the imagination than a sack," Valerie said ruefully, glancing down at her white angora sweater-dress, cut just a little longer than Linda's, with a jewel neckline, long sleeves, and almost no back. The clinginess of the fabric made underwear impossible, and Valerie felt as if she ought to walk hunched over in order to hide her breasts.

"You look fabulous," Linda said with a grin. "I just know we're going to have a great time. Aren't you glad you came?"

Valerie smiled back at her friend. Champagne served by a butler, a townhouse in the East Sixties, marble fireplaces, a bewitching hostess, and a roomful of people—beautiful, successful, New York kind of people. She would try to remember every single moment for Mack; it was the kind of party he deserved to share, even secondhand.

"Hello."

Two hours later Linda and Valerie had separated, each swept up in the sophisticated conversations around them, which were difficult to hear over the onslaught of Beatle records that no self-respecting party in 1964 would have been without. Whenever the girls would catch each other's eye, a small smile was exchanged; invariably they were surrounded by men, old and not so good-looking, old and good-looking, none young, none terrible. Valerie had, only moments before, taken her fourth glass of champagne, which she was nursing, and gone out to the Japanese garden for some air. The cigarette smoke, the sweetness of marijuana, and the constant flow of wit made it difficult to breathe indoors. She looked up from the two little goldfish in their miniature pond to see who had greeted her.

"Hello," she replied, and then frowned as she looked back at the fish, then up again at the imposingly tall, broad frame of the passenger in 4A, David Kinnelon. "Well, hello!" she said again, smiling warmly.

He smiled back, the soft light from the garden's gas lamps illuminating his tanned face, making his gray eyes seem almost translucent, his teeth unnaturally white. "You remember me?" he asked.

"I'm surprised you remember *me*," Valerie said, thinking how attractive he looked in his Edwardian-cut burgundy velvet dinner jacket. "Those Universal uniforms are eminently forgettable," she added.

"The uniforms may be, but not the body in them," David said smoothly. "Do you mind if I join you?" he asked, gesturing at the empty space on the small stone bench.

Valerie shrugged but did not answer. "I'm sorry," David said, realizing he may have offended her. "I didn't mean to be rude. The fact is that I did remember you from the flight this afternoon. I found you attractive then, too."

"Thank you," Valerie mumbled. She decided, hastily, that David Kinnelon might be everything Linda had breathlessly told her he was—she had spoken of little else during the bus ride into Manhattan—but she was not impressed. For all his money and big-time connections, David Kinnelon struck her as just another cocky man, used to getting whatever and whomever he wanted. Still, for Linda's sake, she told herself, she would talk to him. Her roommate would never forgive her if she did not milk this opportunity for all it was worth.

"You're smiling," David commented. "Amusing thought, or did the goldfish do something I missed?"

"I was thinking how impressed my roommate would be if she knew I was talking with you," Valerie admitted, smiling. "She was the other stew in first class, and she was very excited that you were one of our passengers."

"And you?"

"I'm sorry, but I had no idea who you were."

David laughed, a rich rumble from deep in his chest. "You don't seem too impressed even now," he pointed out.

"I don't impress easily."

David's bushy brows went up. "Really? You strike me as somewhat young for such cynicism."

"I'm twenty-one, and I'm not cynical, just not easily impressed."

He wondered if she was being deliberately provocative, but he saw only guileless eyes and flawless skin. "Are you a friend of Angela's or are you here with an escort?"

"My roommate, Linda, used to model for Angela. They're old friends."

"Don't use the word *old* around Angela. Or me, for that matter. We go back a long way together and we're both extremely sensitive about how long." He laughed.

"She's beautiful," Valerie said with feeling.

"For some reason," he teased, "I think I've just been insulted."

As Valerie began to apologize, he put his hand on her sweatered arm. "I'm just joking." He could feel the softness beneath the fabric and damned the intrusion of the material. "And yes, she is beautiful. And wonderful. One of the most wonderful, generous people I've ever known."

"Perhaps we should get back inside or she'll miss you," Valerie suggested, gently moving her arm so that he was no longer touching her. He was too sure of himself, too used to easy conquests, but it was not for that reason that she wanted to be rid of him. A man like David Kinnelon, older, sophisticated, with women like Angela DiChico as his usual companions, could want nothing more with someone like her than a quick roll in the hay, and Valerie had not been avoiding sex the past three years just so she could tumble for David Kinnelon. He was too old, anyway.

"Angela knows where everyone is every minute. She's got built-in radar," David said, again with that delicious rumble of laughter that made Valerie feel as if she had just shared in a delightful secret. "Besides, now that I've found you, I'm going to be very selfish and preempt you for a while longer." He paused, then grinned almost boyishly. "You know," he said, "I just realized that I don't even know your name, and that's unfair since you already know mine."

"Valerie Cardell."

"You're not from New York, are you?"

"Indiana, but Linda and I live in Los Angeles now."

"Will you be staying in New York long?"

"We leave tomorrow afternoon. We only fly this run about once a month. Usually it's the Caribbean or Hawaii."

"Then you both must be senior stews."

Her eyes widened. "I gather you've known a few," she remarked stiffly.

David shrugged. "I put in a lot of air time," was his explanation, but both of them knew how he had come by his knowledge. Valerie got up—she'd had enough of David Kinnelon. There was nothing unlikable about him, except that he was in a league too far removed from her own.

"I'd better get back inside," she said. "It was nice meeting you again, Mr. Kinnelon."

He rose, too, seeming to dwarf her not with his size but with his overwhelming masculinity. He took her hands in a firm grasp. "Why don't we both leave now? You can't possibly have filled yourself up on all those ridiculous dips and canapés, and it would be a pleasure if you'd let me buy you a late-night supper."

Valerie deftly extricated her hands but did not answer until she had retrieved her empty champagne glass from where she had left it by the bench. Then, plastering on her airborne smile, she said, "Thank you, but I think not, Mr. Kinnelon. I'm afraid that your idea of supper and mine would come to a serious difference around dessert time. Besides, as they say, if you've had one stew, you've had them all." And then she was gone, leaving David Kinnelon laughing delightedly at the soft sway of her retreating form.

"You're undeniably, completely, certifiably nuts!" Linda exploded when the two girls met at the airport the next morning. They were passengers on this flight, and were enjoying Bloody Marys as Linda spoke in a barrage of superlatives about the financier she had met at Angela's party. She offered no apology for having spent the night with him, nor any regret that his wife's return from the Golden Door Spa meant that their relationship would be haphazard at best, nonexistent most likely. It was only after an hour of detail and description that Linda had paused long enough to ask Valerie how her evening had been. When she had casually mentioned meeting David Kinnelon, Linda had demanded a verbatim report of their conversation. Her conviction that Valerie had lost her mind was based on Valerie's refusal to go out with him.

"I mean it, Val, there's something seriously wrong with you. How could you possibly refuse an invitation from that man? Aside from his incredible wealth, success, power, and the people he knows, he's also damn good-looking. I mean, so what if he's a little older? You're a very mature person, Val, you have nothing to be intimidated about."

"I wasn't intimidated!" Valerie retorted. "You're unbelievable, Linda, you really are. Just because I'm not impressed with some hot-shot tycoon—"

"Who had dinner with Kennedy at the White House," Linda reminded her.

"Honestly, Linda, he still puts his pants on one leg at a time!"

Linda got hysterical at that, choking on her drink until Valerie had to slap her on the back. "You're terrific, you know that? But tell me, truth now—didn't you find him even the itsy-bitsiest bit attractive?"

"Well, yes," Valerie admitted. "I did, but what does he want with someone like me? Come on, Linda, be realistic. The man, by your own admission, has had and can have any woman he wants. I'm just a stewardess from Galesville, Indiana. A man like him wants only one thing from a girl like me, and no matter how attractive he is, I'm not about to give it to him."

"You can be charming when you want," Linda pointed out, trying to refute Valerie's assessment of David's interest in her. "And you're beautiful. And young. Don't forget young, Val—that counts for a lot."

Valerie shook her head. "Those are all valid reasons, but not good enough. I'm sorry, but this is one trophy," and she pointed at her chest, "that the impressive David Kinnelon will never add to his collection."

"Not even just so you could tell me about it?" Linda asked hopefully.

Valerie laughed. "Not even for you."

When they reached their apartment, exhausted, they had no sooner dropped their suitcases in the bedroom when the buzzer rang. "I'll get it," Linda offered. A few moments later she was tipping a delivery boy and carrying in a white box tied with a lush red sateen ribbon. The card was addressed to Miss Valerie Cardell.

"Val! Come see what you got!"

Valerie dashed out of the bedroom. "Hurry up and open it!" Linda instructed, handing her the box. "Have you been keeping some secret admirer from me?"

"Don't be absurd," Valerie snapped. Quickly she undid the ribbon and turned back the tissue paper to reveal a thick bed of ruby-red roses. One by one she took them out until there were an even two dozen lying on the upturned box top.

"Omigosh!" Linda whispered, awed. "I'll get a vase. Better make it two. And read the card! I'm going to die from the suspense!"

Valerie took the little card from its envelope. It read: "Dear Valerie, I will be in Los Angeles next Friday and would be delighted if you could have dinner with me. Eight o'clock at Perino's. I hope you'll be there. David Kinnelon."

Wordlessly, she showed the card to Linda. "Omigosh!" Linda said again, gasping. "Oh my, wow, jeez!"

"Your vocabulary boggles my mind," Valerie teased.

"Say you're going. Say it. I won't let you turn this down. Now you listen to me, Valerie Cardell, I won't tolerate one word of argument about this. Perino's. Two dozen red roses. I can't stand it. I simply can't." Linda was as excited as if the invitation had come to her. "I don't care if he is suave, debonair, rich as sin, charming, and used to having any woman he wants. You *must* go out with him!"

By now Valerie was laughing so hard that she was almost crying.

"What's so funny?" Linda demanded.

"You. The way you're acting, you'd think Paul Newman himself had asked me out."

"David Kinnelon is better. At least he's not married to Joanne Woodward." She sat down on the sofa next to Valerie. "You will go out with him, won't you?" she asked earnestly.

Valerie looked at the flowers, glanced again at the card which was still in Linda's hands, and was, in spite of herself, impressed and intrigued by the effort the man had gone to—even if it was only to get her into bed. He certainly did things with style, she thought.

"Well?" Linda prodded.

"I'll have dinner with him."

"At last the girl has come to her senses!" Linda sighed theatrically.

"But only this once. I mean it, only once."

Chapter 9

Valerie sat back and wiped the corners of her mouth with the thick damask napkin.

"I can't move," she said with a rueful smile. "You realize, of course, that only because I don't have to fly until next week am I safe from losing my job. After this meal, I'd never pass the weight test."

David Kinnelon smiled and reached out to place his hand on top of Valerie's as it rested on the damask-covered table. "I take it you enjoyed the meal?"

"Very much," she replied, sliding her hand away and placing it in her lap. In fact, she thought, she had enjoyed much more than the delicious meal of smoked trout, veal veronique, endive salad, fresh raspberries, superb wine, and strong espresso. She had found herself so delighting in David's company that only his touch now reminded her that he had not gone to this expense—little as it might mean to a man of his wealth—without expecting a payoff in the end. She wondered how abruptly his charm would shut down when he realized she had no intention of accommodating his expectations.

"What's wrong?"

Valerie was taken aback by the question. "Why, nothing. What makes you ask?"

"Well, that beautiful mouth of yours suddenly got very stern. Did I say something to upset you?"

Startled by his perceptiveness, she answered slowly. "No. I was just thinking."

"Not too pleasant, I gather."

She shrugged and looked down at the sliver of lemon peel in her saucer.

"You're a strange girl, Valerie," David said, his sharp gray eyes noticing much more than she could possibly have imagined. "I think you ought to give me the benefit of the doubt before accusing me," he added quietly.

Her eyes flew to his face, and she was again unsettled by his acute intelligence. "What do you mean?"

"I mean," David said, sitting back in the brocade-upholstered chair, "that you're probably figuring I want a little something by way of a thank-you after the flowers and this dinner." Valerie said nothing, but she did not take her eyes from his, and he went on. "I suspect you've been preparing your defenses, and what I probably should say now is that you shouldn't flatter yourself so, but that would be a lie. Of course I'd like to go to bed with you, but I don't need to, nor am I expecting to."

Valerie was horribly embarrassed. "I'm sorry," she managed. "It's just that I don't understand . . . I don't see why—" She shook her head, leaving the sentence incomplete.

"You don't understand why else I would be here with you except to get you into bed, is that it?"

She nodded, unable to meet his direct gaze.

"Oh, Valerie, how wonderfully innocent you are!"

She glanced up. There it was again—her innocence, as if

it were an extension of herself, an uninvited guest wherever she went.

"I don't see where that has anything– " she began, but David stopped her.

He leaned forward, the lines around his nose creasing deeply as he smiled. "It has *everything* to do with your assumption of my, shall we call it, salacious interest in you. Valerie, my dear girl, there is no arguing the fact that you are an irresistibly lovely female. I can't imagine any man not wanting you, and that most certainly goes for myself. But I also find you delightfully intelligent, charming, and witty. In short, a pleasure to be with. Sex with you would be, I have no doubt, a fabulous icing on the cake, but sometimes I've found a meal can be perfectly fine without any dessert at all."

He was staring at her intently, the power emanating from his gray eyes willing her to understand and believe him. She had no idea how important it was to him that she believe him; had no idea that it was as if helium had been injected directly into David Kinnelon's heart since speaking with Valerie at Angela DiChico's party, making him float with almost youthful exuberance at the thought of seeing her again. Yes, because she was beautiful. Yes, because she was young. And most of all, because she was fresh and soft, totally herself, an original still innocent enough not to know the power she possessed, the effect she could have.

"Valerie?"

At the sound of his voice, a smile slowly began to part her lips, and this time it was she who placed her hand over his. "I'm sorry," she said.

"Does that mean you'll see me again?" David asked, the hopeful gleam in his eyes belying his calm tone of voice.

She nodded, and he smiled, his pleasure evident. Then, abruptly, his expression turned serious. "I'm much older than you," he said. "Does that bother you?"

Only when Valerie had created her own scenario for the evening's end had she been aware of David Kinnelon as anything but a charming dinner companion, an exciting and attractive man she liked and wanted to see again. She had not felt inferior or childish or even unsophisticated as they had exchanged personal histories; the differences in their lifestyles were interesting and amusing rather than unbreachable chasms of dissimilarity. There was nothing old about this man. His virility, his strength, his enormous appeal precluded even a consciousness that he was more than twenty years her senior. He only pointed out to her how much more comfortable she was with someone like him, like Mack, older men of the world, rather than with younger men who still had so much to prove.

"I hadn't noticed," she finally said gently. "Or is that your way of saying that I'm too young for you?"

"You probably are," he admitted, "but if it doesn't bother you, it most certainly doesn't bother me."

"I'm glad."

He looked at her hard, as if assessing her sincerity, then squeezed the hand that was still resting atop his. "Well, now that we've eliminated sex and age, shall we get back to simply enjoying each other?" he asked lightly.

"I'd like that, David. Very much."

After that evening in March came a succession of Sunday afternoons, Saturday nights, weekends, a quick dinner on a Tuesday, a lunch stolen between business meetings on a Thursday, a night at the Hollywood Bowl, an afternoon at the Metropolitan Museum of Art, a day at the New York World's Fair. David conducted his courtship on both coasts, seeing Valerie whenever they both were in Los Angeles or New York at the same time. It was unlike any relationship either of them had experienced before. For David, it was a gradual enchantment, almost a bewitchment as he found himself being true to the words he had spoken during their first evening together. That night in Perino's he had wanted to calm a skittish colt in order that he might lull her for future victory. By the end of one month, with nothing more physical between them than a chaste kiss on the cheek upon greeting, then again upon parting, David Kinnelon had come to believe that he could enjoy Valerie without going to bed with her—an astonishing and altogether thrilling realization for him.

As the first month became two and then three, David admitted to himself that he was only marking time between his visits with Valerie. Whether they shared a nightcap at the Polo Lounge or a ride in a hansom cab in Central Park; met for an eggs-Benedict-and-champagne brunch at the Plaza or sat silently in his Mercedes staring at the lights of Los Angeles from their lookout point high atop Mulholland Drive, her constancy at first impressed, then delighted, and finally totally seduced him. An astute judge of character, David knew that much of his business success came from knowing which buttons to push with an opponent; knowing how to deal with the human being rather than wheel and deal with the business associate. It was this keen understanding that had enabled him, while still a young man, to get what he wanted when he wanted it, as well as to maintain a wide and varied circle of friends. He believed no one was truly as he seemed, and while the people who worked for him did careful studies on the businesses he wanted to acquire, he spent his energy studying the people he had to buy out, buy up, or best. It was not that he was distrusting of all people; it was more that he had learned early on that people's appetites, from greed to need, enabled them to commit a variety of sins and camouflage a variety of weaknesses.

So far, he had found nothing in Valerie but what she openly presented to him. He could spoil her at an expensive restaurant or they could share a simple, home-cooked meal with Linda in the girls' apartment, it didn't matter: her pleasure stemmed only from him. And what drew him to her forever was that the more he sensed her sincerity, the more he wanted to please her. He knew better than to shower her with gifts; her pride would forbid her from accepting them, and the sense of obligation she would feel would taint her attitude toward him. What she seemed to want was him: his ability to make her laugh, his knowledge about places and people. It was his sophistication and experience that seemed to please her, and so he again played Pygmalian to Galatea, but this time with a difference. This time he did not presume to change, but merely to educate, and as he did, it was he who learned about loving.

"Val, I just don't understand you. It's been how many months now?"

"Five," Valerie replied dejectedly. She and Linda were out by the pool of their apartment house, their lean, taut bodies carefully greased against the vicious Southern California sun, a pitcher of iced tea resting on the fake grass mat that surrounded the pool.

"Five! I don't believe it," Linda exclaimed. "Don't you want to?"

"That's not the point," Valerie muttered.

Linda sat up on the chaise, holding her skimpy bikini top to her chest. "But that is the point precisely. If you want to and he wants to, why haven't you?"

"I don't want to discuss this," Valerie said in a clipped voice.

"Well, I think you'd better. My gosh, what's wrong with you? More to the point, what the hell is wrong with him? I don't care if he is forty-five, David Kinnelon is more man than guys half his age, and you can't tell me he's not getting it regularly somewhere else."

"Shut up!"

Valerie felt as if the years had tripped backward and Alice was telling her that if she didn't go to bed with Teddy, someone else would.

Valerie knew that David was waiting for her to make the first move; to indicate that the chaste kiss was no longer enough—for her. And the truth was that it hadn't been for several weeks now—no, almost since the first month. But she could say or do nothing to let him know that she wanted him because by now it had become a matter of her own insecurities and self-doubts. Would she be good enough for him? He was so experienced, so sophisticated, how could she possibly please him? Look what had happened with Roger. Yet, even as she offered those arguments to herself, she knew they were mere excuses and evasions. Her expertise would be the least of his concerns. Why, then, did she avoid it? Why couldn't she bring herself to tell David that she wanted to go to bed with him?

"Do you love him?"

Valerie gazed at her roommate for a moment, hesitating to answer the question she had recently been asking herself. "I'm not sure," she said finally. "I like him, I like being with him. I'd miss him if he stopped seeing me."

Linda took a sip of iced tea, swung her long legs over the edge of the chaise-longue, and leaned over to Valerie with an intent expression in her round blue eyes. "Valerie, tell me something. What do you think love is? What do you think you're missing with David that stops you from calling it love? What are you feeling, Val? Do you ever deal with what you're feeling, or do you just keep going merrily or miserably from one day to the next, assuming you're going to walk on air when true love hits you?" She shook her head. "It's not like that, kiddo. You ought to have figured that one out by now."

"I know," Valerie said, almost to herself. But did she really? Did she really accept that love was not a special sensation, so inimitably different from any other that she would reel from its impact and feel it tangibly as if it were a piece of fabric cloaking her in its magic? Wasn't there still the unshakable belief in the perfection of the right love, all others merely facsimiles to test her strength and resolve until the "real" thing came along? And wasn't this the reason why she was so hesitant not only to go to bed with David but to admit to feelings deeper than fondness?

He was good to her, protective, kind, undemanding, generous. He asked nothing of her but that she be herself. She felt safe with him, sheltered in a cocoon of understanding. It was true that she would miss him if he decided not to see her anymore, but was that because of her feeling for him, or because of the comfort he gave her? She desired him, but not as she had Roger, not with that constant hunger to know his touch, to explore the boundaries of her own body through an uninhibited curiosity about his. At least, that was how she had thought of sex with Roger before actually going to bed with him. Afterward, it had been less than wonderful. And with David, with the lack of that eagerness, wouldn't the final act be even more disappointing?

She didn't know any of the answers. Not to why she refused to sleep with him, not to why she refused to deal with her feelings for him, not to what she was more afraid of: commitment to a man who was undeniably good to her or to her own unrealistic ideals. Never before had she been with a man who seemed to take such pleasure from her with so little effort on her part. Never had she known anyone, man or woman, with the exception of Mack, who made her feel such a sense of rightness about herself. Even if her emotional self believed in the unreality of romantic love, the clear-thinking, intelligent self knew that there was more going on here than idealism. She was distancing herself, protecting herself, for a reason, and it was more than fear of rejection or inability to compromise. It was almost as if, she suddenly thought with terrifying clarity, she expected the worst, and it was therefore easier to let all the decisions, even about feelings, be made for her. Had two foolish love affairs and numerous meaningless dates done that to her? Was she indeed so fragile still that she did not have the strength or the courage to discover what *she* wanted, and instead let a man of David's strength dictate her desires to her? He had not done that—not overtly, she realized. But by virtue of his own gentlemanly behavior, he was leading her to do what he wanted. Well then, she decided, she would make the first move, but because she was curious and for no other reason. If it happened to coincide with David Kinnelon's desires, so much the better; but what she would do, she would do because *she* wanted it.

With a mischievous smile on her face, she looked at her roommate. "I've been an idiot," she proclaimed.

"Ah, at last the girl is using her brains! What, pray tell, has caused this epiphany?"

"You and your damned rudeness."

"Me! Rude! How can you possibly—"

"Oh, Linda, you're wonderful. I don't know what I'd do without you."

If Linda's expression was one of perplexity, it was a flimsy façade to mask the warmth she truly felt. Even after all these years together, she still could not quite determine what made Valerie tick. What she did know was that she could not imagine ever not caring about her, or not taking a certain pleasure in being needed by her.

"Are you sure you want to do this?"

"David," Valerie said with a small laugh, "that makes at least the fourth time you've asked me the same question. Maybe you're the one who's not sure."

"It's just so unexpected." His voice faltered as he took his eyes off the Long Island Expressway long enough to catch the sparkle in Valerie's eyes. She had never looked so beautiful or so desirable—or did she strike him that way because they were about to spend their first weekend together? It had come as such a surprise, her slightly tentative suggestion that after almost six months of seeing each other, they should discover how compatible they were in bed. Had it been only two days ago, when they were having dinner in Los Angeles, a magnificent feast at Scandia, that she had sprung this on him? It seemed as if he had been waiting for that moment since the night of Angela's party, but he had become so resigned to her reluctance to have sex that he thought it would still be months away.

"I wish I understood what brought about this change."

"Oh, David, I've been such a fool. At first I thought your only interest in me was sexual, and when you convinced me it wasn't that at all—"

"Well, a little," David joked.

"I should hope so! But seriously, by then I guess I felt too shy or scared . . . oh, who knows what the reason was, but I figured I had to wait for you to make the first move. Then I realized that you were waiting for *me* to make the first move." She shook her head and grinned. "We could have gone on endlessly that way."

"Not quite endlessly," he assured her.

David had rented a car and they were on their way to the American Hotel in Sag Harbor, Long Island. It was a quaint, historic hotel in the charming seaport village, and getting a reservation there at the last minute, even though it was after Labor Day, had not been easy. He and Angela had been there years before, after they had stopped being lovers but when they had needed to get away to unwind. He had remembered the charm of the hotel, its small bar, its elegant dining room, but had never gone back with either of his wives or any of his girl friends. When Valerie had told him what she wanted, he had known instinctively that Sag Harbor, with its small, wonderful, very private hotel, was the perfect setting.

Now he took one hand off the wheel and placed it on her thigh. She put her hand over his and smiled warmly at him. "I feel like a little boy," he admitted. "I'm nervous as hell."

"Good, I'd hate to be the only one," she said gently. "Oh, David, I just hope I don't disappoint you," she added in a rush.

"You couldn't possibly. Just knowing you want me is more pleasure than I dreamed possible."

Two hours later, they had finished unpacking and were standing, tensely, side by side, looking out their bedroom window that faced Main Street, a block-long amalgam of seashell shops and antique stores that ended at the port of Sag Harbor, populated by magnificent sailboats and large cabin cruisers.

David put his arm around Valerie's shoulders and pulled her to face him. For all her conviction that this was the right thing to do, she was utterly petrified. It had been a long time since she had been with a man; an even longer time since she had wanted to be with one. Now that the moment was here, fear claimed her so completely that she began to tremble under David's touch.

"I know you're not cold," he said softly.

She shook her head, willing herself to meet his eyes

"Scared, huh?"

She nodded and tried to smile. "David, I'm so inexperienced and I'm so worried that—"

"Ssh," he whispered, and drew her against his chest. "It's you I want, Valerie. You. If we did nothing all weekend but walk and talk and browse in the shops, it would be more than enough. Just being with you gives me so much happiness that sometimes it scares me."

Valerie lifted her head from the comfort of his chest, and slowly David lowered his mouth so that it was a breath away from hers. For a heartbeat of time, she wanted to pull away, run down the stairs and out into the street, but then his lips were on hers, just there, not demanding, not prying, just there, something to warm her. Still, she stiffened reflexively, and he pulled back.

"Do you want to go out for a while?" he asked, not releasing her from the circle of his arms.

She shook her head and tentatively put her arms around his neck, drawing him down to her. "Help me, David," she whispered. "Please."

With a groan of long-suppressed yearning, David captured her mouth in his lips, and Valerie opened herself to him, her body yielding to the warmth he was igniting in her as his tongue gently explored, his hands tenderly discovering the soft flesh between her neck and shoulder, the slope of her buttocks, her narrow waist. Feelings, everything was feelings, she thought wildly . . . his quick arousal pressing against her, his heart beating loud and hard against her own . . . her blood throbbing, her bones turning liquid, her need awakening more fully with each thrust of his tongue, each feather stroke of his fingers.

"Oh, Valerie, Valerie, I've waited so long for this," he murmured against her hair, and in answer she pressed herself closer to him, her hands beginning to dance over the buttons of his shirt, eager to feel his hot, masculine strength.

"Are you sure? Tell me, darling, are you sure?" he asked huskily, stilling the flight of her fingers as they tried to push apart his now-unbuttoned shirt.

Valerie said nothing. She stepped away from David and slowly began to unbutton her silk blouse. David did not move to touch her, and she did not take her eyes from his, burning into him the extent of her desire. The blouse made a soft rustle as it slipped from her shoulders to the floor, and still he did not move, nor did she look anywhere but into his eyes, drawing encouragement from their heat.

"I'm giving you my answer, David," she whispered.

"Yes, darling, I know." He clenched his hands at his sides to stop from reaching out to claim her. But he understood her need to do this for him, to make the giving total, and so he stood watching her, the blood racing in his ears, his body quivering with self-control.

She reached behind her and undid the hook of her bra, sliding it slowly from one shoulder and then the other. Not the most practiced stripper could have been more seductive in her disrobing, David found himself thinking. Her guilelessness and her eagerness to please were more erotic than anything he had ever before experienced. She stood before him, naked from the waist up, then moistened her lips and smiled hesitantly, self-consciously.

"Your turn," she said.

"Let me look at you a while longer."

"No. Take off your shirt."

David did as he was told, and she reached out to touch his broad, deep chest, matted with a fine coat of dark hair. He flinched at her first touch, his stomach contracting with his excruciating need for her, but he made no effort to reciprocate. He understood, and he would let her lead until she wanted him to take over. Her hands now traveled over the hard muscles of his shoulders, his upper arms, coming back to his chest, down to the waistband of his pants, back up again to his chest. Unable to withstand any more, he put both his hands on hers and stopped their fluttering arousal. Then, with calm deliberateness, he touched one breast, a gentle caress that nevertheless made her gasp from the flame of sensation it caused. Her head went back, her breasts arching toward him, inviting, demanding. Then his tongue was on her nipple, and her breath began to come in short, ragged gasps. She reached for him, and her eyes opened in surprise as her hand came in contact with the thick hair on his head, nestled against her stomach, his lips igniting her skin.

"David, the bed, please. Let's get into bed."

As an answer, he lowered the zipper of the cotton slacks and slid them down her hips until they formed a heap at her feet. His mouth never stopped working her, his fingers never stopped caressing. She kept her hands on his shoulders as his head lowered, and she did not recognize the guttural groans of pleasure as coming from herself.

"David, please. Please."

He rose slowly, his hands sliding farther up her flesh so that she felt as if every inch of her had been claimed by his massive, omnipotent hands. Silently he finished undressing, and Valerie removed her panties so that they were both, at last, fully naked. There was no guilelessness now as she pushed into the hardness of his chest, her own mouth devouring his lips, his nipples, her fingers greedily touching hot, firm masculinity. Never had she been so excited by a man; never so aware of her body as an instrument that could give such pleasure even as it received it. Suddenly she found that David was holding her head in his hands, looking at her with a mixture of awe and passion. Wordlessly he took her by the hand and led her to the bed.

He began to make love to her, his own insistent need sublimated until he knew she was ready, could feel her heat, the throbbing demand for release. He guided himself into her but then stayed poised above her, all his weight on his hands by her sides, his eyes open, taking in the sight of her sweat-sheened face. Then he began to thrust, the strokes slow, measured, until he saw the way the tendons in her neck seemed ready to burst as her head arched back, until he felt her fingers on his back, urging him into her. He began to move harder and harder, and then he was squeezing her to him, pounding into her hot moistness in a final, breathtaking explosion.

He did not pull out immediately, but dropped his head onto the sweat-salty valley between her breasts. Valerie stroked his head, and waited as her breathing became normal, her temperature lowered, trying not to pay attention to the screeching needs of her own unfulfilled body.

They made love many more times during that weekend, David surprising himself with his energy, proud, like a bull, of his youthful virility. Valerie had heard everything there was to know about faking orgasms, but she did not resort to that ploy. She told David it was due to her inexperience and inhibitions, and that it would happen in time. David had no reason to doubt her or, more important, himself.

Three weeks after their weekend in Sag Harbor, David Kinnelon knew he wanted to marry Valerie. They were in his suite at the Beverly Wilshire Hotel, in bed, the sheets in disarray from their lovemaking. Valerie was nestled against his chest, her mind wondering if the supreme but not complete pleasure she experienced with him was all there was, and if her notion of some indescribable sexual joy was simply another foolish romantic ideal that had no basis in reality. She still did not reach orgasm with David, and she still did not pretend otherwise. She had explained, to his satisfaction, that a woman did not have to fall over the precipice in order to enjoy the trip. He was disappointed, but accepting, and so the pressure to perform was lifted for them both.

"Val, honey?"

"Mmm?"

"You know I love you, don't you?"

She lifted her head, then settled back against the headboard. "You've never said that before."

David nodded. "I know. In the past when I've said it, I've been wrong. I wanted to be sure this time—and, Val, I am sure. I know I'm much older than you, and you probably want someone younger, more energetic, more—"

"David, David!" She laughed, placing her hand on his

shoulder. "Anyone more energetic than you and I'd never be able to walk again."

"Do you love me at all, Valerie?" he asked softly, staring at her. "Could you ever love me?"

She did not respond immediately. He was asking the question Linda had once asked her, the question she had been pondering for so many months now. And the answer was not unlike the one regarding sex. She respected David, admired him, enjoyed being with him, and genuinely liked him. If that, taken together, was love, then yes, she supposed she loved him. Like sex with him, her feelings for David were not an explosive delight, the way she had imagined love would be, but they were warm and wonderfully fulfilling in their own way.

"Yes, David," she whispered. "I love you."

"Enough to marry me?"

Chapter 10

> . . . And wedding bells will be ringing for sought-after man-about-this-town and every other bright spot in the world, David Kinnelon, when he takes lovely stewardess, Valerie Cardell, as wife numero three. David, as we all know and admire, is one of those incredibly rare self-made zillionaires, and we wish him and his bride-to-be years of flying high and happy together. More on the wedding of the year as the very private David chooses to tell us about it. . . .

Alice had read the society column from the *New York Daily News* so many times that the clipping was tearing where her mother had folded it within the accompanying note. And she had stared at the grainy photograph of her sister, stared and read, fueling a fury so virulent that she thought she was being consumed by some terrible disease.

Her mind raced with the vilest, most malevolent thoughts, silently wishing upon her sister any number of catastrophes, any manner of evil to help purge the excruciating weight of jealousy that pressed upon her heart.

Her mother's brief note—explaining that Valerie had sent the clipping to Mack, who had given it to Edith—did not help matters either, she thought disgustedly. She glanced again at her mother's words, which were like knife thrusts: ". . . Valerie has really landed herself a live one . . . the kind of man I dreamed about for you . . . so rich . . . should have been you . . ." *Rich . . . you . . . rich . . . you.*

"Damn it all to hell! And may you not know a moment's happiness all your married life!" Alice yelled, the words a racking sob as she crumpled the newspaper clipping and her mother's letter into a little ball and threw it across her living room.

The oppressive rage and envy could not be so easily crushed. She sat in the living room of her Chicago apartment, unmoving except for the wheels of her mind as they spun around and around, rebelling at the unfairness of the situation, teeming with jealousy-induced invectives, plotting to destroy.

She sat like that for many hours; the next thing she knew, her apartment was totally dark. She remembered having come home from her job as a secretary to an advertising executive and finding her mother's letter, a message of doom. Slowly she got up from the sofa and went into the kitchen. Ten o'clock. She had been sitting there for four hours! With the same deliberate, almost somnambulant steps, she returned to the living room, found the balled-up clipping and letter, and took them back to the kitchen where she put a match to them. She watched the papers curl and disintegrate over the sink, her mind delighting at the idea that somehow this act of destruction was an omen of what would happen to Valerie.

In spite of her hatred, she realized that a part of her could think of her sister with a semblance of objectivity. The picture had been poor, but even so, she had been able to see how the promise of Valerie's beauty was fulfilling itself, as she had known it would since childhood. Her cheekbones had become more prominent as age melted away the excess flesh; her mouth, full and sensuous even as a child, had become more appealing as the structure of her face took shape. Her hair was thick, lush, framing her face like a dark halo; and the eyes, always the eyes, even more startlingly intelligent and beautiful. With that same objectivity, Alice also knew that Valerie had not snared David Kinnelon the way she would have done, had she had the opportunity. Valerie had not used her wiles, because she had none. And she had not used her body, because she would not have had to. A man like David Kinnelon did not marry simply to keep someone in his bed.

David Kinnelon. Mrs. David Kinnelon. Not just a Prince Charming, but truly a knight in armor shining with the glint of newly minted money. Whether her sister deserved such a man was never an issue with Alice. All that was important was that Valerie was getting what Alice wanted more than anything else in the world: money, social position, to be the object of envy instead of the envious.

With no appetite except for a drink, Alice fixed herself a Scotch on the rocks and went back into her living room, turning on the lamp to its lowest power. Sipping slowly, she sat back and wondered anew at her sister's luck. How had she come even to know a man like David Kinnelon? From her mother's letters and calls over the years, little could be learned. Valerie's picture postcards and sporadic letters filled with news about her roommate, Linda, and the places they had traveled to did not imply the kind of life that Alice would have considered promising. Until this afternoon, she had been convinced that she was surpassing her sister in every way.

She closed her eyes, permitting herself to dwell on her family, an exercise she rarely did since it gave her neither pleasure nor insight. In the almost three and a half years since Valerie had left home, the Cardell family had splintered in many directions, all of them leading away from Galesville. Ned had managed to find some poor girl to marry him, Lena somebody-or-other, who worked as a hairdresser while Ned continued to hold down two ever-changing jobs. Even in a city as large as Indianapolis, where he now lived, his temper caught up with him. Billy loved living in San Francisco where he was working in the art department of a gay magazine. Edith hadn't told Alice that the magazine was gay; she didn't know. Alice had found that out herself when she had called

Billy a few months ago to brag to him that she had made it to Chicago. She wondered if either of her brothers knew how far Valerie had gone beyond them.

When she had married Teddy, Alice recalled, she had felt secure that her life would be exactly as planned: the wife of a man who was going places. How wrong she had been. After the first miscarriage, near the end of their first year of marriage, she had unsuccessfully begged Teddy to move them out of Galesville, trying to convince him that she needed to get away from the scene of this terrible failure. But Teddy, who was already staying at the paper later and later each night, coming home a little bit drunker each week, had balked, then flatly refused, telling her that he liked Galesville, liked working on a small-town newspaper, excelling there rather than being mediocre in a large city. Within eighteen months, Alice knew she had chosen both poorly and unwisely so she reverted to the Alice Cardell she had been before marriage. She came home later and later, too, but instead of the smell of liquor, she emanated the stench of sex. When she became pregnant for the second time, Teddy believed the child was his, and since she was not able to determine which of the possible fathers might be responsible, she went along with her husband's belief. Four months into the pregnancy she miscarried again, a painful experience that left her with too much time to think.

Six months ago—a little more than four years after she had married—Alice had moved, against Edith's wailing objections, to Chicago and filed for divorce. She had known Teddy would not object; since the second miscarriage there had been no further pretense that the marriage was merely troubled instead of terminal. Chicago had become her mecca. She had found a small apartment in a brownstone off Lake Shore Drive and a job as executive secretary to an advertising account executive. She dated frequently, usually men of substance she met through the office. She was convinced that it was only a matter of time before the right man came along, the one to place the princess on her pedestal.

With the arrival of the newspaper clipping, she saw her illusions as the delusions they were. No matter how well she succeeded, she could never hope to reach the pinnacle Valerie had achieved through David Kinnelon. But she could, she thought decisively, hope to share her sister's rarefied world until she found a way to usurp her position.

Chapter 11

In early September 1964, two months before their wedding, which was to be the first week of December, David and Valerie were sitting at a banquette in the Plaza Hotel's Oak Room, waiting for Ray Kinnelon. Valerie had been dreading this meeting and had managed to get David to postpone it so many times that she could not possibly ask again without raising suspicion.

Although she and David had never voiced their reasons for being anxious about meeting with Ray, Valerie suspected that David's reluctance came from vanity. The thought of his fiancée meeting a son only a few years her senior undoubtedly disturbed him. For her, it was a far deeper concern. A "stepmother" younger than the son of course caused certain trepidation. More than that, though, was the realization that of all the people she had met through David, and all the people to whom she had been introduced as his bride-to-be, none could afford to pass judgment on her. In whatever way, remote or immediate, they needed David Kinnelon and could not risk alienating him. But Ray Kinnelon was his son, with every right to judge. And so Valerie's fear was that judgment would be passed, and she would fail.

She kept twisting her flawless three-carat marquis diamond engagement ring, feeling, as she had when David had given it to her, that it was too much, too ostentatious . . . and, oddly, too big for someone only twenty-one. She thought his son would think so too. She sipped at her Campari and soda and smiled tentatively at David.

"Nervous?" he asked.

She nodded.

"Well, if it's any consolation, you look lovely."

Her smile did not gain confidence, but she was pleased

that he recognized what pains she had gone to with her clothing. She was wearing a pale blue Courrèges minidress, a gift from David from Paris. Its simple but structured cut and its cool color set off the blackness of her hair and the richness of her body. There was no denying that she was young, and she had made no attempt to camouflage that fact with a more sophisticated hairdo or excessive makeup. But there was about her a self-possession and poise that spoke of maturity. Little could David have imagined, she thought, how out-of-place she felt sitting in a Courrèges dress in the richly decorated Oak Room at the Plaza Hotel. She might look as if she fit in, and she could only hope that she acted as if she did, but her heart's mad beating came not only from Ray's imminent arrival but from the strangeness of her new world.

There was no more time to dwell on any feelings of discomfort because David was whispering in her ear. "Here he comes," he said, and then he was standing up, grinning, greeting his son with a handshake and a slap on the shoulder.

"Ray, this is Valerie. Isn't she everything I said she was?"

Valerie glanced up, expecting to find a younger version of David. He was that—and much, much more. About six feet tall, with the same athletically broad chest as his father, Ray had dark brown hair that was shaggily cut and brushed his jacket collar, and a chiseled, finely structured face, all masculine planes and angles. There were the same intelligent gray eyes, colder than his father's, more overtly probing. His nose was slightly shorter and straighter than David's, his mouth fuller, more mobile. He was dressed in a tweed jacket and tight blue jeans, a rep tie thrown carelessly under the collar of his shirt as a concession to the Plaza's dress code. Valerie absorbed all this as Ray reached out and shook her hand, muttering words of greeting. She heard none of them.

She withdrew her hand and placed it around her glass, needing the cold sensation. She felt as if she were being consumed by a fever, her body unexpectedly sensitized, seeming hot and flushed as if by proximity to fire. The resemblance between father and son was strong, yet Ray Kinnelon exuded a sensuality that seemed almost obscene. It was not just that he was handsome. She had seen other handsome men and they had not made her feel as if she wanted to run away and protect herself. It was the directness of this young man's gaze, appraising her with eyes much older and more cynical than his age. It was his full, wide mouth and square jaw, and the broad forehead with hair hanging lazily across it. There was a carefree comfort with his good looks that manifested in a self-confidence that not even David possessed. No, Valerie corrected herself. Ray Kinnelon was cocky, not confident. Cocky with youth and money and privilege, and that as well as his looks made him devastatingly appealing.

Somehow she got through the next hour, letting the two men do most of the talking while she sat there feeling utterly miserable. Finally, Ray got to his feet.

"I've gotta go, Dad," he said, his voice sending heat waves through Valerie. "Grant and I are flying out early tomorrow morning to check the progress on the Columbus mall, and then we fly down to Baltimore."

"What's happening there?" David asked. "I thought that row of townhouses was already being renovated."

"It is, but there's a problem with the insulation. Grant thinks it may be substandard or close to it, and he wants to check it out for himself again."

David shook his head and grinned. "Got to be the best for that boy, doesn't it?"

Ray shrugged. "It'll pay off when we start selling them as condos. It'll mean a higher buying price."

"I know. Well, I'm glad you stopped by. It would have been a helluva party if you had to meet Valerie there for the first time."

"Oh? What party is that?" Ray looked from his father to Valerie, who glanced at David with surprise.

"I had been toying with the idea of an engagement party, then decided that wasn't right. After all, what does a man my age need an engagement party for? But then I realized that you've never had one." David smiled at Valerie. "I thought that since we'll be leaving for Europe right after the wedding, and that's going to be small, we should celebrate before. Sort of a postengagement, prewedding celebration. Is that all right with you, darling?"

Valerie felt Ray's piercing stare on her, but she smiled warmly at David. "I'd love it. Thank you for thinking of it."

"Then I'll be seeing you there, Valerie. You won't mind if I don't call you Mother, will you?"

Valerie saw the amusement that twitched by Ray's mouth but did not look anywhere near his eyes. *He knows,* she thought, horrified. He knows the effect he's had on me, and he's enjoying it!

He put out his hand and she had no choice but to take it. "Best of luck, Valerie. And, Dad," he added, now shaking his father's hand, "congratulations. I think you've made a beautiful choice."

"So, what do you think?" David asked with parental pride after Ray had gone. "Quite a guy, isn't he?"

"Yes, David," Valerie murmured. "Quite a guy."

"You're nuts!"

"I'm telling you I can't go through with it. Now will you please leave me alone!"

"Valerie, have you completely lost it? Is there something seriously mentally deficient about you?" Linda got up from the dining table in their apartment, where the two girls were having dinner. Despite her engagement and David's entreaties for her to move in with him until the wedding, Valerie had insisted on keeping the apartment with Linda. She needed it not only to feel she was not totally dependent on David, but as a haven from the heady newness of his world.

"Look, you don't understand," Valerie said earnestly. "I can't marry a man whose son I lust after."

"You wouldn't know how to lust if your life depended on it," Linda said as she returned to the table with a pot of coffee. "So the guy is gorgeous and got your juices flowing. So what's the big deal. Don't you think David gets a hard-on every now and then when he sees a beautiful woman? Does that mean he can't marry you?"

"You're disgusting."

"That has long been established," Linda said, sitting down. "I asked you a question. Do you think David's *purely physical* response to another woman would be reason for him to call off the engagement?"

"Of course not. But that woman wouldn't be my daughter! Linda, Ray is David's son. His *son*!"

"You're the one making a fuss over that. Can't you think

of him as just another good-looking man? He's not going to be living with you, after all, so there should be no problems."

"He's gorgeous," Valerie said dreamily.

"I know, I know. You've told me that at least six times already. Val, you're not being reasonable. Why can't you think of him as just another man?"

"Because he's not! He's David's son!" Valerie groaned, folding her arms on the table and dropping her head down.

Linda leaned forward and placed her hand gently on Valerie's head. "You know what? I think you've got prewedding jitters, and this kid Ray is just an excuse—"

"He's not a kid!" Valerie said, her head snapping up. "He's a six-foot, dark-haired, gray-eyed gorgeous hunk of man!"

"Oh shit!"

"See, I told you. This is serious."

"No, it's not," Linda insisted. She contemplated Valerie for a moment, then said, "I'm going to ask you something personal. I mean *really* personal."

"Since when do you ask permission?"

"And you don't have to answer. Of course, if you don't, I'll have an answer anyway."

"Please just get on with it. I'm miserable enough without having to deal with your word games."

"Okay, okay. The thing is, well, it's like this: If you and David were, uh, enjoying . . . oh shit, I can't."

"Linda, come on. What is it?"

"It's none of my business."

"That's never stopped you before," Valerie pointed out, losing patience. "Just blurt it out, okay?"

"Right." Linda took a deep breath and plunged in. "If you enjoyed sex with David, would you be getting so worked up over another man?"

"It's because that man is David's son. I told you."

"But pretend for a minute he wasn't. He was just another guy who sent you into orbit."

"Exactly what are you getting at?"

"I told you it was none of my business."

"Linda . . ."

"What I'm trying to so delicately say is—do you and David have a good sex life?"

"Of course we do!"

"Really?" The question was soft with caring, and doubt.

Valerie did not reply. She thought of how David could never seem to get enough of her, and how much she enjoyed the warmth of his touch, the shelter of his arms, and how many times she had told herself that climaxing did not mean everything. She had wondered these past months if David really believed her when she said it was good for her despite her lack of total satisfaction, or if he thought she was inhibited, unwilling to lose control, or shy, embarrassed to lose control. She liked going to bed with David, and she was more than willing to lose control, if only he would give her time to do so. But she could never tell him that, never. It wasn't that important, considering all the other wonderful things he did for her. But then why had she reacted so strongly to his son? Why had her body seemed to screech with need? Was that purely a physical reaction to someone appealing, or was it her body's way of telling her that she was fooling herself with David? All she knew was that Ray Kinnelon had awakened in her a sensual awareness that she had never known she possessed. And she didn't know what to do with it.

"Val? You angry at me?"

"Nope. Just thinking."

"You're not going to break off the engagement, are you?"

Valerie smiled at the girl who was far more than a roommate to her. "Like you said, he won't be living with us."

"Right."

"I'll probably only see him at holidays and stuff."

"Right."

"And he must have girl friends all over the place. Unmarried girl friends."

"Right."

"And I love David."

"Right."

"I'm serious, Linda. I do love him."

"I know you do, kiddo." But will that be enough? she wondered.

Three weeks before the engagement party, two events occurred in Valerie's life, one which affected her immediately, the other to which she gave little thought.

The first was her meeting with Grant Hollander, Ray's second-in-command in the real estate company. He was the scout for all construction sites and the contractor for all building. David had told her that the thirty-year-old was originally from Sacramento, had worked construction during the day to earn his degree at night, and then had moved east permanently a few years ago. Now he was again going to school at night, this time to get his degree in architecture. David had met Grant two years ago at a Knicks–Celtics basketball game at Madison Square Garden. David had season tickets, and Grant had been lucky with the seat he had bought. Their unabashed pleasure in the game and their extensive knowledge of players and plays had gotten them talking during half-time, then David had invited the younger man to join him and the political aspirant who was his guest for a drink afterward. At the time, Ray had been trying to convince his father that real estate—buying it cheap, renovating, then selling high—was the wave of the future; and so David, liking what he saw and heard in Grant, offered him a permanent job with the real estate venture in mind.

Grant was in Los Angeles, at Ray's request, to check certain construction sites at Marina del Rey, an area that was quickly gaining a reputation for attracting high-income singles. Valerie, dressed casually in white jeans and a turquoise sweater, parked her car in the lot outside Don the Beachcomber, the pseudo-Polynesian restaurant where David had asked that she meet them. David had been in town only for a day and was flying back to New York with Grant that evening.

It took a moment for Valerie to adjust her eyes from the blazing glare of the sun to the darkened, oil-lamp illuminated interior of the bar. She spotted David in a corner booth; both men rose as she approached.

"Hello, darling," David said, kissing her cheek. "Valerie, I'd like you to meet Grant Hollander. Grant, this is my fiancée, Valerie Cardell."

"Hi," she said, shaking Grant's hand. "Please sit down," she added, doing the same. "So at last I get to meet the famous Grant Hollander. I'm not sure whom David speaks of more often or with more affection, you or his son."

"The feeling is mutual," Grant said, returning her smile.

"I understand you're studying to be an architect," she said.

"That's right. I'd like to be able to create some of the buildings we construct instead of just making sure they get built correctly."

"Grant's the best there is," David put in warmly. "You've only met Ray once, so you don't know how stubborn and intractable he can be. Guess he takes after me that way," he admitted with a chuckle. "Ray gets a bug in his head and can get all fired up, missing important points. Grant here has a way of seeing every side of an issue and dealing with each one calmly. He's so levelheaded it makes me sick sometimes."

"I didn't know that," Grant said, genuinely surprised.

David nodded, grinning. "No sense of the impulsive about you. In fact, I've never once heard Ray tell me about your choosing the wrong material or construction foreman, going out with the wrong woman, drinking too much. Nope, all self-control and clear thinking, that's you."

"I didn't realize that was a fault," Grant muttered.

"Oh, it's not," David assured him. "It just makes me feel damn inadequate sometimes."

Grant managed a small grin, but Valerie noticed that his clear brown eyes remained flatly serious, almost flinty. She realized that this young man, who was attractive but nowhere near as sexually intriguing as Ray, was feeling rather inadequate himself. Here he was his boss's protégé, treated almost like family, yet the differences in money and power had to be felt keenly, especially when he was put on the spot, as David had just done to him.

"Don't embarrass him, David," she said, smiling. "It's bad enough the man has to work for you, but you drag him off to meet me and then you pick on him. Not fair."

"Meeting you is a pleasure I've been looking forward to," Grant said. He smiled fully at her, and it was like bright sunshine. Warmth diffused the cold eyes and erased all harshness from his face. She decided that she liked his looks, although his appeal was much quieter than that of either of the Kinnelon men. He was not quite as tall as David nor as muscular. There was about him something of the lean, rangy, but solid physique that Mack possessed, the kind of body that would never turn to fat. He had brown hair dusted lightly with a few gray strands, and he wore it shaggy and long, like Ray's. His face was thin, with a long nose that had a bump on the bridge as if from wearing glasses or getting pummeled a few times with a stray basketball. It was a stern, uncompromising face, especially around the mouth. Small lines had already found their way from nose to mouth, and his lips were thin, but his mouth was wide, so that his smile was a warm, inviting gesture. Valerie thought she had never seen quite such intelligent eyes. They were clear and alive, as if in constant pursuit of information. But they revealed little; she could not tell if they judged, if they enjoyed, if they ever warmed with merriment. And yet they were wonderful eyes, she decided, the kind that would always reflect the truth.

The pleasant conversation continued for another half-hour, until it was time for Grant and David to catch their plane. Grant shook her hand. "Congratulations, Valerie. I'll look forward to seeing you at your party and often after that, I hope."

"I hope so too." Then she turned and let David wrap her in his arms. When his lips touched hers, she gave only part of herself up to the kiss. She could not imagine why, but she felt embarrassed in his arms with Grant Hollander looking on. Later, after David had gone, she found herself foolishly thinking that if Ray had been standing there, she would have encouraged David's kiss, as if to erase some of the smug arrogance she was sure Ray felt about himself. But with Grant, she had felt somehow that she was disappointing him.

The second event also occurred in Los Angeles, this one at the Polo Lounge of the Beverly Hills Hotel. It was an unexpected and undesired meeting, but one she knew she had to keep if she did not want to risk David's displeasure.

Two days after David had left Los Angeles, he had called Valerie from New York to tell her that Angela DiChico would be staying at the Beverly Hills Hotel for a week or two; he wanted the two most important women in his life to get together, go shopping, do whatever it was women did. Since Valerie had given notice at Universal last month, her days had been spent going to the beach, shopping, preparing herself for the wedding. She did not need to share these activities with Angela, nor did she want to.

As had happened often with Linda, whenever Angela was in New York she had joined Valerie and David for drinks or dinner. Despite his affection for the woman, Valerie was unable to warm to her. She thought the older woman a dilettante, jetting from New York to Marbella, to Paris, to Rome, to wherever the good times were. Both David and Linda had patiently explained that Angela had more money than she could spend in a lifetime, and what she enjoyed was spending it, especially on the clothes of new fashion designers whose talents she believed in. To someone of Valerie's background, that kind of aimlessness was not easy to abide. And now she had to be nice to her without David around to help.

Valerie was already seated in the outdoor patio, having a Bloody Mary, when she heard Angela's husky laughter before she saw her.

"Valerie dear, I'm sorry to have kept you waiting," Angela said, pecking Valerie's cheek before sitting down. "I haven't been here in ages, and there were some people I had to stop and say hello to. Don't you love the patio at lunch? It's by far my favorite place in all of Beverly Hills—for lunch, that is. You're looking radiant, my dear. I'm so glad you've let your hair grow out. It was really too mannish the other way. A Bloody Mary for me, too." It was all said in one breathless rush.

Valerie could not help smiling. Whatever her wastrel lifestyle, Angela had energy for an army. And she was the most impeccably groomed woman Valerie had ever seen; even when she was wearing something outrageous or bizarre, she carried it off with a panache that was enviable. Today she had on a black-and-white houndstooth-check suit that Valerie had seen in the current issue of *Vogue:* it was an original Yves Saint Laurent. Her hair, despite her claim that Valerie's short hair had been mannish, was cut in the latest Vidal Sassoon sensation, one section geometrically sliced across one eye, the other side not covering even the top of her ear. Her eyes were rimmed in black, and her lips were painted the same cerise as her fingernails. She was wearing black hose and red

T-strap shoes with three-inch black heels. Valerie felt utterly dowdy in her all-purpose blue Courrèges.

"Angela, you're looking well," she said.

"I feel well, dear. A week in Paris always does that for me. Parisians are a crotchety bunch of misanthropes, but oh, their city. And they do have the most divine taste." She smiled. "And how are you? And Linda?"

"We're both fine. Of course, Linda's busy moaning and groaning about losing a roommate, and not listening when I tell her she's gaining a father-in-law."

"I understand you've met Ray. And Grant."

There was a slight edge to the way Angela said that, without her usual casualness, that struck Valerie as being somewhat out-of-place. Without knowing exactly why, she felt wary, and wondered if there was something more to this luncheon than mere friendliness.

"Yes," she answered carefully.

"Well, what do you think?" Angela prodded, smiling irresistibly at the waiter as he brought her drink.

"I'm not sure I understand your question," Valerie said stiffly.

"What's your opinion of David's boys? I should think the question was fairly obvious."

"Really, Angela, I only met them briefly, hardly enough time to form an opinion."

"My dear girl," Angela said, "you're not what I would call stupid. Even in a short meeting you made some observations, some judgments. I'd like to hear them."

Valerie's anger was beginning to surface as Angela's boldness made her feel increasingly uncomfortable. "Why?"

Angela's elegantly clad shoulders lifted in a gesture of female innocence. "Oh, because I'm curious, of course. Two such young, handsome men like Ray and Grant. I simply want to know what you thought of them—woman to woman, so to speak."

Valerie suddenly realized that Angela had been sent on a fishing expedition by David. Her so-called female curiosity had absolutely nothing to do with the question. David, not wanting to pressure Valerie into telling him what she thought of Ray and Grant, had sent an emissary. Valerie understood how important it was to David that she like the men who were important to him, but she felt it was particularly insensitive and selfish of him to have sent the one person about whom she had openly expressed her dislike.

"Angela, really," she said now, her stewardess smile pasted on, "I'm not as astute as you. It would be impossible for me to have any opinion of them. They seemed nice. Does that satisfy you?"

Angela tapped one lacquered nail against her glass and stared at Valerie thoughtfully. "You don't like me, do you?"

"Of course I like you," Valerie lied. "Whatever gave you the idea I don't?"

"I'm not sure whether it's my history with David that's put you off, or the fact that I'm the only one who doesn't fully endorse this December-May union and you somehow sense that, although I thought I had been rather good at hiding it."

Any pretense of politeness or attempt to control her resentment was tossed aside. Valerie's dark eyes glittered with indignation. "It's neither," she said. "I don't like you because you're one of the most self-centered, self-absorbed women I've ever met."

"You sound envious, dear," Angela said dryly.

"Envious! The only thing I feel is pity that with all you have, you can waste it so casually."

"I think the word you're looking for to describe me is *profligate*. But then, I imagine in your circle you wouldn't have heard it before."

"You're right," Valerie snapped. "Where I come from, we only understand words like *work* and *struggle* and *save*. My family didn't believe in waste and excess because we never had enough excess to waste."

"My, my, touchy, aren't we?" Angela said with a cold chuckle.

"No, Angela, not touchy, just damned angry that you think you have any right to sit there and criticize me."

"I have every right!" Angela hissed, head and neck straining forward so that Valerie was held captive by the fire in her black eyes. "David is my friend, a very close and important friend, and I don't want to see him used and hurt."

"Now who's jealous," Valerie muttered.

"Oh, you foolish child. Do you really believe that? No, you can't be *that* unsophisticated."

Valerie met her glare with an equally fierce one, and waited.

"I love David and I want him to be happy. You're not from his world, and you're over twenty years younger than he. You don't belong together, Valerie, it's as simple as that. David Kinnelon is a forty-five-year-old man of the world, and you're a twenty-one-year-old stewardess from a farm town. Don't give me any crap about love, either," Angela finished harshly, "because I'm not as gullible as David. I don't believe it."

Valerie sat there for several moments while the pounding of her heart slowed. Rage and shock kept her speechless. Anything she might have managed to say would have been met with total disbelief anyway, she realized. This woman who was so intent on looking out for David's interests did not trust her; worse, she had condemned Valerie without a trial. Angela DiChico had decided that she was a self-serving fortune hunter. Well, so be it, Valerie thought. She'd be damned if she would defend herself to a woman like her.

"Don't try to stop this wedding," Valerie said softly as she took her pink cloth napkin from her lap and placed it on the table. "David would never believe you anyway."

Angela sat back in her wrought-iron chair and gazed thoughtfully at Valerie as she rose to leave. "Prove me wrong," she said. "For David's sake, I want you to prove me wrong."

Chapter 12

More than three hundred guests celebrated at David and Valerie's prenuptial party, held on the roof of the St. Regis Hotel. It was a night of dazzling glory for Valerie, who swept through the evening feeling like Cinderella at her ball. Not even Angela's brittlely false friendliness could dull the sparkle of her pleasure.

In the weeks that had followed their run-in, both women

had maintained a patina of courtesy, but their hostility lay close to the surface like a lesion ready to reopen. Whenever David spoke of Angela, Valerie pretended an equal enthusiasm for her, and the few times the three of them had been together, both women skillfully pretended that nothing was amiss. If Valerie was unhappy about anything during these weeks, it was having to hold to that hypocrisy. That, and being without her family. But she and David had agreed on a small, civil ceremony in his home, and knowing how impossibly costly the trip would be for her family, she had agreed to his wishes. The only guests would be Ray, Linda, Grant, and Angela.

Billy had sent a beautiful wedding gift of eight Rosenthal crystal champagne flutes. From the rest of her family, nothing, except a brief, cold note of congratulations from Alice. Valerie wondered from time to time if perhaps she did romanticize them too much, but then she dismissed the thought. They were what they were, and she had no right to expect more. David and Mack each supplied more than enough love and security.

Dear Mack, she thought with a sigh as she sat back on the couch in the living room, where she had been listening to music. How she missed him. Over the years there had always been letters and calls, but he had never been able to arrange to meet her. In her heart, though, she knew his wisdom and warmth and good wishes would be as much a part of her wedding as if he were there.

The vast expanse of David's living room had been transformed into a cloud of white flowers, everything from roses to carnations, tulips to mums. One of Angela's friends, an occasional supper-club pianist, had volunteered to provide the music on David's white baby grand Steinway. Bottles of LaFitte-Rothschild champagne '37 were chilling, and the hors d'oeuvres, catered by William Poll, included everything from smoked trout to imported Iranian caviar. Only moments before, an hysterical Linda had left the bride in the master bedroom to finish dressing.

Valerie was wearing a white *peau de soie* Lanvin suit with lapels of hand-sewn seed pearls. An Alençon lace short veil attached to a seed pearl cloche curved around her dark head. It was an outfit that spoke of style and taste...and great expense.

At twelve forty-five, the pianist was seated, and David stood proudly in his morning suit before Judge Connelly, who was officiating; Angela, Linda, Grant, and Ray were several feet back. David's son was best man, Linda maid of honor. With a slight nod from Angela, the pianist began to play a selection from Vivaldi's *Four Seasons*, a choice that David had suggested and Valerie had enthusiastically endorsed.

The strains of the music filled the room. Slowly, Valerie descended the stairs, clutching a bouquet of white lilies; her stomach was knotted, and a strange lightheadedness made her dizzy. She kept her eyes on the judge's face until she felt sure she would reach the bottom step without tripping. Then she looked directly at David, and a small smile touched her mouth and shone from her eyes like light refracting off crystal. The radiance of her beauty touched each person in the room. Tears welled in Linda's eyes, tears of joy and love. A frown flickered briefly on Angela's brow, and the fleeting thought came to her that never had youth been more beautiful nor had she ever missed her own more. Grant Hollander saw perfection in the flawless body, the creamy skin only partially hidden by the veil, the thick black hair. He saw perfection and was intimidated by it. Ray Kinnelon shared a very private, very masculine look with his father, a look that telegraphed admiration and envy. And David Kinnelon felt his chest swell and his throat constrict with an almost painful surge of pride and love. The young woman walking toward him so regally was about to become his wife. As she took her place by his side and they both turned to the judge, he found himself thinking the most humble thought of his life: whatever happiness he might bring to her, it could be only a mere fraction of what she had given him just by permitting him to know her.

The wedding of David Kinnelon and Valerie Cardell went off smoothly. Even the bride's aim was perfect: the bouquet fell into Linda's hands. A chauffeured, white stretch limousine, Grant's gift to the couple, took them to the airport. From there they flew to the south of France for a two-week honeymoon.

Even though it was off-season, there were enough people David knew in Cannes, Monte Carlo, Juan-les-Pins, Cap d'Antibes, and St. Tropez to fill the Kinnelons' days and nights with luncheons, dinners, and parties. They sunbathed and drove around in their rented Peugeot, ate and drank, gambled and shopped, and for two weeks they each, together and privately, believed they had found paradise.

Only sex marred the perfection of Valerie's honeymoon. She did not try to avoid it, and she still would not fake her pleasure in it. She was willing to accept it the way it was, but that did not prevent her from experiencing an occasional feeling of disappointment, or having an unexpected fantasy about what these glorious two weeks along the romantic Riviera would have been like with someone whose touch she hungered for and who could fulfill that desire and leave her wanting more. She loved David completely; the two weeks with him convinced her of that. His generosity, the way he taught her about foods and wines, the history of the towns; how he always treated her with deference and respect in front of his friends. He was good to her in every way, and she knew how much he loved her. But when there was nothing left for him to teach her, would she still be willing to dismiss her needs, still be willing to accept a halfway measure of physical pleasure? She asked herself that question only once during their honeymoon. They had made love that afternoon. When David fell asleep afterward, she rose and stood by the french windows of their suite at the Carleton Hotel in Cannes overlooking the Mediterranean. Rain pelted the glass, and La Croisette was almost deserted; the giant leaves of the palm trees waved frantically in the gusty wind. She turned to stare at her husband, sleeping peacefully, his face softer in repose, the lines of age and ambition smoothed away. Her guilt was so fierce that she shuddered and had to wrap her arms around herself to keep the chill of her conscience from overpowering her. She got back into bed and put her arm around David, and when she finally fell asleep, the question was buried far back in her mind, where she would not have to deal with the answer.

After six months of marriage, another dissatisfaction created a chink in the perfect veneer of Valerie's life, and this one could not be so easily buried.

Ever since they had returned from Europe, her life had been a whirlwind of parties in both New York and Los Angeles. There were premieres, gallery openings, Broadway shows; private parties for foreign businessmen and small dinners for domestic luminaries. At first she had loved every social minute, loved getting dressed each day to have lunch with the wives of the men David knew, but that had palled even more rapidly than the nightly social circuit. She was tolerated by these women, and patronized. They talked around her, dropped the names of people and places that were only references in a newspaper to her. And at night it was a performance as David's adjunct that was played. She began to feel like an ornament, a valuable possession to be dressed up for special occasions so that he could show off what he had acquired.

She tried to fight her feeling of dissatisfaction, but it would not go away. She knew she could never discuss it with David; he would be hurt and confused, and then he would blame it on the difference in age between her and his friends. She knew her youth had nothing to do with her increasing restlessness and resentment. She also realized that while her guilt over these emotions was enough to stifle them for the moment, it would not always be so.

Chapter 13

"All set?" David asked as Valerie came downstairs. Suitcases, a cosmetic case, and a four-suiter, all elegant Mark Cross pieces, waited at the foot of the stairs. She and David were meeting Grant at LaGuardia Airport, the three of them off on a puddle-hopping trip to potential construction sites.

"I'm so excited I can't stand it," Valerie said. "You're finally going to meet Alice and Mack. I can't believe it!"

"Do you think she'll like the wedding gift we got her?"

"Who wouldn't like Baccarat stemware for twelve!" She laughed. "Believe me, it's much more than she got for her first wedding."

Two months ago, almost on the day of Valerie's six-month anniversary, she had received a postcard from her sister postmarked Bermuda. The message had been: "On my honeymoon." Valerie had called her mother and learned that Alice had married Richard Appleton, the owner of an advertising agency. They would be living in Lake Forest, one of Chicago's "wealthiest" suburbs, according to Edith. Valerie had been as surprised by her sister's sudden marriage as she had been by her divorce from Teddy; Alice had never given her any indication of either event.

When David had told her about this trip, she had invited herself along and suggested a stopover in Chicago. Fortunately, Mack had a trade show scheduled there at the same time. It would be the reunion Valerie had long dreamed about.

"A hotel in Washington?"

David and Grant exchanged sheepish looks. They were having dinner at the Fairmont Hotel in New Orleans, the third stop on their trip. For the past three days, Valerie had listened attentively as the two men discussed possible uses for land they were considering buying in Detroit, Dallas, and now New Orleans. Gradually she had come to be impressed by Grant's controlled enthusiasm for a project, his way of showing David all sides of an issue, and his quiet, wry sense of humor, which enabled him to treat David with a certain irreverent affection. She was enjoying herself tremendously away from the New York scene, and grateful that it was Grant who accompanied them, not Ray. She had seen David's son on a few social occasions in the past eight months, and invariably he had been with a beauty. His behavior toward Valerie was always charming, polite, and totally correct. Her reaction to him never changed: her senses reeled every time she saw him.

"What in the world do you two want a hotel for?" she asked. "I thought you were into shopping centers and renovating apartment buildings."

"We are," Grant said. "The Dallas project will be a

revolutionary one for us. It's going to be the first upscale shopping center."

Grant grinned, and Valerie was fascinated by the way life sparkled from what she had first thought were cold and unrevealing eyes. Real estate and building thrilled this man, and she found herself warming to him. The intensity of his commitment to his work animated him, making her aware of how handsome he was.

"We're thinking of calling it Plaza d'Oro—the Plaza of Gold," Grant said, "and renting out the space to the top retailers across the country—Saks, Bergdorf's, I. Magnin's. Hopefully, we'll have a branch of Neiman-Marcus there too, to really capture the Dallas money crowd. Architecturally," he went on, his brown eyes shining with his vision of the future, "it's going to be the sleekest, most un-shopping-center center in the world. And I want restaurants there too. Not the fast-food places, but a good French restaurant, elegant and expensive." He glanced at David. "You're really going to let us go ahead with this?"

David grinned and shrugged. "What choice do I have? Ray hasn't spoken about anything else for weeks, and now that you've got your degree, I figure it's time you put it to some practical use." He laughed. "Ray's impossible sometimes. He tells me it's just some acreage near Dallas. He never told me what you two had planned for it."

"It sounds wonderful," Valerie said, smiling warmly at Grant. "Now what's this about a hotel in Washington?"

"I was thinking that with office complexes, shopping centers, and apartments, the builder's money can be tied up for a long time—until the return on the investment comes in by way of renting out or selling the space," David explained. "Interest rates are moderate now, but that could change at any time, and I was looking for something that would have a quicker, more secure return on my investment."

"Like a hotel," Valerie said.

"Exactly. If it's done correctly—and, more important, if it's in the right location—you get money coming in immediately. A hotel in Washington, D.C., where there are tourists as well as dignitaries, foreign and domestic, on big fat expense accounts, seemed a natural."

"For someone who thought real estate was just a plot of

land with a tract house on it, David has learned quickly."
Grant said.

Valerie smiled proudly at her husband. "I think it's fantastic. Tell me more."

"Grant's going to design it, so let him tell you."

"Well, it's going to be all glass," Grant said, "so that every room will have a view of the various monuments. It's going to be the last word in luxury, with everything from individual terrycloth guest robes to fully stocked bars for the suites. And I've been considering making the top ten floors co-op apartments."

"Since when?" David asked, surprised.

Grant smiled. "Well, I haven't really planned it all through yet, but what do you think?"

"Does Ray know about this?" David asked, ignoring Grant's question.

"Uh, no."

David said nothing for a moment as he looked at his protégé thoughtfully. "It's a great idea, Grant. Go with it."

"You mean it?" the younger man said with undisguised eagerness, and Valerie smiled at the almost childlike excitement lighting up his face.

"I mean it. The important thing is the hotel management team. Let's do it right—"

"—Or not at all," Grant finished for him, laughing. "Boy, wait till Ray hears about this. You won't be sorry, David, it's going to be the most fantastic—"

"And expensive," David interjected dryly.

"Listen, you two moguls," Valerie said. "We've got a nine-o'clock flight out of here tomorrow and I'd like a few hours' sleep."

"Val's right," David said, leaning back and running his hand through his thick, dark hair. "I'm kinda beat myself. You're off to Los Angeles, aren't you, Grant, to check out that office complex in the San Fernando Valley?"

"I was, but now with your okay on the hotel deal, I'd better head home. Ray'll need to get started working out the purchase details. We can't be the only smart developers around, so we've got to move fast."

"Then this is good-bye until we're back in New York
Valerie said.

Grant looked at her, and Valerie thought she saw the most intense flash of warmth directed at her, but then the moment passed, the brown eyes veiled once again.

"It's been wonderful traveling with you, Grant," she said. "I've learned a lot."

"Don't tell me we've got another budding real estate tycoon in the family," David joked.

"Not yet." Valerie laughed, finding the idea equally amusing.

David had made reservations for five for dinner in the Cape Cod Room of the Drake Hotel in Chicago. The first to arrive was Mack, and as he entered, Valerie jumped from her seat, rushing to meet him in an embrace that was so unrestrained it brought smiles to several of the sedate diners observing them.

"It's been too damn long," Mack said, holding her around the waist as they made their way back to the table. "And you're even more beautiful than I imagined you'd be."

Valerie reached up to give him another kiss, then turned, beaming, to David, who had risen, hand extended. "At last," he said.

Mack shook David's hand and smiled warmly at him. "I know. I was beginning to think you weren't real either."

Drinks were ordered, but before they could be served, Alice and her new husband arrived. Valerie stood up, arms opened wide to hug her sister, who she thought looked lovelier than ever. In the four years since they had last seen each other, Alice's storybook features had settled into a certain sharp angularity, but they became her, Valerie decided. The blue eyes were still that pure, remarkable cerulean; the skin pale and creamy; the hair perhaps just a shade lighter than the natural blonde she remembered. Alice was more beautiful now, more enchantingly feminine.

Valerie did not get a chance to hug her sister because Alice did not get close enough. Instead, she pecked Valerie lightly on the cheek, her attention focused totally on David. Valerie's smile slowly retreated, and her hands fell back to her sides. "Alice, you look wonderful," she said. "It's been so many years."

"Has it?" Alice turned to her husband. "Richard, this is

my sister. And this is Mack Landry, one of Valerie's closest friends. How are you, Mack?"

"Alice, good to see you."

David glanced at Mack not missing the cold politeness in his voice.

"I'm David Kinnelon," he said then, offering his hand to Richard Appleton and to Alice. "It's a pleasure meeting you, Alice. Val has been so excited about this trip, seeing you and Mack again. And now I can understand why. Please, let's sit down."

Two drinks later, Alice was leaning toward David, smiling attentively at him, ignoring Valerie, Mack, and her husband.

"You mean she never told you about when she ran away from home?" Alice laughed lightly. "Oh, it was just terrible. Papa had the police after her." She turned to Valerie. "Remember that, Val, when you ran away to Eddington and Papa had to—"

"Alice, I don't—"

"Really, David, you should have seen her then. Poor little Val, so miserable and lonely she had to run away. You can imagine how difficult it was on our parents."

"Alice . . ."

"Now, Mack, come on. You know a new husband loves to hear about what his wife was like as a child. Didn't *you*, Dickie?" she asked, rubbing the back of her fingers along her husband's cheek. He jerked his head away, smiling indulgently but saying nothing.

"Besides, Mack," Alice went on, "I should think David would want to know all about you and Val. I swear, David, for a while there our father thought Mack and Val . . . well, you can just imagine what he thought. Every time Val went to the big house, he just about had conniptions, even though she wasn't more than a maid, but still, his imag—"

"Alice!"

"My goodness, what's wrong, Mack? It's all true, isn't it?" she said, blue eyes wide with innocence. "Before you two got so, well, I guess *close* is the right word, Val did clean and polish and dust and stuff, and you did pay her for that."

"Oh, Alice, come on!"

"It's okay, Mack," Valerie said softly. "Perhaps we should

order now." She looked hopefully at David, who only nodded, his mind registering each nuance that was being exchanged.

Alice placed her hand on David's arm. "I'd love one more drink." As an afterthought, she remembered her husband and turned to him. "You don't mind, sweetie, do you?"

"Well, I am kind of hungry," Richard said, feeling the strain as much as the others did, and not understanding it.

Alice faced David, her eyes holding his, using the look that had gotten her any male she had ever wanted. "Please?"

"Alice is right, David," Valerie said with feigned enthusiasm and a frail smile. "This is a celebration dinner and we should drink and have a good time. After all, two marriages and a reunion are pretty special. Isn't that right, Mack?" The desperation in her voice made David wince. He would do as she wanted now, he thought, and learn what was going on later.

During the next round of drinks, Alice's voice grew louder, her hand on David's arm more lingering, and her conversation more disparaging of her sister: how glad her family had been when Valerie went to stewardess school, since they had thought she might end up a waitress all her life; how Valerie had had trouble in school; how Valerie used to hide and read all the time because she couldn't get along with anyone; how Valerie had had to wear her hand-me-downs. The more Alice talked, the quieter Valerie got. The burning pain in her chest made it impossible for her to do more than nibble when the seafood dinner was finally served. She tried to talk with Mack and to get to know Alice's husband, but the evening had become a disaster. She wasn't angry at Alice. It was impossible to be angry with her. Hadn't Valerie married a wonderful, famous, wealthy, powerful man? Wasn't she leading the life that Alice had dreamed of for herself? So her sister was jealous; Valerie understood that and forgave her mean-spirited behavior. Still, David would never understand; and Mack, she knew, was doing a slow boil.

At last coffee was over and David asked for the check, not bothering to extend his usual invitation for a brandy. Valerie sensed that this dinner had been difficult and confusing for him, and he wanted it over as much as she did.

"This has been a most interesting evening," David said, looking from Richard Appleton to Mack, and not glancing at

Alice. "Mack, we'll be in town another day; maybe you and I could meet tomorrow and go over those plans we were talking about earlier." It was a totally impulsive lie, and Valerie stared at him, her surprise obvious. There had been no discussion between them. What was David doing? But Mack nodded with complete understanding, and then he reached over to squeeze Valerie's hands, as if to say that everything would be all right.

"Good idea, David. Say lunch? How about a steak at Blackhawks?"

David nodded, gratitude in his eyes. He would find out exactly what was going on from the one person he instinctively trusted to tell him the truth.

In the lobby, Alice hugged her sister with more warmth than she had shown during dinner. "Want to go shopping tomorrow?" she asked. Valerie felt a tremendous surge of relief; everything was just as she had thought. Her sister had been jealous and that had triggered her nastiness. Now she wanted to make it up to her.

"Valerie, maybe you'd like to visit the trade show?" Mack offered, feeling David's warning gaze on him.

"To see farm machinery?" She laughed. "No thanks. Shopping with Alice will be fun." She kissed her sister's husband lightly on the cheek, then hugged Mack. "I've missed you so," she whispered.

"He's a good man, Val," Mack said in an equally low voice.

"I know." Then she pulled away and smiled brightly at him and her husband. "I don't want you two saying anything bad about me at lunch tomorrow, understand?" she teased.

"I think that's already been taken care of," David muttered, frowning.

Alice heard. "Oh, dear me, I hope you didn't think I was deliberately being unkind about Valerie," she said in a rush, glancing at the three men with a frown of self-reproach. "I thought you would all enjoy those little stories. I mean, Valerie has come so far since those days."

"Alice, I think we understand," her husband said. "Thank you, David. It was wonderful meeting all of you." With his hand firmly on his wife's elbow, he steered her out of the hotel.

The Kinnelons said nothing until they were in bed. David waited until Valerie had nestled against his outstretched arm before saying, "Okay, now what the hell is the matter with your sister?"

Valerie's heartbeat accelerated with anxiety. She felt the color drain from her face, felt the tips of her fingers suddenly go cold. She had been dreading this, hoping that it wouldn't happen, knowing that it would.

"What do you mean?"

"You know exactly what I mean. That bitch hates you."

Valerie moved away from the comfort of his arm. "Don't be ridiculous. I'll admit there was a little sibling rivalry showing tonight, but—"

"Sibling rivalry! Come on, Val, don't be deliberately obtuse."

"David, you're making a big deal out of nothing and I'm tired. By the way, what's this sudden desire to meet with Mack?"

"This sudden desire, as you put it, came as a result of watching you and your sister. I'm counting on him to tell me what my own wife has never thought to speak to me about: her life before she met me, her family, and this damned curious relationship with her sister."

"There's nothing to tell," she said stiffly.

"Fine. Then tell me about nothing," David insisted, frustration bringing an edge to his voice.

"I want to go to sleep."

David knew better than to force a confrontation. Gently he put his hand on her shoulder, and her hand came up to hold it in a tight clasp. If Valerie saw her sister as guilty only of sibling rivalry instead of the treachery he had witnessed tonight, then he would have to shield her from the worst kind of enemy, the one she did not recognize.

"Thanks for picking up so quickly last night," David said the next day when he and Mack were seated at Blackhawks, a steakhouse named for the Chicago hockey team.

"Alice really had her claws out," Mack said. "I could see you were confused. Obviously, Valerie hasn't been very forthcoming about her family."

"That's an understatement."

"You've got to keep Valerie away from her sister," Mack began. "She's dangerous."

David's gray eyes became flinty with wariness. "In what way?"

"You saw it for yourself, didn't you? You saw how that little bitch operates. Christ, how many times when they were growing up I wanted to slap her silly." Mack shook his head at the recollection. "Little Miss Innocence. Alice in Wonderland they used to call her because she was such a good little girl." He snorted derisively. "That little girl was screwing her brains out in the backs of trucks when she was thirteen. That little girl could lie so smoothly that you'd end up believing her even when you had evidence that she was full of shit."

Mack took a deep swallow of his drink, so caught up in the memories that he was oblivious to the strange expression on David's face, an expression of such loathing that his skin was flushed, and he was clenching his teeth so hard that a muscle began to twitch in his jaw. He was grasping his glass of Scotch with both hands, his fingernails white with the pressure.

"That little girl tricked the man who wanted to marry Valerie into marrying her," Mack then told him.

"What!"

"Oh, I'm glad she didn't marry him, believe me, but the truth is that Alice tricked Teddy Chambers into marrying her."

"I think you'd better explain everything, Mack. From the beginning."

Two hours later, David was in his suite, waiting for his wife to return. He had canceled three meetings he had scheduled for the afternoon. Valerie took precedence over everything; in truth, he wouldn't have been able to concentrate on anything had he kept those appointments. He had listened, rapt, to a remarkable story, and he knew that somehow he had to share the truth with his wife. It would be difficult; Mack had explained how very difficult. Valerie had never been able to reconcile betrayal with any member of her family. Slight jealousy, occasional meanness, an act of selfishness once or twice, yes, these she would acknowledge, but true enmity? treachery? deliberate harm? Never. A family, flawed as it might be, was something inviolate to her. When it came to her sister, she was blind. It was up to David to show her the truth.

He heard the key turn in the lock, and he straightened in his chair. He had to be careful, had to handle this right. . . .

"Hi, darling," Valerie said, dropping several packages from Marshall Field and Carson Pirie Scott on the carpet, and going over to give him a kiss. "Did you have a nice lunch with Mack?"

"Sit down, Val. I want to talk to you."

"Sounds important." She felt a sudden queasiness. "Don't you want to hear about what a nice time I had with Alice?" she asked, sitting down in the brocade club chair that was separated from his by a small Queen Anne table.

"I can see by the packages that you had a good time."

"It was wonderful. We caught up on the past four years, and she told me about her move to Chicago. It was just great. And we had lunch at this charming restaurant at Marshall Field. Really, here we were, two ladies out on the town and—" She knew she was babbling, and stopped, but she dreaded hearing what David had to say. She had a feeling that it would be a continuation of the conversation he had started last night, and she did not want to deal with Alice's faults. Hadn't the pleasure of the past few hours mitigated them all?

"Val, I want to tell you a few things, and then you decide if you want to have anything more to do with your sister."

"David, I don't want to discuss this," she said, getting to her feet but not knowing where to go.

"Please sit down, Val. At least give me the courtesy of hearing me out."

Slowly she sat back down, her eyes riveted on a distant point in the room. David, in a quiet, steady voice, repeated to her what Mack had told him. He told her how, before Alice had left Galesville for Chicago but after it had become evident to everyone in town that her marriage to Teddy was a farce, she had started spreading the rumor that Valerie was responsible for the trouble in her marriage, that she had been in touch with Teddy, saying she had never stopped loving him, and that Teddy had told Alice he wanted a divorce so he could be with Valerie.

He repeated to her how Alice had told everyone that it

had been her idea to send Valerie to stew school because Valerie's notoriety with men, her promiscuity, was proving such an embarrassment to her family.

He told her of Alice's lies to Teddy Chambers; how she had manipulated and maneuvered him into marrying her. He had learned the truth only after a bitter and cruel fight with Alice during which she had blurted it all out.

The hotel room crackled with the sordid stories David related, much as he had crackled with rage earlier when hearing them from Mack. Finished, he sat forward in his chair, hands resting on his knees, his face a taut mask of concern for his wife. Valerie said nothing, continuing to stare straight ahead, without so much as blinking.

Finally, David went to her. He crouched down and put a hand on her thigh. "Val?" he said softly. "Honey, you okay?" Still she said nothing. "I'm sorry, Valerie, but I felt you had to know. I don't want you to have anything more to do with her. She's dangerous. She only wants to hurt you, and I swear," he said fiercely, "I'll stop at nothing if anyone tries to hurt you."

Carefully, Valerie lifted David's hand and started to rise; he was forced to do the same. She looked at him fully for the first time since he had begun speaking.

"I don't believe you," she said in a pleasant conversational tone, as if discussing where to have dinner. "I think you and Mack, as men, simply do not understand the kind of relationship that exists between women, especially sisters, and I would prefer you never to discuss this subject with me again."

David was thunderstruck. "You can't mean that!"

"Oh, but I do."

"Val, don't do this to yourself. If you don't believe me, then you have to believe Mack."

"It's not a question of belief or disbelief," she continued, edging toward the door. "I resent you two having discussed me and my sister, and I resent you thinking you have a right to tell me who I can and cannot see. You're my husband, not my keeper."

"But it's for your own good," David protested.

"More damage has been done for the sake of someone's

good. No, David, I will not tolerate any more of this. Is that understood?"

"No, dammit, it is not!" David bellowed. "How can you stand there and defend that bitch? How can you dare to refuse to protect yourself! Don't look so appalled, Valerie. *Protection* is exactly the right word, from the most vicious, evil enemy you—"

"Stop it! Stop it!" she shrieked, and then she fled. The sound of the door slamming shut reverberated in David's ears like cannon fire.

Valerie stood waiting for the elevator, willing her heart to calm, believing that if it did not stop its ferociously hard thudding it would burst through her chest. When she got to the lobby, she headed for the bank of pay telephones, fumbling in her jacket pocket for change. It took her two attempts to dial her sister's number; her fingers were so clammy and cold that they could barely move. Alice picked up on the third ring, but Valerie had to swallow twice before being able to respond. She opened the door of the telephone booth to get air. A fine line of sweat erupted above her upper lip.

"Alice?"

"Val, is that you? You sound so funny."

"Alice, did you ever tell Teddy Chambers that I had an abortion?"

"What!" Valerie heard the incredulity, and something more, something slightly forced.

"Please, Alice, I need to know the truth. Did you ever tell Teddy that I had had an abortion, that I had sex . . . sexual problems?" She closed her eyes and leaned against the back of the telephone booth. The receiver felt like a part of her ear, so tightly was she holding it.

"Val, I don't understand what's gotten into you. We just spent a lovely time together and it's not forty minutes later and you're calling me with these ridiculous questions. What's going on?"

"Answer me. Did you or did you not talk to Teddy about me?"

"Well, yes, but where in the world did you get the idea it was about sex? You and sex! That's unbelievable. Don't you remember how prudish you were?"

"What did you say to him?" Valerie asked dully.

"I told him how much you hated Galesville and how you had been dreaming about leaving ever since you were a little girl and that I didn't think even he could get you to stay."

"Why? Why did you have to tell him that?"

"Oh, Val, come on. Who knows why. We were probably working late one night and just got to talking. You know how these things happen."

"And did you get to talking the night he stood me up for the Christmas party?"

"Of course not, this happened long before that. In fact, I thought about it later and I really felt guilty. I mean I felt kind of responsible because if I hadn't said anything to him about you hating Galesville so, he might not have stood you up. I guess he was real hurt by it and didn't know how to deal with it."

"*He* was hurt," Valerie repeated, mindlessly spewing back what she was fed.

"Val, you can't blame him. He really cared for you, and when he thought that might not be enough for you, well, that had to come as a shock. You can understand, can't you?" Her voice was like spun sugar—soft and smooth and flawlessly innocent.

Valerie ran her tongue over lips that felt cracked and caked. "One more question, Alice," she said. "It's not true that you told people you were responsible for me going to stew school, is it?"

Alice laughed; the sound scratched against Valerie's ear. "Of course not! Where did you get that idea? Everyone in town knew that Mack was behind it. In fact, I had my hands full after you left because of it."

"What do you mean?"

"The rumors were flying for months. Everyone just kind of assumed that Mack had sent you off because either you were pregnant or because it was getting too hot and heavy between the two of you."

"Oh dear Lord," Valerie whispered, nausea washing over her. To think that she and Mack... it was the ugliest, sickest...

"Of course I set them all straight, but it was tough for a while. Why do you ask such a silly thing?"

"I've got to go, Alice. I'm sorry I bothered you."

"Stay in touch, Val. Don't forget you promised me one of those fancy New York parties."

"Of course. Anytime. 'Bye."

David said nothing further to his wife about Alice, and Valerie told him nothing of her conversation. But for hours, and then days, and finally weeks afterward, she would read a line in a book, hear some dialogue on a television show, catch a few words in a conversation, and she would shudder and her stomach would contract. The reference would be either directly or obliquely about sisters; the very word had come to take on an ominous meaning for her. If Alice was guilty only of what she had admitted, then they had been youthful mistakes, forgivable if not totally understandable. If Alice was guilty of what Mack had told David, they had been deliberate, intentional acts of maliciousness, neither understandable nor forgivable. Valerie could not bring herself to acknowledge the truth. She knew, though, and that was why she would shudder and her stomach would contract. She knew.

BOOK III

Chapter 14

Tears streamed down Valerie's face, blending with the snowflakes melting on her cheeks. Her hair was covered in a black mink shako cap that matched her black mink coat, but a chill ran through her as if she were standing naked in the grim December air.

The tears that fell as the last of the earth was shoveled over her father's grave were for the man she had never known, the father he might have been had circumstances been different. They were for all the times she had needed to run to him for comfort, and could not; all the times she had been forced to run from him. They were for all he had missed in life, and all he had never understood.

She watched motionlessly as Mack and her mother placed flowers on the fresh mound. No one else from the family was there, she thought sadly. Only his wife, and the one daughter who had made his life even more of a hell. Ned had been dead eight months now, blown to bits by a land mine in the Mekong Delta. He had moved to Indianapolis, married, separated, enlisted, and died all in a few short years, a stranger to her. Billy had refused to come to his father's funeral, and Alice had been unable to attend. Twice in the past year she had continued the pattern set when she was sixteen: reckless driving. The first time, she had demolished a brand-new car, miraculously escaping with only a few scratches. The second time, a week ago, she had not been so lucky. She had been driving her husband to the airport early in the morning in a dense fog, and had missed seeing another car turning. She had been going too fast and had crashed head-on, resulting in a broken arm and a dislocated shoulder; the other driver walked away unscathed.

So now, only a few days before Christmas 1968, Eli Cardell was put to rest, with few of the family for whom he had worked so long and hard there to pay their respects.

"Come on, Mack, jus' one more drink. What's a wake without gettin' drunk. Eli would want us to have a few for him."

David glanced at Val as she poured her mother another drink, her fourth straight Scotch since they had returned to Mack's house after the funeral. David did not like Edith Cardell, and he had not liked Eli either, but he had not been willing to let Valerie come back here alone. Perhaps if Billy had planned to attend, he might have considered remaining in New York, but the thought of Valerie being alone with her mother, even with Mack around, had not pleased him.

He had met Edith and Eli once, during the second year of his marriage to Valerie. He had taken an immediate dislike to both of them, annoyed by their constant references to his wealth, and by Edith's glowing praises of her other daughter while Valerie waited on her hand and foot. He had never met Ned, but he had seen Billy several times when he and Valerie had gone to San Francisco, where Billy was now a successful graphic artist, living with another young man, Rob, whom he introduced as his roommate, but who David knew was his lover. In Billy, David had instinctively sensed a friend to his wife, the only member of her family who was. Alice had become a closed subject for them. If Valerie was in touch with her, and he suspected she was, she kept it from him, and that was just as well.

"David, can I get you anything?" Valerie asked, rousing David from his glum thoughts. "Mack, what about you?"

"I'm fine, darling," David said, and Mack nodded his agreement.

Valerie sat back down and reached for her mother's hand across the kitchen table. "Mama? You okay?"

Edith threw back her head and emitted a deep, harsh laugh. "I ain't never been better, and that's the truth. The only thing I'm mournin' is the damn time I've wasted." She grinned slyly at Mack. "Ain't that right, Mr. Landry, sir? Helluva lot of time wasted. But now we can—"

"Edith, I think you've had enough," Mack said, avoiding Valerie's curious look as he tried to take the glass from Edith, but she was too quick for him. Another burst of grating laughter shook the quiet of the room as she hoisted the Scotch to her lips.

"Never enough, never!" she declared, gulping the liquor. Abruptly, the sly merriment in her watery blue eyes turned to sadness. "I wish my princess were here," she mumbled.

"Alice would have come but she's not well," Valerie said softly, again reaching for her mother's hand. "But I'm here, Mama."

Edith shook off her daughter's grasp. "You! You're not my princess. You're not my sweet Alice." She stuck out the empty glass. "Get me another drink."

"Mama—"

"Get it!" With another quick switch, she gazed at Mack imploringly. "Oh, Mack, honey, it's just not right her bein' there and me here. Maybe now we can go visit her, huh? Will you take me to see my princess?"

"We'll talk about it, Edith."

"That's all you ever tell me," she exploded. "'Later, Edith.' 'We'll see, Edith.' 'We'll talk about it, Edith.' Well, later is now, dammit! Eli is dead and I've waited long enough!"

"Edith, please..."

"Mama...?"

"Val, maybe we should take a walk. Let your mother—"

Val ignored her husband and looked at Mack. "What is it, Mack? Why is she being this way?"

Mack shook his head and got up from the table. "It's nothing," he muttered.

"Hah!" Edith said. "Nothing, is it? That's a nice thing to call what we—"

"Edith!"

Mack's voice rang loud and hard, and when he turned around, the fury in his eyes fixed Edith into silence. She mumbled something as she took another swallow of Scotch, and her eyes remained downcast.

"I'm sorry, Val, David," Mack said in a normal voice,

although the expression on his face was hard with self-control. "Eli's death, the funeral—I think the tension's just getting to her. Why don't you two go on upstairs and rest awhile. You must be tired from the trip."

David glanced quizzically at Valerie, but she shook her head. "I think I'll take that walk now," she said. "Alone, David. Do you mind?"

"Are you sure?"

She nodded. "I won't be very long."

She put on her coat and hat, then bent over to kiss her mother. "I'll see you later, Mama."

Edith caressed the soft black fur, laying her cheek against the sleeve of the coat. "My princess would look so beautiful in this," she whispered. "So beautiful."

Valerie sensed the anger in David's eyes but did not look at him as she turned quickly to leave. She walked and walked, past the school that had been the scene of so much unhappiness for her, past the white fence and hedges that were as scraggly now as they had been back in 1956. Nothing was ever fixed, improved, brought up-to-date. There was the library, and the post office, and the office of the *Courier*. She stood in the road, gazing up at the window, remembering the first time she had ever climbed those steps and met Teddy Chambers. He was no longer there, she knew. She didn't know who ran the paper now; it didn't matter.

She kept walking, stopping again outside the hotel. She wondered what young girls were waiting tables; if any of them wanted to get out of Galesville, and if any of them would. She had chosen to forget how unchanging it was, how endlessly the same the days and the nights and the people and the life were here. Her own world had become so limitless, her existence so filled with new experiences that she had allowed herself to cover the painful memories under a sheen of imagined joys. How foolish, she thought as she trudged back. And how sad.

By the time she reached the Cardell cottage, night had fallen, and the snow was coming down faster and thicker. She hesitated at the front door. She had not been back in the cottage since arriving in Galesville that morning. She and David had rented a car in Indianapolis and driven straight to Mack's, where they were staying until tomorrow's flight back to New York. There was no room in the cottage for them; besides, she knew that as much as David claimed he understood her background, the reality of it was much harsher.

Slowly, she entered, and stared around at the small living room for a few moments before climbing the stairs to her room. Nothing was different. The orange-crate stools by the makeshift vanity were just as she had left them, the mirror still cracked, covered with a fine layer of dust and a cobweb peeking out from behind it. There was even a dusty tube of Tangee Coral Flame lipstick still lying there. Her throat began to feel scratchy and she knew it had nothing to do with the dust. She went back downstairs and into the kitchen, blinking back her tears. On the table was one of her mother's confessions magazines. No, nothing had changed. What had ever given her the idea that it could?

She sighed deeply and left, needing to go only next door to Mack's to recapture what was good about Galesville, and some of her tarnished innocence.

"David?"

"Mm?" He turned over in bed so that he was facing Valerie.

"What do you think about bringing Mama back to New York with us?"

David sat up and turned on the bedside lamp. "What gave you that crazy idea?"

"It would be good to get her away from here," Valerie explained. "Away from memories of Papa and Ned and everything. Look at her, David. She has no life here, she's just wasting away. At least with us—"

"It's out of the question."

"David, be reasonable! It's not as if we don't have room."

"I don't want to hear another word about this, Valerie," David said sternly, unmoved by the beseeching look in her eyes. "Your mother belongs here. She would be miserable in New York, not to mention what she'd do to your life. Besides, if you're so concerned about her welfare, let Alice take her. Then again," he added dryly, "I don't see her little princess extending such a foolish invitation."

"Why are you being so selfish?" Valerie cried. "Look at this town, it's nothing. And that house she lives in is nothing.

Her whole life is one big nothing. I've never asked you for a thing, David, not a thing, except this. I just want to share a little of what I've been given. Is that so terrible?"

"If she deserved it, I'd find it all very commendable, but she doesn't. And besides," he rushed on, seeing Valerie about to protest, "you're forgetting something very important. However small and seedy this town and this life of hers may seem to you, it's where your mother belongs, whether you want to believe that or not."

They stared at each other in silence for several moments. Finally David turned out the light. "Good night, Valerie," he said, but she made no reply. She stayed awake for quite some time afterward, and in the morning she did not bring up the subject again. She did not have to. When she went next door to say goodbye to her mother, she found her sitting at the kitchen table in her housecoat, reading the confessions magazine. Edith did not hear Valerie come in, so what her daughter was able to observe in those few seconds was the truth of David's words. Her mother was in her element; she belonged here. Just as Valerie belonged far away.

Chapter 15

Perhaps to try to make up for the losses she had suffered, or perhaps because he would soon be fifty and was more aware than ever of their age difference, in April 1969 David acted on a promise he had made to Valerie early in their marriage. On occasion she had teasingly complained that the New York townhouse reflected none of her own taste and that she would like to decorate a home for them. So he bought her a rambling ranch house in Bel-Air, set behind a natural fence of sky-high cypress and eucalyptus with a majestic view of the smog-tipped San Gabriel Mountains.

The only flaw in David's generosity, as far as Valerie was concerned, was that he wanted Angela to help with the decorating. Since the older woman was staying in Malibu for as long as her current relationship with a sculptor fifteen years her junior lasted, Valerie had no acceptable excuse not to see her.

Angela, Ray, Grant, and David were out on the patio that surrounded their blue-tiled swimming pool while Valerie was in the kitchen preparing salads for lunch. David had become bicoastal the last few months, depending on business commitments, and on this trip he had brought Grant with him. Valerie had not seen him or Ray since New Year's in New York. Only Linda was absent from this unplanned reunion. She was still working as a stewardess and trying to convince her boyfriend of the past year that it was time to get married. She was the only one who knew of Valerie's true feelings for Angela, and she had stopped telling her that she was wrong a while ago, seeing that it was useless. In all the years that had passed, and on all the occasions when Valerie had been with Angela, nothing had occurred to make her change her mind about her.

"Anything I can do to help?"

The paring knife slipped from Valerie's hand as, startled, she looked up to find Ray at her elbow. She suddenly understood the old cliché about the heart skipping a beat. She willed herself to wipe the inane grin from her face, to tear her eyes from his steady, slate-gray eyes. He was tanned from a week's vacation in Acapulco, the firm, youthful muscles of his arms and chest golden, the brevity of his swimming shorts exposing his lean, hard thighs to perfection.

Valerie laughed self-consciously and retrieved the knife. "You surprised me," she said with a slight tremor in her voice. Despite time, despite distance, Ray's appeal for her was as strong as ever. He was always proper, always polite, yet lurking near the surface was a knowing insolence, as if he was waiting for her to make the first move.

"Need me to bring anything out?" he asked. She shook her head, and a tendril of hair fell over one eye. Slowly he brushed it back, his fingertips seeming to scorch her skin.

She jerked away and moved quickly to the refrigerator. "You can take this," she said, holding out a pitcher of iced tea.

He did not immediately take the cold pitcher, but stood

there a moment, arms folded across his chest, a soft smile playing on his full lips.

"You're flushed," he said in a low voice.

"It's hot in here."

"No it's not. The air-conditioning's on."

His hand came out and she thrust the pitcher at him, looking away from the invasive familiarity in his eyes. Then, abruptly, his smile broadened, became more genuine, as if he had tired of the game. "We could probably use something stronger. All that talk about the Florida hospital is making for some interesting conversation out there."

"You're not into building hospitals now, are you?" Valerie asked, relieved.

"Grant's found this old pink-stucco hospital down in Key Biscayne. It's right on the ocean and it's been abandoned since after the war. He's trying to sell Dad on the idea that we should buy it and turn it into a luxury resort hotel."

"Sounds like a good idea."

"It is. I've gotta admit, Grant's a genius sometimes. He's got an eye for development possibilities that's incredible. I guess that's why he's the architect and I'm the deal maker. I would have looked at that building and seen just an old empty hospital."

"Maybe, but deal making takes talent too."

"Thanks," he said quietly, and she felt the flush of warmth from his look steal up her body. Their eyes locked only briefly, but long enough for Angela, unseen at the entry to the kitchen, to understand exactly what she had observed.

"Charming, very charming," she remarked dryly, entering. "I've always wondered if the right Kinnelon married you, Valerie."

"Can it, Angela," Ray said sharply. "Speaking of charming, where'd you leave the rest of your bathing suit?" he added, his eyes roaming boldly over her scanty string bikini. Not bothering to wait for an answer, he opened the sliding glass door that led to the patio, and left.

Valerie pretended to busy herself slicing an avocado, but her face felt hot and her stomach was churning with anger.

"You don't give up, do you?" she asked.

"What do you mean?" Angela replied with feigned innocence as she reached for a carrot stick.

"You're still waiting for me to slip up, show you that I'm only after David's money or whatever it is you think I want from him."

"I haven't noticed you changing your opinion about me either, although I must commend you on your performances. David has no idea how you really feel."

"Why should he? I love him. I don't want to see him hurt, and if he knew how you and I felt about each other, that would hurt him."

Angela leaned against a counter and watched her thoughtfully. "I guess old sarcasms die hard," she said slowly.

"What's that supposed to mean?"

"It means I'm apologizing for what I said about you and Ray."

Valerie's brows went up with surprise, and she waited warily.

"The truth of the matter is that I've been wanting to talk to you and there just hasn't been the right opportunity."

"Angela, give me some credit," Valerie said hotly, putting down the food and the knife. "I've been out here since April, it's now July, and in those months we've seen a lot of each other—too much. You've had plenty of opportunities to talk if you really wanted to."

Angela conceded the point with a slight nod. "I guess I don't like to admit I'm wrong."

"Oh?"

"And that's what I'm trying to do now."

"Why all of a sudden? It's been years since you first let me know what you thought of me. What brought on the great change?"

"You're not making this easy for me."

"I don't intend to."

Angela laughed briefly, ruefully. "I suppose I deserve that. And you're right. I have been waiting for you to show your true colors. Even when I've been alone with David, I've looked for a crack in his happiness, one false note." She shrugged. "Hell, I knew a long time ago I was wrong about you, I just wasn't generous enough to admit it."

"Why now?" Valerie pressed.

"Because I think it would be better to try to be friends than civilized adversaries. Because I think I could help you, and because I think you could learn to like me." She laughed again. "Who knows why now, except that I wanted to do it. Look, Valerie, we've had the truce and it's been tough on both of us. I don't think we have reason to be enemies, so all I'm saying is let's try it as friends."

Valerie said nothing, weighing the sincerity of Angela's words, looking into the black eyes bright with intelligence and conviction and finding no sham. She frowned, confused not only by Angela's admission but by her own totally unexpected sense of relief. She had been determined not to like Angela; but now, just knowing that the older woman had finally granted her approval, she felt she could admit to herself that Angela wasn't so bad either. What a child she was sometimes, she thought with amazement.

"You're still the most self-centered, self-absorbed woman I've ever met," Valerie muttered, a small smile teasing her mouth.

"I won't deny it!" Angela replied. "I waste my time, my money, and my talent. I sleep with men who are too young for me, buy them gifts that are too expensive, and tell them they're great artists when I wouldn't let them paint my bathroom. But you know what? I'm having such a damned terrific time I don't want to stop!"

A rich giggle escaped from Valerie, and before she knew it, both women were helpless with laughter. "I won't stop, you know," Angela said finally.

"Stop what?"

"Being nasty and sarcastic, especially if I see a look like I just saw between you and Ray. He's extraordinarily attractive, but you know that, don't you? If he weren't David's son, I'd be tempted myself."

"He's too old for you," Valerie reminded her with a catty grin.

"Grant's the one you should pay attention to."

Valerie's expression turned completely serious. "Look, Angela, I'm glad we cleared the air between us. At least for David's sake we don't have to pretend we like each other any more; it can start to be genuine. But leave Ray and Grant out of this. I love David very much. I still can't seem to convince you of that, can I?'

"I'm convinced all right," Angela said, "and I wasn't

referring to Grant as an object of romance, so don't be so sensitive or I'll think you're guilty of something."

"Go on," Valerie said impatiently.

"I've known you for a while now, Valerie. I've watched you, seen you change and grow. You love David," she said carefully, her eyes riveted on Valerie. "I really do believe that now. Maybe it's not with red-hot passion, but there's tremendous feeling there, and it's been good for both of you."

"Then what's the problem?"

"David's greatest joy with women comes from teaching them. With you he's fulfilled every Pygmalion fantasy he's ever had, much more so than with his other wives. But you've been a very quick learner, Valerie, quicker than I think he realizes. What's going to happen to both of you when you don't need him to teach you anymore? What's going to happen to him when you get restless—and it's going to happen, believe me."

Valerie opened her mouth to protest, then stopped. Hadn't the same thought crossed her mind, only to be guiltily shelved? Hadn't her recent suggestion to David about taking courses at New York University been a first, tentative step toward doing something on her own? And hadn't the visit to Galesville, seeing her mother's vacuous existence, frightened her more than she wanted to admit?

"What does Grant have to do with this?" she asked softly.

"Learn from him, Valerie," Angela told her. "Real estate is a wide-open field, a woman can do something there."

"But why Grant? Why not Ray?"

"Grant knows more," Angela said matter-of-factly. "And he has taste and talent. Ray has the burden of the great David Kinnelon to carry, so sharing doesn't come easily to him, but Grant doesn't have that to worry about."

Valerie shook her head slowly. "This is ridiculous," she mumbled halfheartedly, avoiding Angela's penetrating stare. "I have no interest in real estate."

"Then find something else! Believe me, Valerie, the day is going to come when the life of leisure is going to strangle you."

"It hasn't hurt you any," she commented sharply.

"I planned my life this way. I tested myself when I was

young, and I succeeded, and now I can afford to tell the whole world to go to hell because I know who I am. But you haven't done that yet and you're the kind of person who's going to have to. Right now you still need David, but the day will come when you're going to need yourself, Valerie, and all I'm saying is be prepared."

Valerie looked hard at Angela, hearing the words, but in her heart she knew she was not yet ready to listen to their meaning.

The next several months were spent in the laborious process of decorating the house; finally, just before Christmas, it was finished. David and Valerie decided to throw open their doors in a massive celebration of the new decade and a housewarming, and so on December 31, 1969, more than three hundred people oohed and aahed over the imported Austrian crystal chandelier in the dining room, and the gold fleur-de-lis inlaid marble entry foyer, and the room that had been turned into an entertainment center with hidden stereo speakers and banquettes of thick gray velvet and an all-mirror bar. The house sparkled with diamond-bright conversation and shimmered with silks and satins as actors and directors, business moguls, athletes and rock stars, photographers from decorating magazines and gossip columnists from Hollywood trade journals drank the Kinnelons' champagne and ate their catered food. Linda was there with a new engagement ring, Angela with a new young man. A ravishingly beautiful woman clung to Ray's arm, and even in the dazzling atmosphere of her own triumphant party, the sight of his arrogant masculinity made Valerie's pulse race.

"You've never looked lovelier."

Valerie put her empty champagne glass on the tray the uniformed maid was holding, then glanced up to see who had paid her the compliment. Her smile was wide for Grant.

"Thank you. And you look fabulous in a tuxedo. Why aren't you here with some starlet like your partner is?" she teased.

Grant shrugged. "I'm kind of old-fashioned that way. I like an adornment I can talk to."

Valerie tilted her head, studying the calm, steady expression of this man she liked so much. "I imagine you would.

But not tonight, my serious friend," she added gaily, looping
er hand through his arm. "Tonight is pure frivolity. After all,
t's the start of a whole new decade."

"And what do you want for the next ten years, Valerie?"

"Oh, nothing more than what I have right now—a house
ike this, a husband like David, and friends like you and Ray."

Grant's smile was small and did not quite make the
ourney to his eyes. "Well then," he said, grabbing a glass of
hampagne for Valerie, "here's to all that you want."

She lifted her glass, and her blue-black eyes twinkled
vith the beauty of her happiness as she looked up at him.
And here's to all that you want, Grant. And to finding an
dornment you can talk to!"

Valerie spent most of the evening wandering among her
uests, showing off the house, accepting compliments with a
ophisticated graciousness that charmed everyone. The only
lisappointment in an otherwise perfect evening was the
bsence of three people she had very much wanted to be
here. Billy was with his roommate, house-sitting a friend's
partment in Hawaii; Mack was in Curaçao, recovering from
ronchitis; and Alice's family had prevented her from flying
ut. Confined to bed for the last six months of her long-
waited pregnancy, Alice had finally been able to carry full
erm, and had given birth a few months ago to a baby
laughter, Maggie. But the child had contracted pneumonia
nd was now home from the hospital for the first time in
hree weeks. Valerie wished her sister could have come to the
arty tonight; the glitter, the famous people, and the heady
tmosphere would have delighted her. It was just the kind of
vening Alice would have loved.

Four days later, David left for Brazil to check on some
ew talent for his soccer team. Valerie drove him to the
irport, extracting a promise from him that when he returned
hey would take a much-needed vacation together, someplace
vhere there was nothing but endless beach, blue water, and
o telephone.

She rushed home to dress for a charity luncheon she was
ttending at The Bistro. Afterward, she planned to shop for a
ift for Maggie. She loved buying things for her niece,

pictures of whom accompanied every one of Alice's frequent letters.

As she put the finishing touches to her makeup, Valerie considered whether she wanted a baby, as she had on occasion since getting the first photo of Maggie, which Richard had taken when the child was four hours old. David had asked her about it early in their marriage; she had not wanted one then. She had felt too young herself, and much too new in David's world to take on responsibility for another. But seeing Maggie's adorable face, and knowing through Alice's letters how complete a woman her sister now felt, created a certain longing in Valerie. Yet, she wasn't sure. Was she being selfish? Maybe. But there was David to consider. Would he want to start a new family and all that that entailed at his age? That might be more than he had bargained for when he took a young bride.

The doorbell rang then, interrupting Valerie's musings. Slipping on her Baume and Mercier watch and grabbing David's anniversary gift to her—a black Hermès alligator bag—she went to answer it.

She opened one-half of the double front door to a woman in her late thirties with badly overdyed platinum hair, the black roots extending several inches. Her purple eyeshadow was smudged, and her coral lipstick was cakey, as if she'd been chewing her lips. The woman wore a red cloth coat belted with a black fake-leather sash, and under her arm she carried a black fake-leather clutch bag. Small brown eyes were set close to a puglike nose; her lips were thin, her mouth abbreviated. These underscaled features were in a face so round and angleless that Valerie had the swift impression of a kewpie doll, and not a cute one. Feeling unaccountably and suddenly on edge at this stranger's presence, she started to close the door, but the woman's black-cloth-gloved hand shot out against the doorframe, maintaining the open space between them.

"Valerie Kinnelon?" she asked in the flat midwestern drawl that Valerie knew well.

"Yes?"

"I'm Lena Cardell. Your brother Ned's wife. I want to talk to you."

Chapter 16

New York sparkled on this May afternoon: the sky was cobalt, the temperature in the high sixties, and the tulips along the Park Avenue center isle plump with color and bloom. From his thirty-seventh-floor office in his Park Avenue building, David Kinnelon was oblivious to everything but the ledger on the desk in front of him.

"Dad, you're not listening to a word we're saying," Ray Kinnelon complained.

"Sorry, Ray," David said, his eyes darting back to the ledger. "Something about the hotel in Key Biscayne, right?"

Ray frowned at Grant, who shrugged. "Dad, what's wrong?"

"Nothing. Now, where were we?"

"*We* were in Key Biscayne. You were obviously someplace else," Ray rejoined.

"David, we've been trying to tell you that we're going to come in seven hundred fifty thousand dollars over budget," Grant said.

"Hmm," David murmured, his brows furrowing, the ridges around his nose and mouth deepening. "Well, take care of it."

"Don't you want to know why?" Grant asked, sharing a look of surprise with Ray.

"Dad, come on, this isn't like you. Usually if we're five thousand over budget you're furious. What's going on?"

"I'm not quite sure," David admitted, "but I'll deal with it. As far as running over budget is concerned, I'm sure both of you are convinced it's unavoidable, so go ahead and do what's necessary. I'll see you later."

It was an unmistakable dismissal. With a concerned glance at his father, Ray got up and walked to the door, Grant following.

"Dad—"

"I said I'll see you later," David repeated, his attention fully on the ledger.

Alone, he reread for the fifth time the statements of deposits to and withdrawals from his wife's personal account. His family accountant had, with reticence and awkwardness, suggested that David take a look at them because several unusually large withdrawals had been made over the last few months. When they were married, David had opened an account for Valerie so that she would not feel she was on an allowance and have to ask him for money every time she wanted to buy something. She paid for her charge accounts from it, as well as the day-to-day household expenses. David made sure there was never less than $10,000 in the account, an amount Valerie had frequently told him was exorbitant. David never paid attention to the account; he left it entirely to his accountant to make sure that the $10,000 was always there.

At first, when he saw the January withdrawal for $3,500 made out to cash, David had thought his accountant was being petty. So what if Valerie had bought something for $3,500; she was certainly entitled. But then in February, March, April, and now two days ago, there had been that same withdrawal of $3,500, made out to cash. There was nothing to show for the large expenditures—no new fur coat, no new furniture, no particularly expensive new outfit, no jewelry, no unusually luxurious gifts. Nothing to warrant a total withdrawal of $17,500 over five months. In fact, he reflected, the only thing that had been unusual during this time was his wife.

He tried to recall when he had first noticed that Valerie was not herself; it had begun the weekend he had returned from Brazil, when she had moved back to New York. They had gone to Paradise Island shortly afterward for that promised vacation, but instead of the romantic interlude he had anticipated, it had been ten days of an almost forced gaiety. He now remembered having mentioned it to Valerie, and how her casual dismissal of his concern had been enough for him; he had concluded that she simply was tired from having decorated the Los Angeles house. He had accepted that as her excuse for not being interested in sex, or in the lesser pleasures of sightseeing, sailfishing, and even the elegant meals the hotel provided.

Business had kept him busy in recent months, especially his booming real estate subsidiary, and he had been traveling more than usual. After one trip he had noticed that Valerie looked particularly gaunt, as if she had lost a great deal of weight suddenly. Her normally healthy glow seemed sallow, and shadows flickered across her eyes when she thought he wasn't watching. He had wondered if she was ill and had insisted she go to a doctor. To pacify him, she went, and received a clean bill of health. Their life had resumed, if not with that sense of permanent honeymoon that had marked their years together so far, then with a comfort that David did not find unpleasant. Valerie started taking courses at New York University and spent a great deal of time reading and studying; he had attributed her disinterest in keeping up her social life to that. But now, faced with the evidence of these withdrawals, he wondered if something else could be behind the changes in his wife. He shook his head at the very idea. He was imagining something sinister where nothing existed. There had to be an easy explanation for the shadows, the reticence, the sexual indifference.

He had always believed he knew her so well, he mused. Uncomplicated, generous, loving, forgiving to a fault. But perhaps he did not know her; perhaps there was more to the sweet-natured child/woman he had come to need so intensely, more that she had been able to conceal until now.

Suddenly David's fingers flattened on the ledger and his eyes closed briefly as if to banish the notion that had come, uninvited, unexpected, to mind.

Was it possible . . . oh, *no!* . . . was it possible that she was planning to leave him?

"Let's have our coffee in the den," David suggested after dinner that evening. "I want to talk to you about something."

A flash of alarm darkened Valerie's eyes as she followed him into the den. Her heart began to hammer out a hard rhythm that had become achingly familiar over the past months. Guilt permeated every natural response, every instinctive act. It had made it impossible for her to enjoy her husband in bed; impossible for her to have a carefree conversation with a friend; impossible for her to be interested in David's work or travels; impossible for her to concentrate on anything but the nightmare her life had become. She went through the days like an automaton, motions of habit that bore no resemblance to living. How many times had she sat across from her husband at dinner, or lain next to him in bed, the blood pounding mercilessly in her head as she waited anxiously for him to demand an explanation for her behavior. The months had passed and there had been no questions, but her guilt had not lessened, nor had her anxiety. She almost wished he would confront her so that she could stop the duplicity and subterfuge. Yet, once he knew, there would be nothing left for her, not even the nightmare existence, and she feared that even more than she feared the torment.

"Mel was by to see me today," David began when they were seated.

"Mel Davis, our accountant?"

David nodded, and Valerie avoided his eyes. He knows, she thought frantically. It's finally going to come out. Oh my darling, I'm so sorry!

"Anything wrong?" she asked, her voice cracking.

"You know I don't pay much attention to your personal account, Val. That's yours to do with as you wish."

"Yes?"

"Well, Mel noticed, I guess the best thing to call it is an irregularity over the past few months and thought he ought to bring it to my attention."

"Yes?" she said again in a breathless whisper, her eyes immense now as she watched her husband's face.

"Valerie, you've withdrawn seventeen thousand five hundred dollars since January. On the fifteenth of every month, you've written a check to cash for thirty-five hundred. I think I—"

"Oh, David!" she cried, covering her face with her hands, her shoulders sagging.

Gently he pulled her hands away and held them in his. "What is it, Val? What's been going on?"

"I can't tell you, I can't!" she cried, shaking her head. She tore her hands from his grasp, rushed to her feet, and began pacing the room, unable to face him.

David went to her immediately and, placing his hands firmly on her shoulders, forced her to stand still. She refused to look at him, her head bowed as sobs continued to ravage her.

"Were you planning to leave me?" The words came out in a voice lead-heavy with emotion, and Valerie could feel the trembling of his fingers through her dress. To have him think that was even worse than what she had been going through; crueler in every way.

"David, darling, no, never!" she wept. "I would never leave you, never. I love you so much, David, and now, now . . ." She broke off, and as she turned away from him, she could not see the lines of worry and age vanish from her husband's face.

Like a child, Valerie let him take her by the hand and lead her back to the sofa. He then went to the bar and poured them each a brandy. Her eyes were enormous in her drawn face as she took the snifter, her fingers icy when they made contact with his.

"Will you tell me what's been going on now?" he asked, sitting down. "I can't help you otherwise."

"It's been so awful I don't know what to do anymore," she said. "I've wanted to talk to you so many times, but I couldn't, I just couldn't drag you into this."

"Valerie, whatever it is can't be that bad—not if you let me help. Please, darling, trust me."

"You'll hate me."

David's smile was small and weary. "Hate you? I don't think I'm capable of anything but a frightening love when it comes to you. No, Valerie, I could never hate you, no matter what you did. You must believe that."

She wanted to, desperately. She gazed at him, at this man who had made her world safe and warm, and knew that she had been destroying him as surely as Lena Cardell had been destroying her. She could not continue to do that to him. For his sake, she would risk the truth.

"I'm being blackmailed." The words came out less audibly than a breeze. Her eyes were haunted, the pupils dilated with shame and fear. Her fingers were curled around the brandy snifter, meeting so that her nails pressed into her flesh with deliberate pain. Her tongue darted out to moisten her lips, and she swallowed several times, but still she could feel the scratchy dryness at the back of her throat. She watched her husband warily, unblinking, waiting for the expected explosion.

But all he said, calmly, as if he had known this was the case and had merely been waiting for her to confirm it, was, "By whom?" She could not know how his heart thundered in his chest and roared in his ears, how his relief was so deep, so complete that he felt like laughing. He could deal with blackmail. "By whom?" he pressed when she did not answer.

"Lena Cardell."

"Who is she?"

"My brother Ned's wife."

"Sweetheart," David said lovingly, "I don't want to have to drag everything out of you. This isn't an inquisition, and whatever's been going on, I'm here now and I'm going to help. So please, just tell me from the beginning."

"Lena Cardell was Ned's wife," she repeated. "They were already separated when he went into the army, but they were never legally divorced."

"When did you meet her?"

"On January fourth. When I got back from taking you to the airport to Brazil, remember?" He nodded. "I was getting ready to leave for a luncheon and there she was at the front door."

"This started in Los Angeles, then?" he asked, surprised.

"Yes. I had never met her before that afternoon." She took a gulp of her brandy, and the watchfulness slowly faded from her eyes, replaced by a flicker of anger. "I hadn't heard from Ned since I had left home for Dallas years ago. I never would have known he had even been married if my mother hadn't written me about it."

"How did she find you? Did your mother give her our address?"

"No. In fact, I asked this woman that, and she laughed at me. Said she had her sources, the same sources that had given her the information that would make her a rich woman." Valerie shut her eyes briefly and shuddered at the recollection of the conversation.

"Go on," David encouraged. "Tell me what she threatened to expose you with."

"Oh, David, they're all lies. Horrible, vicious lies, but I had to pay her, I *had* to!"

"I know, darling, I understand. Now come on, what was it?"

"When I was around fifteen or sixteen, Mack's younger son, Wayne, tried to rape me." She saw her husband's eyes widen with surprise. "I never told you because, well, because there seemed no reason to—it was ugly and it was in the past. Anyway, he tried, but he didn't succeed. This woman said...she said that she knew the real story. She said she knew the truth was that *I* had seduced Wayne, and Mack had believed the supposed rape because I was his mistress! She said she knew Mack had left Galesville not because of what his son had done, but because I wouldn't let him break off with me and it was the only way to get rid of me." She pressed her fist against her mouth as if to hold back the nauseating lies. "None of it's true, David, none of it! Wayne Landry did try to rape me, and Mack left because he couldn't help me anymore—my father had made that impossible. But I was never his mistress, and I never took anything from him until he gave me the money for stew school. This woman was threatening to tell you these sick lies, so I *had* to pay her. You understand, don't you, David, I had to pay her to protect us!" She was sobbing again, quietly now, as if she no longer had the strength to be hysterical.

"But, Valerie, why couldn't you have just told me about it when it first began? I would have believed you and this could have been stopped immediately."

"I've been so confused...I thought...I thought that even though you would say you didn't believe it, you would. The lies would be like some kind of demon seed and once planted it would take root and suspicion would grow in your mind." Valerie saw the way a tendon in David's neck throbbed, and knew she had wounded him deeply.

"I didn't trust your love, David," she admitted. "I thought you'd walk out on me. You'd start to doubt me and that would be the end. I couldn't bear it. I couldn't bear the thought of your leaving me."

With a sigh, David sat back and closed his eyes. She wanted to touch him, to say, with a gesture, how sorry she was, but she did not dare. Not yet. Because he hadn't yet shown her that her fears were unfounded.

"David?" she tried tentatively, when the silence became too loud. "Darling, please say something."

He opened his eyes and stared at his wife, seeing the frightened child she was. If he could get his hands on Lena Cardell at this moment, he would not be responsible for his actions, he realized. To have caused Valerie such anguish, to have threatened the very security he had so carefully nurtured for her, was no less a crime than murder in his mind. For him, that was what Lena Cardell had done—killed the happiness of the woman he loved. But right now Lena Cardell was not important. Only making Valerie whole again mattered.

He put aside his brandy glass, took hers away, and opened his arms. She came into his embrace hesitantly, not quite believing she was being welcomed this way. When she felt the warmth and strength of her husband's arms around her, she experienced a rush of well-being that she had forgotten could exist for her.

"What are you going to do about her?" she asked.

"Where have you been sending the checks?"

"To a box number in Indianapolis."

"That's easy enough to trace."

"Do you think you can get back the money?"

"I doubt it. With someone like her, she probably had it spent before you gave her the first check. The money's unimportant. What I'm curious about, though, is who told her about you and Mack and his son in the first place. That's the person I really want to get."

"It must have been Ned," Valerie said, surprised that he would think it could have been anyone else. "He knew about the incident with Wayne."

"But Ned's dead," David reminded her. "If he had told her, it would have been when they were together and that was a while ago. Why didn't she try to blackmail you when Ned first went into the army? Why wait?"

Why indeed? Valerie wondered.

Nine days later, at dinner, Valerie squirmed impatiently while her husband told her about a bank he was deliberating taking over in Tucson and about two dinner invitations they had received, and reminded her to buy a birthday present for his secretary. Her neck ached from so much polite nodding. What she did not know was that David was stalling intentionally. For the first time in his life, David Kinnelon felt utterly helpless. As he sat at the table, trying to pretend life was going on normally, his mind feverishly sought a way to avoid telling Valerie what he had learned. If he revealed the truth, she would hate him—if she even believed him. And if he did not tell her, he was endangering her.

"David, please tell me what happened!" she finally demanded.

"It's all been taken care of."

"That's it? That's all you have to say—it's been taken care of?" she repeated incredulously. "You get Lena Cardell's address, fly off to confront her, and come back to say it's been taken care of! Well, I'm afraid that won't do, David. I want more information than that, if you don't mind."

He shrugged, his eyes riveted on his fresh-fruit cup. "What's there to say? I saw her, she admitted the blackmailing, and that's it. She spent the money, of course." He looked up, and Valerie found his unconcerned expression offensive. "Come on, honey, let's not dwell on it. It's over. Be thankful for that."

Valerie waited to see if he really was not going to speak further of it, then said, "All right, David. What aren't you telling me?"

"Nothing." He flung down his napkin. "Dammit, let it go. Okay? Just drop it. I said it's over so let it rest, will you!"

"No, David, I will not let it rest." Her voice was calm, her face implacable. "Now what is it you're failing so miserably at keeping from me? Tell me, David. I have a right to know."

He breathed deeply. He couldn't lie to her, yet the truth . . . the truth . . . He exhaled with one word: "Alice."

Valerie frowned. "What about her? What in the world does my sister have to do with my being blackmailed by Lena Cardell?"

"Your sister," he began, his voice sharp with bitterness, "your sister told her about Wayne and Mack. Your sister is responsible for telling that woman a good many things, all with one purpose in mind: to hurt you."

Instinctively, Valerie grabbed herself around her midriff, so acute was the pain that shot through her stomach. Her eyes, sparkling heatedly only moments ago, seemed to have turned a matte blue-black. Blood pounded in her head, and the thunderous beating of her heart hurt so much that she winced.

"I don't believe you," she managed.

David reached for her hand. "Don't you think I would have done anything in my power to have spared you this? Don't you know it's killing me? But it's the truth, Val. Dammit, it *is* the truth!"

She shook free of his hand. "I don't believe you," she repeated. "The whole idea is absurd. What reason would Alice have to do such a thing?"

"Who the hell knows why!" David shouted in his fury. "For the same damn reason she's done all she can to destroy you throughout the years. Valerie, you've got to come to your senses about that woman. If you don't, there's no telling what she might do to you. She's relentless."

"Tell me everything," she said remotely.

David looked at her questioningly and saw that she was not watching him, that her eyes were as blank as a doll's. Her posture was so rigid that it seemed as if she were tied to the chair. He wanted nothing more than to hold her, comfort her, but having come this far, he knew he had to tell her the rest.

"According to Lena Cardell, your sister called her on New Year's Day with the excuse that she was getting in touch with all of the family for the New Year."

"Had they ever met?"

"No, and according to Lena, your sister knew she had been separated from Ned, but she was still family as far as Alice was concerned." He paused, thinking of his sister-in-law's monumental nerve. Had she been in the business world, she might have gone far with such a conscienceless nature.

"Go on," Valerie instructed. "Then what?"

"It seems that Alice wanted to make Lena feel like one of the family, and what better way to do that than by sharing some of the Cardell secrets, especially yours—Alice's version, that is." He related everything emotionlessly, but rage churned within him. "As Lena said, Alice was, and I quote, 'quite filled with worry that Valerie could get into trouble.' When I asked her what she meant by that, she got the most disgusting look on her face." He shuddered, remembering the woman's small mouth pinching with greed, the bug eyes gleaming.

"And what *did* she mean by that, David?" Valerie prodded. "That if any of this sordid information ever got into the wrong hands, I would be vulnerable? Is that what she meant? Is that what Lena claims Alice told her?"

David nodded, miserable.

"In other words, you're telling me that from this conversation with Alice, Lena decided to blackmail me?" She laughed brittlely." For someone so smart in business, David, you seem to have difficulty putting two and two together."

David's eyes narrowed. "What the hell is that supposed to mean?"

"It means," Valerie went on, scorn rimming her voice, "that you have no proof for accusing my sister. So what if she called Lena Cardell, and so what if she told her some things about me that admittedly she shouldn't have? That's hardly what I would call irrefutable evidence. In fact, it's what I would call making a case to suit your own purposes. I'm sorry, David, but you hate Alice so much that you've made a connection where none exists. I don't buy it."

The wind coming off a frozen lake in the heart of winter would have been more warming than the color and emotion in David's eyes at that moment. "I don't believe you. I really don't believe you. I can't believe that someone I consider intuitive, intelligent, sensitive can sit there and be so damn stupid! Are you crazy! I think you are, I really think you must be. That's the only permissible explanation for what you've just said to me!"

"David, I understand, I do," she said sweetly, not rising to his anger. "You've disliked Alice since that time in Chicago, and nothing can make you change your opinion of her. So, okay, here's another incident and Alice is involved—on the periphery, mind you, but nevertheless involved. It's so easy for you to make her the culprit because you're looking for it, but, David, there's no motive. Don't you see? Alice has no *reason* to do this to me. I'm sorry, darling, I really am, but all we're dealing with is some greedy woman who wanted her share of the pie and she twisted a few harmless incidents into a basis for blackmail. Unfortunately, I was too shocked and too frightened to do anything but pay. But believe me, Alice had nothing to do with it." She paused, then: "Did she get any of the money?"

"Of course not!" David retorted harshly, astonishment and frustration making the taut muscles in his neck quiver.

"That wasn't the purpose. Jesus Christ, Valerie, when will you understand, when will it penetrate that all Alice wants to do is hurt you. The end justifies the means with that bitch, and the end is to destroy you!"

Valerie said nothing, staring at her husband, willing him not to continue. She did not know if she could keep up the pretense a half-second longer.

She did not dare get up, because she was convinced her knees would buckle and an exit of dignity would become a wobbly display of weakness. She did not dare reach out to touch her husband, because the glacial temperature of her fingers would be too revealing. And she hoped she would not have to speak on the subject again, because undoubtedly her voice would crumble like a rotted board.

In her heart she believed every word David had said. But she could never let him know that.

She still was not ready to walk away from Alice. She did not like her sister, she admitted to herself now. And she did not like how her sister invariably made her feel: duped. She recognized herself as being the perfect victim for Alice: trusting, loyal, forgiving. And so, time after time, since they were children, she had excused any wrongdoing on her sister's part, rationalized it with any explanation that would fit, would be acceptable. Or she had relegated it to a corner of her mind where it would accumulate dust and be forgotten.

But none of it had ever been forgotten, and the dust could easily be blown off the relics of treachery. Even now, though, knowing that her sister had been the cause of such anguish, even now Valerie did not hate her. And she was not willing to let her go. She was her *sister*. That had to count for something fine and loving, despite the maliciousness. No one's *family* could be that deliberately evil. Valerie's life was so full that it was understandable if jealousy sometimes governed Alice's actions. And when I was younger? Valerie asked herself. Was she jealous then too? Did she see in me what Mack had, what David did, and could deal with it not with love but only with hate? Did she, as Linda said once, want not so much to get for herself as to take from me?

"Is that all you have to say on the matter?"

David's voice snapped Valerie back to the moment. "There's nothing else to say, is there? I think you jumped to conclusions that are totally absurd. Would it make you feel better if I called Alice, asked her to explain herself?"

David's laugh was derisive. "What good would it do? She'd come up with some wonderful lie that would fool you just like all the other times."

"They don't fool me, David," Valerie said softly, looking down at the table.

"Then why—"

When she glanced up, her eyes were hard with defiance. "She's my family, David. Do you understand that? *Family.* And they must be forgiven—even when they don't deserve to be."

"Until when, Valerie? When does family cease to be sacred and start to be human?"

"I don't know."

"Will you ever know? Will that day ever come when you'll stop forgiving?"

"I hope not, David. I really hope not."

Alice pressed her foot on the accelerator of her new red Mustang convertible until the speedometer registered seventy-five miles per hour. With the top down and the highway traffic light, she reveled in the freedom of speed. Without her car, she would go crazy. On the road she could think, plan, breathe.

Her hands gripped the wheel harder and her foot pressed down until she was going eighty. An image of her husband and her baby daughter flickered feebly before her, and she idly wondered how they would fare if anything were to happen to her. But nothing would. The road was her special domain where, like any ruler, she reigned above the law. Dick often warned her that she was tempting fate with her careless, high-speed driving, but she knew better. Here, in a car, going fast and free, she and the gods had an agreement. Here she could be special.

But nowhere else, she thought bitterly, the speedometer inching forward. The rest of her life was like a bottomless pit of desperation from which all attempts to escape failed.

Reading about her sister's spectacular New Year's Eve party, seeing the pictures of her house, the guests, listening to her on the phone bubbling and brimming with happiness had made Alice writhe with jealousy. So what that she had been invited to the party? The fact remained that she couldn't be there; the fact remained that it was her sister's party, not her own; the fact remained that it was her sister's house, her sister's guests—her sister, not her.

She had needed to strike back, to prove, if only to herself, that she had ultimate control. That with a word, an action, she could shatter the fragile perfection of her sister's world. And she had succeeded for a while.

Lena Cardell had been an inspired choice, an entry in her memory bank that she had never thought she would need. Calling her had confirmed what she had suspected by virtue of her having married the worst of the Cardells: that Lena was selfish, greedy, gossipy, and stupid enough to do what Alice wanted without realizing she was being used. The perfect victim. And even though the game was over now and the bitch had told David Kinnelon who had been the source of her information, there was no way Alice could be held responsible for the blackmail. David might suspect it, might even convince Valerie of it, but her sister would do nothing about it except to feel confused and hurt.

Oh, to have watched her suffer would have been a delicious treat, and an opportunity that she could have used to her advantage. If only she could have been with her more, with David more. These past months would have been an ideal time to show David how much more lively, loving, sophisticated she was than her "troubled" sister.

Well, there would be another opportunity. She would create one if she had to. As astute an adversary as David was, as ruthlessly protective of Valerie as he might be, he did not worry Alice. Valerie, like Lena Cardell, was a perfect victim.

Alice turned into the middle lane, oblivious to other cars. The shrill blare of a horn forced her to look into her rear-view mirror. A driver was shaking his fist at her for having cut him off, but she just grinned and drove on. She could get away with anything in her car. And somehow she would channel that strength against her sister. One way or another, she would get her. Even if she did not achieve the glory that rightfully belonged to her, she would make sure

Valerie did not have it either. One way or another . . . and Valerie would do nothing except to feel confused and hurt. She never did anything. She never would.

Chapter 17

After the incident with Lena Cardell, Valerie devoted herself to her studies with an eagerness that continued for many months. She enjoyed being a student, even an older one, thriving on the new freedom of the young and adapting to it easily despite the difference between her regular lifestyle and that of the undergraduates. She went to school three days a week, studying a variety of courses from the Romantic period in English literature, to the history of America during the two World Wars. She took to wearing slacks and sweaters instead of pantsuits; in cold weather she even wore boots and jeans. Never one to use a great deal of makeup, she now found a light brush of blush and lip gloss sufficient, her own healthy complexion enviably doing the rest. The naturalness of her beauty had never been so dazzling, and even David could not complain about her new style. When they entertained, her wardrobe reflected time, taste and money, but now she wore the designer clothes with a confidence and poise that created its own style: casual elegance. Valerie had learned how to toss a scarf a certain way; to put a barrette in her hair at a certain angle; to twist a long belt around her hips with a certain jauntiness. She had developed a personal flair that could take the traditional and make it individually hers. Pictures of her appeared regularly in *Women's Wear Daily*, and "insouciance" became *her* word.

That same confidence reflected itself in her conversations and her interests. She no longer sat prettily while Ray and Grant and David discussed business; she asked questions, voiced opinions about everything from construction of a new apartment to the shame of a Spiro Agnew. At luncheons and fund-raisers she could not avoid, she tried to engage other women in conversations about Kent State and Vietnam, the significance of the musical *Hair*, and the issue of the Pentagon papers, but aside from a desultory comment or two, the ladies preferred to talk about Bill Blass, Geoffrey Beene, and their illicit affairs.

Lately, she had been getting restless with the effort to improve the quality of her social conversation; restless with her position as an adjunct to David instead of his partner; restless even with her studies, seeing them as goalless, forever incomplete. And so on this day in June, 1971, three months after her twenty-eighth birthday, the exam in American Studies she had tomorrow could not hold her attention as her mind wandered back to an incident that had occurred right before Christmas.

She and David had wintered in Bel-Air, spending a lot of time comforting Linda, whose marriage had broken up after ten months when her husband ran off with another man. Valerie's spirits since the debacle over Lena Cardell had been fully restored, and she felt a new sense of freedom and ease with her life. It was spoiled when she received a letter, in California, from a doctor in Eddington informing her that her mother needed round-the-clock care for her alcoholism.

Afraid that this was someone's ploy to again extort money, she had David check it out while she did the same by calling Mack and her sister. It was confirmed: Edith Cardell was in such bad condition that she needed to be institutionalized, but she refused. The only alternative was a full-time private nurse.

Valerie leaned back now against the loveseat in the New York den and closed the textbook in her lap. Without wanting them to, her thoughts returned to that last devastating conversation she had had with her mother more than six months ago. . . .

"Oh, if it isn't the rich fine lady herself. And why does this lowly subject merit a call from royalty?" was her mother's slurred greeting.

"Hello, Mama. I called to say hello, find out how you are."

"I need money," Edith complained in a whine. "You don't send me enough money."

"I thought the five hundred dollars a month was more than you needed. That's what you've always told me."

"Well, I want more. Alice would send me more if she had it. She's such a good girl. Why can't you be more like your sister?"

"If you want more, I'll speak with David. I'm sure there'll be no problem."

"Why should there be a problem? You're rich enough to send me twice that amount, three times! Alice told me how rich you are with that fancy new house of yours and all those fine clothes. Alice, poor as she is, she manages to send fifty dollars every three or four months, but you with all your fine and fancy friends, you can only spare a coupla hundred."

"I'll send more, Mama. I will. Mama, there's something—"

"Poor Alice, you don't know how you hurt her. You're so selfish, Valerie, always have been. That poor girl has gone through so much, those terrible miscarriages, a bad marriage to that awful Chambers boy, a husband now who doesn't provide what she deserves. And you—you won't help her. She tells me everything. How you never invite her to your parties, how your husband hates her, how you send her newspaper clippings of yourself just to rub her nose in her poverty. You're so selfish I don't know how I raised a child like you. No wonder you and Mack got along so well. Two of a kind."

"Mama, I got a letter from your doctor in Eddington and—"

"What!"

"He said you've got a problem, Mama, you're sick."

A cackle shot its way across the miles, making Valerie shiver with its meanness. This was her mother, her mother! And she was sick. Valerie had to keep reminding herself that the viciousness, the ugly, unjust lies and accusations were from a woman whose mind had been poisoned by alcohol. She wasn't speaking from the heart, but from the bottom of a bottle.

"Of course I'm sick. You'd be sick too if your life had been ruined."

"Mama, the doctor said—"

"I don't care what that quack said! You listen to me. You don't know nothin', nothin', understand! That holier-than-thou pal of yours, that self-righteous bastid, ruined my life. He drove me to this. He did it, you hear me!"

Valerie's mouth went dry, and she clutched the phone with both hands to stop them from shaking. "What are you talking about, Mama? Who ruined your life—Papa?"

"Papa! Hell no, not your damned papa! All that fool ever did was work hisself to death while the big man diddled with his wife."

"What did you say?" Valerie's breath caught in the back of her throat like a lump of sour bile. She swallowed repeatedly, but it would not go away.

"I'm talkin' about your hero, your great pal, the man who sent you away from me. The man who couldn't see the specialness of my precious Alice, my sweet baby, and he knew all the time she meant everythin' to me, everythin'. I'm talkin' about big old Mack Landry, that's who! Surprised, Valerie? Bet you didn't know about him and me, didja? Didn't know him and me were lovers for years and years. Yup, years."

The lump of bile had settled in; Valerie had to gasp for air. She began to cough, then retch. "Hold on a minute, Mama, I'll be right back," she said, and ran into the powder room to throw cold water on her face and cup her hands under the faucet, gulping water, frantic for relief.

"Mama? You there?" she said, coming back to the phone.

"Shocked ya, didn't I?" her mother went on as if she hadn't been interrupted. She laughed that nerve-severing cackle again, and Valerie trembled as if someone had walked over her grave.

"Well, it's the truth. I swear it, you hear! The truth! That damned bastid played me along and I fell for it, thought he'd marry me, but did he? Did he? I believed him when Eli was alive, believed him when he said I couldn't get a divorce, but after Eli was gone, the bastid had no more excuses and he still didn't marry me. I was good enough for his bed, but not good enough for his name! That doctor is right, my stupid daughter. I am sick! I been sick for years. I wasted my whole life waitin' on him, waitin' to become Mrs. Mack Landry and live in the big house. And whadda I got to show for it—nothin'! Nothin' but an empty house and a full bottle and now they want to take that from me too! Well, I won't let 'em, you hear! I won't let 'em. . . ."

Valerie got up from the couch now and walked over to the bar to pour herself a short brandy. Every time she thought of that conversation, she was as appalled as she had been the first time; but as David had remarked when she told him about it, she shouldn't have been surprised. That day in Mack's kitchen after Eli's funeral had been strangely tense; the clues for what had been going on had been there, if they had only known to look for them.

But it was not merely her mother's illness or her secret life that replayed in Valerie's mind. The impact went deeper, touching off a fear she had begun to feel after her father's funeral but had deliberately ignored.

She began to wonder what would happen to her if David was no longer there for her; no longer providing not the security of financial comfort but the security of his love, his protectiveness, his acceptance of all responsibility for her life. She began to realize that she was as dependent today as she had been at eighteen, at eight. Her life had been a series of dependencies: her father, for a roof over her head and food in her stomach; Mack, for sustenance to keep believing; her husband, for security. Never once had she truly risked herself.

And that, she understood now with a startling clarity, was Mack's promise of long ago. All this time she had thought she had fulfilled his promise that she would leave Galesville. But that had been only the dream. The promise was that she had it within her to do anything, be anyone, accomplish whatever she wanted. She had spent years believing that she had proven herself, but all she had proven was that dependency could be made frilly and pretty to hide its basic flaws, but the weakness of the position never changed. And it was that very weakness that made her mother's conversation so terrifying to her. Take away the expensive clothes, the beautiful homes, the powerful, wealthy, influential, protective man, and what was she—nothing.

Angela had said in the kitchen that afternoon in Bel-Air not so long ago that the day would come when Valerie would need herself. She did not know what she would do or how she would do it; did not know how to tell David that she was ready to fulfill the promise, not just the dream. All she knew was that Angela had been right, and the time was now.

A few nights later, Valerie waited anxiously for David to come home from a dinner meeting with Mayor Lindsay to discuss a special week-long salute to Seventh Avenue. She was waiting for him in bed, trying to read Leon Uris's latest best-seller, *QB VII*, but her tension made the words a blur.

Telling one's husband that one wanted to go to work should not have caused such nervousness, she realized, but with David the anxiety was warranted. Little had changed in the years of their marriage regarding his Professor Higgins attitude toward her. He still enjoyed showing her off as his most prized possession. She knew he would not be pleased with this show of independence, but she had to do it, or she would feel a self-betrayal that would make her hate him someday.

She greeted him warmly when he came in at eleven o'clock, then waited until he was in bed. "David?"

"Hm?"

"I'd like to talk to you about something."

"Later," he muttered, reaching for her.

"Now, David. Please."

He hiked himself up against the headboard. "Okay. What's so important it can't wait till morning?"

"David, you know I enjoy going to school."

"Yes?"

"I mean, it's been a really terrific experience."

"Val, I'm delighted you like school—go ahead and get your Ph.D. if you want. But I'm exhausted and I'd like to make love to you before I fall asleep."

"School isn't enough, David," she went on doggedly. "I want something more. I want to *do* something."

"Do something? And what exactly would you like to *do*?" He made no attempt to disguise his impatience or the mockery in his voice.

"Work. I want to get a job and go to work."

"You must be joking."

"I'm quite serious."

"What in hell do you know how to do—serve people on

an airplane?" he snapped. "Be serious, Valerie. You're about as equipped for a job as . . . as a diamond is for cutting glass. Sure you could do it, but why spoil a good thing?"

"David, I'm not happy. I want more out of my life than what it is right now." She tried to keep her voice steady, to mask the resentment that was building in her.

David laughed, an unpleasant, derisive sound. "You sound like every other bored housewife who doesn't know a good thing when she's got it. Look, Val, I won't have *my* wife running around in one of those little Madison Avenue boutiques or opening some fancy-shmancy art gallery. You're not equipped to do anything except what you do very well—and that's being my wife. If you're so damned bored, take a few more courses, study French, learn how to bake bread from scratch." He threw up his hands. "Christ, I don't care, but just forget this lunacy about working."

Valerie's eyes took on the cold, imperturbable look that had signaled her defiance with her parents. "What are you afraid of?" she challenged.

"Oh, don't give me that crap, Valerie." He glared at her, and the slatelike hardness of his eyes told her how disgusted he was, but she would not stop. Her own anger and humiliation gave her courage.

"Obviously you're afraid of something, or you wouldn't be so irrational on the subject. Is your precious masculinity at stake? Is that it?" she pressed, her voice oozing sarcasm.

"Stop, Valerie. Stop this right now."

"No, David, I won't! Dammit, what's wrong with wanting to be more than just your appendage? You don't need a third arm, a second head, so why do you treat me like that, like I'm something unique to whip out when you want to impress people. Why can't you let me be a woman? Why can't you let me grow up!"

Shock cast a gray pallor to David's face, aging him mercilessly. Valerie's skin looked as if it had been painted thickly and artlessly with red blotches from a palette of fear and fury.

"I didn't realize I was hampering your maturity," David said finally, his voice chillingly soft.

"That's not what I meant and you know it!"

"Then please explain yourself."

"I'm tired, David—tired of waiting for you to tell me who I am."

"That's ridiculous!"

"You're not worried about the wife of David Kinnelon working because it might diminish you in front of your friends," she went on relentlessly. "You're too secure and self-confident to worry about *them*. Oh no, David, the only thing that's bothering you is how *you* might not be able to handle it."

"You're crazy," he said with what was intended to be withering disdain, but he looked away from the fiery intensity challenging him.

"You're afraid to lose control. Right now you have me exactly where you want me, and that makes you feel very, very good. But if I went to work, if I suddenly started to be something on my own, why, David, look at the risk. You just might end up with a wife who was more of a woman than you bargained for, and that, my husband, scares the hell out of you."

"I can't believe what I'm hearing."

"You'd better believe it, because it's the truth and you know it. Refute me, David. Go ahead, I'd really like to hear you tell me I'm wrong. But you know what you fell in love with about me was my innocence, my malleability, my looking up to you and absorbing all you had to teach me. The trouble is you haven't bothered to take a look recently to see how much I've learned."

"Valerie, of course I see what you've become and I'm proud of you, but that has nothing—"

"David, don't you see? Don't you understand?" she broke in impatiently. "You've made me in the image of what you wanted in a woman, and I'm eternally grateful for it. But now I need more. You should understand that better than anyone. If I were married to a different kind of man, maybe this wouldn't have happened. But look at what you are, David—your strength, your intelligence, your success. Didn't you ever stop to think that living with that day after day, being influenced by it in everything I did would have its effect? Didn't you ever stop to realize that one of these days I would need to generate my own self-respect as you have yours?"

"Then why are you accusing me now of hampering you from going further?"

"Because you are! You're afraid that if I take the next step I might not want you anymore. That's what this is all about, isn't it, David? Isn't it?"

"This is ludicrous," he said flatly.

"What's ludicrous is your denying the truth. What's ludicrous is your insecurity. Don't you know that the more you let me be, the more I'll love you for it?"

He looked hard at her, and her eyes never wavered from the probing concentration of his stare. Then he shook his head. "I don't want to discuss this again, Valerie. We'll work out these differences in some way, but the issue of your going to work is closed. Now I'm tired. Good night."

"David, I—"

"I said, good night."

The next several days were like an armed truce, a polite and strained cordiality that was as enervating as a raging battle. They spoke to each other to confirm social plans or to discuss pressing household matters; other than that, no words were exchanged. When they were guests at a party for Beverly Sills, they did not speak to each other until it was time to go home, circulating with an intensity that would have been laughable had it not been so painful to each of them.

At the end of a week, they both had had enough. When David returned from work, Valerie was in the living room. He approached her and silently she rose and went into his arms. They held on to each other, their mutual love and apology tacitly communicated in the embrace.

"I've been such a fool," Valerie said.

"And I've been an old idiot. Val, sit down, let's talk."

Her eyes glittered like crystal as they held steadfastly to his. "David, I'm so sorry," she began.

"Let me go first, Val. This past week has driven me crazy, and if I don't get it all out now I might not have the nerve again." He smiled gently at her, then plunged in. "You were right. About everything. I am afraid to let you go. Not so much because I might lose control but because the thought of you out there with all those young men makes me sick with jealousy."

"But, David, you couldn't possibly—"

"Anyway, not to belabor the point, go to work if you want. I'll back you all the way."

She gaped at him. "You're not serious!"

"I am, totally. If that's what you still want."

"Oh it is, it is!" she quickly assured him. "You know, I was all prepared to tell you I was wrong. That wanting to go to work was a lousy reason to destroy a marriage. It just wasn't worth it."

"That's the same conclusion I came to—once I stopped trying to convince myself that you didn't know what you were talking about," he admitted ruefully. "Now, what do you want to do?"

"Work at Kinnelon," she responded without hesitation.

He frowned. "Kinnelon? You want to work for me?"

Her eyes danced merrily. "Why not? What could be better than being married to the boss. At least then I'm guaranteed preferential treatment," she teased.

"What would you like to do there?" He paused, looking at her thoughtfully. "I have a feeling you already know exactly."

"Real estate," she said. "Making something from nothing, creating a building for people to work in or live in or have fun in, like a hotel—that intrigues me. And it's an exploding business. I think there's room in it for an amateur to learn."

David considered for a moment. "You've thought this through?" She nodded excitedly. "All right, then, we'll meet with Grant and Ray."

Valerie wrapped her arms around his neck and raised her face to be kissed. His hands came around her slowly, almost reluctantly, as if the naked, defenseless emotion he had shown had left him more vulnerable than he liked. Then he crushed her to him, hugging her so hard that she felt breathless. And in that moment, Valerie realized the power she held over this man, and silently vowed never, ever to abuse it.

Chapter 18

The first six months of Valerie's apprenticeship were a never-ending round of questions and explanations until words such as *tax abatements*, *fiberglass*, *asbestos*, *building unions*, and *building permits* rolled off her tongue like the ingredients of a beloved recipe. She delighted in her job and learned something new every day, but then came an incident that threatened to turn her world upside down.

One of the only aspects of her new life that she did not relish was her proximity to the man whose appeal for her had never waned, but as the days passed, and even evenings working late, she came to believe that Ray was merely a crush, not a problem. When a trip to St. Louis was scheduled to look into a site for a luxury apartment building and Grant and Ray suggested she join them, she thought nothing of it. It would be her first trip with them, and only the excitement of the experience was on her mind.

They were staying at the airport hotel, and after a mediocre dinner had gone into the cocktail lounge, which was also a discothèque. After thirty minutes of blasting rock and roll, Grant excused himself.

"I'm packing it in," he said, getting up from his barstool. "The beer is flat and the music's too loud. The combination is making all that white gravy from dinner come gurgling back up." He grinned down at Valerie. "Don't let him keep you up too late. He can boogie all night if you let him." His eyes turned hard for a moment as he stared at Ray. "Don't do anything dumb, Kinnelon," he muttered, then left.

"What did he mean by that?" Valerie asked.

"Who knows." Ray shrugged. "Grant gets off on being the wise old man and sometimes he's a pain in the ass."

"I like him."

"Hey, so do I. That doesn't mean he can't be a pain in the ass sometimes."

Valerie changed the subject. "I'm glad I came on this trip. I think I'll learn a lot about the luxury end of things you seem so interested in now."

"It's the way to go," Ray said authoritatively. "By the way, how did David take it? Knowing how possessive my father is, I'm surprised he let you go."

"David doesn't *let* me do anything," Valerie said stiffly, then realized how arch that sounded. "Besides, he knew I was safe with you and Grant."

Ray grinned at her, his gray eyes flashing with that familiar knowing glint, and Valerie immediately wished she could take back her words. At that moment, she knew she had been a fool to believe this man wasn't a problem. For the first time, she was alone with him, in a strange place that held no history for her. The temptation to put her conscience aside for even a little while brewed in her like a fever. She knew she should get up from this barstool and go to her room, away from his nearness and the hot pulse of the music and the warmth from the drinks. That was what she should have done.

The music turned soft and slow, and without asking her, Ray got to his feet and took her hand, leading her to the dance floor. When he put his arms around her, his body heat penetrated her clothes so that it was all she could do not to gasp. He glanced down at her, his mouth a tight smile of awareness, but he said nothing as they moved to the music.

Against her will, Valerie shut her eyes and imagined what it would be like to go up to her room with him, to extend this moment to its natural conclusion, to yield to her desire. She imagined what it would be like to feel his bare chest against hers, his hands touching and igniting her, his mouth on hers.

"Come on." Valerie's eyes flew open at the husky voice in her ear. It was only then she realized that the music had stopped and they were still on the dance floor, and she was still in Ray's arms. "Come on, Val. We've waited long enough."

"Ray, no, this isn't—"

"Ssh." And he took her by the hand out of the discothèque.

She didn't resist. It was as if David were a stranger from her past, and here, with Ray, in this small hotel, was everything she could possibly want in the present. She said nothing as he led her into his small room, the large bed declaring its purpose as if a red ribbon were wrapped around the pillows.

"Drink?" he asked, going to the bottle of vodka and bucket of ice he had on the dresser top. She shook her head, warily watching his every movement.

"Sit down," he urged, moving to the bed. She followed, sitting on the edge, tensing for what she knew would happen, wanting it to happen, hating herself for wanting it.

"Come here," he whispered, taking her in his arms. "You don't know how long I've wanted to do this."

His mouth brushed hers gently at first, but for Valerie it was as if she had been kissed by fire. Every nerve in her body twanged with longing, and she leaned in to him, demanding more closeness. When the pressure of his mouth increased, she met it eagerly, her hands going around his neck, entwining themselves in his thick hair. He pushed her down on the bed and slowly undid each small pearl button on her silk blouse, the touch of his fingertips making her ache. His head lowered to her neck and her arms wrapped around him as he nibbled at the sensitive flesh and began to move lower. She strained against him, her breathing ragged as her mouth sought his again.

"Jesus!" he managed, whispering the word hoarsely as he leaned away from her and looked into her eyes shimmering with passion. "Either my father isn't a very good lover or you're hotter than I figured," he said with a short, crude laugh.

Had David stepped into the room at that moment, the effect on Valerie could have been no less chilling. Reality slammed against her senses, sending her reeling up and off the bed. She recoiled inwardly, nauseated by herself.

She rebuttoned her blouse and picked up her purse.

"Hey, where're you going?" Ray asked. "Val, don't be a child about this. You're no virgin, so what the hell. We both want it, for Christ's sake. What's the big deal?"

"David is the big deal."

"What he doesn't know won't hurt him."

"Maybe to your way of thinking, but not mine. David is my husband and I love him very much. And if I were ever to cheat on him, it certainly wouldn't be with his own son." She moved to the door, then turned around. "I'm sorry, Ray. I didn't mean to let this get so far."

Sleep came slowly to her that night. She wondered if she would be able to work with Ray again; if he would tell Grant what had almost happened. She thought about quitting, but how could she explain that to David? And she thought about the next time. If she stayed on the job and found herself in a similar situation, on the road in a dark lounge with too much to drink and too-vivid fantasies, would she be able to stop herself again? Ray Kinnelon knew her too well. He knew his effect on her, and he knew her vulnerability to him. If she did stay on the job, she would have to be very careful about protecting herself from him. No, she thought as she finally let sleep claim her, that wasn't the problem. She would have to learn how to protect herself from herself.

What occurred over the next several months was far different from what Valerie had anticipated. She need not have worried about a sexual tension between her and Ray; countering his attitude took all her attention and energy.

Every suggestion she made had to be defended; every opinion that was at odds with one of his had to be debated. Even after a year, he still treated her as if he was indulging a whim of his father's, condescending to her as if she were a secretary instead of a woman with a flair and an aptitude for the real estate business. It was the posture he had adopted since the first day she had started at Kinnelon; the incident in St. Louis had neither alleviated nor exacerbated it. In the beginning Valerie had looked upon his endless criticism as a challenge, a way for her to reach for the right answers; months later, it had become a restrictive chain that would have hampered her progress had it not been for Grant's unwavering support and patience.

She saw in Grant a self-control and poise reminiscent of David. He had an uncanny way of diffusing potentially explosive situations, and an engaging ability to endorse ideas that Ray might not like without antagonizing him and arousing his volatile temper. She had once witnessed Ray rip into a job foreman for a slight mistake, then wrap his arm around the man's shoulder in the next instant, the gesture meant to eradicate the humiliation of the dressing-down. Ray believed that people understood and forgave him not only because he was the boss's son but because he deserved to be understood and forgiven; he was smart and successful, and that gave him certain rights. Grant never trod on another's self-respect. He encouraged and, when a mistake was made, enlightened. He was a natural-born leader of men, Valerie had come to realize, whereas Ray was a natural-born leader of businesses.

She knew that she was a cause of dissension between the two men, but she had no idea how frequently. On this particular September morning, more than a year since she had started working, she was again the subject of an argument between them.

"I think you're wrong, that's all. You support her too strongly and that's only because you've been dying to get into her pants. I ought to know—I have, too—but for a stepson it wouldn't be seemly."

Grant clenched his hands into fists to stop himself from throwing a vicious punch at Ray's smug face. They were in Ray's office on the eighteenth floor of the Kinnelon Building on Park Avenue, and Ray had been telling Grant that he did not like the way he handled Valerie.

"You're a pig, you know that?" Grant said with less heat than he felt.

Ray laughed, his gray eyes cold with insolence. "Yeah, and there's not a damn thing you can do about it. That's the beauty of being the boss's son."

"Too bad you didn't pick up some of your father's class, too," Grant retorted.

Ray shrugged. "The point of all this is that I'm fed up with both you and her and that cute little tutorial program you've had with her for more than a year now. I've told you enough times, the more you encourage her, the worse it is, but you don't give up, do you?" His eyes narrowed. "Sure you're not getting any on the side?" At that, Grant started to rise from his chair, his face dark with fury. "All right, all right, calm down," Ray said with another laugh. "Just testing."

Grant sat back down slowly and removed his tortoise-shell glasses as a delaying tactic to restore his composure. In all the years he had known and worked with Ray, he had accepted the differences between them and had learned to use them productively. Ray was brash, he was deliberate; Ray was cocky, he was cautious. The combination had flared into heated arguments, countless screaming matches, all ultimately resolved over a beer. Except the battle over Valerie.

"You've been against her since the first day David brought her in here to work and I still don't understand why."

"I've told you before, she doesn't know a damned thing and she doesn't care. This is just a way for a rich broad to idle away some time."

"You don't believe that for a minute," Grant argued. "You know she's extraordinarily intelligent, Ray. She's picked up more this past year than some people do after a long time of specialized training. And she's good, very good, and she's getting better, if you'd just give her a chance. You've tried this idle-broad number on me before and it won't wash. You don't want her around for another reason, and I've got a good idea what it is."

"Oh yeah?" Ray asked warily.

"Yeah." Grant grinned, enjoying himself. "What are you afraid of—that Valerie might see you're not as great as Daddy?"

"You're a stupid bastard, Hollander. She's a waste of important time, that's all. My father has nothing to do with this."

"Or the fact that you find her attractive," Grant supplied lazily.

"Believe me, if I wanted her, I could have had her a long time ago."

Grant's brows raised, rage again swelling his chest, but he said nothing.

"Listen to me, will you?" Ray went on. "If we have to have her around here, there's nothing we can do about it; my father's still boss, after all."

"Odd, I thought you already had him out to pasture."

"Just don't be so damned supportive," Ray finished with a fierce glare. "Deal?"

Grant stood up slowly, brushed a hand through his hair, and moved over to the edge of Ray's desk. He placed his palms on a mound of papers and leaned over so that his face was only inches from Ray's. "No deal, Ray. You and your father may pay my salary, but you sure as hell don't have the right to tell me how to treat people."

"You stupid son of a—"

"I've been knocking but no one heard."

Grant quickly straightened and turned around. Both he

and Ray stared self-consciously as Valerie stood in the doorway, arms laden with blueprints.

"Uh, sorry, we didn't hear you," Ray said.

"Obviously," she replied. "Artistic differences?" she asked, sharing her smile with both men.

"As good a way to put it as any," Grant remarked dryly. "Sit down, Val. We were just discussing those old brownstones on East Seventy-eighth Street."

"That's what I wanted to talk to you two about," she said, placing the blueprints on Ray's desk and sitting down in the other guest chair. "I think it's a mistake to tear them down. These apartments are structurally sound. Why not sell them as is, to the people already living in them?"

Ray lifted his eyes from the sight of Valerie crossing her legs and shot an amused glance at Grant, who kept his expression impassive.

"What's your reasoning, Val?" Grant asked.

"Who cares?" Ray said dismissively. "We could get more money if the apartments are new, plus the tax advantage is better."

Valerie's eyes went to the window that afforded a magnificent view of a cloudless September sky, but she was as mindless of the vista as she was of the tension between the two men. Excitement filled her, and the pause was to gather her thoughts so that she could best win her argument.

This latest project was Ray's: to tear down some older brownstones that were fully occupied and build luxury co-ops on the site. She had studied the blueprints and given the plan a great deal of thought, and her idea was in complete opposition to Ray's concept, but she felt instinctively that she was right. All she had to do was convince Ray of that.

"Well, Val?" Ray prodded.

"Okay, here goes," she said with an engaging grin. "I think that within ten years, probably less, the rental-housing situation in New York City is going to explode with costs so prohibitive that only corporations and diplomats will be able to afford them. People aren't going to have a place to live."

"So they'll have to buy," Ray pointed out.

"Exactly. But not all of them will be able to afford the luxury condos and co-ops you want to build."

"There's more money out there than you realize," he

said. "And more schmucks ready to spend it. They think that if you charge them a lot they're getting something special," he said with a grin of superiority.

"That's not the point," Valerie argued.

"Well then, by all means explain your point." He made an obvious show of looking at his watch. "Be fast, though, I have another appointment."

"Take your time, Val," Grant said. "Don't let this bully intimidate you."

Valerie gave him a grateful smile, then continued. "Since most people won't have the money for luxury rentals or co-ops, there's got to be another solution for them. Plus, the cost of construction for less-than-luxury buildings is so high that there's a poor return on investment. But what if we turned current rental units into condos and co-ops and let the people now renting *buy* them at an attractive insider's price. It's the perfect answer!" She paused, looking from Ray to Grant, then back to Ray.

"I'm listening," Ray said reluctantly.

"First, people will buy because they'll feel they got a bargain and because they'll be able to stay in their homes. Second, they'll buy because they'll figure that if the rental market is so tight, others will have to buy, too. In that case, they'll sell—at a profit. Then they'll have more money and just might use it to move upward, into one of the luxury buildings." She sat back in her chair, dark eyes flashing with conviction.

"Well, say something, you two!" she finally urged with a nervous laugh after several long moments of silence. "What do you think? Grant, come on, tell me, is it a terrible idea?"

His brown eyes crinkled and his usually stern mouth softened with a smile. "No, it's not a terrible idea at all." His smile broadened as he looked directly at Ray. "In fact, I think it's brilliant."

"Hey now, just a minute," Ray quickly put in, flashing Grant a warning look. "It's not a bad idea, I'll concede that, but who needs it? Let the small-time operator have the small-time conversions. I want Kinnelon to stand for luxury."

"That's a poor argument," Grant protested. "There's not a damned thing wrong with Valerie's proposal, Ray, and you know it. You're being ornery for the sake of orneriness." He smiled at Valerie again, and she watched the two men carefully, wondering which would win: ego or intelligence.

Ray's eyes hardened. "I didn't say there was anything wrong with it. I'm saying who needs it. There's not enough money in it for us."

"But there can be," Valerie explained. "Kinnelon buys up the buildings, we *own* them, Ray, and our costs are minimal to fix up a lobby, put in a new boiler, that kind of thing. Then we sell. Maybe it's not the megadollars you're used to, but there is money in this. And that money can make money as people buy and sell."

"Val's right about one thing," Grant offered. "Rental housing in this city is going to become nonexistent, and people have to live somewhere."

"Let them move to Queens."

"It's going to happen there, too," Grant said, undaunted by Ray's sarcasm. "We can still build the luxury apartments, meanwhile making money off these smaller units. I think it's worth investigating."

Ray opened his mouth to speak, then shook his head and looked pensively at Valerie. "Dammit, I don't even believe in my own arguments enough to fight you on this!" he finally admitted, smiling. "It *is* a brilliant idea, and I should have thought of it first. My father better watch out. You learn fast, Val, damn fast. Next thing we know, you'll be taking over the soccer team!"

"Thank you," she said softly, her eyes locking with his in an expression that totally excluded Grant from its warmth.

For the next several months, Valerie felt more fulfilled and exhilarated than ever before in her life. The Watergate break-in came and went, as did Nixon's subsequent landslide election. Troop pull-out continued in Vietnam, as did the failure to have peace with honor. People were talking about Tutankhamen as if he were a prized dinner guest instead of a mummy, and acupuncture clinics sprouted in California so that, from the notorious Esalen Institute in Big Sur to the quick quacks in Los Angeles who specialized in everything from LSD therapy to "tattoos for a better you," the state became a mecca for misfits and miscreants. When David and Valerie spent a few weeks in Bel-Air, every party they attended, even those with the most conservative guests, featured an artisan-crafted pottery dish with hand-cut cocaine, the new form of afterdinner mint. The men took to wearing tight jeans and shoulder-length hair or, lacking enough, combing their back hair forward, then teasing and spraying it, and looking like shrunken heads when they finished. Displaying chest hair became a masculine obsession, wearing gold medallions a masculine prerogative. And in New York, revolutionary causes enticed symphony conductors to make fools of themselves, and actors and actresses to voice their own lines with stridency and self-importance. But for Valerie, all this played in the background. Going to the office, stretching her abilities, learning, gaining on her potential—that was what her life was really about.

After a March day spent enjoying the scent of spring while walking along the hidden streets of Greenwich Village and studying the details of the houses in Washington Mews and Grove Court, vestiges of elegance long forgotten in the postwar mass construction boom, Valerie arrived home eager to draw up sketches for door and window designs for a renovation they were planning in Hoboken, New Jersey. One of the areas in which she had recently discovered a talent was designing. She knew she didn't have the vision to be an architect, but when it came to details such as doorknobs, shelving, cabinets, fixtures, she had a flair that even Ray encouraged.

She picked up her mail from the glass-and-brass table in the foyer. "David?" she called out.

"In the den."

"Hi darling," she said, kissing him.

"You look happy," he said, getting up to pour her the glass of white wine he knew she liked in the evening.

"I am. I've got some terrific ideas for the Hoboken project, and I got letters from Billy *and* Mack. What a windfall, and it's not even my birthday."

"Not for another two weeks," he said. "Do you realize you're going to be thirty?"

"Ugh. Don't remind me."

"Are you kidding? I've been waiting for this birthday for years. Now you'll finally be over the hill. Ugly, old, no sex appeal," he went on with mock solemnity. "I guess I'll follow tradition and trade you in for a newer model. Isn't that what men my age do?"

"Men your age should be grateful for whatever they can get," she retorted. "Now let me read my mail."

She opened Billy's letter first. "He's been made a partner in his firm," she said. "Isn't that great? And he and Rob are going to Tahiti this spring. Can you imagine the two of them in Tahiti?" She grinned. "That island may never be the same." She refolded the letter, then opened Mack's.

As she read, her face paled and an odd kind of ringing, like out-of-tune guitar strings, thrummed in her ears. Where she held the letter turned sticky with the clammy perspiration from her fingers.

"Val? What is it? What's wrong?" David asked, alarmed by her sudden change.

Wordlessly, she gazed at him, through him, the letter still clenched in her hands. Her eyes were like glass, shiny but opaque, and their unblinking, unfocused stillness increased his anxiety.

He reached for the letter, but she drew away, and began to read aloud, her voice a sound as flat and gray as an endless stretch of highway.

> "Dear Valerie,
>
> I am writing you now because I have many things to say and probably not much time left to say them. I can picture you as you are reading this, a shadow falling over the beauty of your face, the warmth leaving your eyes. I have taken the coward's way out by writing, but if we were together now, it would not lessen the pain or ease the burden, and this way, we are both able to maintain the dignity of our feelings.
>
> I have known for a long time that I am dying, but does one ever really *know* such a thing? Yes, it's there in our minds as something far off, something to deal with after we are too tired to enjoy more than the sounds of the birds returning after the winter, the colors of the leaves when they burst into ripeness, when tasting the sweetness of the first apple of the season hurts our teeth more than it

pleases our palates. That is when we think that maybe, only maybe, it is time for death. But certainly never before, when there is still so much to learn and do. So for over a year now I have known, but I have not known because I still believed that I could cheat it until I was ready for it. But I'm a very sick man, and the doctors have given me only a matter of weeks. I know what you're thinking, and no, I could not tell you before. It's ugly, unpleasant, unhappy information, and why should you have carried that around with you?

Because death is close at hand and because knowing that makes a person too aware of his frailties and transgressions, I want to tell you something that I should probably go to the grave with. Indeed, 'confessing' is not really good for the soul, just easier on the conscience. You know your mother is a very sick woman. Not sick as I am, but in a way she has a more terrible disease. Unhappiness. For as long as I have known her, she has seen and believed only what she wanted, never what really was. She did this with you and your sister, and still does it. When I see her, there is always a remark about Princess Alice, always a belittling comment about you. You probably will never understand what a threat you were to your mother, a threat that was passed on to your sister. I was able to get you away from one, but you must work at staying away from the other. That is one of the messages of this letter, Valerie dear. Listen to your husband and to your true friends when it comes to Alice. Even if you don't believe us, trust us. She is your enemy, as is your mother. Don't keep giving her second chances, new opportunities to hurt you—she'll use them. I'm sure you're reading this and getting angry, but consider it the right of a dying old man and a loving friend to offer advice one last time.

Let me go back to your mother. By now you undoubtedly know that she and I were once lovers. No, it's unfair to that word to use it for Edith and me. We availed ourselves of each other, but your mother, in her self-delusion, believed that it was more; believed that I would marry her once your father died. I never told her I would; I never promised her anything. She believed what she needed to believe, and I need you to believe that I am telling the truth. I am not the cause of her sickness, but I might have helped it along by never convincing her of the reality, and that I do regret.

One last thing I want to share with you. You are approaching a milestone in your life, your thirtieth birthday. I would like so much to be able to celebrate it with you, but I'm staying in Boston with Ty for the end. So I want to wish you the joy I have always wanted for you, just more of it.

Ty will be handling the will for me. I've spoken with him and Wayne, and neither of them want the 'big house' in Galesville. They like living in Boston, Ty with his law practice and Wayne with his fancy men's-clothing store. And I'm glad, since I have always wanted you to have the big house. And that is my bequest to you, my dear Valerie. The big house where we discovered each other, and the farm, and my love, which will last long after I have gone.

Mack"

Tears streamed down Valerie's face. She did not look at her husband, did not go into his arms to be comforted. She sat with the letter held tightly in her lap, her heart pumping hard as wave after wave of conflicting emotions stormed over her. Resentment that this man she loved like no other, this man who had been father and friend and savior was leaving her, billowed and crested. Pain at the loss slapped against her soul; cold fury pounded mercilessly. How dare he be taken from her? How dare he leave her? How dare he die! Grief was affecting her like a pebble tossed into a pond, each thought generating another in an ever-widening circle of anger and anguish until finally nothing was left but the reality of her desolation.

When she could no longer bear to be alone, she lifted her tear-glazed eyes to her husband and saw him sitting there watching, waiting for her.

"Oh, David, David," she sobbed, and collapsed into his outstretched arms.

Three days later, David, in order to put a stop to his wife's carping, went for a complete medical checkup. The next day, he met her for dinner at the newly opened Windows on the World atop the World Trade Center, and reported on his clean bill of health.

"Happy now?"

She nodded. "I know you indulged me, and thank you. It's just that with Mack, I got scared."

"I understand, sweetheart." He paused while the waiter served their cocktails. "Val, I know you said you didn't want to visit Mack now, but that was right after you got the letter. It's been a couple of days—do you still feel the same?"

"That was the whole point of Mack's letter, David," she explained. "He wants his dignity at this time, and even calling him would be wrong." She shook her head. "No, I'll do it his way, even though there's nothing I want more than to be with him."

"Are you pleased about the house?" he asked. "We haven't even discussed it."

"Very much so. I may never use it, but just knowing it's there and it's mine makes me feel good."

"Children would like it." David said the words softly, his eyes carefully on the onion in his Gibson.

Valerie hesitated before answering, her eyes narrowing slightly at the unexpected remark. "Yes," she said slowly, "they would like it. What makes you say that?"

David shrugged, hoping his expression was more casual than he felt. "No reason."

"David?" she coaxed. "Come on, something's on your mind. Did the doctor tell you you're getting too old to have children?" she teased.

"Not exactly," he replied, "but he did ask why you and I haven't had kids. To tell the truth, I didn't know what to answer. I know we agreed when we first got married to wait until you felt ready, and that's the last time we ever discussed it. I feel like the most inept, insensitive clod, but it never entered my mind again. I guess I figured that if you wanted a child, you'd tell me. And then with the letter from Mack, I got to thinking about our mortality." He grinned self-consciously and rubbed one finger around the icy rim of his glass. "I suppose what I'm leading up to in a not particularly graceful way is—what do you have to say about the subject?"

Valerie's expression was guarded. "Would it upset you very much to be a father again at your age?"

"Not if that's what you wanted."

"I'm not sure if it is. That's the trouble. I've thought about it, of course, what woman doesn't, but I'm just not sure."

"Are you afraid?"

"No more than it's wise to be afraid. I'm certainly not concerned because my sister has a history of miscarriages," she assured him. "No, I think what makes me hesitate is you. I wouldn't want you to be indulging me. I would hate that, David. And you'd resent me and the baby for disrupting our lives."

"Val, to tell you the truth, I think it would be kind of terrific to have another child. An old man my age with a baby son—I like the idea!"

"It could be a daughter, you chauvinist."

"You'd have to stop working, of course," David said.

"Oh really?" Valerie's eyebrows rose and a knowing smile played about her mouth. "So that's what this is all about—a way to get me back in the house, waiting docilely for you every night with pipe and slippers."

"Well, you would have to stop working," he repeated. "Wouldn't you?" he added with less conviction.

"Nope. Women work right up to their last month, even in their last month if they can. And then go right *back* to work after they give birth."

"Is that what you would want to do?" David asked, genuinely startled by his wife's attitude.

"Sure. Oh, David, don't be so old-fashioned." She laughed. "I haven't worked hard this past year and a half just to toss it away. My job means a great deal to me."

"Wouldn't a baby?"

"Of course, but I can manage both. It's been done before, you know."

"But still . . ." Confusion clouded his eyes.

Valerie took his hand in hers. "Darling, don't you think we're being a little premature," she said gently. "I haven't even conceived yet."

Valerie worked until the middle of her eighth month, when the sheer weight of carrying the child in the cold of December became more than she could handle. With the exception of two weeks of morning sickness, her pregnancy had been trouble-free. Each passing stage had been an event to be shared with David; each change in the contour of her body an excuse for him to bring her another trinket, another bauble. He behaved with fatuous pride, and Valerie thrived. There was an energy in everything she did, and at work, both Ray and Grant were stunned by her output and intimidated by her insistence that they stop hovering over her nervously—she had no intention of giving birth in the office.

Toward the end of December, David suggested they hire a private nurse, but Valerie refused.

"If you're worried, let's ask Angela to stay," Valerie said one evening. "She's good in emergencies."

It turned out that Angela was leaving within days for a three-week cruise to South America with Carlos, a twenty-six-year-old jewelry designer.

"How about Linda?" David offered.

"I can't ask her," Valerie protested. "She's got her new husband to take care of. Darling, be reasonable, I really don't need anyone. You're just a phone call away." She snuggled closer to him on the long living-room sofa, her stomach making the position awkward. "I'll be fine, David, honest. You're worrying for nothing."

David rubbed his hand lovingly over her roundness. "Maybe so, but having a nurse here would make me feel better."

An idea began to form in Valerie's mind. She wondered if she dare suggest it, even though it was the best solution.

"David, no nurse. I mean that," she said emphatically. "But if it'll make you feel better to have someone here, I have a suggestion."

"Name her. Anyone you want."

"Alice," she said matter-of-factly, but then her hands flew to her stomach, and she was not sure if the baby's kick or the hard hammering of her heart had caused her to flinch.

Such utter amazement blazed in David's eyes that his silence seemed hyperbolic. Finally, he began to laugh, a dry, brittle sound like crackling wood in a roaring fire. "You really are a glutton for punishment, aren't you?" he bit off. "Of all the women in the world who can be with you at this time, you choose your worst enemy." He moved away from her. "Forget it, just forget it, and I'll try to forget you even said it."

"But, David, it makes sense. She—"

"I said no!"

"Just listen to me, please."

David jumped to his feet and stood glaring down at her. "The answer is no. End of discussion. Is that clear?" There was a quiver in his voice, the tremor of fury barely leashed.

"You're totally irrational on the subject, you know that?" she said hotly.

"Damn right I am, and with good reason. Christ Almighty, what does it take to get through to you?" he bellowed, giving in to the passion of his astonishment. "The woman hates you. She'd sooner see you dead than help you have a baby." He began to pace the living room, then pivoted and strode back to tower before her. "There's a small war raging inside me now, Valerie, between guilt at not doing what you want during this time and absolute conviction that I'm right. I'm afraid I'll live with the guilt. No Alice."

"You're wrong, David," Valerie said with a calm that surprised her. "She's my family. She would never do anything to hurt me or this baby, but I can see there's no point in arguing with you."

"Damn right. Now, who'll it be?"

"Oh, hire your stupid nurse, I don't care. But you have to do one thing for me."

"Anything, just name it," he agreed readily, sitting down again.

"I want Alice here when I have to go into the hospital. Now, don't go getting all stubborn on me, David, and listen.

This would mean a lot to me and it's a compromise for both of us."

"But why? I just don't understand you when it comes to your sister. Why have her here at all?"

"Because this is a time when a woman wants her family around her. My mother is too sick and—"

"But I'm your family, Valerie. And Ray."

"You are, darling, but it's not quite the same." She saw the hurt in his eyes and hoped she could make him understand.

"David, I know how much you love me, and I know you think Alice is bad for me, but trust me about this, please. Having this baby is so important to me, and I want . . . well, I just want someone who's 'old' family with me, someone who knew me when I thought babies came from vitamins!" She laughed, but the tension in his face did not disappear. "I know this doesn't make much sense. It's just that a sister . . . a sister is a special kind of relationship and I want mine with me at this time."

"She didn't feel this need for you when she had Maggie," David pointed out.

"We're different."

"I think this may be the only time I've ever wanted you to be more like your sister," he commented dryly.

"Will you do this for me, David? Please?"

Lack of understanding was evident in the furrow of his thick brows, the sharp concentration in his eyes, the tightening of his lips. After several moments he shrugged. "Call her and arrange it. But just for the last few days, Valerie, no longer. When does the doctor think it's due?"

"Between January fourteenth and nineteenth."

"That's right, I forgot he could practically pinpoint the hour. I think I liked it better when doctors kept the secrets to themselves and let us be surprised."

"Well, we don't know the sex, silly," Valerie said, glad for the shift in subject.

"Now, we have a deal, right?" David pressed.

"Right. You get a nurse and I get Alice."

"At the last minute."

"Yes, David," Valerie said with feigned patience. "At the last minute."

* * *

The nurse proved helpful and unobtrusive, easing Valerie's qualms about having her in the house, and Alice did not have time to annoy David because she arrived on January twelfth and Valerie went into labor the evening of the fourteenth. After thirteen hours of excruciating labor, the obstetrician performed a cesarean; it was either that or risk both the mother's and the baby's lives. Valerie was built too narrowly; the baby could not come out unless it was lifted out.

Two weeks later, Valerie held her baby in her arms for the first time. After an eternal moment when she feasted on the sight of her daughter, she feebly looked around to see who was in the room with her.

"Welcome back," Ray said, moving to her side and taking her cold hand in his.

"Ray," Valerie's voice was a gossamer veil of sound, as light and weightless as air. "Isn't she beautiful?"

"You're beautiful, and you gave us one helluva scare."

"Where is everyone? Where's Alice? And David? David's not here. Where is he?"

"You've been very sick, Val," Ray explained carefully. "You had a cesarean two weeks ago."

"Two weeks!"

"Val, please, don't get excited. The doctor'll kick me out of here if he thinks I've upset you. You've had this place frantic."

"I'm sorry, Ray. Go on. I don't remember much of anything."

"You've been in and out of consciousness. It seems that you were storing up all the poisons in your system; the organs that get rid of them weren't functioning properly." He grinned. "This is kind of embarrassing."

"Please, Ray, just tell me."

"You got all distended, bloated, as if you never gave birth. The doctor was worried that the incision would burst. Nothing seemed to work to expel the wastes, and you were getting sicker and sicker and the danger was increasing. Drugs weren't working, special catheters weren't working. Do you remember any of this?"

Valerie shook her head; her eyes, like huge, highly polished blue-black marbles, were riveted on his face. "All I remember is thinking how tired I was, so tired that I didn't think I'd ever be able to hold my baby."

"Well, finally they gave you a shot of something or other, something powerful because the next thing you were doing what you should have been doing two weeks ago. And now here you are." There was a smile on his mouth, but Valerie found it curious that he would not meet her eyes, that he kept looking at her hand, or the foot of the bed, or the vase of freesias on the dresser.

"Ray, where's David?" she asked again, putting as much strength as she could in the question.

"Val, look, you need your rest. I'll be back later." He started to pull away his hand, but she held on tightly.

"Ray, where is my husband? Why isn't he here with me now?" Like a crack in a cement wall, a tremor of panic split her voice.

"There was a little trouble here," he mumbled.

"What kind of trouble? Dammit, Ray, tell me!"

He inhaled deeply, then sat down on the edge of the bed and held her hand in both of his. "Val, when you first came out of surgery, the doctor brought the baby to you. Alice, David, and I were here with you when the doctor brought her in. She was the most beautiful thing I've ever seen, like a soft pink duck." His smile was fleeting, the memory a weak weapon against the tension.

"Go on," she urged.

"We were standing here, marveling at her, not worried about you yet because we didn't know anything was wrong. We all came over to the bed to get a closer look at the baby, and Alice, Alice . . ." He stopped and shook his head, unable to continue.

"Tell me, Ray," Valerie whispered, conveying her urgency in the hard squeeze she gave his hand. "What did my sister do?"

"Oh Christ, Val, it was horrible," Ray burst out in a hoarse voice. "She stared at the baby, really just kept staring at her like the poor little kid was peculiar or deformed or something, and then she turned to David with this smile, I can't begin to describe it—it was demonic, like something only a warped imagination could create. Her eyes, I'll never be able to forget her eyes, they were like two blue diamonds, glittering and cold, so cold." He shut his eyes and shivered, but the image could not be dispelled by a shake of the shoulders.

"What did she say, Ray? Tell me, tell me!" The panic was stronger now, no longer a crack but a lesion, and her words came out haltingly, with breathy gasps.

"She turned to David and with this smile on her face, that coldness in her eyes, she said, 'Oh, David, she's beautiful, which is no surprise, of course. And to think Valerie believed she could get away with her little secret. But then, you knew, didn't you? I mean about her and Ray?' And she laughed, this husky, almost seductive kind of sound. It was obscene. Dad and I just looked at her—goggled, actually—and she said, 'You're really a grandfather, David, but congratulations anyway.' And then she walked out. She simply walked out."

"And David?" Valerie managed, convinced that her heart would slam through her chest in one final convulsive beat of repulsion.

"He went berserk," Ray said. "I've never seen him like that, he just went crazy. He started to storm out after her, but I held him back. He tried to wrestle out of my grip, his strength was unbelievable, and he kept groaning this animal bellow from deep inside him, not saying anything, just roaring. I've never seen such rage, such fury. And then . . . then . . ." Again Ray halted; this time when he tried to get up and move away, Valerie let him.

"What happened to him, Ray?" she cried. "Something's happened to my husband! You've got to tell me!"

With his back toward her, unable to deal with the fear and shock he knew he would see on her ravaged face, he spoke in a voice roughened with the abrasive edge of soul-twisting anguish.

"David had a heart attack, Valerie. He's been in intensive care ever since. We don't know if he's going to make it."

BOOK IV

Chapter 19

In July 1975, as the heat and humidity of New York began their inexorable journey to the oppressiveness of August, Valerie was immersed in her work, as she had been unrelievedly since her husband's death two weeks after her daughter, Christianne's, birth in January 1973.

Since that time, Nixon had resigned, Ford had taken office, books on the Watergate scandal had made pop celebrities of journalists, pollution had become the revolutionaries' new cause, and a film producer named Irwin Allen had made a fortune out of misfortune. For Valerie, the events of the world occurred but did not touch her; it was as if she viewed life with peripheral vision while her major focus was on her daughter and the half-control her husband had bequeathed her in all of Kinnelon Enterprises. Despite her holdings, she left the various businesses to those best equipped to handle them, and devoted her energies to the ever-expanding real estate endeavors.

Finding a substitute, if not a replacement, for her husband would have been easy. She met men constantly on her job, and there were always invitations from women in the social circle she had shared with David to meet eligible men, as there were invitations from the husbands of these women to fulfill their fantasies and increase their conquests. Valerie said no to them all, her social life circumscribed by Grant and Ray, both of whom had become closer to her and surrogate fathers to Christianne; and by Angela and Linda, as steadfast as ever. Valerie had had no contact with her sister since Christi's birth. A condolence card sent by Alice and her husband had been shredded and burned; occasionally a call would come for her in the office, but Valerie's secretary had been instructed never to put her sister through to her. She was dead as far as Valerie was concerned. What Mack and Angela and Linda and David had wanted for her all these years had finally come to pass, and if there was remorse for this turn of events, the inescapable loneliness in the townhouse; the blaring silence of the Bel-Air estate; the interminable emptiness in her bed, overrode it.

This afternoon, with the sun a magenta ball in the western sky, and the bleat of horns signaling the Friday exodus to country and shore, Valerie tried to concentrate on the cost estimates Grant had provided on a suburban waterfront condominium complex in Westport, Connecticut. It would be the first for that bedroom community that prided itself on expensive single-family homes, but Grant believed that luxurious suburban condos were the wave of the future, and if Kinnelon got the municipal go-ahead for these plans, it could be the beginning of a whole new form of development for them. The problem was that Valerie's mind kept slipping from charts and graphs to Ray, something that had been happening too frequently lately.

She wondered when she would finally give in to his invitations, which had ceased to be familial more than six months ago, as if he had been waiting for the sake of propriety only. It was never a question of *if* she would yield. Since David's death, work and her daughter had become convenient shields from a freedom to have Ray if she wanted him. And she did. She had never stopped wanting him.

Occasionally the thought came to her that it would be much better if she could feel about Grant Hollander as she did about Ray. With Grant there were no psychological tangles to confuse her, no memories to shadow their association. But for so long now Grant had been as familiar and dear to her as Linda, a friend, quietly there, quietly supportive, and comfortable, someone from whom she did not have to hide herself. But it was not Grant whom she thought of when she read an erotic passage in a book or watched a love scene in a movie. It was Ray; it always had been.

Fortunately, Valerie did not have to lie when Ray invited her to his place in Southampton this weekend, as she usually did, making up a variety of lame excuses to avoid being with him an entire weekend. Linda had called earlier in the week, crying hysterically, announcing that she was coming to New York. Her second marriage was over; she had finally kicked Mark out last weekend, and she needed to be with Valerie. And on Monday Ray was flying out to Chicago for a few days. By the time he returned, perhaps he would have decided to stop trying. That would be better for all concerned, Valerie told herself without a trace of conviction.

"Isn't she gorgeous?" Valerie stage-whispered, smiling broadly as she gazed down at the sleek, dark head of her daughter. She glanced up at Linda and at Nancy, the nurse, and her smile turned self-conscious. "I know, every mother says that."

"Well, in this case it's true," Linda agreed. "Night, sweetie," she said, leaning over the crib and kissing her goddaughter's velvety cheek.

"Good night, my love," Valerie said, doing the same. "Good night, Nancy," she said to the nurse, and she and Linda left.

In the kitchen, Valerie poured coffee. "Sure you don't want anything stronger?"

"Liquor'll just get me crying again," Linda said, "and I've done enough of that this whole week." She sighed. "Two marriages, Val. Count 'em, two. Is it me?"

"What do you mean?"

"Am I too demanding, difficult, bad in bed, a lousy cook—what the hell is it with me? The first one runs off with another guy, and this one thought I was a Joe Palooka doll, punch her and she bounces right back for more. Where do I find them?"

Valerie smiled indulgently. "In bars, on airplanes, in the aisles of grocery stores, in your gym."

"Are you trying to tell me I have lousy judgment in men?"

"Well, let's just say not too discriminating." Seeing her friend's hurt expression, Valerie quickly said, "I didn't mean that the way it sounded. It's just that you need to be with someone all the time. That can lead to mistakes, I guess."

"Then I'd better learn to be alone. Though I couldn't do it as long as you have."

Valerie sat back and sipped her coffee thoughtfully. "Sometimes I don't think I can do it another day," she admitted.

Linda looked at her with interest. "You know, I've been blabbing nonstop since I got here, typical me. Talk, Val."

"There's nothing to say. It was just a comment."

"It's Ray, isn't it?"

"What in the world gave you that idea?"

"How well do we know each other, Val? Who was it you told so many years ago that you couldn't marry David because you were hot for his son? That hasn't changed. You've been good about it, but I've seen you when he's around. I've watched how careful you are to be polite and cordial and indifferent. But I know what that cost you. I think you feel about Ray today exactly as you did eleven years ago when you first met."

"Don't be ridiculous," Valerie said, carefully avoiding her friend's keen eyes.

"Now I'm positive. That 'don't be ridiculous' line is one of your more obvious giveaways."

"Linda—"

"And that's another one. Don't 'Linda' me, Val, you know it won't work. Does he know?"

"Does he know what!" Valerie exclaimed with a tinny laugh. "It's remarkable how you never change. You've got the two of us in bed when we haven't even been formally introduced."

"Okay, so he doesn't know," Linda went on blithely. "But something's been happening, I can tell."

"Since when did you get so perceptive about feelings?"

"Touché," Linda muttered, and Valerie apologized.

"I'm sorry, that was mean. I just don't like this conversation, that's all."

"Forget it."

"Good. Now, what shows do you want to see while you're here?"

"No, forget the apology. I'm not finished talking about you and Ray."

"Linda, please . . ."

"You do still care for him, don't you?"

"Well, what if I do? It's impossible. It's wrong. He's David's son."

"Was David's son. *Was*. As of two years ago, he became a very eligible man for you."

"He has asked me out a couple of times," Valerie confessed, and had to laugh at Linda's, "Ah-ha, I knew it!"

"So what's stopping you?" she asked.

"He's David's son!" Valerie repeated. "Somehow that seems so . . . so improper!"

"That's an idiotic excuse. Try another."

Valerie grimaced. "Think how humiliating it would be to face him in the office every day if it didn't work out."

"Hey, what's a little humiliation between co-owners of a multimillion-dollar company? He can't fire you, right?"

"I'm not his type," Valerie pointed out, offering the arguments she had been using on herself. "He likes models, like the red-haired cover girl he's seeing now."

"Valerie, I like models too. Broad-chested, tight-assed, dark-haired hunks. Does that mean I would turn down a bald-headed guy with three-inch glasses if he excited me? Come on, who're you kidding? You've got a case on him and you're scared to death."

"It's been so long," Valerie said softly, her eyes reflecting her nervous pleasure at the idea of being with Ray. "I haven't been with anyone but David, I might not—"

"Oh pooh," Linda cut her off. "Just do it. For once in your ordered, proper, controlled life, do what you want and to hell with the consequences."

Three days later, Valerie received a telephone call from Angela, who had returned from a quick trip to Chicago to attend an exhibition of works by a sculptor friend of hers.

"There was a fabulous dinner afterward at Le Perroquet—I just love that place—and it was really strange," Angela said. "I saw Ray there with your sister."

Valerie ogled the receiver as if a venomous snake had somehow been put in her hand.

"Isn't that odd? I mean, what in the world would Ray be doing with Alice?"

Valerie planned to ask him that the next time she saw him, but instead, he invited her out for dinner and she accepted, and because going out on a date was such a new experience for her, and because the man she was having the date with was someone she had wanted for so long, she completely forgot about it.

Two months whirled by in a succession of baseball games and Broadway plays, brunches at the townhouse, dinners at La Grenouille and La Côte Basque. Each weekend they took Christianne and Nancy and trundled off to Ray's Gin Lane home in Southampton.

One night in mid-September, Valerie found herself in Ray's apartment for the first time. She had told him, when he had once invited her there early in their relationship, that she preferred not to, offering no explanation, and Ray had said that he understood how she might feel uncomfortable, maybe even unfaithful to David's memory in some way. It wasn't that at all. Valerie knew that she felt safe in a restaurant or her own apartment or even the house in Long Island; she did not have to confront her constant longing for him, the hunger that she woke with each morning, twisted and turned with each night. But in his apartment, on his territory, she would have no excuse that they might wake the baby; no way to say good night and make *him* leave. She was afraid that in Ray's apartment, she would give in to herself.

But after a lovely dinner at Windows on the World, in the cab going back uptown, Ray had given the driver his address, and before Valerie could object, he had put his finger against her lips.

"Ssh. It'll be fine," he had whispered, and she had decided that it would be.

"I can't believe you've never been here before," he said now, coming up behind her with a flute of champagne in each hand.

Valerie turned from the window-wall that overlooked Central Park. "I guess there wasn't a reason," she said, taking the glass. "It's a beautiful apartment," she added.

Ray had the twenty-first-floor penthouse in a magnificent prewar Central Park West building. The two bedrooms and den had a view of the Hudson River; the living room, dining room, and kitchen faced the park. The decor in the living room, where they were now, was masculine with its burgundy suede couch, its two marble cube coffee tables, its black leather Le Corbusier chairs, its simplicity and architectural coldness, but there were comforting touches of warmth scattered about that relieved the austerity. An enormous Mexican rug woven in vivid oranges, yellows, and sunset purples punched heat and light into the room with almost physical force; a mound of overweight pillows covered in thick Moroccan cotton lessened the severity of the brass-framed fireplace; a back-lit étagère that held wooden miniatures of all the Kinnelon constructions added whimsy and youth.

"This is wonderful," Valerie exclaimed, looking at the collection. "What a great idea."

"Grant started it for me," Ray explained. "After we designed the hotel in Washington, D.C., I refused to let him toss the working scale. He told me that since my office was larger than his, I could keep it if it meant that much. The next thing I knew I was taking it home, and then he found some of the old ones he had been keeping in a storage room in the office. Ever since, it's become a way for me to keep track of our growth. Plus they're attractive, of course."

She smiled at him, and wondered if he could tell how nervous she was and how much she wanted him to touch her and take the decision out of her hands. He was so handsome, his long, thick dark hair only slightly touched by gray near the temples, his slate eyes so shrewd like his father's, so confident; his wide, full mouth almost obscenely sensual. Age had thinned his face, indented creases from his nose to his mouth that added a certain virile harshness to his appeal. She wanted to taste that mouth, feel his lips capturing hers. She needed to run her hands on the hard, muscular expanse of his chest and know what it would be like to be close enough to hear him breathing, feel his heart against hers, thundering with desire as hers was now doing.

She turned suddenly, her blue silk Oscar de la Renta dress swirling against her calves. She did not dare keep looking at him. Her longing had to be obvious.

The soft strains of Frank Sinatra singing "Fly Me to the Moon" filled the room. "Let's dance," he said.

Facing him, she marveled that she had ever thought of his gray eyes as cold, when heat made them smolder like coal. He took the glass of champagne from her and placed it on the window sill, then opened his arms for her. Now is the time to go, she thought. Before it's too late, before you won't be able to say no. Go, now.

But then she felt the soft wool of his jacket brushing against her silk dress, and she was taking small, slow steps with the music. A gentle nudge and she was closer, her lips against his neck, his hair feathering her cheek.

"Oh, Valerie, Valerie," he murmured, and her blood ignited, fire spreading in her thighs so quickly that she felt weak-kneed.

"Ray?"

"Mm?"

"Why haven't you ever married?"

He held her away from him and stared down at her speculatively, a quirky half-smile curving his mouth. "You ask the damnedest questions at the damnedest times."

She said nothing as she continued to meet his eyes, her own bright and glowing.

"Don't you know why?" he went on. She shook her head, daring to dream of the answer, not daring to voice it. "I've been waiting for you. From the beginning. From that time in the Plaza when I saw you sitting there with my father, watching me, judging me. And all the time since then."

Her eyes turned darker with pleasure at his words. "And you've wanted me, Valerie," he said in that same warm caress. He brought her close again, each word a skin-scorching breath on her flesh. "You wanted me since that evening and all these years, too, haven't you? Haven't you?"

She did not trust herself to speak, sure that her voice would be thick and the words unintelligible. She nodded against him, a movement as slight and short as a musical note. Sinatra's mellow voice played on, but they stopped dancing. An ambulance siren wailed twenty-one floors below. Valerie heard nothing, the roar of her heart excluding all else. With tantalizing slowness, Ray lowered his head, and then, finally, he was kissing her. Unlike that time in the St. Louis motel room, tonight she would take what she had long wanted.

Her mouth opened to him, their tongues meeting, exploring, inflaming. She felt the thrust of his hips, and responded by pressing closer to him. He lifted his head and her mouth felt deserted, but then his lips found the column of her neck, and the tender place by her shoulders, and the promising hint of cleavage. When he tugged off the straps of her dress, and his mouth met the crest of her breasts, she had to bite her lip to keep from urging him to hurry. Exquisite yearning throbbed within her, and she did not want to wait, did not want gentle seduction. Not this time. This time she wanted to be taken fast, hard, immediately.

"Ray, hurry, please," she whispered as his hands found her breasts, straining for more than his touch. Her hands played along his back, then reached between them, boldly searching for him, telegraphing her need with each stroke. Fleetingly, she wondered what was happening to her, where this shameless aggression came from. She felt like a stranger to herself, her arms and mouth and flesh demanding and taking instead of following and accepting.

"The bedroom," Ray said, and led her by the hand down a hall. She could not wait for him to undress her; while he was still taking off his own clothes, she stood naked and wanting. When he faced her again, he did not have a chance to utter a word. She was covering his face with kisses, discovering his back and arms and chest with hands that could not be stilled. They tumbled onto the king-sized bed, limbs entwined, tenderness abandoned as they punished each other with passion.

And when it was over; when their bodies turned cold and the gasps for air became measured breathing, Valerie understood, at last, what had been denied her all those years with her husband.

Valerie let laughter and frivolity back into her life. She would leave the office at four o'clock to prepare dinner *à deux*. She bought three hundred dollars' worth of new bras, panties, teddies, camisoles, and slips, and five hundred dollars' worth of nightgowns and peignoirs. She giggled as she walked down the street, embarrassed at the freeze-frame image that flashed in her mind of Ray and her in the shower, his erotic style of getting clean a fantasy fulfilled. She shared almost every detail with Linda, who applauded loudly from the sidelines. To Angela she confided the momentary lapses she still experienced: Was this right? Should she be feeling so good with David's *son*? And Angela always said, "David would approve." Sometimes, when she spent the night alone, Valerie would look at the picture of David she kept on the mantel in the den, and she could almost believe that he would.

Only occasionally did Valerie think that the storybook combination of sexual fulfillment and deep, tender love were still eluding her. Ray's cavalier attitude toward Christianne sometimes bothered her; he always brought her gifts, but he gave nothing of himself to the child, not even a stroll in Central Park. He continued to badger Valerie professionally or, worse, condescend to her when he was forced to admit she was right. He had a selfish habit of showing up two hours late for a date, with an excuse about work, or unplanned drinks with a client, or sometimes no excuse at all. And his increasingly curt attitude toward Grant—belittling his ideas, canceling his decisions, disapproving his plans—disturbed her greatly, causing her to consider whether Ray's arrogance at being a Kinnelon had swelled now that he had her, as if she were the final challenge in proving that he was as good as his father.

What troubled her the most about her relationship with Ray was how Grant had changed toward her. The easy camaraderie that had so long been between them seemed strained now. Grant was more formal with her and always had an excuse when she invited him to the house. She did not understand this new distance, attributing it to an old-fashioned, gentlemanly awkwardness since he knew that she and Ray were sleeping together.

But these were all minor flaws compared to the perfection she found in Ray's arms. Much could be forgiven for the sake of sexual ecstasy.

Chapter 20

"Mommy, Mommy, come here, look at what I did!"

Alice clenched her jaw and gripped her coffee cup in

both hands, hoping her daughter's screeching would stop if she did not reply.

"Mom-my! Come here!" came the whine seconds later. Furious, Alice put the cup in the saucer with such force that some of the liquid slopped over the rim.

"Shit!" she said, and stormed out of the kitchen and up the stairs to her daughter's room.

"Maggie, what is it? Don't you know I'm busy!" she snapped, the sight of her child's prettily flushed face and fingerpaint-splattered smock doing nothing to soften her.

"Look, Mommy, look at what I made," Maggie said, proudly holding up her fingerpaint portrait of her mother. "See, it's you. But I couldn't make it as pretty as you really are," she added, looking at her mother with the same shallow, pale blue eyes, only their innocence was genuine.

"That's nice, Maggie. Now I'm going back downstairs and I don't want to be disturbed. Do you understand?"

Maggie nodded solemnly, her blonde curls bobbing. "I'm sorry, Mommy. I won't yell again. Do you have a headache?"

"Yes," Alice replied, and started to leave.

"Mommy?"

"What is it now, Maggie?"

"I love you."

"I love you, too," Alice answered without feeling, and then left, shutting the door to her daughter's room with a clang.

Back in the kitchen, she wiped up the spilled coffee, then poured herself another cup but did not drink it. She went through four pots of coffee a day, and rarely took a sip. It was the same with food. She always prepared a large breakfast for herself after Dick had gone to work and Maggie to school, but she never ate so much as a piece of toast. She went out to lunch with the women she knew and played with a chef's salad but never ate. Dinners were the most difficult because she was never alone. Either she was at home with Dick or they were out with friends or clients. She had to struggle to bring a forkful of food to her mouth, and it was torture to swallow, but she was tired of being lectured by Dick and everyone else about how thin she was getting.

What the hell did they expect? Who could have an appetite when your insides were being consumed?

Dammit, she couldn't stand living like this much longer. It wasn't fair, it just wasn't fair. Her marriage had become a charade played for the benefit of a six-year-old. In the years since Valerie had stopped speaking to her, Alice had taken to adultery the way a Frenchman takes to the kitchen; her affinity for duplicity found a perfect outlet in a series of liaisons. At first they were enough to diminish the loss of her sister's generosity. At first. But then the thrill of clandestine meetings and the sweet triumph of seduction palled as inexorably as dreams become compromises, and when Dick had discovered one particularly indiscreet affair and threatened her with divorce, the pleasure in illicit sex had died, leaving her alone with her desperation.

Had she known the snowball effect her remark that day in the hospital would cause, she would have tried to control herself, but seeing Valerie in that bed, surrounded by loving friends, and looking at the puffy ball of life in her arms and knowing the advantages that child would have, had been too much for Alice. She had needed to strike out as viciously as possible, and so she had attacked with the remark about the baby being Ray's, about David being a grandfather. She had underestimated his loathing of her and his capacity for rage, a rage so ferocious and deep that it had killed him. She had been similarly startled to find herself cut off from Valerie. She had never expected that, never imagined that her sister could be so strong. And for this long.

When she had finally realized that Valerie would not weaken as she always had in the past, Alice had decided that more strident measures had to be taken. If she could not get to her sister, then she would find another way, but that life would no longer be denied her. She was not getting younger; her looks would soon stop carrying her on a free ride. She needed to act and soon. So, a few months ago, she had tried to trap Ray. It had been a nervy thing to do, calling him out of the blue with the excuse that Dick had asked her to learn when he would next be in Chicago since he had some business to discuss with him. When she had met him at Le Perroquet, alone, claiming that Dick was violently sick with a stomach flu, she had felt confident that he would be a much easier target than his father. She had made it clear that she was eager to go to bed with him, but Ray had only thanked her. Thanked her! He had said he was flattered, found her enormously charming and appealing, but thought too much of her for a one-night stand, which is all it could be. Bullshit! Pure bullshit!

And now the columns and magazines were filled with pictures of her sister again, only this time it was with Ray Kinnelon that she was photographed. Young, dashing, impossibly wealthy Ray Kinnelon who was escorting her sister to the parties and discos. Her sister was doing it again, but this time she would not succeed. No matter what it took, this time Valerie would lose.

What Alice had been thinking for many weeks now, since she had seen the first photo of Ray and Valerie; what took away her appetite and made her short-tempered with her daughter and shrewish with her husband—was how to hurt Valerie. In order to destroy her, Alice had first to get close to her again; lull her into trusting her once more, regretting the two years of silence, guiltily welcoming her back into her life. Only when Valerie was vulnerable would stealing Ray from her give Alice the glorious satisfaction she craved.

Alice knew that to get back with Valerie she needed help, someone to nudge open the door; she could make the final push herself. But who? Her mother was out of the question, a hopeless alcoholic finally institutionalized last year. Angela and Linda would lay down their lives for Valerie, especially if it meant thwarting *her* in any way. She didn't know Grant well, but her instincts told her he was a Kinnelon man through and through, devoted to David and probably equally devoted to his widow. She didn't dare approach Ray again. He was too quick, too cunning; he would see through her. Unlike Teddy Chambers those many years ago, Ray would not swallow any tale she might tell; he would confront Valerie, and that would serve no purpose.

Who then? Who was close enough to Valerie to be used? Trusting enough to be manipulated?

She sat there a long while, staring into her cold coffee, chipping away at one red lacquered fingernail. Her mouth began a familiar twitch. In and out, in and out went her lips, like the metal click beetle toys of childhood. Chip at the polish, click went her lips; chip, click, chip, click.

And then she knew. In the quiet of her Lake Forest kitchen, she laughed out loud, and when her daughter called out, "Mommy? Are you okay?" Alice did not hear her, because she was laughing so hard. Her cheeks flared pink with triumph, and her blue eyes glittered coldly like the chrome handle of the refrigerator as she opened the door. Suddenly ravenous, she took out a pound container of potato salad and ate directly from the plastic tub until there wasn't so much as a parsley flake left.

"I don't believe it, not a word. You're up to something, Alice, same as always. What is it this time? You have money, you have a daughter, a loving husband, a nice home, so what could it be? Or is it the same old thing—get Valerie for the sake of getting her?" Billy Cardell took his cloth napkin from his lap and tossed it disgustedly on the table at Ernie's, where he was having dinner with his sister. "You never change, do you?"

Alice made an effort to keep her composure. She wanted to take the glass of ice water and toss it in her faggy brother's face. At thirty-five, he looked ten years younger except for the loss of his wispy blond hair, now just a crown around his ears. His proper, expensive-looking three-piece suit, his manicured nails, his trim body bespoke a successful businessman, perhaps an art gallery owner, someone refined and educated. Not a fag, she thought derisively, quelling the urge to call him exactly that. But she did not want to make a scene in this noted restaurant, and she had not flown out to San Francisco to leave without getting what she wanted.

"Billy, you're misunderstanding me completely," she said, dripping sweetness. "I'm concerned, that's all. I really am. Don't you think I have a right to be?"

"Actually, I think it's none of your damned business what Valerie does."

"Obviously I'm a better sister to her than you are a brother."

He laughed harshly. "That'll be the day. You've had it in for her since the day she was born. What she hasn't told me I learned from Mack and David. You wouldn't know how to be a good sister if your life depended on it."

"That's unfair," Alice protested, feigning offense. "There may have been times when I was . . . well, I guess unnecessarily selfish is one way of putting it—"

"Yeah, one way," Billy interjected.

"But that was a long time ago and I really am worried about her now. And Christianne," she added somberly.

The wariness and contempt that had alternated on his face all evening now disappeared, leaving only genuine interest. "What about Christianne?"

"That's what I've been trying to tell you, Billy," Alice said, her eyes opening wide with the seriousness of her message. "Our sister is squandering all David's money, and soon she'll be getting into Christi's trust. Is that right for our niece, Billy? It's one thing to set a terrible example for her daughter by sleeping with her stepson—and anyone else she can get her hands on. At least Christianne's too young to know what's going on, but the way she's spending money . . ." She shook her head, deeply troubled by her sister's enormous transgressions. "Billy, that child is going to end up with nothing, absolutely nothing."

"Valerie's a very wealthy woman, Alice. I can't believe she could possibly spend what David left her in her lifetime, even in Christi's."

"You wouldn't think so, I agree, but it's true. She's redone the house in Bel-Air, and keeps two cars there now but never uses them, just keeps these two big Mercedes and pays a private mechanic to take them out for runs. She's completely redecorated the townhouse, too, and now she's spending thousands on having her office redone."

Billy studied his sister hard for several moments before speaking. "How do you know all this, Alice? You haven't seen Valerie in two years. I think you're making up the whole thing, every damn word. Why? What the hell are you up to?"

"I'm not up to anything," Alice insisted. "I care what Valerie is doing to herself and her child, that's all. And as for not being in touch with Val, well, I'll have you know that we share many of the same friends, and whenever these women are in Chicago, they're quick to call me and let me know what's going on."

Billy said nothing, weighing her words. She reached out and took his hand in hers, swallowing hard to gulp back her distaste for touching him.

"She's changed, Billy. Our considerate, sweet-natured sister has become a stranger." Alice's voice held just the right note of regret. "First, all those men not even six months after she buried David. And some of them the husbands of her friends! Wasting all that money, leaving her child alone with one old hag of a nurse after another. Do you know that no reputable nurse will stay there longer than two weeks because Valerie is never there, and when she can spare an hour from her good times, she doesn't even want to be bothered with what the nurse has to say! Christianne probably doesn't even know who her mother is at this point. And now the disgraceful affair with her own stepson. It's awful, Billy, just awful, and we've got to do something."

"It's none of our business," he repeated, but with less conviction than earlier.

"If we love her, it *is* our business."

"Maybe she's just going through a phase. We've all done that, so now it's her turn."

Alice shook her head. She had been hoping it would not be necessary to use her last card. She did not like her brother, but she had no need to hurt him. Yet, if her lies hadn't convinced him, perhaps anger would.

She removed her hand from his and sat back in the velvet tufted dining chair. She lowered her eyes in a perfect expression of distress. "I don't think it's just a phase when she talks about her brother the queer," she said softly.

"What!"

Alice lifted her eyes, forcing a look of gentle remorse. "I'm sorry, Billy, I didn't want to have to tell you, but it's true. She ridicules you to her friends, calling you names, making no secret of how ashamed she is to have a homosexual brother." She watched, delighted, as his face went white with shock, his blue eyes flashing with disbelief.

"I don't believe this! You're making it up. Valerie would never speak of me that way, never!"

"Why would I lie about such a thing, Billy? I hate hurting you this way, but you've got to understand how desperately our sister needs help. If you don't do something soon, who knows what could happen."

"Me? Why should I do anything to help? If being gay isn't good enough for her, then fuck her," he stormed, anger fueling his hurt into a bitchy meanness.

"She needs you, Billy," Alice implored. "You're the only one in the family she's ever trusted. Besides, she won't let me near her. I can't even get through to her on the phone."

"Then let her go to hell."

"I know you don't mean that. You're just angry, and I don't blame you, but, Billy, please, go see her. Tell her we know what she's been doing and we want to help her. Tell her how much I miss her, and that this estrangement has gone on long enough." For the first time that night, Alice's voice sang with sincerity, but Billy was too self-absorbed to differentiate this sound from the virtuoso performance that had been played for him.

"That hypocritical bitch," he muttered.

"She's not a hypocrite, Billy, she's just not herself. That's why you've got to talk to her, convince her that without her family, without you and me, she's got nothing. You've got to see her!"

His pale blue eyes washed over Alice. She did not dare take a breath, did not dare blink against his unwavering stare. She had nothing else left to use against him, and no one else left to use against Valerie. He had to agree to see her; he *had* to.

The movement was brief, curt, small; nevertheless, she saw it. An unmistakable nod.

That night, Billy had an argument with Rob. He needed to retaliate for his pain, and Rob was handy. Billy did not tell him what was wrong, so when he left the next day for the airport, Rob had no idea where he was going or why.

Nor did Valerie. Billy tried calling her at home, but she had already left for the office; when he called there several times, she was either in meetings or out, and he did not want to leave a message. So, when he arrived at Valerie's townhouse late that night, he was totally unexpected.

He had to ring the bell several times before Nancy let him in. Too tired, too tense to be polite, he demanded to know where his sister was, then harshly informed the nurse that he would announce himself. He dropped his overnight bag in the foyer, then strode in the direction she nervously indicated.

He pushed open the door to the den. There, on the brown tweed loveseat, was his sister, wearing a floral-patterned peignor that left the length of her legs exposed. Her dark hair was tousled, her head thrown back, eyes shut and a feline smile of contentment on her lips. With her, one hand on her bare thigh, his face partially hidden in the crook of her neck, was Ray Kinnelon, jacket off, the top three buttons of his shirt unbuttoned. Billy need not ever have met him to know who he was immediately, instinctively.

He took three steps farther into the room, then stopped, his hands clenched into fists at his sides.

"Bitch," he snarled. "Filthy, hypocritical bitch."

In one startled movement, Valerie's head came forward and her eyes opened. "Billy!"

Ray jerked away from her as she got to her feet, hastily closing her peignoir. "Billy, what are you doing here?" she exclaimed, rushing toward her brother. Her impulse was to wrap him in a warm welcome, but there was a strange, dead expression in his eyes that halted her motion. She glanced back at Ray, then looked at her brother again, and smiled shakily. "Billy, I had hoped to intro—"

"Slut. You're nothing but a slut. I can't believe how wrong I've been about you." With those words, Billy turned his back on her and walked out of the room.

"Billy, come back!" she cried, racing after him. She reached out for him, but he shook her off; she shuddered from the revulsion she saw in his face.

"Billy, wait, don't go. Let me explain," she begged. "It's not what you think, it's not—" She swallowed the words as the front door was slammed in her face.

Slowly she turned around, clutching the peignoir closed with both hands. She saw Nancy and Ray standing there watching her carefully.

"Val?" Ray ventured. "Who was that?"

"Go to bed, Nancy," she said, ignoring Ray.

"Are you all right, Mrs. Kinnelon?"

"I'll be fine. Please. Go to bed."

When the nurse climbed the stairs and the sound of her door closing echoed through the house, Ray went over to Valerie, who still had not moved from her position by the door. He put his arm around her shoulders and led her back into the den.

"Who was that?" he asked again.

"My brother Billy," she said dully.

"What was that all about?"

"I don't know. I've never seen him like that."

"Shock, that's all," Ray said. "He wasn't expecting me, it's nothing more than that." He grinned. "Brothers have trouble believing a sister is also a woman. Of course, he got what he deserved for barging in on you unexpected."

She shook her head. "No, it's more than that. Did you hear what he called me? Those names, those vicious names. Billy would never talk to me that way. We've always been so close." She clutched Ray's arm, her eyes beseeching. "Something horrible has happened, I just know it!"

An hour later, two brandies had calmed her sufficiently that she asked Ray to leave, assuring him that she would be all right. She told him that she would call Rob in the morning; maybe he would know what was going on.

But by the next morning there was no reason to call California. At nine-thirty, two uniformed policemen arrived at the townhouse to inform her that her brother had been found three hours earlier, in a hotel on Tenth Avenue that catered to homosexuals, his wrists slashed. A note had been found, for Valerie Kinnelon at this address.

"Alice? It's Valerie."

"Valerie! Oh, good gracious, how wonderful! I can't believe it! Oh, Val, I'm so excited. You've finally called, finally! I've been praying for this for so—"

"I'm flying out this afternoon. I'll take a cab from O'Hare to your house."

"But—"

The phone was already dead.

Valerie sat in her first-class seat, eyes closed, oblivious to the stewardesses and to the turbulence that caused the plane to drop and bump. In her lap was the note left by her brother, crumpled like the bottom of a toothpaste tube in the tight trap of her fingers. There was no need to read it again; by now, she had memorized each excruciating accusation of betrayal, each tragic lie. And the hurt. The pitiful, pathetic hurt that had driven Billy to suicide. He had been so devastated by what he believed to be her life-long hypocrisy that he could not even consider talking to her, convinced that what he had witnessed was confirmation of the truth instead of an unfortunate coincidence giving credence to lies.

She did not have to conjecture about the source of the lies; Billy had spelled it out clearly in his note: the visit from Alice, and his conviction that she was lying giving way to his conviction that she was speaking the truth. Indisputable was Alice's mastery at deceit and deception, and so at long last Valerie's innocence gave up the struggle against the loathing she had pretended was indifference. By shunning her sister, she had believed that she also shunned feelings any more disruptive than apathy. But Billy's death had plucked the crust of civility from her emotions as deftly as one peels away the thin, cracked veneer of dried wax from a piece of fake fruit. Nothing remained in her but the need for revenge, a scalding drive that would not rest until, with as much pain as she was capable of causing, she impaled her sister on the ragged blades of her lost innocence. . . .

When Alice opened her front door, the smile she wore was as smooth as her silk shirtwaist.

"Oh, Valerie, it's so wonderful to see you again," she said warmly, spreading her arms wide for a welcoming embrace. Valerie walked past the gesture and into the center hall.

"Where's Maggie?" she asked.

"In school, of course."

"And Dick's at work?"

"Yes, what—"

"Shut up, Alice."

Alice stared at Valerie as if a mad stranger had set foot in her home, but her voice was steady as she said, "Would you like some coffee? A drink?"

"I didn't come here to be sociable. I didn't come here to forget the past two years and make up with you." Without waiting for a response, she pushed past her sister and went to her left, assuming from the layout of the entry that she would find the living room. She sat down on the long sofa and crossed her legs, her brother's letter still gripped like an extension of her fingers. She waited for Alice with an expression of condescension tightening her mouth, deadening her eyes. Nothing Alice could say or do, no lie, would she let penetrate the ice-hard control she had on herself.

"Valerie, what's wrong?" Alice asked carefully, sitting down on the edge of a beige brocade armchair across from her sister. "You seem so—so cold."

"Billy's dead," she said, feeling an enormous sense of pleasure at the way Alice's blue eyes widened with horror, the way her perfectly manicured nails grasped her silk-covered knee; at the sound of her shocked gasp.

"What happened?"

"You killed him."

"What!" Alice was on her feet, and Valerie's pleasure fattened.

She waved the crumpled letter but would not relinquish it when Alice made an attempt to take it from her. "It's all here, every single cruel, vindictive lie you told him about me. He couldn't take it so he killed himself, but you might as well have been the one who held the razor to his wrists. What did you hope to accomplish, you sick, conniving, evil bitch. *Tell me!* Why did you have to go and do this to him, why! Wasn't it enough that you've spent your entire life trying to destroy me? Why Billy? What did he ever do to you! WHY DID YOU HAVE TO DO THIS!"

"You're crazy," Alice said, returning to her seat. "I don't know what's gotten into you, but obviously you're not yourself. Let me get you a drink, a Valium, something to help."

"I don't need a pill, damn you!" Valerie screamed, and then she inhaled deeply, shut her eyes, and willed herself to regain her self-control. To be anything but completely calm and self-possessed would be to defeat the purpose of this trip. She had to show Alice that she had lost.

"All these years, every time someone would tell me about you, warn me to get away from you, I wouldn't listen. Oh, maybe there was a part of me that believed what they were saying, but I wouldn't listen when they said you were evil, you were my enemy. I thought you were just jealous, and I decided I could understand that." Valerie's voice took on the rhythmic, singsong quality of a monologue long rehearsed, never performed.

"When I found out about you and Teddy, I so wanted to believe that you weren't capable of hurting me that way that I went against two people who truly loved me. When I wanted you to share in the richness of my life, you tried to ruin that with your filthy insinuations, still I forgave you. Time and time again, I forgave and forgave. When Mama told me some of your lies, I made myself believe it was her drinking that created them. When you manipulated, oh so shrewdly I must admit, to get that woman to blackmail me, I found every excuse, every rationale I could to deny that you had any hand in it. Even when David died because of the vile, outrageous things you said, even then I didn't hate you. I knew it would be better not to have you in my life, but even then I wouldn't let myself hate. But now you've gone too far. Now you've killed Billy, and you know what, Alice, sweet little Princess Alice?"

"You're crazy," her sister repeated, stunned.

"It feels good, Alice. It really feels terrific to let my hate come through." Valerie's voice scratched as the last piece of hardened rind on her true feelings was picked away. "And let me tell you something else. Whatever has driven you to hurt me all these years can't compare to what I feel about you. *Hate* is too mild a word. You're beneath contempt, you're a loathesome stranger, you're a sick, foul, evil slug under a moss-infested rock who should be stomped until you squirm, begging to be put out of your misery. You should be dead, Alice."

Abruptly Valerie got to her feet and stalked over to where Alice sat cowering in the armchair, her eyes enormous, her white face as bleached of life as a sun-weathered crab shell.

"I take that back," Valerie said, glaring down at her sister, the letter by her side as if it were a ceaseless round of ammunition fueling her fury. A smile that held no kindness tricked her mouth into a curve, and her blue-black eyes burned the agony and rage of her pain into her sister's face.

"You shouldn't be dead," she said as softly as an undertaker's footfall. "You should writhe like the slug, desperate with unhappiness, each second of each minute of each day a long wail for release from your misery. That's what I wish on you—not death, but that the rest of your life be spent knowing the torment you have caused others, with no relief, not a breath's time of relief."

Valerie stared at her sister, transfixed by the twitch of her lips, in and out, in and out, like a metal snapping toy. Was this the beginning of her sister's torture, a small sign that the suffering had already begun? Her smile grew broader, her eyes fiercer at the thought.

Valerie retrieved her purse from the sofa and moved to the doorway. "I lost a brother and a sister today," she said quietly, turning to face Alice one last time. "Billy killed himself because of your evilness, and for the rest of my life, this is the day you died for me as well." She paused; then, even more softly: "The saddest thing of all is that I've died a little, too."

She opened the front door and walked, eyes noting nothing, to the taxi she had instructed to wait. It was only on the way back to the airport that Valerie allowed the tears to come, great racking sobs that tore at her eyes and clawed at her throat, that twisted her heart and cramped her stomach. Such loss, such needless loss. Yesterday, she had had a family, weak as it was, distant as it was; she had believed in it against all truths, even against love. Today it was gone, and with it the last tattered scrap of her innocence.

Alice heard the front door close, but it may have been many minutes or even an hour before she moved from the beige brocade armchair. Time traveled away from her; she was caught in the moment of Valerie's closing the door.

As she sat there, she thought not of what she had caused; her brother had been weak, foolish, another disposable victim like Lena Cardell and Teddy Chambers . . . and Valerie. She had gambled and lost. The fierce determination that had marked her sister at an early age, like a scar, had burned hot and red today, as it had those many years ago when she had defied them all and gone to Texas. She had underestimated her sister then, and she had overestimated her brother now. Neither mattered. She would not end up like her mother, waiting for Mack Landry, waiting until there was no time left.

She would take what she wanted, and to hell with everything else. Ray Kinnelon would be hers, no matter the cost.

Chapter 21

Valerie went on with her life, and if it was with slightly less joy and perhaps a hint more cynicism, she did not regret the change. She pushed herself hard at work, enjoying traveling to new or developing sites more than being in the office. It was when she was in Westport, overseeing the condo development with Grant, or going over blueprints with him on an airplane to Memphis to check their new shopping center, or talking with him late into the night at a hotel bar about her ideas for a luxurious senior-citizens' condominium village in Denver, that brightness twinkled in her eyes, and excitement rang in her voice.

She had stopped speaking of her plans and ideas to Ray; he never endorsed them, never encouraged her, and lately he had even taken to dismissing them as so much feminine fluff. It would have been too easy to measure their personal relationship by his professional disregard, but she decided that would be pointless. She understood Ray's chauvinism, as she had his father's, and she forgave it, secretly happy that at least she had Grant as a friend in whom she could confide her dreams. Ray gave her laughter and pleasure and an exquisite sense of womanliness. If that comfort she had found in David's arms was missing, if that sense of rightness and belonging that she had always believed accompanied love was absent, she easily reconciled the loss with the gain of youthful exuberance he provided, the masculine arrogance she had come to appreciate, and the still-surprising sexual longing he alone could arouse. And so, on March 24, 1976, her thirty-third birthday, when he asked her to marry him, presenting her with a six-carat emerald with four one-carat diamonds, one at each corner, she accepted both the ring and the proposal.

* * *

"Sweetheart, there's something I've been wanting to speak to you about," Ray said one evening in April as they were having dinner at Romeo Salta's. The Italian restaurant had become a favorite of theirs, and they went there at least once a week for their angel-hair pasta, Caesar salad, and unwavering service.

"What about?" Valerie asked, tasting the fine pasta.

"Grant. I've decided not to renew his contract as president of Kinnelon, Inc."

Valerie put down her spoon, and took a sip of her soave before speaking. "What in the world are you talking about?"

"His contract is up next month and I've decided not to renew it," Ray explained with a casual shrug. "I'm chairman of the board, so I can hire and fire whomever I want." He grinned. "Except you, of course."

"Don't I have a say in this?" she asked tightly, her eyes challenging his.

"Of course, but what's to say? Val, darling, you've been so busy with your little plans that you don't know what's been going on."

"I see," she replied, feeling indignation well in her chest. "And what exactly has been going on that I've missed with my little plans?"

Ray laughed at the sarcasm. "Come on, Val, don't be so defensive. You know this job is just an indulgence for you. After all, what you know about real estate I could put in a thimble. And that's the trouble. You have no idea how Grant has screwed up. I can't keep him on, he's costing the operation too much money."

"Everything he's ever built is running at a profit," she pointed out.

"True, but what about all the opportunities he's missed. The Scanlet Corporation has been buying up prime real estate across the country from under our noses and building massive center-city hotels. That's what we should have been doing instead of fooling around with condos and co-ops and those fancy places in Florida and Washington." His eyes hardened as he leaned forward. "When Grant should have been scouting prime urban land for us, he was out in the boonies, designing award-winning buildings instead of money machines. He's got to go."

"I thought the two hotels were doing well," she remarked, carefully tempering the tone of her voice.

"They're doing okay, nothing more, and we don't get businesses at either of them. It's conventions, sales conferences, that kind of thing that keeps a hotel going," he asserted, nodding for emphasis, "and that's where Scanlet has us beat. Los Angeles, Dallas, Chicago, Nashville, Cincinnati, the list is endless. Not to mention—especially not to mention—here in New York," he added with disgust. "Three damned hotels they're putting up, and talk about prime locations. They're going to have the tourist and business trade sewn up. By the time we get into the act, if it's not too late, the damned land will be so expensive it won't be profitable to build." He tossed his napkin onto the table. "That man has cost us a fortune and I've had it with him."

"But, Ray, David didn't want us to get into that kind of business," she reminded him.

"That's where we've all been wrong. My father liked making money. When he told us to stick to the smaller constructions, it was because he thought that would be more profitable in the short run. He was near-sighted, as we all were."

"Oh, then you do blame yourself in part?"

Ray's look was knife-blade sharp. "Damned right I do," he snapped. "I should have been paying more attention to what Hollander was up to instead of trusting him so completely. Well, no more. I'm taking over the real estate end totally, and I'll hire a few good contractors to work under me, the way it was when Grant first started with us. Enough of this artsy-fartsy stuff and enough superior materials and the rest of that crap. I'm going to build hotels and office buildings in the heart of every major city and best Scanlet at his own game. The competition will be good for both of us."

Valerie said nothing, her astonishment freezing her into silence. It was difficult to believe what she was hearing, and yet she did not know how to argue against him. When Ray's mind was made up, as it obviously was about Grant, little could convince him that he was wrong. She had seen him this way when it came to her own projects; when he spoke about some of the personnel in other Kinnelon businesses. Ray could not tolerate a missed opportunity, and even if it was he who had decided to forgo it, when a mistake had been made, it was always someone else who got blamed for it. How different from his father, she thought. David had always accepted the responsibility for error; as head of the company it was his job to do that, he had often told her. But not Ray, whose ego was too vulnerable, too susceptible to slight, built as it was, she realized, not on a self-made foundation as his father's had been, but on inherited strength, extrinsic power.

"I think you're making a terrible mistake," she said.

"I don't really care what you think."

Valerie's eyebrows went up.

"Sorry." The apology was automatic and meaningless. "I don't want to take this out on you, but I'm fed up with Scanlet, and Grant should have been on top of what was happening in commercial real estate. Look, I know you like him, and I know he's been good to you. Hell, he's my best friend. But this is business, Val, pure and simple. Grant's out."

Valerie would not give up. "I think David would be horrified by what you're doing. You know how he felt about Grant."

"David's dead, Valerie," Ray said harshly. "*I'm* in charge now, and I want Grant out. End of discussion."

"What about me? Are you firing me too?"

Ray laughed, a brittle, unpleasant sound. "I can't."

"But you'd like to," she said, feeling the accelerated beat of her pulse, tasting the sourness in her mouth and hating him, quickly, momentarily, for making her feel this way.

"Well, to tell you the truth, I did want to talk to you about your job." Ray's wide, mobile mouth, which she so loved to feel on her skin, suddenly struck her as small and mean, and she was fascinated by its sly ability to speak cruelly with the same ease as it offered tenderness.

"What about it?" she managed.

"Once we're married," he said authoritatively, "I want you to quit. It's not right for my wife to be traveling around the country, traipsing in muddy construction sites, talking with hired help. And I don't want you in the office either. My father may have indulged you your little job, but I refuse to.

It's inappropriate, and I don't need to hold your interest by giving in to this folly of yours." His voice was a vocal strut, a swagger of self-righteousness.

Valerie had the fleeting thought that she had been sleeping with a stranger; had fallen in love with and agreed to marry someone who looked like this man but bore no inner resemblance to him. Had she mistaken this tyrannical male chauvinism for masculine arrogance? Had she thought him forceful, determined, confident, when in fact he was merely a bully? Was his cavalier attitude toward her child, their dates, and her work really a monumental selfishness that, because of her sexual awakening, she had refused to acknowledge? Could she have been so wrong?

An ugly, unwanted image of her brother lying in a pool of his own blood crisscrossed with a memory flash of her sister sitting in an armchair calling her crazy, offering her a tranquilizer. She shivered, and then Ray was holding her hand.

"Sweetheart, I know this has all come as a shock to you," he said with a note of gentleness, "but trust me, I know what I'm doing. I love you, and I want this marriage of ours to be perfect. Not having you work is important to me." He brought her hand up to his mouth and kissed each finger. Then he smiled, that warm, sensuous movement that made her knees weak and her stomach hard with a knot of desire. She could see nothing small and mean in that mouth now. "Baby, I've waited a long time for you," he murmured. "Such a long time. I don't want anything to spoil it."

She could always go back to work after a while, she thought.

Grant returned a few days later from a three-week vacation to London, and Valerie tried to get him alone, but he always had something pressing to handle. When she invited him to dinner, telling him that Christianne was going to forget what her uncle Grant looked like, he demurred, claiming prior engagements. This went on for two weeks, until Valerie forgot her intention to warn him of Ray's plans as she got more and more involved in preparations for her mid-May wedding.

One evening, after an exhausting day of working with

the people at the Hotel Pierre, deciding on floral arrangements and the dinner for the small wedding reception, Valerie begged off from seeing Ray, needing the solitude of a warm bath and an empty bed. As she was relaxing in the den, trying to read the latest issue of *Vogue* but not being able to concentrate, she decided to call Grant at home. He couldn't be out every night, she thought, and she missed talking with him.

"Hello?"

"Well, hello, stranger," Valerie said warmly. "I was beginning to think you were a phantom."

"Valerie?"

"See, you don't even recognize my voice anymore, that's how long it's been since we've spoken."

"Is something wrong?"

"Yes, something's wrong. I've missed you. You took off so fast for London I never even had a chance to formally invite you to the wedding. So, you're now formally invited." There was silence from the other end. "Grant? Are you still there?"

"I'm here," came the flat reply. "Look, Valerie, I'm really busy. Can this wait until morning? I'll see you at the office."

"There's nothing special I wanted to talk to you about," she explained, wondering at his curtness. "I just haven't seen you in a while and I wanted to say hello. Lately we seem to talk about nothing but business. Can't friends share more than that?"

"Of course they can. And that's what we are, friends."

"Grant, are you, uh, I don't know, are you angry with me?"

"Should I be?"

"Well, you sound so peculiar, and come to think of it, you haven't been very accessible recently. If I didn't know better, I'd think you were trying to avoid me," she said with a nervous titter.

"I've been busy, that's all."

"Will you have dinner with me soon? Christianne really misses you and so do I. Who else will tell me my cockeyed ideas aren't so crazy?"

"Ray." The one word had an odd, accusatory sound.

"Grant, I want to see *you*," she said, ignorant of the

torment each word caused him. "Nothing's changed between us just because I'm going to marry Ray. I hope you don't think—"

"I have to go, Valerie. I'll see you in the morning."

She was left with a dial tone.

The next day, she never got a chance to question Grant about his strange attitude, because he was closeted with Ray in the morning and had meetings all afternoon. When she and Ray were having drinks later that evening, she asked if he had told Grant that his contract was not being renewed.

"Not yet. I still need him for that apartment unit in Seattle. Besides, I'm not going to fire the guy."

"You're not?" Valerie asked, surprised.

"Nope. I'm not going to renew his contract, that's all. He can stay on if he wants, but not as president. He can go back to contracting."

"He'll never tolerate that."

Ray shrugged. "Then I guess he'll have to resign."

Valerie stared at him, understanding dawning. "That's what you've planned from the beginning, isn't it? Forcing him out?"

"It's done all the time. I'm not going to be labeled a bastard by those suppliers who love Grant, they're too important to me. This way, he leaves on his own, and we'll both look good." His eyes flashed with satisfaction.

"By the way, Val," he continued, "I have to go to Detroit tomorrow morning for a few days. There's a company out there that manufactures industrial furniture and I'm thinking of buying it. This new high-tech stuff I've been reading about might be a good thing to get into."

"Will you call?" she asked, more out of habit than feeling.

"I'll try, but you know how crazy it can get when I'm locking up a deal."

Ray did not call the next night or the day after that, but Angela did.

"Hi," Valerie said when her secretary put her through. "Are you going with me tomorrow to Laurent's to check out a wedding outfit?"

"That's one of the reasons I called. I can't make it

tomorrow. I'm flying out in around two hours to Puerto Vallarta."

Valerie groaned good-naturedly. "How old is he this time, nineteen?"

"That's unnecessarily vicious, darling," Angela retorted. "I'll have you know that Enrique Marques is a mature thirty with the photographer's eye of a knowing fifty-year-old."

"You're incorrigible." Valerie laughed. "Well, have a wonderful time. Isn't this kind of sudden, though, even for you?"

"The truth is that if I have to appear at your wedding without a tan, someone might guess my real age. I need a little time in the sun, darling, to cover up the liver spots."

When Valerie stopped laughing, she asked, "What's the other reason you called?"

"Oh, yes." Angela's strong, husky voice lost its tone of mirth. "Val, did you ever ask Ray about that time I saw him with your sister in Chicago?"

"No, I forgot. Why?"

"Did you see today's copy of *Women's Wear Daily*?"

"No. I usually save it for the end of the day. Why?"

"Darling, I've really got to run, but check out the paper. I don't like to bring you bad news, but since tactfulness has never been my strong suite, I've got to tell you that something stinks in the stockyards. I'll call you when I get back to the city. Adiós."

As soon as she hung up, Valerie took the paper from her briefcase and flipped through the fashion photographs and line drawings, finding nothing unusual. Then she saw it, in the "Eye" gossip column—a picture of Ray dancing with her sister! She stared at the photograph, then scanned the column for a mention of the couple. There it was: "The notorious Mr. K., Jr., is making his last bachelor days swing, but at least he's keeping it in his fiancée's family."

Hands trembling, heart thudding, Valerie refolded the newspaper and neatly placed it back in her briefcase, each movement precise, as if calculated and deliberate motion would quell the havoc within. She sat back in her desk chair and tried to make sense of what she had read. What was Ray doing in Chicago when he had told her he was going to Detroit? More important, what was he doing with Alice? He knew what had happened between them, knew how much she hated her sister; how could he be with her, laughing, dancing, allowing his picture to be taken for everyone to see?

It became impossible for her to concentrate on her work. She left the office with a terse message to her secretary that she was going home and that if Mr. Kinnelon called, to tell him to phone her there, it was urgent.

It was an interminable wait until Ray finally called at seven o'clock.

"Hi, babe, miss me?" he asked.

"Hello, Ray. How are you?" Valerie said warily. Tell me what's happening, she urged silently. If you volunteer the information then I'll know you have nothing to hide. Don't make me ask you, please.

"Closed the industrial-furniture deal. This could be big, really big."

"That's nice."

"Sure is. And there's a piece of property here, an old single-room-occupancy hotel near the Chicago Convention Center that I want to check out, so I'll stick around a few more days. It might make the perfect location for a hotel."

"I thought you were going to Detroit?"

"I got confused. I meant Chicago. All these midwest cities smell the same," he said, laughing.

"I see."

"Hey, you okay? You sound funny. Everything all right at the office?"

"Of course. Why shouldn't everything be all right?"

"Well, listen, I've got to run. I'm staying at the Drake if you need me. I'll be back in a day or two. Love you."

"'Bye, Ray."

She sat in her kitchen, staring at the dead phone in her hand for several seconds before hanging up. With mechanical rigidity, she went upstairs to Christianne's room. The sight of the dark curls, the chubby pink fingers curled around the Snoopy doll, reassured Valerie that here, with her daughter, was a purpose and a sense to her life, reality without confusion.

Tiptoeing out, she went downstairs to the den. She poured herself a brandy and sat on the sofa, bewilderment and loneliness joining her on either side. Had Ray really mixed up Detroit with Chicago or had he deliberately lied to her?

Why hadn't he told her he had been with Alice? If it had been innocent, unplanned, shouldn't he have mentioned it? And why couldn't she have swallowed her pride and asked him about it outright? Maybe marrying him was the wrong thing to do, she thought. He was so used to being a bachelor, a different beautiful woman in his bed every week. Now he was going to be married to a woman with a child. Maybe he didn't want the responsibility. Or maybe he wanted one last fling before settling down. But why choose her sister?

She gulped the last of the brandy and got up to pour another. She needed to talk with someone, but whom? Angela was off in Mexico; it was only four-thirty in California, which meant Linda was still at her job as a stew instructor. The one person she really wanted to talk to had been treating her as if she had an infectious disease. She needed Grant now, needed the warmth and understanding and support he always provided. He would be able to make sense of what Ray was doing, and of her own doubts. But he was probably out with one of the girls he had been dating lately, every night with someone new.

By her fourth brandy, Valerie's mind was racing in a tableau from the past. Here an image of Lena Cardell, dirtying up Mack and David. There a recollection of Billy's note . . . David treating her like a prized possession . . . Ray manipulating her mind through his expertise with her body . . . Grant, supportive, kind, loving . . . and Alice, always Alice, trying to poison everyone against loving her. Maybe she had finally succeeded, Valerie drunkenly decided. Here she sat, alone, wondering if the man she was supposed to marry loved her. And if she loved him. Had she ever really loved anyone? Or had she polished feelings of gratitude and security with the same waxy veneer she had used over her hatred for her sister?

Distraught, confused, lonely, and drunker than she had ever been in her life, Valerie craved reassurance. She dialed the operator and placed a long-distance, person-to-person call to Ray at the Drake Hotel in Chicago. By the clock on the table, it seemed to be five minutes after eleven, but now Valerie's vision was as wobbly as her emotions and she was not sure it wasn't five minutes to one. As she was trying to make up her mind about the time, the connection was made.

"Hello?"

"Ray?"

"Oh hi, I wasn't expecting you. Anything wrong?"

"No, I just . . ." She stopped. She shook her head, trying to clear away the sound of warm giggles in the background, but it persisted like a headache.

"Valerie, are you all right?"

"I'm fine." She took a deep breath. "I just wanted to tell you I love you." The brandy did not come with sound effects, she told herself, not with that tinkling, bell-like giggle that she had heard once before, years and years ago when Teddy Chambers had pushed her from his life.

"Me too, babe. Anything else you . . . Wait a minute, Val." He muffled the phone, but she could still hear his voice, speaking to someone in the room. "Sorry. Listen, if there's nothing else I—Alice, stop it, will you, just wait a minute." There was a dead stillness across the wires. "Oh shit. Valerie? Are you there? Val?"

She had already dropped the phone, left it dangling against the sofa cushion. She bounded up the stairs to her room and slipped on a sweater and a pair of slacks. Racing out the door, thought and action were out of control; only the need to run from the pain propelled her down the street and into a taxi. Unguarded, unprotected impulse brought Grant's address to her lips. She did not wait while the doorman announced her but headed straight to the elevator. When she got to his apartment, he had the door open, and he was standing there, waiting for her. An image of unrestrained strength printed itself on her brandy-fogged brain. So tall and broad, so comforting in that beige sweater, so unthreatening with his tortoiseshell reading glasses making the deep brown of his eyes even darker, warmer.

She slowed her step as she approached, and when he closed the door, neither of them said a word. Self-consciously, she touched her disheveled hair and glanced down at her hastily thrown-together clothes. Then she looked up at him, her eyes ink-dark with tears, and he opened his arms to her.

"Oh, Grant!"

He held her, not speaking, just wrapping her in his warmth, letting her cry, his own eyes squeezed shut against the rage he felt for whomever had hurt her, for his own helplessness.

At last the tears stopped, and she was still in the protection of his arms, still gazing up at him with heartbreaking need. Slowly, inevitably, their lips met, gently, softly, and then with a crushing demand that left them both breathless.

Long into the night their bodies reinvented pleasure, sometimes tenderly, sometimes brutally, legs and arms thrashing, mouths hungering, nails clawing for a closeness that would shut out reality. A lifetime of loving went into that night; for one, a loving long suppressed; for the other, a loving long unrecognized.

In the morning, Valerie dressed quietly, careful not to awaken Grant. She stood for a moment gazing at him, the lines by his eyes, his mouth, erased, leaving only kindness. She leaned down and kissed the rounded muscle of his shoulder, then she left.

When Grant awoke less than an hour later, he did not have to search the apartment to know that Valerie had gone. He couldn't have checked the other rooms if he had wanted to; he barely made the bathroom in time as self-disgust and remorse heaved out of him in one convulsive wave after another.

Valerie paid the cabdriver and tipped him generously for the drive from the new Eddington airstrip. She took out her suitcase and stood in the path to the house, looking around her, reacquainting herself with the giant apple tree, the overgrown front lawn of the caretaker's cottage, now lived in by a new family; the smell of corn growing and wild daisies and yesterday.

Slowly she walked up the path to the big house, her home now. She would have to get used to sitting on the worn leather couch without Mack there to tell her the mysteries of the world; to being in the kitchen and not having a glass of milk and a batch of Mae's oatmeal-raisin cookies. And she would have to get used to being without her daughter and to trusting her nurse completely; to waking up each day without a briefcase of blueprints or designs speeding her on her way.

She would have to get used to being by herself, thinking for herself, making choices and decisions by herself and for herself. Isn't that what Mack had known she would need when he had left her the house?

BOOK V

Chapter 22

"Mom, come on, we're going to be late."

"I'll be down in a sec, Christi," Valerie called out to her ten-year-old daughter. "Make sure Davey doesn't forget his Rams jacket."

"He's wearing it. Hurry or we'll miss the plane. The cab's been waiting five minutes already."

Valerie glanced at herself in the mahogany-framed mirror over the matching eight-drawer dresser in the master bedroom of the big house. Tomorrow, March 24, 1983, she would be forty years old, a milestone birthday. So much had happened since that morning in May 1976 when she had fled Grant's bedroom for the solace of Mack Landry's legacy to her. Seven years had passed, with the world experiencing the tragedies of Jonestown and Khomeini, the losses of Sadat and Princess Grace; when her own youth seemed irrevocably lost the day Elvis died; when the youth of others was aborted by Lennon's murder.

She slipped on the peach-colored jacket of her Perry Ellis suit, and thought what these seven years had meant for her personally. There had been the joyful discovery of her constantly growing love for the man who was truly right for her, and the indescribable thrill of giving birth to their son, Davey, who would be four in a few months. She had known sadness, too, for the final goodbyes she had had to say to the family to whom she had clung with crablike tenacity. She had . . .

"Mom, come on!" Christianne's squeaky voice of authority shook Valerie from her musings. She pushed up the sleeves of her jacket and turned to grimace cheerily at her reflection. Light brackets marked her mouth and slender fans spread from the corners of her eyes, but for forty, she thought, not bad!

Once on board the airplane bound for Los Angeles, Davey and Christianne settled in with books, magazines, and headphones, while Valerie relaxed with a glass of white wine. She wanted to scan the screen of memory and isolate times that she knew could never be forgotten. Yes, tomorrow was a milestone birthday, she thought, but a milestone in another way, too, marking seven years of ponderous effort and struggle. Remembering made the happiness she now knew that much more precious. She leaned back against the headrest and closed her eyes, recalling that day seven years ago when she had returned to New York from her self-imposed exile to Galesville, when the new phase of her life really began to take shape. . . .

"Just let me say everything I have to, Grant, and then you can talk, okay?" Valerie spoke with more assurance than she felt as she sat in his living room one month and three days after she had fallen into his bed.

"Look, Valerie, I know you've been through a lot. You don't owe me an explanation, you don't owe me anything. It happened, let's leave it at that." Grant was extremely uncomfortable. He would sit down on a cotton-covered pillow chair, jump up, pace the room, sit down at the end farthest from Valerie on his art-deco green-velvet couch, pop up, stride over to the window that faced Gracie Mansion, back to touch a ceramic ashtray, a Steuben glass walrus, sit on the leather ottoman that went with the brown leather recliner, up again. His deep brown eyes proclaimed his embarrassment as loudly as if he were shouting his feelings through a megaphone.

"Will you please stay in one place for five minutes," Valerie requested, smiling. "You're making me even more nervous than I am already."

"How about a drink?" Grant asked, still standing.

"At eleven o'clock on a Saturday morning? No, I think not. Now, will you sit?"

He tried again, this time back on the cotton-covered pillow chair, which was diagonally across from her. He sat on the edge, his fingers spread on his chino-clad knees, his hair tousled as if he had just awakened, which he had. Valerie had arrived twenty minutes ago, unannounced, the doorman's insistent ringing on the intercom and her own knocking on his door finally rousing Grant. With great haste and awkwardness, he had showered and dressed, and was now trying to avoid dealing with the woman he had not seen or spoken to since making love to her more than a month earlier.

"I'll try to make this fast," she said, "otherwise you might run clear out of the apartment on me."

"Sorry," he mumbled, looking down at his hands.

"What I came here to tell you is that I love you."

She had spoken as matter-of-factly as if she were delivering an annual report to a board of directors, and Grant's eyes on her were completely void of comprehension.

"Did you hear me?" she said more softly. "I said I love you, Grant Hollander."

The brown eyes slowly filled with understanding, then with an astonishment as deep and as real as his heart's secrets. A warm smile brightened Valerie's face. "Yes, that was my first reaction too," she said. "When I left you that morning—no, even before that, when I came here, drunk, depressed, so hurt by Ray that I thought I would die, all I wanted was your comfort. I think I must have always known that you cared for me, but I was too blind and too selfish to deal with it." She paused, got up, and went over to the window, her back to Grant as she continued to speak.

"That night I used you. I used your feelings for me, I used your kindness, I used all that is good and fine about you because I knew you would let me." Her voice was a husky whisper, her back stiff as she went on with her confession. "It's funny, usually the man takes a woman for granted, but that's what I had been doing with you for years. You were always there for me and I assumed you would be there for me that night. I didn't care what *you* might feel, all that mattered was that you take care of *me*, that you give me what *I* needed."

She turned around, her eyes meeting his with an honesty that had taken her a month to find the courage to reveal. "When I woke up that morning, I knew I had to leave everything, especially you. It was bad enough that I was wrecking my own life, I didn't have to do the same to yours."

"Val, please, don't do this to yourself," Grant urged, but she stopped him, putting out her hand as he started to go to her.

"Why shouldn't I do this to myself? You'll never call me selfish, or stupid because I didn't see Ray for the shallow man he is. You'll never tell me what a fool I was." Her voice grew more heated. "Do you know he had the nerve to call me in Galesville, and tried to explain about Alice." She laughed bitterly at the recollection. "He thought I would believe him when he said he'd been drunk, thought I'd forgive him." Her mouth twisted with self-disgust. "Why shouldn't he believe that? He knew I'd forgiven my sister time and time again, so how could he think much of my intelligence."

"Valerie," Grant said slowly, this time ignoring her gesture to stay in his chair as he went over to her. "Don't do this to yourself, please. You made a mistake, that's all. We both did." His hands moved up as if to touch her, then dropped back to his sides.

She stared at him, her eyes penetrating his for the truth. "Is that how you really feel?" she asked. "Do you regret that night?"

His hands clenched into fists, and his eyes shuttered briefly. "No," he said. "No."

She stepped closer to him and put her arms around his neck. "Hold me, Grant," she whispered. "Please. Hold me."

Slowly his arms came up to circle her softness, and when he felt her nearness, he groaned, burying his lips against her hair. "Valerie, oh Valerie, I love you so much."

"And I love you. I've been so stupid, so—"

He stopped her with a kiss of such longing and tenderness and rightness that the blood pounding in her ears seemed like music and the bursting feeling in her heart a pain she had relished for a lifetime.

When they broke apart, Grant gazed down at her, eyes brimming with love. He smiled ruefully and caressed the side of her face. "I can't believe this is really happening," he murmured. "Somehow I have a feeling I'll wake up and this will be a dream, like the dreams I've had about you for years."

"Then don't wake up, ever. I want you to feel this way about me for a long, long time."

"Forever, if you'll let me."

They went into his bedroom, and this time when they made love, there was none of the desperation of that other night. Their passion welled from feelings; their pleasure from the knowledge that there would be no more running away.

Later, as Valerie lay contentedly in the crook of Grant's arm, he said, "Ray wants me out of Kinnelon."

She said nothing for a moment, not wanting to spoil the lazy sensuality she was experiencing, but then she propped herself against the headboard. "So he finally spoke to you."

"You knew? Why didn't you say something to me?"

"I tried," she protested, "but that was when you were treating me as if I were a pariah."

"I was jealous as hell," he admitted. "I couldn't bear the thought of you being with Ray, so instead I acted like a pouting teenager." His expression was contrite. "Some kind of jackass, huh?"

She bent over to kiss him lightly. "The kind I love." She paused, then: "What are you going to do?"

"Start my own business, I think. Hollander Construction—how does it sound?"

"Not bad, but I have a better idea."

"You're both crazy," Ray shouted, slamming his hand down on his desk. "Not only that, but you're nuts!"

"You can't stop me, Ray, I own half the company," Valerie said coolly. "And since Grant and I are going to be married, you—"

"What!"

Valerie regarded the man she had almost married, the man she had told herself she wanted for more years than she cared to remember. The physical appeal was still there, probably always would be for her, she admitted to herself. And she would always be grateful to him for the pleasure as well as the pain he had caused her. Without both, she never would have known what was truly right for her.

"I don't believe it," he said, his eyes darting from Valerie to Grant, back to Valerie. "Is this true?"

"Sometimes I think I'm hallucinating," Grant said, grinning and reaching across the distance between his chair and Valerie's to take her hand, "but it's true."

"Well, congratulations," Ray muttered through tight lips, his eyes the color of a sunless winter sky.

"Please, Ray," Valerie said, "be happy for us. You and me, well, let's just say when it was good, it was very, very good."

"Yeah, I know. And when it was bad, I screwed it up." He stared hard at Grant. "You're a lucky s.o.b., you know that?"

Grant squeezed Valerie's hand. "Yeah, I know. And I owe it all to you."

"Spare me your gratitude," he grumbled. "Let's get back to business. Your plan is out of the question. Why in hell should I walk away from the real estate company and let you two run it?"

"Because we love it, Ray, and for you it's just one more Kinnelon enterprise," Valerie supplied. She removed her hand from Grant's and leaned forward in her chair, earnestness glinting in her eyes.

"You don't need it, Ray," she went on. "By letting me buy you out, Grant and I can build what we want the way we want it, and you won't have to worry about a Scanlet Corporation getting too big, or a supplier resenting you, or anything. For you, it's just another way to make money. For us, a way to build dreams."

Ray remained silent, his eyes metallic with speculation. Valerie and Grant watched him carefully, each wondering if the shrewd businessman before them would relinquish his hold on lucrative Kinnelon, Inc. A week ago, Grant had been convinced that Ray would sooner sell his father's soccer team, the bank in Omaha he now owned, and probably three other operations before giving up the real estate business, but Valerie's arguments were sound—or was it that he just wanted this so badly? The idea of building the very best apartments, hotels, and offices, leaders in design and material, thrilled him even as he questioned the practicality of such an endeavor. Ray was not wrong when he pressed the issue of cost effectiveness or spoke of convention hotels that could cheat on room refinement for the sake of additional revenue-producing bars and lounges. He was not wrong; it was simply not the kind of work Grant wanted to do, nor, he discovered, did Valerie. She never forgot any of David's teachings: attention to detail; the cost of the small extras often reaping great rewards; spend money to make money. Ray had accused his father of being short-sighted, she told him, but Ray was mistaken. David Kinnelon had been proud of his name and what it stood for. Grant and Valerie wanted to perpetuate that pride, if Ray would let them.

"I'll make a deal with you," he said now, shattering the tense silence. "I won't sell out, not yet." He tilted his desk chair back and a cunning smile came to his face. "You stay on for five more years as president, Grant. I'll step out of the picture entirely during that time. If by January 1, 1981, Kinnelon does not surpass Scanlet in profitability, I'll buy Val out. If you do," he shrugged, bringing his chair forward, "you buy me out. How does that sound?"

Valerie and Grant exchanged a puzzled look. "It doesn't make sense," Valerie said. "Why keep Grant on when you wanted him out? And why wait five years when you've been chomping to get Scanlet now? You know our plans call for a totally different kind of construction."

"Exactly," Ray said. "This way I give you two a chance to fall on your faces and I look like the good guy." The slick smile he wore vanished, replaced by a brittle arrogance that settled in his eyes. "For years I've watched you, Grant, with your ideas, your details, your careful attention to every little thing. My father loved you for it. He knew I was strictly the nickel-and-dime guy, the one who got in, made the bucks, and got out. Do you have any idea how much I resented you for your talent, for your taste?" He laughed, not a bitter sound, not a kind one either. "Now you're even going to marry the woman I wanted. Believe me, I'm going to enjoy watching you fail."

"Ray, you're joking, aren't you?" Valerie said quietly, not believing what she was hearing.

"No, Val, I'm not. I'm damned fed up with trying to be as good as Grant, knowing all the while I don't stand a chance. Well, now I'll just sit back and watch where you end up without me to handle the nickels and dimes. Should be interesting, don't you think?"

Valerie tugged her eyes from the hard, ugly slash of Ray's mouth. Who was this man, this insecure, pride-poor stranger? It struck her as preposterous that once she had thought she loved him. She doubted that she even liked him.

Grant too was startled by Ray's revelations. He had long suspected that Ray resented him, but he had no idea it went this deep. Now he was throwing down the gauntlet, pitting ego against pride, business savvy against talent and taste. The challenge appealed to Grant.

When Grant spoke, there was a strength in his voice that riveted Valerie's attention. "I'm agreeable to your plan, Ray. On one additional condition."

"Sure, name it."

"Whatever I build in the next five years has the name Hollander on it."

"Go to hell!"

"I like it," Valerie put in, grinning with delight. "That way when we buy you out we won't have to change the name on the new buildings."

"You're both out of your minds."

"Is it a deal?" Grant pushed.

"Yeah, yeah, it's a deal. A sucker deal." And the sound of Ray's confident laughter boomed through the office.

In September of that year, Valerie became Mrs. Grant Hollander in a small civil ceremony at Angela's home, with Christianne and Linda in attendance. If the memory of another time, another ceremony, another man brought a momentary pang of loss, one glance at Grant and the devotion shining in his eyes vanquished it. They spent their two-week honeymoon in Galesville, setting a pattern of escape and isolation for the future. In Mack's kitchen, in his bedroom, in his beloved study, Valerie and Grant firmly established their love, both the lightning that had sparked it and the caring that would make it last.

Before they returned to New York, they made a brief stop in Los Angeles. One afternoon while Grant was at the Kinnelon offices in Century City, Valerie was strolling down Rodeo Drive with Linda. As they reached the corner of Wilshire Boulevard and Rodeo, Valerie suddenly stopped, staring thoughtfully at the Beverly Wilshire Hotel and at the Brown Derby, a landmark at this location for years; she had heard that the restaurant might be for sale.

"What is it?" Linda prompted. "You don't want to have lunch here, do you? The food is awful."

"No, no, I'm just thinking," she replied absently. "Wouldn't it be wonderful to build something really spectacular here, right here on this corner?"

"Come on, Val, let's go into Giorgio's, I need a new sweater."

"Wait a minute, Linda, hear me out. Think about it—something unbelievably magnificent, taller than anything Beverly Hills has ever known, and architecturally perfect, not like those atrocious Century City monoliths." Valerie's eyes sparkled like fresh snowflakes as her vision began to take shape. "It could be a monument to David. Yes, the Kinnelon Tower. Retail space on a few floors, an absolutely top-rate restaurant, and both residential and commercial space." She focused her attention on her friend, who was staring at her, mystified.

"You don't see it, do you?"

"To tell you the truth, I haven't the foggiest idea of what you're talking about," Linda admitted. "I thought you and Grant were going to establish the Hollander name. What you're describing sure doesn't sound like Grant's kind of project."

"But it is," Valerie said excitedly. "It can be everything that both Hollander and Kinnelon stand for, everything that David and Grant respected about each other. And it'll revolutionize Beverly Hills. Look at what's happening around here already," she said with an expansive wave. "Rodeo Drive is becoming a Faubourg Saint Honoré. The money that is spent here is phenomenal and it's going to increase so that the cost of a square foot of space will zoom. And people will pay because they want to be where the money is—Ray Kinnelon lesson number one!" she added with a smile.

"I'm still baffled," Linda said. "I can understand how retail space could be profitable, but why would anyone want to live down here?"

"Are you serious? The corner of Wilshire and Rodeo—Linda, we are talking about the primest of the prime, an address that people would sell their souls for. Of course people would live here, and they sure as hell would lease office space here." She paused, her face dancing with animation as ideas and plans took shape. "You know what? Forget leasing! We could do co-op offices, people could *buy* their offices—it's the natural next step!"

She grabbed Linda's hands, gripping them firmly. "I'm going to do it," she vowed, nodding with absolute confidence. "I'm going to build the Kinnelon Tower right here, and it'll be the most extraordinary, spectacular, fantastic thing this town has ever seen! Ray and the Scanlets and the Trumps and the Helmsleys will be called second-rate by the time Grant and I are finished!"

Grant's enthusiasm for the Kinnelon Tower mirrored his wife's. Together they planned and designed long into the night, blueprints and papers strewn about their New York den. In sketch after sketch they created their dream. It would be a thirty-story building with an atrium entrance where people could sit and read a newspaper, or have a cup of cappuccino or espresso from a small concession. The first three floors would be devoted entirely to retail space, those shops of international repute whose names were equated with expense and elegance. An outside elevator would whisk people to their homes or offices or to the tower's Michelin-star-quality restaurant. The top fifteen floors would be residential space, only two apartments to a floor, each with a wraparound terrace for a magical view of the city, each with no less than three thousand square feet, each with such luxuries as Boulton stereos in every room, in-floor safes, computerized security systems; jacuzzis and hot tubs, cedar-lined closets, recessed lighting, all-marble baths, individual washers and dryers, and teak floors. The starting price for the apartments would be one million dollars, all customizing extra. Grant and Valerie laughed over this, acknowledging Ray's influence. Architecturally, the building would be a glass obelisk, a glittering missile piercing the sky. The Kinnelon Tower would be a monument not only to David but to design excellence, and they couldn't wait to get started.

When they tried to buy the site of the Brown Derby, their problems were only beginning.

Chapter 23

"We're in trouble." Grant tossed a handful of reports onto his desk. "Val, the timing couldn't be worse for us. If something doesn't start clicking soon, we are in the proverbial shit pile."

Valerie stared gloomily at her husband of not quite two years. "What are we going to do?"

"Who the hell knows?" Grant replied with unusual roughness. "That condo we opened in Miami Beach is sitting three-quarters empty, and that's with throwing in a new Lincoln Continental. Who would have thought Florida would lose its appeal."

"We've still got plenty of time," Valerie said. "We've got a lot of new developments started, and if we get the Brown Derby site—"

"Better accept it, Val, that's just a pipe dream. Even if they give in finally and sell to us, we don't have the money to buy it now, let alone build. Do you have any idea how much money we've sunk into our various projects?" He picked up some of the papers he had tossed down. "The shopping mall in Nyack, New York, has one tenant—Sears—that's it. Now that's a big chunk of business, true, but it's also a big mall. The shopping center in Worcester, Massachusetts, has three tenants, all specialty shops, all very, very minor leases. We opened the resort lodge in Aspen during the wrong season and it's been losing money for us steadily. The hotel in New Orleans has had such structural problems that for the first time in my professional career I'm being criticized for sloppiness and greed, and you know what—the critics are right. I had no business opening that damned place as early as I did—elevator doors jamming, electrical wires exposed, rugs coming up, leaking faucets." He pounded his fist on the desk top. "That bastard's gonna win, dammit!"

Valerie took a deep breath, got up from her chair, and went to the window. When she spoke, her voice was low, her eyes gazing off into the distance. "Maybe that's been our problem."

"What do you mean?"

"We've been concentrating so hard on getting constructions started, assuming quantity equals profitability, that we've forgotten why we're in this race in the first place." She turned to him, a knowing sparkle in her eyes. "We've forgotten what makes you so outstanding in our rush to give Ray what he wants. Well, what about what *we* want?" she asked with increasing vigor. "What about the great designs, the impeccable standards, the desire to establish the Hollander name as synonymous with quality? And for that we need patience."

"The trouble with patience," Grant remarked dryly, "is that it could lose us our deadline."

"I don't think so," she argued. "Do you really think Ray gives a hoot how many buildings we open for him? It's the money he cares about—the whole deal is based on profits, remember? Scanlet has focused entirely on urban buildings, and with rising construction and labor costs, they're going to feel the pinch in a way we won't, if we do what we know best—and that's give quality, do a few things really well instead of a lot of mediocre jobs. And do one thing absolutely spectacularly, like the Kinnelon Tower!"

"You have to forget that, Val. Really, for now it's impossible."

"I won't forget it and neither will you!" she insisted. "Don't you realize that a building of that stature can have a ripple effect on everything else we do?"

He looked at her with interest, the cold, dismal cast to his eyes lifting slightly. "I appreciate what you're saying," he conceded, "but the risk is enormous, and we still don't know if they'll even sell the site to us."

"Then we'll just have to keep fighting for it," she said, going over to him.

"That building means a lot to you, doesn't it?"

"Yes, Grant, it does. Call it an expression of love if you want, because I think that's how I see it. Love for you and David, and for Mack, too. It's very important to me."

He rose, and cupped her face in his hands. "And you

think quality is the answer, huh?" he asked with a new jauntiness.

"And patience," she said. "Don't forget patience."

"That I have. I waited long enough for you, didn't I?" He hugged her close. "And it was worth it."

"This will be too, darling." She entwined her hands in his thick hair, and kissed him, putting all her conviction in the strength of that kiss.

That conversation took place in April 1978, and for a while it seemed that Valerie's belief in their success would be prophetic. The following winter, their lodge in Aspen, known as Hollander House, a Kinnelon, Inc. construction, became a haven for the rich and the playful. The luxury condominium in Miami Beach eventually sold out, although the two shopping centers still had less than full tenant occupancy. Even more exciting, and a strong indication that they were doing things right, was Grant's earning two design awards for suburban industrial parks in Connecticut and Rhode Island, starting a trend that was picked up nationwide.

Then, in June of the next year, when Valerie was thirty-six, she gave birth to David. It was a much easier birth than her first, the decision to have a cesarean made from the beginning so there were no long, excruciating hours of labor, no danger period afterward. Christianne assigned herself the role of surrogate mother, pampering the baby named after her father with almost suffocating devotion, and making a fiction of sibling rivalry. Compared to the joy of having Davey, the Hollanders' professional difficulties seemed like a thin layer of dust in their lives: insignificant, irrelevant, removable. An atmosphere of endless possibility surrounded them like a golden halo. This lasted for four months, after which they finally achieved what they had long sought: they were able to purchase the site of the Brown Derby. The soaring costs of labor and supplies and the impossibly high interest rates had created a devastating real estate slump, however. They needed time—time to ride out the national financial crisis, time to see a return on their investments, time beyond Ray's deadline.

Two months into the new decade, they seemed to have run out of time.

* * *

"I can't believe what I'm reading," Valerie said disgustedly, handing Angela the copy of the national magazine. "What kind of a rag would print such garbage?"

Angela shrugged her elegant shoulders, as stylishly clothed as ever in a Giorgio Armani jacket. Her black hair had been permed into a bubble of short, tight curls, and a recent facelift had removed fifteen years. They were by the pool in the Bel-Air house, Christi splashing merrily in the shallow end, Davey asleep in the guest bedroom that had been turned into his nursery. Nancy, still with the family, used the den as her room.

"I don't understand what's going on," Valerie said. "This is the fifth or sixth article I've read about myself recently. What started this?"

"Probably some hungry hack eager for a headline. Ignore it."

"How can I?" Valerie objected. "It's already begun to affect business. Grant was at the bank yesterday to request an additional building loan and he was turned down. Can you believe it, with his record? Said they didn't want their money invested with, and I quote, 'people of such dubious ethics.' If this keeps up, we'll be sitting with a foundation on Rodeo and Wilshire and not much else. And the rest of our projects will lie fallow too. Hollander Real Estate won't just be ruined, it won't even be, period!"

Angela could voice nothing but empty platitudes, and that she would not do. Valerie's outrage and concern were well warranted. According to the various articles and items that had been appearing recently, David Kinnelon had died not of a heart attack but mysteriously, the cause not quite determined. Speculation was gaining credibility that his very much younger wife, who had inherited half his vast holdings, might know more than she was saying. Her engagement to his son and her subsequent takeover of the real estate operation made the untimely and strange death suspicious and worthy of investigation.

"What does Grant say?" Angela asked.

"What can he say? We're both stymied. It's all so absurd, yet look at the damage it's causing. It's as if someone has deliberately set out to make sure we fail." Fierce indignation glinted in her eyes like the sun on the blue water in her pool. "After reading the first couple of articles, we thought Ray might be behind it."

"Now it's you who's being absurd."

"The man does hate to lose," Valerie reminded her.

"Sure, but he doesn't have to stoop to lies and innuendoes in order to win."

"I know, I know," Valerie agreed wearily.

"What are you going to do?"

"What can I do except ride it out. But it's killing us, Angela, it really is. January first is the deadline. If we can't turn this negative publicity around, the Kinnelon Tower, Holland Real Estate, everything we've worked so damn hard for will be lost." In place of the indignation, a shadow of such infinite sadness came over Valerie's eyes that Angela shivered in the midday heat.

A few nights later, Grant and Valerie were in bed, unsuccessful in their attempt to make love. Disgusted with herself, she moved over to her side of the bed and faced the wall. "I'm sorry," she said in a muffled voice. "I don't know what's wrong with me."

Grant placed a hand on her shoulder. "It's this mess, Val. We both know that's what's doing it."

"It's getting worse and worse," she said, close to tears. "It even made the TV news tonight. Why won't Ray put a stop to it? That's the only way it'll end. He's got to make a public statement."

"I called him about that today."

Valerie turned around and sat up. "You did? Why didn't you tell me?"

"Because what he had to say wasn't too encouraging."

Valerie's eyes were fixed on her husband's face, and her heart somersaulted at the grim expression she saw. "Tell me," she said stiffly.

"He's conducting his own investigation. He's hired an attorney to look into the allegations." His tone was tired, a surrender to circumstances beyond his control.

"I don't believe this!" she exploded, stunned. "I can't believe he would do this to us!"

"He said that only after an investigation cleared your name would a public statement by him make any sense or serve any purpose. Until then, he thinks people will believe he was covering up for you because of your past relationship. Nothing I could say could persuade him to change his mind."

"This can't be happening. It's some kind of nightmare. It's blackmail, that's what it is!" she cried, slamming the word into the air. "Only this time it's not just money they want, it's our entire futures, our lives!"

"This time?" Grant repeated sharply. "What do you mean?"

She dismissed the question with an impatient shake of her head, but Grant persisted, grabbing her by the arm, forcing her to look at him. "I asked you a question. If Ray or anybody else can find something in your past to use against us, tell me. We can lose everything if you don't."

She shook off his grip, glaring at him with eyes flinty and unyielding. "There's nothing in my past, Grant," she assured him icily. "Your trust in me leaves me speechless."

"Well, what the hell else did you expect me to say! You talk about blackmail as if you're damned familiar with it!" He looked away from her cold stare.

"I'm sorry," he mumbled several moments later. "This whole thing has me thinking crazy. I feel so damned helpless. It's like we have to sit back and wait for the next salvo of trash and do nothing to defend ourselves. And each day that passes brings us closer to that lousy deadline."

"Grant," she said softly, "once, many years ago, someone did try to blackmail me." She saw the flame of distrust glow in his eyes, and rushed on. "I was totally, completely innocent of everything except being very young and very foolish, and not trusting my husband enough. You must believe I've done nothing that could in any way hurt you." She hesitated, the appeal in her eyes strong, urgent. "You must trust my love, Grant, and then we can fight this. It *is* a form of blackmail, but the person behind it can win only if we stop believing in each other."

Grant studied her, thought of how she had exposed her soul to him in countless conversations, given him her heart with unquestioning confidence that he would not abuse her love. She was not capable of subterfuge and deceit. If there was anything she did not want to tell him, it was more out of embarrassment for herself than any possible damage it could cause him. He pulled her close to him. Her arms came around his neck, and she pressed her mouth into his shoulder. He felt the hot sting of tears on his flesh, and held her away, gently tilting her chin so he could look at her.

"Don't cry, Val, please. We'll fight this, I promise you. And we'll win. I love you more than anything else on this earth, and if you were a young fool, I've been an old one for having even one doubt about you." He tried to smile as he tenderly wiped away her tears. "Since you've had some experience with this sort of thing," he said as lightly as he could manage, "do you have any suggestions on how to proceed?"

She gazed into the depths of the brown eyes that never reflected anything but devotion to her. She saw the way the ridges of age cut unkindly into his face and how the stern mouth was rimmed with lines of worry. She felt the endless strength of his love in his hold on her, and for the first time in her life she understood what it meant to need a man. Without Grant, she did not want to conquer the invisible enemy; without Grant staunchly by her side, the victory could be only a hollow one. And she knew that without his unwavering trust in her, eventually she would not have him. The enemy had to be stopped for reasons far more meaningful than their business.

"Let Ray have his investigation," she said finally. "We're going to hire a detective and find out who's behind this."

"A detective?" Grant repeated dubiously.

She nodded, a new determination settling on her face. "That's what David did when he had to find the blackmailer that other time. We can hire a professional at this kind of thing, someone who knows how to get to the source of these stories."

"Val, I don't know. . . ."

"What choice do we have? It's better than just sitting back and waiting for the next salvo, as you call it."

Grant mulled over her words, then said, "You're right. We have no choice. Do it, the sooner the better."

Angela gave Valerie the name of the detective David had used to get Lena Cardell's address years ago. Angela herself had needed him on a few occasions when a spurned boyfriend had decided to be more greedy than was wise. At the end of ten days, Ray's attorney had concluded his investigation and Ray made a statement to the press, but by then Valerie had the detective's report, and she was so poisoned with hate that the exonerating words in the newspapers meant nothing to her.

"This time I'm going to get her," Valerie vowed to Grant the evening she received the report. "I'll make her wish she were dead."

They were having dinner at L'Orangerie on Sunset Boulevard, but for all that Valerie tasted of the fine French food they could have been eating at McDonald's. In her purse was a three-page report naming her sister as the author of the smear campaign. Affidavits from two writers gave conclusive proof against her, and more could be gotten, including letters, unsigned and typewritten, that would no doubt match a machine at Alice's disposal. Even more damaging were the postmarks on an envelope one of the writers had kept—Lake Forest, Illinois. It was almost as if her sister wanted to get caught, Valerie thought.

Since reading the report late that afternoon, Valerie had stalked her home like a caged animal, seething, a storm of such vindictive brutality churning within her that she felt sapped, drained of energy for anything but hatred. Her first impulse had been to race to the telephone and whip Alice into a frenzy of fear, taunting her with threats of retribution and revenge so diabolical that she would never be able to take another easy breath, never know how and when a strike against her would occur. Valerie paced, thoughts of such evil proportions making her physically sick to the point that she found herself retching with the venom that welled in her like a geyser. Images of her sister lying dead, a dagger in her heart, brought a smirk to her face. Images of her sister lying mutilated under the tires of an eight-wheel truck made her laugh with glee. Images of her sister wandering alone in the tunnel of night in a desert, with no water, her lips caked with the scabs of blisters, her skin ravaged by the sun, the condors circling hungrily, made her wrap her arms around herself and hug with pleasure. These were hours of self-discovery for Valerie. Earlier, she would have scoffed if anyone had told her she was capable of such malevolent thoughts. But now she knew she was capable of even worse in order to see her sister finally rotting in hell.

Eventually she calmed down, and only then did she call Grant at his office to tell him what she had learned. He had offered to come home immediately, but she needed to be alone to expel some of the vitriol so that she could think and plan carefully. This time there would be more than words; more than idle curses that left a mere bee sting of pain. This time she would deal with her sister in the only way her sister would understand: with treachery and a callous disregard for anybody's feelings but her own. This time Valerie would be satisfied with nothing less than Alice's absolute destruction. She had hurt too many people; at last it was her turn to writhe, tormented, in the darkness.

"Val, it's over, let it rest," Grant said to her now. "I'll call her, tell her we know everything. I don't want you to have anything to do with that witch."

"I'll do whatever's necessary, and you can't stop me." There was an air of self-possession about her that was chilling in its intensity. It silenced him.

"I'm going to make sure that Alice never again feels she has the right to call herself my sister," Valerie said calmly. "I'm going to see that she shivers with fear and dread at the mere mention of my name. My sister will never again be capable of hurting me or anyone I love. Never!" The last word was a slice in the air, a whistling dart of bone-hard resolve.

"What are you planning to do?"

She shook her head, and a smile reminiscent of the Valerie he loved came to her face. "No, darling, that I won't tell you. There are some things you deserve to be shielded from, and my sister is one of them. What I have to do is between her and me. I don't want you to be part of it, to have anything to do with the kind of ugliness I have to use as a weapon against her." She laughed mirthlessly. "You know, in a strange way I wish my mother's mind weren't so pickled by alcohol. I think I'd enjoy having her watch what I'm going to do."

"Val, are you sure this is right?"

"Right? Right? No, of course it's not right, Grant. But

that's been my mistake all along, trying to do what's right with a creature as deadly as a scorpion. Do you do what's right when your life is threatened? No, you do what's necessary." She reached out and held his hand. "Please, darling, don't look at me like that. I'm not crazy and I'm not going to do her bodily harm, if that's what you're thinking."

Grant shrugged, unable to take his eyes from the fierceness smoking blue-black in hers. "It's just that I've never seen you like this. You're so hard, Valerie, so . . . ruthless." He put his other hand over hers and offered a small smile. "I think you're frightening me a little."

She nodded her understanding but said nothing more. There was nothing more to say.

Valerie did not take a step to confront her sister in person for another month. She used that time to gather as much damaging evidence as was available. When she had hired the detective to follow her sister, she had had no idea what he would find. A photograph of her typing a letter to the newspapers, perhaps, or a tape-recording of a call would have been sufficient. Instead, she got a bonanza, and with it the discovery that there was nothing she wouldn't do, no duplicity that she was loath to commit if it meant ruining Alice. And she finally understood, too, how this same drive had infected Alice all these years. For the very first time, Valerie acknowledged the sickness of hatred that had ravaged her sister's life.

At the end of a month she was ready to force the issue. She told Grant only that she was flying out to Chicago, and would be back in New York, where they had been for the past month, that night. When she reached O'Hare Airport, she called Alice, and heard not the tinkling giggle that would remain forever in her mind, but the wary voice of an enemy trapped.

"Valerie, is this really you?"

"Yes. I'm in Chicago."

"Are you coming to the house?"

"No, I think it would be better if we meet somewhere. You're familiar with the Drake." It was a statement, not a question, not a suggestion.

"Do you realize how long it's been since we've seen each

other?" Alice said with a slight show of confidence. "Why, it's been—"

"Not long enough," Valerie said curtly. "I ought to tell you something, Alice. This afternoon won't be nearly as pleasant as the last time I saw you. You do remember that, don't you?"

"Valerie, if you've flown out here to accuse me of something outrageous again, I refuse to put myself through it. I have enough troubles of my own without—"

"You don't know what trouble is."

Valerie heard the gasp of surprise, and plunged ahead. "Meet me at the bar at the Drake in forty-five minutes. I'd advise you to be there, Alice, if you value your marriage."

"What!"

Valerie quietly replaced the phone without answering, but she did not immediately open the door to the booth. She leaned against the glass, her eyes closed, and breathed deeply many times. Her heart was pounding out of control, and her teeth were chattering even as sweat moistened her palms. Her determination to attack was strong with desperation, but her ability to perform was weakened by alienation with the role. Only the profound desire to protect those she loved impelled her to move.

Alice was sitting in a booth when Valerie arrived. She stood in the doorway to the lounge and studied her, this lifelong enemy. She could well appreciate the ease her sister had with men; she had ripened with age, an overt sexuality emanating from her like a scent. Her face was harder around the mouth, duller in the eyes. The blonde hair was now more obviously from a bottle, the makeup applied with a heavier hand, but the same old arrogance was present in the arch of the neck, in the knowing smile. And the beauty was still evident, like the gaudy wrapping on an empty box. As she walked over to the booth, the urge to wipe that smugness from Alice's face gave Valerie a new rush of courage.

"Hello, Alice."

"Valerie. I suppose I should say it's good to see you, but I doubt that's true." Valerie sat down and saw her sister slip into a smile as artificial as polyester. "You're looking well," Alice said. "Having babies obviously agrees with you, despite your age."

Valerie did not answer, but sat, fingernails drumming rhythmically on a manilla envelope she had placed on the table.

"Don't you think you should order something?" Alice remarked coldly. "It won't look right if you just sit here."

"I don't plan to stay that long." Her voice was as smooth and serene as a nun's smile, and it made Alice recoil.

"Why are you here, Valerie? What's this all about?" Alice brought her hand up to her mouth. She could feel it starting—the tic, the dreaded twitch.

Valerie took her sister's hand and put it back on the table, then watched her mouth click in and out, in and out. "Nervous?"

"Just tell me why you're here so we can get this over with. I don't have time for you."

Valerie's eyebrows rose with false surprise. "You don't? Since when? I thought I was the only thing you did have time for." She patted the envelope and smiled nastily. "When you're not sleeping around, that is."

Alarm jumped into Alice's face, and Valerie felt the first stirrings of mastery. Alice reached for the envelope, but Valerie clutched her wrist, shoving it away. "All in good time, Alice, all in good time."

Like a chameleon, Alice's expression went from tense to passive. "I think that business of yours is making you a little weird, Valerie. Maybe you should just accept the fact that you don't have what it takes to be a career woman. Your place is in the home, taking care of your husband and children. All this running around creating empires is turning you into someone hard and ugly, and rather unstable, too, I might add." She shook her head dolefully. "I really find it most unbecoming."

"You mean I should be more like you and Mama?"

"Well, yes, actually. You've never heard us complain."

"I see." Valerie pretended to give thought to her sister's advice. "In other words, I should be bored and dissatisfied and sleep around, but I shouldn't complain. Is that what you're trying to tell me?"

"That's the second time you've accused me of that. How dare—"

"How dare I? Why, it's quite easy. You always were

Mama's favorite, and I guess if she and Mack did it, that made it all right for you."

Alice's eyes fluttered wide with shock; the twitch quickened. "You knew about Mama and Mack?"

"Yes, I knew. And I know about you and, let me see, what is it, about twenty, I think. Yes, you and about twenty men. Do you think Dick would be interested in this information?"

Alice gaped at her sister. Her hands seemed to have nowhere to go; they fell ineffectually into her lap, onto the table, around her highball glass, to her mouth, her hair, back to her lap. Valerie opened the envelope and several black-and-white snapshots dropped out. When Alice made a grab for them, Valerie again grabbed her wrist and pushed it away. "Not yet, Alice. Not quite yet."

"What are you doing to me?" she hissed, leaning forward so that her breath ruffled Valerie's hair. "Where did you get those?"

"From a detective I've had following you for a month," Valerie replied. She wondered if her heart would hold out, or if the accelerated pounding would suddenly stop, her heart unable to tolerate the pressure. "I must say, Alice, fidelity is not one of your finer attributes. But diversity certainly is. Just look at these."

She picked up a photograph of her sister, naked, between the legs of a man. Another picture showed her on her back, a similar act being performed on her by another man. In yet a third photograph, Alice was on her side, her head thrown back for the camera to catch the expression of ecstasy as two men serviced her.

"Active, aren't you?" Valerie said, assembling the photographs and replacing them in the envelope.

"What are you going to do with those?" Alice asked stonily. "Give them to Dick, I presume."

"Actually, no, that wasn't what I was planning," Valerie said conversationally. "You see, what I thought I would do is keep these until the day I'm told you've been buried. I don't trust you to give up the witch-hunt until then."

"Here we go again. More of your crazy accusations."

"You're right. You're absolutely right. I'm crazy to accuse you of having made anonymous calls and sent anonymous letters telling the press that David died mysteriously and that I should be investigated." Her eyes took on a marble-cold hardness, and her fingers clawed the envelope as if it were her sister's face. Her words came out in a snarl of hate. "And yes, I'm crazy to think that you deliberately set out to seduce Ray. And yes, I'm nuts, certifiable to imagine for one minute that you have spent a lifetime trying to destroy me!"

"I don't have to listen to this," Alice muttered, and started to rise, but Valerie's hand shot out like a riata, a noose-tight grip keeping Alice in her seat.

"You'll go when I'm good and ready to let you go. I have two more of your anonymous letters—the typing is a perfect match on the sample the detective took from your machine one afternoon. And—"

"He was in my home!" She gasped, horrified.

"And," Valerie went on evenly, "a tape of you calling the *Chicago Tribune*, after, *after* Ray totally cleared me in the press."

"I can't believe you did this to me, I can't believe it," Alice murmured, burying her face in her hands.

"There was no stopping you, there never has been a way to stop you. You're like a vicious tapeworm, eating your way through my life. What better way to retaliate than to eat my way through yours. For one entire month, this stranger followed you; for one entire month he and I have known every step you've taken, every call you've made, every morsel of food you've eaten, when you've made love with your husband or with another man, when you've slapped your daughter. Every single moment of every day for an entire month," she repeated with calculated cruelty. "Think of it, Alice, not a moment of privacy. Invasion on every level." She sat back, her smile a stiletto's slash.

"You're sick. You're crazy!"

"All I wanted from this detective was to catch you in the act of doing something against me," Valerie went on with the same robotic deliberation. "I was worried it might be a waste of time and money, but I didn't know what else to do. Ray had given his statement to the press, so I assumed you'd stop harassing me that way—yes, Alice, I've known you were behind it for quite some time," she said with amused scorn. "I knew you'd try something else, I just didn't know what or when. But you didn't stop. What was going through that twisted mind of yours, Alice? Did you convince yourself that a baseless scandal was better than no scandal at all? Keep up the hint of trouble and sooner or later it would get you the desired results? You must be so desperate. It would be kind of pathetic, I guess, if it weren't so evil."

"I'm leaving."

"Shut up and sit there," Valerie snapped. "What you want doesn't mean a damned thing to me." She waited a moment, as if to gather strength for the final assault. "When the detective came up with the windfall, I knew I had you. I knew that finally I was going to beat you." Her grin was mirthless, merciless. "You've turned into quite a performer, haven't you? Of course, I should have known you'd be like that from the time I caught you in the wood shed with Ty Landry. Some things never change, do they? Tell me, Alice, does screwing all those men relieve the burden of your jealousy, of that hate you carry around in you? I can't imagine that it does. I know that making you miserable hasn't eased the weight of my loathing of you."

By the time Valerie spoke her last words, tears were streaming down Alice's face. Valerie watched, emotionally depleted. There was no more rapidly pumping heart, no fuzzy dryness in her mouth, no cramping in her stomach. A heavy calm had settled over her, like a tarpaulin on a playing field, shutting out all but the cold.

"You don't know how horrible my life has been," Alice managed through her sobs. "You've gotten everything I've ever wanted, and I've had nothing, nothing but this face and body. That hasn't been enough! Don't you see—it hasn't been enough!"

"I think you've had quite a bit," Valerie said quietly. "You just wanted more, you wanted everything, and you wanted it the easy way, as if it were your right to have it."

"But it was my right! I was the princess! I was the one who was supposed to have the riches, the fame, the glory, not you! That's what Mama promised me and I believed her. Oh, Valerie, forgive me, but I believed her!"

Valerie gazed at the face contorted with despair, and then quickly looked away as she felt the old, dangerous stirrings of doubt and compassion. Her sister's tragic belief in a fairy tale was a poor excuse for a lifetime of treachery; there could be understanding, but never again forgiveness.

"Why didn't you stop?" she asked. "Why couldn't you just be satisfied with what you had?"

"Because it wasn't enough," Alice admitted. "Every time I read about you, saw your picture, imagined the life you were leading, I died a little. I didn't want to hurt you, but I couldn't help myself."

"And all the people you used and hurt along the way—what about them, Alice? What about Billy? What about the lies you told him and David? What about Lena Cardell, the times with Ray . . ." She broke off, and shook her head. "You could have stopped anytime you wanted to, Alice. You just didn't want to."

Alice nodded miserably. "I thought if I could just be part of your life, everything would be all right. I thought that if you would just let me share a little of your spotlight, I'd be happy. I didn't care who got hurt along the way if it meant getting what I believed was my due."

Valerie's eyes flashed. "I tried to let you share. Time after time, I tried, but whatever I gave you wasn't enough. You wanted too much, Alice."

"I wanted what I believed I deserved!"

"What about all these men?" Valerie asked, tapping the envelope.

"Meaningless. A stupid way to feel I had a power you didn't." A wave of nausea rushed through Valerie at the pathological jealousy that consumed her sister, but she said nothing.

"What have I ever had except sex?" Alice went on tearfully. "Even when we were kids, I knew that compared to you, I was second best. Sex was a way to prove I existed, to prove I could be wanted."

"But you had everything when we were younger," Valerie reminded her. "I was the one who was treated like a stepchild, and you, as you just told me, were the princess," she added bitterly.

"Yes, I was the princess and I believed I would have everything I wanted because I *needed* to believe it. If I didn't, I'd be face to face with what I really am—an ordinary, unenviable, mediocre woman leading a mediocre life. I wanted more—from you, from everyone. And the men gave it to me; they helped me pretend I was special."

Valerie closed her eyes, the sadness of her sister's empty life and for her own loss overwhelming her. "Did trying to destroy Grant and me and all we worked for make you feel special too?" she asked with that same bitterness.

"I'm sorry, Val, sorry for everything. You can never understand how desperate I've been."

"Oh, yes, Alice, I understand. In fact, I finally understand that I've probably hurt you as much as you've hurt me, but I can't apologize for what I've become, I can only feel sorry that your life is such a disappointment to you."

"Don't shut me out, Val," Alice said with an urgent quiver in her voice. "Give me another chance. Please," she begged, reaching out to place her hand on Valerie's. "I'll change, you'll see. I'll never do anything to hurt you again, I promise. Things will be different between us, I swear it. I'm sorry for everything, but I couldn't help it. You understand that, don't you? Don't you?"

Gently, Valerie slid her hand out from under her sister's grip. She felt a strange burning ache in her chest, an excruciating pain that robbed her of the ability to speak. She recognized the torment within as guilt warring with conviction. Her sister was a pathetic woman and she saw that now with a brutal clarity. It would be so easy to yield to the guilt and give Alice another chance. But another chance for what? Alice would never change. As she herself admitted, she couldn't help herself. And if all she believed she had were her face and body, what would she be capable of doing when they went? Valerie shuddered inwardly and knew that this had to be the end. There could be no more second chances, not even for her family.

She tucked the envelope under her arm, put the strap of her purse over her shoulder, and stood up. "I'm going now, Alice."

"Valerie, please, don't do this to us!" Alice cried. "We're sisters! We're all we have!"

The fire in Valerie's heart was raging now, and she felt the hot, stinging tears in her eyes, but her voice was as firm and sure as her decision. "You should have remembered we were sisters a long time ago. I'm sorry, Alice. I really am."

She stared down at Alice for one long moment, then left, knowing that the last image of her sister, her face red-streaked, her hand outstretched, her mouth open in an unspoken plea, would stay with her until the day she died.

All Valerie told Grant the next day was that Alice would never bother them again. She was as sure of this as she was that there would be a new tomorrow. And Grant knew better than to press her for details. It was enough for him to have her back, completely.

"I think the publicity is dying down, too," he said as they got ready for bed. "I might be able to swing that additional loan now."

"That would be wonderful, darling. Maybe we can ask Ray for an extension on the deadline. The Kinnelon Tower would be worth it to him, don't you think?"

The ringing of the telephone forestalled Grant's response. "Hello?" he asked.

"This is Dick Appleton, Valerie's brother-in-law. Is she there?"

Grant held out the phone. "Val, it's for you. Your sister's husband."

"I don't want to speak to him."

"I'm sorry," Grant said into the phone. "She's unavailable right now. May I take a message?"

"This is urgent. Tell her it's about Alice."

"I don't think that'll impress her," Grant remarked dryly.

"Put Valerie on the phone. Please!"

Grant placed his hand over the receiver. "Val, the guy sounds frantic. I think you'd better talk to him."

"What is it, Dick?" she asked without preamble.

"Valerie, I know something terrible happened between you and Alice, but you've got to fly out here right away. She's in the—"

"I thought you told my husband this was urgent," she cut him off curtly.

"It is! Alice is in Cook County General. She was in a horrible car accident. She was probably going too fast as usual and couldn't brake in time . . . I don't know . . . but she smashed into an oncoming van with about twelve kids in it. Thank goodness they're all right, but, Val, Alice is in serious condition.

Her car was totaled, and she went through the windshield. Her face is smashed to a pulp. She was in surgery for over fourteen hours. You've got to come here. You're all she has."

Valerie clutched her stomach and expelled a long breath. The room temperature was comfortable, but she felt as if she were out in a blizzard. And she knew that she had to fight now for more strength than she had ever before needed in her life.

"She doesn't have me, Dick," she said finally. "Not anymore."

"You don't understand. She's never going to look the same again. Do you know what this will do to her? How can I handle this? You know what her face meant to her. She's maimed for life. You're the only one who can help."

"I'm sure you and the doctors will do a fine job for her. Besides, I can't imagine my presence accomplishing anything but increasing her pain."

"Will you just listen to me and stop this childishness! There's not a tooth left in her mouth, and her gums are so lacerated with bone chips that reconstruction is out of the question. She'll never be able to eat solid food again! One entire side of her face was slashed to ribbons and her cheekbone is in splinters—there isn't even enough bone left to put it together again. Don't you realize what's happened? This is her face, dammit, her *face*! You've got to be here for her. She needs you. Dammit, Valerie, you're her sister!"

For Valerie, a lifetime seemed to pass in the seconds of silence after her brother-in-law had spoken. A recollection of wishing her sister mutilated by a huge truck flashed in front of her. Guilt singed her, but it was a pain she knew she had to withstand.

"I'm sorry, Dick," she said slowly, dully. "There's nothing I can do."

"What do you mean! You've got to help her. Don't you care about your own sister? Valerie, without her face, her life is ruined. She might as well be dead!"

"I lost my sister a long, long time ago, Dick. The person you're talking about doesn't mean a thing to me." With that, she hung up the phone, her hands shaking, her shoulders hunched under a cape of desolation. She felt the warm touch of Grant's fingers on her arm, a reminder of life and love.

"What have I done? Oh, Grant, what have I done?"

He held her tightly, saying nothing. She shut her eyes, but the image remained. Her sister lying bandaged in a hospital bed, her face gone. That face that she had pampered and shown off, used as a passport, relied on the way a genius relies on his brain. Gone. Forever gone. Like Valerie's own illusions about family, about her sister's ultimate goodness.

She shuddered in her husband's arms as the last tremor of guilt died within her, a pale specter of remorse to stay with her always, as indelible and as heavy as the memory of beauty would be for her sister.

The deadline of January 1, 1981, came and went. Neither Kinnelon's new constructions nor profits exceeded Scanlet's, but Ray offered to sell to Grant and Valerie anyway. It was impossible for him to deny their professional superiority in real estate; whatever they created was, simply, the best. Pride in workmanship was something Ray could not put a price tag on, and he decided he did not want to. Valerie and Grant refused to buy him out, however. Without the Kinnelon name and money and support, they never would have achieved what they had. It would continue to be a mutual endeavor, only from now on, all the buildings would carry the name Hollander, the third full partner in Kinnelon, Inc.

Valerie and Grant forged ahead; she concentrated totally on the Kinnelon Tower, he on all other developments. The Tower had become a symbol to her of the men in her life: of Mack Landry's gift of opportunity to be what she could; of David Kinnelon's unconditional love; of Grant's unwavering support. Not to complete the building would be to cheat these men of what she owed them.

By early 1983, Hollander Hotels had been started, or plans drawn up, in six major cities. In the next seven years, Hollander industrial parks would sprout in suburbs from Massachusetts to South Carolina. The Kinnelon Hotel that had been renovated from the old hospital in Key Biscayne had been turned into a time-sharing vacation resort. Grant's idea had proven so successful that the name was changed to Hollander Villas, and he had recently bought land in Nassau to build another. They had gotten out of the shopping-center market entirely, and deliberately avoided challenging the monopoly the Scanlet group held on urban construction. The Hollanders had weathered financial crises and surmounted emotional turmoil, but finally their dreams were becoming reality.

Chapter 24

The practiced silkiness of the stewardess's voice requesting passengers to adjust their seats forward and fasten their seatbelts brought a fond smile to Valerie's face. Tomorrow, March 24, 1983, she would be forty years old. It was more than twenty years since she had experienced the thrill of having her own stewardess's wings, of believing that the universe was small, all things in it possible. More than twenty years of unexpected pleasures, unforgettable pains.

"Excited, Mommy?" Christi asked.

"I sure am. Tomorrow's going to be quite a day for us."

"Are photographers going to be there?"

"Yup, maybe even television crews, too."

"TV," Davey exclaimed. "Oh boy!"

"I suppose I have to wear a dress," Christi complained.

"No jeans, no sneakers," Valerie instructed.

"Not me," Davey said firmly. "I'm wearing my E.T. sneakers for television!"

"Mommy?" Christi asked thoughtfully. "What would we have done if all this didn't happen while school was on spring vacation?"

"Arranged for you to get your assignments and take them with you. It's just lucky for all of us that the timing worked out the way it did."

"Sure is," Christi agreed heartily. "Who would want to do phooey old homework in California."

Valerie smiled. "California's for sun and fun, right? The big house is for rest, and New York is home."

"I like home best," Davey put in.

"Me too," Christi said.

"I like wherever you two and Daddy are," Valerie said. "That's home for me."

Grant was waiting for them at Los Angeles International. He greeted them warmly, having been unable to spare the few days' vacation that he had insisted Valerie take if she were to survive until her birthday.

"You look wonderful," he said, holding her at arm's length. "Not a day over twenty-five."

"I feel even younger. You were right to make me go. It's funny. All those years I couldn't wait to get away from Galesville, and now I look forward to the times I can go back. No pleasing a woman, I guess," she said, laughing.

"We'll see about that later," he whispered in her ear.

Later lasted long into the night, with conversation and loving alternately keeping them awake. At one point, Grant swept back the dampened hair from Valerie's forehead and looked deeply into her eyes.

"Happy?" he asked.

"More than I ever thought possible."

"Do you know how much I love you?"

"Do you know how much I need you?"

His eyes widened with surprise. "I think that's the first time you've ever said that."

"I've been afraid of the word," she admitted. "I thought it meant dependency, weakness. You've shown me it can mean loving."

"You're about as far from weak and dependent as any person I've ever met," Grant said.

"Now, but . . ." She shrugged. "Before you, darling, I wasn't really able to be me, at least not without a struggle, so I came to view my needs as dependencies."

"You mean with David?"

She nodded. "And Mack too. They were both wonderful to me, but we were never equals and they never saw me clearly, weaknesses *and* strengths. With them, there was always an expectation of how I was supposed to act and think, and most of the time I gave them what they expected because I needed their support, their security. That's why I confused need with dependency."

"And with me?"

"I need *you*," she answered readily. "Who you are, what

you are, how you love me. That's given me strength and courage."

"I think I'm blushing," Grant said with undisguised pleasure.

"Blush all you want, but it's true. When I was a little girl—actually, when I was a big girl, too—I really thought there was such a thing as a Prince Charming. He would be handsome and smart and loving and kind and—" she grinned at her husband, "great in bed. I believed one person could be all that, but that I wouldn't have him. And then I discovered you, my mythical Prince Charming."

"You didn't discover me, Val," Grant explained gently. "You discovered yourself."

"Yes, I suppose you're right."

"You stopped trying to be what someone else wanted," he went on, "stopped trying to deny what you needed and wanted out of life. That freed you. I just happened to be the lucky guy who was around at the right time."

"I didn't even know what I was searching for until I found it," she murmured as she moved closer to him, one arm around his chest. "You're my Prince Charming, my husband, my lover. But most of all, you're my best friend."

"Val, honey, if we didn't like each other so much, the loving would have stopped long ago."

"I always believed that, I just didn't know I could have it. I wanted someone who would love me not just for what I am but for what I could be, someone who would teach and learn, listen and hear. That's you, Grant. You've never been afraid to let me be me, no matter where that might take us or the mistakes I might make."

"The same holds true for me," he pointed out. "You've helped me let loving into my life, and affection. Do you have any idea how frightened I was to care deeply about anyone, that's why I've always put so much emotion into my buildings—they couldn't turn around and disappoint me. But with you, well, you would never take advantage of my love, so I'm free to give it and free to enjoy taking it."

"I think maybe we've both been very fortunate," she said, kissing him lightly. "It may have taken forty years to find you, but it'll take twice that long for me to ever let you go."

In response, Grant crushed her against him, their heartbeats sounding like one in her ears.

The next morning, Grant and the children gave Valerie birthday presents that included a beautiful pearl and diamond bracelet and a Steuben glass replica of the Kinnelon Tower. The miniature obelisk was only eight inches high, but the most intricate detail had been replicated, down to the name plaque in etched glass.

By noon they had finished one celebration and were on their way to Rodeo Drive and Wilshire Boulevard, where another event would mark this momentous day in Valerie's life: the ribbon-cutting ceremony to officially open the Kinnelon Tower.

The uniformed doorman who would be presiding over the entrance to the Tower opened the door of the leased limousine for Valerie, and cameras clicked rapidly as she stood, gazing up at the monument to her dreams, the symbol of her love and gratitude to the men who had brought such fullness to her life. For her husband, she knew this building was an architectural triumph that would win awards and set standards for years to come. For Kinnelon, Inc., it was a real estate accomplishment achieved against almost insurmountable odds. But for her, it was so much more.

She stood at the curb, not moving despite the light pressure on her elbow from Grant. She kept looking up at the soaring strength that reminded her of Mack. At the perfection of details that was a testimony to David. And then she brought her eyes to her husband's face, and knew in her heart that, like having him, the Kinnelon Tower was the fulfillment of a promise.

She let Grant lead her to the glass doors, where a two-foot-wide red satin ribbon had been tied through the large brass handles. She spotted the plaque set into the concrete wall, the words: "Dedicated to the Memory of David Kinnelon" etched boldly into the brass.

She turned to face the throng of people, recognizing many celebrities in the crowd. To her immediate right was the mayor of Beverly Hills; next to him were the mayor of Los Angeles and the three men whose banks had financed, sometimes reluctantly, the entire endeavor. To her left was

Ray, his smile warm and proud; and then Angela and Linda, beaming love as if from a beacon. The mayor of Beverly Hills stepped forward.

"Ladies and gentlemen, this is a day Beverly Hills will long remember," he said in a resonant voice. From an aide he took a pair of scissors. "It is with great pride and pleasure that the Kinnelon Tower officially opens for business—and with a waiting list of buyers and tenants, I might add!" The crowd laughed appreciatively. "But most especially we commemorate this day with tremendous gratitude to Valerie Kinnelon Hollander for her enduring determination and perseverance to see this magnificent building completed." He held out the scissors to her. "Mrs. Hollander, if you would do the honors, please?"

As she snipped the ribbon, applause rang in her ears, but the thundering of her heart was louder. She faced the crowd again, heard, as if from a distance, words of congratulations and the popping of champagne corks; felt embraces, kisses, handshakes. Then there was the unmistakable sound of voices singing "Happy Birthday Dear Valerie" as a ten-tiered birthday cake in the shape of the Tower was wheeled up to the entrance.

The twinkle of stars in a clear midnight sky and the glitter of the jewels on her wrist were poor rivals for the joy that blazed in her eyes. She felt the burn of tears and willed them unshed, but the cause of them could not be as easily controlled. Almost three years had passed since she had last spoken with her sister, but not a day had gone by without a pang of sorrow for the loss. There was no one left of the family she had fashioned from fantasy, and so the unshed tears were not only for what this day was but for what could never be.

And then she felt her daughter take one hand, her son the other; felt the warmth and comfort and love of Grant behind her, his fingers resting gently on her shoulder, and she smiled, needing no effort of will to banish the tears. She was surrounded by the family she had fashioned from reality, and like the Tower that had been created out of love, this family, *her* family, would endure.